"How long is forever? Sometimes, just a second."

— LEWIS CARROLL

MAD WORLD

Echoes Loom

BRANDON T BERNARD

MAD WORLD: Echoes Loom

First Edition 2025

ISBN: 978-1-966486-00-8

You let my imagination run wild even though you never fully understood. I can't tell you my stories, but I can still hear you everyday.

I miss you Mom.

MAD WORLD

•ECHOES LOOM•

BRANDON T. BERNARD

ADAMAS
HALMA
BRIARWELL
THE DRAUGHTS
CAISSAN MOUNTAINS
CLYPEUS
THE WEALDS
ROOKWOOD
ROOKRIDGE
THE WASTES
THE WINDS
THE HOLLOW
SPIRE SIDE
VIRIDIAN MOUNTAINS
RUTRUM
CLAVA
SOUTHERN WEALDS
QUEENWOOD
AVIUM MOUNTAINS
THE WRECKS
GREYFIELD
FALX MOUNTAINS
THE WETLANDS
MIRUS
GREYHARBOR
BRIGHTON
SAXUM CAPE
THE WARRENS
ILEX
THE WILDS
N
S
WONDERLAND

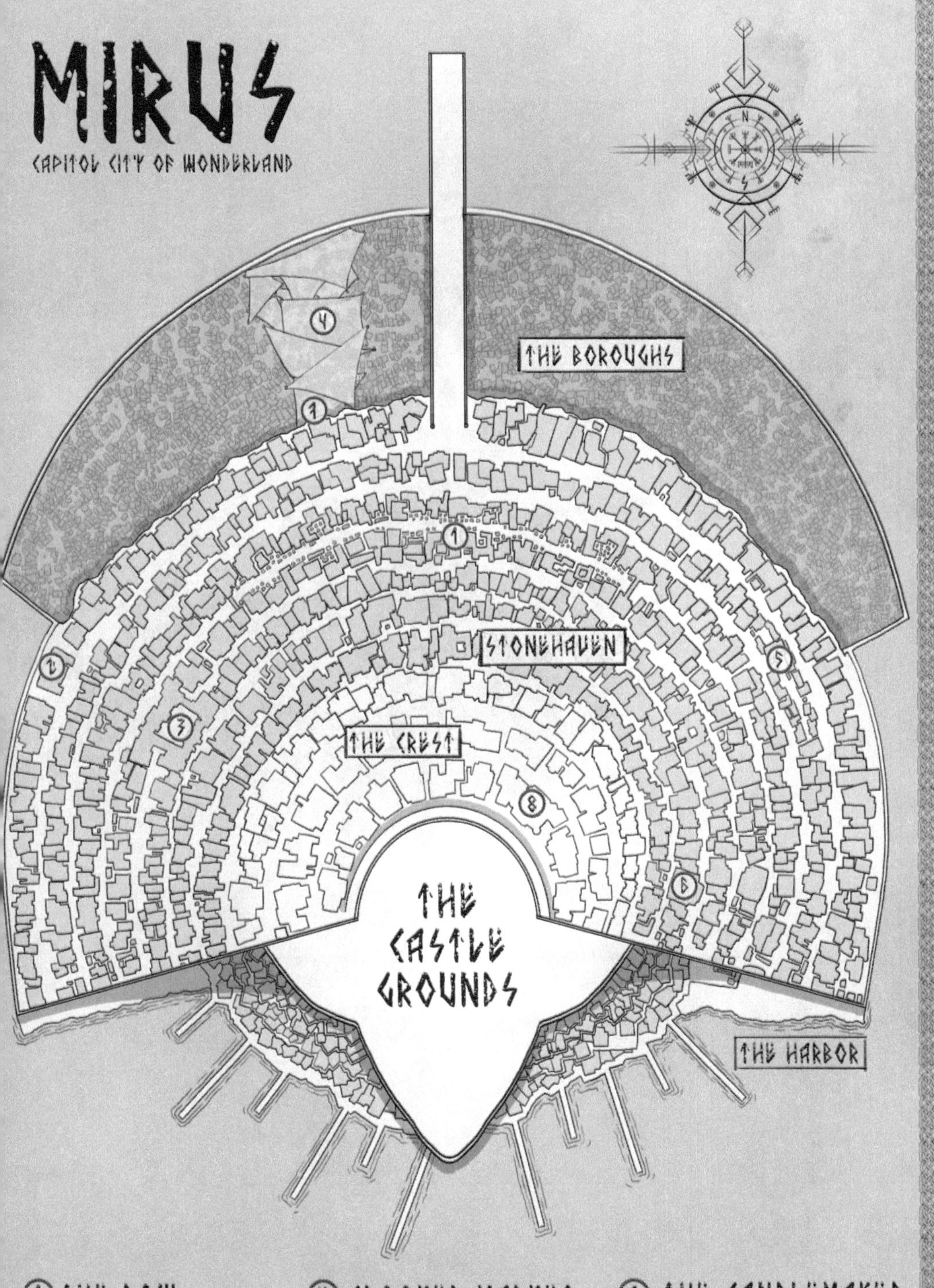

1 THE ROW
2 HANGING CELLS
3 QUADRANGLE
4 CROOKED MARKET
5 THE FORGE
6 COROLLA GARDEN
7 THE CANDLEMAKER
8 BRONWYN'S MANOR

THE STORY THUS FAR…

Cheshire and Jonathan searched for March and Mary after they were kidnapped, and the bodies piled up to get the answers they needed, but March and Mary Anne ultimately escaped from a dungeon cell, put there by Lysander and Uriah's schemes.

The cult leader, Sheridan, offered an ultimatum: surrender Mary Anne or pay the price. With her blood, he unleashed a blood-thirsty horde onto the city. To save the people, Mary Anne offered Cheshire the Mask of Light and the Mask of Shadow in return for use of the catacombs.

March parleyed with Lysander and Uriah for their help to defend the castle, during which time she had to cut off part of Dormy's arm to save her life. March then took a harrowing journey to the Hollow to get more of Jonathan's elixir, which was destroyed by the cult. On the way, she encountered the legendary Juju Bird and the Bandersnatch, discovering they hold their own secrets.

Jonathan helped the Mirusian soldiers save as many people as possible from the horde but ended up lost in the city. Sheridan and his lackeys confronted Jonathan, but he killed them before succumbing to his injuries and lack of elixir.

Cheshire visited Time, the last living Old One, who gave Cheshire the location of his mother's grave. Unwilling to believe Time's lies, he dug up the grave to find a stranger's corpse. Afterward, Cheshire tricked the Ace into the city, using the assassin's hatred and ax to mow down the horde, and the Mask of Shadow to send the rest to a watery grave in the harbor.

March returned too late to help but did bring news of Lysander and Uriah's armada sailing to Mirus. Cheshire returned to Time and killed him, dooming Wonderland to never move forward in time again. Mary Anne found a hidden vile of Jonathan's elixir, saving him, then pardoned Cheshire of his past crimes, and the throne room doors finally rumbled open for her.

Part I

CHAPTER 1

MARY ANNE

The giant iron throne room doors stand open. Despite the days, weeks, or months it has taken to reach this moment—she cannot recall how long—hesitation keeps her foot poised before the threshold. This fear will not hold dominion over everything she has accomplished to this point. She swallows, closes her eyes, and takes her first step into the throne room and into her future.

Mary Anne's heartbeat thunders in her throat and hands, fire fills her cheeks, yet her chest is cold and hollow, as if her heart tries to escape the beauty, the mystery, and the overwhelming sensation of hope and dread forever intertwined together. The sharp pats of her feet upon the stone floor cut through the overpowering silence, the emptiness of the throne room.

These windows should not exist, cannot exist, this deep within the belly of the castle, yet the morning sun illuminates the most incredible view Mary Anne has ever laid eyes upon. The Grand Arcana, the magic flowing through Wonderland, must indeed be powerful to recreate the sun and sky. Even for an illusion, the warmth reaches out and caresses her skin.

Particles of dust shine like ethereal gold and drift through the dawn's soft, curious gaze. Sunbeams glow through tall gothic windows with frosted glass at the far end of the room and highlight the edges of four towering columns at the center of the room with brilliant white outlines, as if carefully painted by a master. This should not be.

Chandeliers the size of small boats glimmer and hang from giant golden chains overhead, vibrant tapestries larger than mainsails adorn the walls, and plush benches and chairs with curved arms circle the throne room's perimeter, accompanied by sparkling silver candelabras as tall as saplings.

Mary Anne crosses between the massive columns, monuments to Wonderland's history, which disappear high into darkness beyond the dawn's reach. She runs her hands along one of their cold surfaces, covered with recessed Old Prodigium runes running the full height, or at least she believes so, as they become too small to discern toward their tops. The columns' circumference is unlike anything she has seen before; it would take over thirty of her standing fingertip to fingertip to surround a singular column.

A memory resurfaces. The columns resemble the one she passed on her first carriage ride to Mirus and those the Duchess pointed out atop the castle's tower, rising from Wonderland's lush landscapes and piercing the sky.

Whether out of fear or wanting to build anticipation, she cannot be certain, but Mary Anne finally turns her attention to the area of the chamber, the one wall she purposefully neglected. Everything might be nothing more than a dream and vanish before her eyes. A thin section of stone wall sits between large windows—a shadowed mountain between two rivers of colored glass and light. Mary Anne tries to swallow her heartbeat back into her chest and fill the void lingering since the doors swung open upon her touch.

The throne of Wonderland, in all its magnificence, sits on a raised dais, blurred from her tears, and waits for her behind the gossamer curtains of sunlight.

The tears twist in her stomach, swell in her chest and eyes, finally falling to her cheeks. Her lips, pressed tight, tremble at the miracle. She dares not utter a sound in this hallowed place. The pristine white marble of the throne catches the morning light and glows, drawing, no, beckoning Mary Anne closer. She treads softly, unsure of each footstep, afraid at any moment she might awaken from this dream.

Any storybook illustration, master's painting, or author's text can never capture and depict the simple, pure beauty and the power of the throne. All others in the world, should there be others, must pale in comparison. The smooth white marble stands in stark contrast to the darker stones of the floor and walls. Intricate carvings, filled in with silver, resembling diamonds, hearts, acorns, cups, shields, and other symbols cover the edges of its back and arms. Surely more sophisticated symbols would adorn a throne, though Mary Anne soon notices those symbols repeat throughout the throne room, upon the borders of each tapestry, in the twisting metal of the candelabras and chandeliers, and the white marble ornaments hanging from the golden tassels of the sweeping red canopy high above the throne.

She reaches out and caresses the smooth arm, with only a fleeting moment of hesitation in her heart. She will not wait any longer. A chill runs up from her fingers to the bottom of her feet and the top of her head.

"At long last," she says through her tears. The soft echo of her voice, even whispered, startles her.

If this is the prize for the hardships endured, the battles were well worth it. Not the prize, merely the precursor to what lies ahead of her: Jonathan, magic, power, and her ascension to the queen of Wonderland.

She steps onto the dais and stands in front of the throne, not yet ready to sit. The breadth of the grand chamber brings a knot to her throat. With the sunlight to her back, she can see every detail with newfound clarity. She realizes the mighty columns, like the throne, are of a stone unlike the rest of the chamber, out of place, similar in color to the gray limestone surrounding her, but something about their appearance whispers they do not belong. Something red catches the sun and sparkles in the deep recesses of each rune. Red jewels perhaps, similar to those on the Wonderland map in the cartographer's room.

Her imagination conjures hundreds of smiling and adoring townspeople filling both sides of the chamber. Down the aisle, at its center leading from the doors to the throne itself, Jonathan approaches ceremoniously, smiling, and kneels before the dais. She commands him to stand with a gesture. He steps upon the dais in front of her, his wide shoulders blocking the rest of the people from sight, and lifts her chin and kisses her sweetly—a taste of the future.

Her unrequited love and the others fade like smoke in the sunlight. She is alone again. Her heart races once more. This is a time to celebrate, not be alone. Mary Anne must tell someone—anyone.

Before she has time to think, her feet carry her from the throne room. She wants to run for her bedchamber deeper in the castle and wake Jonathan to tell him, to show him her accomplishment. A selfish thought. He still needs his rest to heal after his ordeal with the Cult of the Mother. True, Cheshire wiped out the masses, but Jonathan's bravery cut the head from the snake. He will always be her hero and will learn soon enough of her triumph.

The Duchess perhaps should have been her first choice. Mary Anne runs through hallway after hallway, curve and turn, and up and down staircases. The castle whips by in a blur. Her head tingles from her pure exhilaration and her quick breaths. It gives her body the sensation of floating, as if the magic, the Arcana, a gift bestowed to the queen, courses through her veins like icy fire. She keeps running and, in the enjoyment of the sensation, realizes she does not know where to find the Duchess at this early hour, or where her chambers are located.

After several more empty hallways, she stops to gain her bearings. An ill sensation takes over her body, similar to when setting foot on a dock for the first time after days at sea. Jolted by the decrease in momentum, the body takes time for the senses to adjust, missing the rush the way a drunkard misses the bottle. The top of her silk robe hangs open and the bottom flaps behind her, only secured by the tie at her waist. She did not notice this entire time, nor did she care.

Mary Anne changes course, holding her robe closed at first then relinquishing herself to the freedom, and returns to her chambers to find Grace, her handmaiden. The weightlessness of her body wains as she runs, the weight and the tiredness of her legs becoming apparent. Every fiery breath she takes quells the cold rush carrying her before. Regardless, she keeps every ounce of passion and hope in her thundering heart.

Grace must have heard the slapping of Mary Anne's bare feet against the floor. Her handmaiden meets Mary Anne halfway down the corridor from her chambers. Though her half-mask conceals her eyes, the corners of her lips curl with concern.

Mary Anne stops running, and the sting from the bottom of her feet travels up her legs. She fights against the pain to keep a smile through her panting breaths to reassure Grace nothing is amiss.

"Morning." Mary Anne rests her hands on her knees and summons whatever saliva she can to coat her parched mouth. "Take me to the Duchess. Immediately."

Grace hesitates a moment too long for Mary Anne's liking.

"Now."

The tone startles Grace. It surprises Mary Anne as well. She has never been so insistent with her handmaiden before, but time slips away. Mary Anne's heart beats like a ticking clock, counting every second away from the throne room.

Grace nods and shuffles as fast as her gown will allow, Mary Anne following behind her. The metal-lined cage of Grace's dress clicks and scrapes the faster she moves. Her neck and shoulders twinge with pain every few paces. Mary Anne recalls when she discovered the metal piping within her handmaiden's dress. Any movement besides small steps and standing with perfect posture must cause intense discomfort. Grace has not worn anything except her gilded gown and mask since Mary Anne's arrival in the castle. Mary Anne pities Grace, truly, but if her handmaiden must endure pain for a short while for Mary Anne's succession, surely she will understand its worth. There will be time to apologize later. However, queens do not apologize.

After several more seemingly never-ending corridors and upward-winding stairs, past lavish paintings and sculptures, and through a gallery of thin tapestries, they reach a wide, arched door at the dead end of a hallway. Grace stands yards back, gripping her shaking hands. Mary Anne knocks loudly upon the thick oak. Proper decorum dictates knocking gently and waiting for a response before knocking again. However, a queen is never wrong, so Mary Anne knocks again, louder than before, even though muffled shuffling comes from the other side.

The Duchess unlatches what must be at least six locks and bolts from the inside of her bedchamber and swings the door open, gripping her own lavish feather-collared robe. Her cheeks flush without a hint of rouge. No heart-shaped color upon her lips, dark-plum eyeshadow, or wide wings of black liner to conceal the wrinkles at their corners. Without the harshness of her makeup, the Duchess's soft features, her age, and her gentleness shine in the morning light from the windows behind her.

"Mary Anne?"

Mary Anne weeps the moment she meets the Duchess's gentle eyes. The trickle of tears become full torrents. She looks upon her as when a child would see a parent return home after a long voyage. Though the Duchess's worry turns to a smile, plump cheeks rising to make crescents out of her eyes, this outburst of emotion seems out of place, as if not meant for her eyes. Someone else should stand in the Duchess's stead, but who? Whatever words Mary Anne planned to say, and whomever Mary Anne thought of, slips away. The words truly important to her finally pour out with her tears—the words she needed to hear and needed to say since she first reached the castle, perhaps before.

"I am worthy. I am worthy. I am worthy."

CHAPTER 2

CHESHIRE

Cheshire walks freely through the castle corridors. His mother's purple sash drapes around his neck, trousers, vest and cloak bundled on his back, and his cock dangles and bounces between his legs. This is how he spent most of his years growing up in the castle—his castle—in the areas where he was allowed to venture. The only reason to lay claim again is to see its inevitable destruction.

At the moment, he has no need of the Mask of Shadow or the Mask of Light, though still concealed within his laced gloves, should he need them. After a millennium of skulking in shadows, Mary Anne's unexpected, yet gracious, absolution of his past crimes proves advantageous.

Halfway down a long corridor, Cheshire returns to a familiar solitary door, forces it open, and steps into a grand chamber he has not set foot in for over a thousand years. He discovered it among many others on his nightly excursions as a child when he would sneak from his bedchamber while the rest of the castle slept.

This chamber houses remnants from the Age of Kings, who thought their wealth and status must be apparent in everything. Rather than destroy, burn, or dispose of 'the history', as his mother, who possessed simpler tastes, would refer to them, she'd had them sequestered to less used parts of the castle.

Several gaudy curved-back sofas and chairs, along with draping ferns in tall painted vases, divide the large chamber into separate areas. Three dozen nude marble statues of athletic men and women in dynamic and dancing poses—though none comparable to Jonathan or March—call this chamber home, long forgotten and frozen for eternity in a never-ending dance. Here he learned to admire and appreciate the detail, the beauty, and the strength of both the male and female form, which piqued his curiosity. Another reason he frequented this chamber.

On the north and south walls, giant golden-framed looking-glasses, at least twenty feet in height, give the illusion the room continues into infinity. The three dozen figures turn into three thousand in their lies. Or is it truth? Both often intertwine.

Cheshire approaches one of the looking-glasses on the north wall and runs his hand along its ornate swirling frame. Far behind it, his fingers find a concealed button he had to tip-toe to reach when younger and presses it. A soft click releases one side of the looking-glass, and the sole entrance opens to reveal a shallow hidden sitting area spanning the length of the chamber and a pathway behind the eastern wall to a similar area behind the looking-glasses of the south wall.

Within the walls, the looking-glasses become windows. Plush couches as gaudy as those outside rest against the back wall for hidden eyes to indulge in voyeuristic desires. However, these couches bear years of dust, unlike those within the chamber—a sign the soldiers nor anyone else have discovered this secret.

Since his world has become so much smaller, giving up the knowledge of the catacombs under Mirus and the hidden passages of the castle, it pleases him to have a place known to him and him alone. He follows the pathway around to the south end of the room, lays his bundle of clothing on a dusty cushion, and wraps his mother's sash back around his neck. His clothing will be safe here.

He slides from behind the looking-glass, closes it, waiting for the click, then sits on the tepid stone floor in front of it as he did as a child. These looking-glasses would expand his small world into infinity. Here he would converse with his reflection—the only friend besides his mother he had for many years.

Cheshire stares into his own eyes—purple shards of glass in concentric circles. He waits in silence while searching them. They become blurred. His breaths quicken. In their reflection, he sees the gentle gaze of his mother's eyes, and he blurts out crying without warning. His sobs echo against the high ceilings.

"Hello," his reflection says through the tears. "It has been a while."

"Yes. Yes, it has." Cheshire takes his time to regain control of his breath. "Then again, I guess we have both been rather preoccupied."

A laugh bubbles up. "Do you remember" — his reflections pauses — "when we would sneak out and walk behind the servants to test how quiet we could be? We would walk the entire length of the castle, wing to wing, matching their every footstep."

"Yes, but do you remember when we would use our passageways to move and reposition the knights' armors to scare the Chamberlain?"

"Or when we would steal his gloves and fan?"

"He thought a ghost followed him."

"The way he screamed."

"The way he ran."

They share a laugh at the Chamberlain's expense. It slips away, and silence thumps in Cheshire's ears.

"Do you remember our—" Cheshire begins to ask.

"A silly question," says his reflection.

"Silly or not, allow me to finish it."

"What is the point? You know the answer."

"I know," Cheshire says after a long pause. "I held on to her for as long as I could, but she faded with time. I did not mean to lose her. I remember her words, her songs, but after a thousand years I am not sure if the sound I hear in my head is her voice or one I conjure." A knot grows in Cheshire's throat, tears swelling. "I remember everything, every fucking detail. Why not her? Why have her beautiful face and lavender eyes become smudged in my memory like a mishandled painting?" Cheshire weeps again, stomach spasming, unable to close his mouth. "I miss her."

"As do I." His reflection wipes his own tears away.

"This is not what I thought it would be."

"Returning to the castle?"

"Yes."

"There was so much good, but also so much pain. Good once filled these halls. Now it has been covered over like old furniture with dirty linens to gather dust and be forgotten."

"And the Duchess will die for it."

"Yes, she will."

"I cannot say this to anyone but you." Cheshire puts his hand on the looking-glass, and his reflection reaches out to touch his. "I hate that our home does not feel like a home anymore."

"Would it? After being gone for so long? Besides, we have a new home now. One not of mortar and brick."

"Jonathan and March. No matter the months, years, or decades in between my visits. Their scent, their warmth, their touch, their laughter, their singing—they are home."

"They are home because they wait for you. They spend sleepless nights thinking of you. They love you without question, hesitation, or condition. They are home because you can always return to them. But not here."

The reflection shakes his head.

"Not until I find our mother."

The urge to cry pulls at Cheshire. He struggles against the tears, the grimace of his face, and the trembling of this body.

"Do not fight it."

"I must," says Cheshire in a broken voice, body shaking uncontrollably. "I must or it will consume me."

"Let it," his reflection says through the tears. "As you have every other ounce of pain."

Cheshire listens and lets the wave of sorrow embrace him. He cries out loud and long, filling the infinity of the chamber with his pain. His reflection weeps with him, and they have more breath to give, their lips cracked and eyes swollen and red.

After his short, choppy breaths subside, his reflection grins. "We have not spoken in quite some time."

"I know." Cheshire's lips tremble. "I was afraid."

"Of what?"

"For some reason, if I dared glance in a looking-glass, stream, or puddle and said something, you would not be there. I am sorry. I did not mean to leave you here in this horrible place."

"You didn't, silly ass. You took me with you."

Cheshire has no energy left to cry. All he can let out is a struggled wheeze. Before he can thank his reflection, a voice turns the humid air to ice.

"Cheshire." The voice, his mother's unmistakable voice, bounces through the chamber.

Cheshire whips around, heart pounding in his chest, not trusting the reflection beyond himself. The statues remain frozen in time—no movement anywhere. He turns back to his reflection, who is just as shocked.

"Did you hear?"

His reflection nods. "Yes."

An empty chasm grows in his gut.

"Come with me." Cheshire leaves the looking-glass and searches the menagerie of sculpted bodies in the endless reflections, running his hands over each one to make sure they are indeed marble, wishing for a glimpse of her, but shakes the thought.

"I conjured it," he says to reassure himself. He looks at a different looking-glass.

His reflection scratches at his hair. "Falling back into old habits brought a piece of her back."

"More than a piece. I can bring her back. I can find her. I will find her."

Cheshire wipes the tears from his cheeks, chest, and thighs and leaves the chamber to continue his unsettling search. Down neighboring corridors, he forces open other locked doors to reveal nothing of importance: vast empty chambers, which at one point were servant quarters, smaller rooms, storage closets, and smaller sitting rooms.

He looks into the breastplate of one of a dozen suits of armor lining the hallways. Though the image is dull, his reflection says, "Nothing," clear as the dawn.

Any evidence of his mother, her kindness, her soul, has been erased. His mother's bedchamber filled in with bricks at the Duchess's orders. But nothing can ever truly be erased, no matter how hard the Duchess may try. Cheshire is living proof, as well as the sash, his mother's sash, around his neck. Something must remain hidden in the castle. Cheshire will turn every chamber upside down to find the truth.

The trail he will blaze starts with the Gryphon—liar, falsifier—who knows more than he divulged to Cheshire and ends with the Duchess, gargling on her blood at Cheshire's hands. Gods help whoever stands in his way.

Servant women who happen upon him when they round a corner gasp, cover their mouths, and avert their eyes, unsure where to look. Others choose to stop and let their gazes linger, their eyes swinging back and forth like the pendulum of a clock.

Cheshire nears the kitchen as a rumbling grows in his stomach. The warmth of the kitchen pulses through the hallways. Ovens have been burning and the cooks working since before dawn. The back of his jaw tingles, and his mouth salivates. The sweet smell of freshly baked breads, biscuits, and spiced tarts waft through the air the closer Cheshire draws. Perhaps his trail does not begin with the Gryphon but with food to regain his strength.

Intrusive memories, visions of his childhood, come in waves like the heat. His mother meets him with a basket filled with fruits, meats, cheeses, biscuits, anything he could desire. Sneaking out of the catacombs to steal a few more snacks in the middle of the night before the cooks returned to their duties. His mother's smile as she sings him the lullaby every night of his life with her.

In the kitchen, the older women, the cooks, have little patience for his shit. They keep busy kneading dough, chopping meat, and pulling apart and snapping vegetables. Flour covers their foreheads, cheeks, and aprons.

"What is this nonsense?" one asks, slamming three freshly plucked turkeys on a wooden table.

"We're just opening the castle to everyone still? Didn't most of everyone leave?" asks another with flour and dough up to her elbows.

"You'd think they'd have half a mind to wear half of something," another cook says, snapping carrots.

He can taste the myriad of warm aromas filling the air. Trays with stacks of bright, colorful tarts and pastries cover an entire table. He shoves an entire custard tart in his mouth. The crunch of the flaky crust and the sweet smoothness of the filling squishes in his mouth and sends shivers from his tongue to the top of his head and down to his toes. His eyes lose focus, and his stomach swirls with gratitude. He pops several more in his mouth, grabs another three, stacking them on top of each other, plus an apple from a large bowl on another table, and a warm loaf of bread with a thin layer of flour on its beautifully cracked crust.

"Wait," says the woman covered in flour as he turns to leave.

Against his better judgment, Cheshire turns back, mouth full. The woman's eyes narrow and scrutinize him. His body glistens with sweat from the heat of the ovens. He expects another comment about his lack of clothing. Instead, she tilts her head from side to side, sifting an idea back and forth. A glimmer of what Cheshire suspects to be a hint of recognition sparkles in the twinkle of her eyes.

No. No one in the castle knew of his birth except for Pat and Bill, the Gryphon, the White Paladin, and, unfortunately, the Duchess. All those with knowledge kept his existence secret for his safety, being born a bastard child. It broke his mother's heart to keep him from the world, so she gave him a world of his own, the catacombs, which are, unfortunately, no longer his—at least those within the castle and beneath Mirus.

The cook's eyes bounce back and forth from his eyes to his hair to his chest to his sash—his mother's sash. Her lips form a thought.

Before she can say a word, Cheshire throws his apple across the kitchen and shatters a large serving dish on a shelf along the wall. Its large white pieces rain to the ground and break into smaller shards.

The unexpected event breaks the woman's concentration, and she joins in the other cooks, collectively cursing and shouting at him to leave with the most colorful language Cheshire cannot help but appreciate. He takes his food in hand, along with another apple, and walks out casually to search the castle and enjoy his meal.

Silly of him not to consider some of the older servants in the castle would not recognize his mother Queen Dinah's sash. It would be difficult to draw the connection. Most would consider it a dishonorable trophy—to wear the sash of the queen he was accused of slaying by the Duchess.

While Cheshire eats and walks through the hallways, he shifts candelabras off their center, pushes the bottoms of towering paintings askew, and wipes his hands on tapestries as he passes.

The servant girls closer to his own age who pass him giggle at first then blush at how long they stare, before running off to other parts of the castle.

Wait.

Over the past three days and nights, scouring every level of the castle, Cheshire crossed the paths of servants, castle guards, and caught sight of the Chamberlain and Pat and Bill wandering the halls. Yet, there are two more players missing from the board. There has been no sign of the Gryphon, *which means he is not in the castle. He more than likely seeks refuge in the city. Cheshire is a man divided.*

The Gryphon is wise enough to know Cheshire hunts for him to seek answers and retribution for his continuous lies. Cheshire would have happened upon him or a trace of him. He wastes his time searching the castle room by room for his prey, and the Gryphon probably counted on it. Damn him.

The Duchess awaits Cheshire's methodical and intentional torment before he takes her life. She holds answers but has made herself more elusive than the Gryphon, hiding somewhere in the castle.

Jonathan and March wait for him to join in unadulterated bliss.

Logic serves the Gryphon should be first. Between him and the Duchess, the Gryphon would be more willing to answer if tortured. His answers, should he reveal them, would save time searching the castle, and if he remains resolute in his lies, his death will leave Cheshire free to attend to the others.

The end is near. Once Cheshire finds his mother, he will open the floodgates of every hell and bring their fury upon the city and the Duchess and make her pay for every year, every day, every hour, every minute, every second she stole from him and his mother.

"Cheshire."

The sound of his mother's voice brings tears to his eyes and a knot to his throat again. He turns around to an empty hallway. Not empty. A servant girl far down the corridor fidgets with the edge of her apron and watches him walk away. She snaps her head down when she realizes she has been caught and disappears around a corner. The voice could not belong to the servant girl. It was, is, his mother's sweet tune, her cadence, said with the same loving inflection as when she would find him in the middle of just-completed mischief.

This is no mere coincidence. Cheshire would imagine his mother as he drifted off to sleep. However, now, his eyes are open. He does not slumber, yet he hears her voice clear as the temple bells of the city. Not only is he divided, he is pulled apart. How he has longed to hear his mother's voice, let alone call to him? But her voice, though soothing to the heart, is stained with the smallest hints of doubt and foreboding.

Despite his unwavering confident grin, an unexpected volatile mixture of emotions swirls in the pit of his stomach—the welcome, familiar warmth of being in the place where he grew as a child; an unwanted, yet expected, chill of knowing its harrowed history; the pain where comfort should be; the sense of being alone, surrounded by people. Forever caught in between.

The Gryphon must wait. Cheshire must settle his mind and focus his thoughts before the beginning of the end, which means discovering the source of his mother's voice.

CHAPTER 3

MARCH

March opens her eyes to a new morning, rocked by the gentle tide of Jonathan's breathing—slowly pushing her away and always pulling her back in the wake of his body. The sweet song of his dreams drifts from his lips to her ears. She inhales deep as she wakes, breathing in her love's scent and realizing Cheshire and, thankfully, Mary Anne have left.

Her hands hover over the bruises covering his body like a leaf dancing on an autumn breeze, not ready to settle on the forest floor—first his thighs, then his torso, his chest, and then the side of his face. The tonics the castle physicians administered have done wonders for the swelling of his injuries. He heals, but the bruises from the battle with Sheridan, the cult leader, linger and turn pale green and yellow. She kisses him ever-so-softly on his forehead and rises from the wide bed, careful not to disturb his rest.

A small scroll lies at the foot of the bed. March collects it and knows the scribe of the tightly wrapped parchment immediately. This is the second scroll she has received from the Gryphon. The red wax seal bears his sigil—a lion's open roar, teeth bared, framed by long wings.

Damn it all.

She breaks the seal and unrolls the scroll. The words 'Your presence is required outside the gates' are scratched with an elegant hand lost in these times. March has not ventured out of the castle since her return from the Hollow, but it appears her place is in the city this morning. She wonders how much of the city has been repaired after the attack by the cultists. In the end, it matters little. What she is to worry about is the assault to come.

A glance back to the bed tugs at her heart. She prefers to stay in bed with Jonathan and wear nothing, be one with each other, their bodies pressed into indistinguishable heat, with Cheshire joining them soon, increasing their passion, moaning in glorious harmonies.

Leaving Jonathan's side was not among her plans for the day. She should not. The past two she has bathed him with gentle cloths and, in the small conscious moments the tonics allow, fed him spoonfuls of broth and makes sure he takes his elixir. When he wakes, she should be by his side, regardless of the dangers outside their walls. But they are not *their* walls. They are not in the Hollow, but in the castle of Mirus. They are not safe here, and so she will see what need the Gryphon has of her, only to see her loves protected.

"Every step away," she whispers.

A small and slow twitch at the corner of his mouth responds—the first sign he can understand. He will complete their simple ballad when he wakes.

March pushes through the gossamer curtains surrounding the bed and sets the scroll on top of one of many large trunks in the corner of Mary Anne's bedchamber—all of their bedchamber, now—and makes a decisive selection of wardrobe for this day. The creak of the heavy wooden lid reminds her of the Mill's breaths, ever so slight, yet ever-present as their wooden home stretches with the new day. March steps into a loose-fitting pair of leather trousers and heavy boots, wraps and ties a narrow linen band around her chest, and attaches leather bracers to her trousers and slides them over her shoulders.

The latch to the chamber door clicks and lifts. March pauses and glances over her shoulder, cautious but not worried. Her collection of swords waits an arm's length away, all ready to bathe in crimson. Mary Anne's handmaiden, one of the Sarafan, enters, hands clasped, head bowed, and waits by the line of wardrobes.

What does Mary Anne call her? Grace or something foolish. Not her real name.

Her presence brings March's blood to boil and her skin to crawl, unwilling and unable to accept all this woman and her uniform represent. The servant girl should occupy her time with Mary Anne, but without their queen-to-be present, she appears lost, out of place, like the rest of them. The girl stands waiting for some command or order. March does not want to address her, but the sooner she leaves, the quicker this disgusting film will leave her skin.

"She is not here. Do you not know where she is? Is this not your entire duty and purpose now—to wait on her? Rather poor service, if I do say so myself. If I were you, I would go find her."

Without the prying eyes of the Duchess and Mary Anne, the handmaiden allows her docile facade to slip, releasing a bit of the anger caged behind her half-mask, lips twitching. A familiar expression to March, and one she does not wish to look upon any longer.

"Be off with you." March slips on a leather back harness with two of her swords, Absolom and Monpart, oiled, sharpened, sheathed, and buckles a belt of daggers around her thigh. Even though March cannot see the handmaiden's eyes, they crawl upon her still, until the slightest turn of her head toward Jonathan.

"Take your eyes from him before I pluck them from your skull," says March, cold as the steel on her back. "Linger one moment longer and I will consider it a mercy to end your suffering and servitude for you."

The handmaiden knows none of March's threats are idle, so she lowers her head and stumbles backward, metal clinking within her gown. She winces from the pain and rushes out of the chamber without looking back.

"I fucking hate this place," says March.

She slips a tall, thin half-empty bottle of rum from her stash at the side of their trunks without it clinking against the others. She uncorks it with her teeth, spits the cork into her free hand, and takes a long swig, welcoming the warm, sweet flavor, washing the brief encounter with the handmaiden from her mind. This has been the first close encounter with any of the Sarafan roaming the castle since arriving in Mirus, and will hopefully be the last. March finishes the contents of the bottle, corks it, and returns it to the floor.

She turns back to the bed and her heart swells. Cheshire, in all his disheveled glory, perches crouched on top of the headboard, looking down at Jonathan and then raising his lavender gaze to meet her.

Within the span of two blinks, Cheshire closes the distance and stands toe to toe with March, reaching up and running his fingers down her arms like gentle raindrops. She welcomes the shiver he brings to her body.

"Where are you away to so hurriedly?" He unbuckles her harness and lowers it to the floor. His fingers slide inside her braces and run their length from collarbone to waist, caressing her breast and dipping them inside of her trousers.

Not fair at all. Cheshire has done all the work for her, appearing wearing nothing but his beautiful swollen cock and sash, depriving her the delight of hearing the stitches and seams pop and rip from this clothing as she pulls it from his body. Her thumbs circle his nipples, and she watches his cock jump and flex at her command. The slightest pinch causes its head to swell full and hard and his stomach muscles to shake.

"I am summoned by the Gryphon."

He kisses her, gently at first, then deeper, consuming her—tongue forcefully eliciting a sweet moan from her. He holds her bottom lip between his teeth, their breaths mingling together. "To the Gryphon, you say?" His lips move against hers with every word. "And when are you to meet him?"

She grabs the scroll from the trunk and holds it up. His eyes dart to it before she slips it into her pocket then grabs the back of his hair with her free hand, their lips circling one another.

"He waits even now, I presume." She kisses him deeply, her tongue overpowering his. His moan is low and rumbles at the back of his throat.

"He shall wait a moment longer." Cheshire pushes the linen wrap over her breasts and exhales as if it were the first time looking upon them. It is the way he always looks at her, and it brings an untold joy to her to feel the love in his shimmering eyes.

He kisses her chin. Damn him. She stretches her neck for him to kiss his way down her neck. Kisses fall on her skin like gentle, autumn leaves upon the grass, and his breath leaves trails of his desire. His gentle lips find their intended target, her right nipple, and envelopes the tip of her breast with his entire mouth. His tongue circles and teases, the heat of his mouth circulating through her chest.

March pulls him by the hair and moves his face to her other breast, which he accepts almost greedily, showing the same attention and reverence. Her free hand rakes down his shoulders and arms. Cheshire would and has spent the better part of a day at her breasts, taking pleasure and giving it in return. She takes hold of the base of his cock, thumping like a heart in her hand, and squeezes against its pulse. Cheshire pants and rubs his cheeks and chin across her breasts, dragging his lips and pressing against her skin with his tender and rough touch.

Unable and unwilling to leave him, March places the scroll on the trunk and reaches down to play with his heavy, full balls. He stands and massages her breasts with firm hands, locking eyes with her, his intentions clear. He winks and glances off to the left. Her eyes meet

Jonathan's—open, and with a crooked smile upon his face, and her heart jumps a second time. If not apparent before, it appears the Gryphon must wait, not just from Cheshire's bidding, but from Jonathan as well, and a union they all need.

CHAPTER 4
JONATHAN

Jonathan wakes before his eyes open from the familiar scent of home and a gentle shadow beyond the darkness, like a cloud passing above the oak of the Hollow sharing its shade. It does not help he has not moved in days, sleeping in the same position, barely conscious from the potions the castle surgeons administered. The bruises and soreness have taken root in his muscles. His bones are branches on a weathered tree, and he fears they will crack if he moves too quickly. Swords fresh from the blacksmith's forge might as well pierce his ribs and stomach.

His eyes slowly let in the light and a vision of the heavens sits above him on the headboard—Cheshire. His love's twinkling eyes, ever-mischievous grin, and his body shaped by the gods hangs above him like a dream from which he would never want to wake. Cheshire winks at Jonathan, welcoming him back to the world.

Jonathan can hear a slight shuffling across the room—March, he hopes. Every move he makes, from the flex of his foot to his smallest finger, ignites a fire across the rest of his body, but he manages to raise his head to gaze upon his other love, March, dressed and ready with swords for whatever this day brings.

Presumably unwise, but from the throb of his own cock, Jonathan cannot let Cheshire and March go so quickly, now finally awake. And from the look of Cheshire above him, cock as hard as the thick bowsprit of a ship, he shares the same idea.

He lies his head back down on the silk sheets, catches Cheshire's eyes again, then glances to March. Cheshire knows Jonathan's thoughts, and in the time he takes to look up again, Cheshire is across the room.

Jonathan suffers the pain and pinpricks in his fingertips and the cold rush creeping across the back of his head in order to raise it again and watch his loves. A more beautiful, powerful, and heavenly sight—the pairing of March and Cheshire—does not exist in all of Wonder, past, present, or future.

There is something especially sensual having March fully clothed and Cheshire without a stitch besides his sash. Their hands caress each other. They kiss hard, tongues lashing and teeth biting. Cheshire raises March's top to reveal the full curves of her breast match the curves of his ass, and Jonathan hungers for both. Jonathan's cock bounces, glistens, and flexes involuntarily, faster and faster, craving more as he watches them enjoy each other.

March catches Jonathan's voyeuristic gaze and returns a wondrous smirk. Though he could not see her, he felt her heat next to him while unconscious, ever at his side.

"Welcome back, dear heart." March strokes Cheshire. "You wish to watch?"

Rather than risk nodding his head, Jonathan's eyes widen to saucers. "Yes."

March keeps a tight grip on Cheshire's shaft and leads him through the sheer curtains to her side of the bed. Jonathan needs, no, he must get out of bed. He braces himself, grips the sheets ready to swing his legs to the floor—chest, thighs, arms, and back screaming.

"Darling," says Cheshire. "What the fuck do you think you are doing?"

The pain persists, but the anticipation of the exquisite pleasure to unfold before Jonathan dulls his senses. Cheshire stands behind March, kissing at her neck and biting at her ear, all the while both staring into Jonathan's soul. Cheshire's hands circle and massage her breasts and slink around her body to untie the linen wrap, tossing it to the floor. Her arms reach back over her head, arching her back, stretching her body to fondle Cheshire's hair—a maiden figurehead to match his bowsprit.

How formidable and sensual March appears, wearing her trousers and the bracers running down the sides of her breasts. Jonathan has seen her wear this many times throughout the years, and her strength and grace never cease to amaze him. Coupled with Cheshire and his fearsome physique, sinewed muscles, unbridled confidence, and animalistic nature, it is as if Jonathan looks upon a goddess and god in human form, and he does not know what he has done in his life to deserve a modicum of what they give him.

Before Cheshire can finish unbuckling her trousers, March spins around behind him and pins one of his arms between them, lowering it between her legs. By her gasp and the press of her hips against Cheshire's backside, his fingers have found their intended target.

From Jonathan's angle, it appears as if March fucks Cheshire from behind, and Jonathan recalls the beautiful night at the center of the hedge maze, where he witnessed March use their mold of Jonathan's cock on Cheshire, and he wants to see it again even more now.

With her free hand, she reaches around and strokes Cheshire's length, twisting and sliding her hand on top and below. His open-mouthed grin grows as he pants and places his tongue against the front of his top teeth. Jonathan's heart races, his cock jumps and drips upon his stomach, and his ass quivers.

His loves never break eye contact with him. March whispers to Cheshire before licking the curve of his ear, leaving her hand in place.

Cheshire heeds her desire and thrusts into the grip of her hand over and over again, both of their hips pulsing and pushing together. Jonathan uses every ounce of strength to fight the urge to sit up, but his body compels him.

March and Cheshire see the temptation in his eyes and break from each other. March steps from her boots, lets the bracers and trousers fall to the floor, and lies on his right side. Her breath dances upon his lips, teasing him with her heat. Cheshire climbs on the opposite side of the bed and gently kneels next to Jonathan's head, teasing him as well, stretching his shaft across his face not to satiate Jonathan's palate but for March's waiting mouth. Jonathan said he wanted to watch, and they mean to put on such a performance.

By the fucking gods, March asked if he wanted to watch, and they will make sure he damned well does. The worst of it is Jonathan cannot reach his own cock, yearning, screaming to be touched, held, stroked, and consumed.

March leans over Jonathan and takes more and more of Cheshire into her mouth, tongue licking the bottom of his shaft, kissing the tip of his head each time, and moaning along the journey. Cheshire pulls her hair back tenderly and tucks it behind her ears, keeping strands from falling by running his fingers through her hair. March releases Cheshire's cock, and it grazes across Jonathan's lips too quickly for him to taste.

Jonathan could stretch his neck up and touch Cheshire's glistening shaft and March's lips with his tongue, but a gentle hand from March to Jonathan's shoulder keeps him in place, leaving him no choice but to endure and enjoy the performance.

He cannot stop his own hips from thrusting, squeezing his ass each time. His body aches, yet he will endure. As with any injury sustained in the past, the more he moves, the sooner the soreness of his muscles will fade.

Cheshire makes his way to March's side of the bed, where both kneel together, Cheshire behind March, next to Jonathan's waist. He presses hard against her back, and his wet cock head slides out from between her thighs. He turns her head back for a kiss with one hand and, with the other, massages her breasts. March circles her hips and slides her sensitivity back and forth along Cheshire, moaning and whimpering into his mouth.

Whether a stroke of luck or purposeful, they straddle Jonathan's right hand. He pushes past the ache of his body and cups Cheshire's balls, massaging them while his loves kiss. His hand works up the wet shaft until he finds March's warmth. Jonathan slides two fingers inside her beautiful body while keeping hold of Cheshire's sliding shaft—an awkward grip, but their faces and breaths through gritted teeth make it worth it.

They grind hard against his hand. Cheshire places one of March's arms over his shoulder to see the exquisite spectacle. Jonathan's thumb traces the tip of Cheshire's cock as it pushes out every time, and when it slides back, his thumb massages March's tenderest spot. Jonathan wants them both to reach out and grab his own shaft, inches from them, but fears at their first touch he might explode. He still might just at the sight of them.

Jonathan grips Cheshire's shaft, asking him to stop, tired of being teased, and guides Cheshire's head inside of her. March winces, pushes her hips back, and releases a long, drawn-out moan to fill the chamber.

As always, Cheshire begins gently with March, his girth almost too much for even Jonathan to take. Her body rocks with each thrust, slowly taking more of Cheshire and losing her breath the deeper she welcomes him. Jonathan keeps his hand on their lustful, magnificent union, massaging both, feeling, kneading, and pressing as Cheshire's momentum builds. The rhythm of their bodies slamming together, the ripple of their motion, March's quick inhales, and Cheshire's groans are almost too much for Jonathan to bear. Damn the pain—he reaches for his own cock with his free hand, but Cheshire grabs his wrist, making him wait.

For fuck's sake. Frustrated, but grateful, Jonathan heeds Cheshire, not wanting this waking dream to end. His lovers' bodies, however, shake, their breaths quicken, nearing their end, but stop, alike in mind, their climax already planned.

Cheshire slides from March, who quivers at his absence. After catching her breath, she moves to the head of the bed and swings her leg over Jonathan's face, straddling him as if mounting a horse. Before Jonathan can raise his head to kiss her wet skin, Cheshire kneels behind her again, and this time, her hand guides him in. With March accustomed to Cheshire's girth, he does not slow his pace. Their breaths and moans grow wilder, louder.

Between their legs, the heat from their sex is palpable, bringing sweat to Jonathan's face. Their scent is more intoxicating than any tea in Jonathan's possession. He watches this divine union as long as he can bear, dripping down upon him from the heavens. Jonathan tenses his arms to test the pain. Bruised, but nothing broken. It can and will be endured. He reaches up, fighting past the shooting pain in his arms and back, wraps his arms up around both of their thighs, and pulls them down, smothering his face with their love.

They do not stop, nor would Jonathan wish them to. He turns his head, allowing his loves to glide over every side of his face, gasping for breath, and kisses and licks as he can. The faster Cheshire fucks March, the harder Jonathan pulls them down, almost suffocating himself with the flesh of his lovers. They grind harder on his face as they did his hand. The fullness of Jonathan's tongue reaches and laps at March's sensitivity, tickling the edge of Cheshire's head as it peeks out, and runs down the full length of Cheshire's shaft until his large, low-hanging balls slide across his face. Over and over again, they press and grind across his face, wetter every time.

Their thighs quake violently in his arms, shaking the entire bed. Whatever pain Jonathan feels leaves his body for this conjunction of souls. Cheshire pulls from March and reaches around to strum her, as Jonathan pulls her onto his waiting mouth. She gasps, holds her breath as she releases her climax, gifting it to Jonathan to drink, which he does willingly, swallowing and licking until she finishes and beyond. Cheshire plays with Jonathan's tongue with his fingers as it passes. March finally catches her breath, however, Cheshire is not finished.

He slides back into March and thrusts hard again and again, to March's half-moans and half-laughter. Their sweaty, sticky bodies slap together furiously. Cheshire's shaft swells and hardens before Jonathan's eyes. His moans turn to screams, wild and animalistic. March must feel the stretch in her body. She slides from Cheshire, moves to the side of Jonathan, and guides his cock into Jonathan's waiting, parched mouth. His love, swollen, nearing his end, falls to his hands, and cannot help but continue to thrust, panting and whimpering, sliding deeper into Jonathan's throat every time.

Cheshire's cock swells in Jonathan's mouth, just as he pulls away, leaving only his head in Jonathan's lips. He roars into the air as his climax fills Jonathan's mouth, mixing with March's. Though he tries to swallow, Cheshire's gift escapes the sides of his mouth, which March quickly collects with her tongue. After what must be six of seven bursts, Cheshire slides deep into Jonathan's throat once more, his balls flush against Jonathan's eyes, and finally pulls free.

Jonathan catches his breath, eyes blurred, thinking it over, thankful for the quickening of his soul from his lovers. Cheshire and March lie at his sides, still careful not to touch the rest of his body, and each grab his cock with one hand. They are not finished. They stroke in unison with wet hands, and every time they pass the rim of Jonathan's head, his body jolts. Pain should overtake his body, but all he feels is their touch, their love, and the tingling sensation in the back of his head and deep within his stomach. March and Cheshire take turns kissing and licking the tip of his head until Jonathan can hold back no longer.

He raises his head again to watch his own climax as they continue to stroke and twist his cock, shooting long white ribbons across his stomach, chest, and face—almost rivaling Cheshire. The pits between the muscles of his torso fill with white and clear pools. His loves continue to stroke until Jonathan has nothing left to give. They kiss and lick their way up his body, collecting and drinking from each pool, not missing a single drop, until they reach his lips. They swallow and smile at him—angels from on high, his guardians—and leave long, lingering kisses on his lips.

The quick jostle of March and Cheshire collapsing on the bed next to Jonathan brings the pain back to his body. They gently rest their foreheads against his shoulders. Despite the afterglow of their time together, a knot forms in Jonathan's stomach, knowing they must again part ways; March to the Gryphon, Cheshire to his mischief, and Jonathan to Mary Anne. He closes his eyes and breathes them in. More than their sex, their scents—the oaks of the Hollow, parchment, linseed oil, and citron from March, and the forests beyond, leather, and earth from Cheshire; they smell of home. They are his home, though they find themselves thousands of miles away.

"Do us all a favor." Cheshire kisses Jonathan's shoulder. "Recover soon."

"I know there are many tasks yet—" Jonathan winces.

"You misunderstand me," says Cheshire. "I do not care for your tasks around the castle. I want to fuck you." Jonathan chuckles the best he can. "And I want to watch March fuck you with the wonderful toy Pat and Bill made for you, from you."

"Is that so?" asks Jonathan.

"Oh, I am quite captivated by it. And while I look forward to March using it on me again, I cannot wait to see you take your own cock."

"Agreed," says March.

"Shall we invite them to join us again?" asks Jonathan.

"You have both played with them?" March raises herself to her elbow.

"Yes." Cheshire raises to match her. "It was quite unexpected but thoroughly enjoyable." After a quick exchange of glances, Cheshire looks down at Jonathan. "Have you two fucked them before?"

The question takes Jonathan by surprise. The simple answer is yes, but they have never broached the topic with Cheshire since they never crossed paths. An odd sense of hypocritical jealousy fills Jonathan. Though he and March have shared Pat and Bill, the thought of Cheshire with anyone else brings Jonathan's blood to boil.

"It started with the making of the mold," says Jonathan. "Difficult to not be aroused by three sets of hands on my cock. And on the odd, unfortunate detour to Mirus, we have, on occasion, crossed paths. Do you think us wicked?" Jonathan asks Cheshire.

Hundreds of scenarios spin behind Cheshire's eyes. "I think you selfish. Where was my invitation?"

"Difficult to invite you when you disappear for years on end," says March.

"Fair," says Cheshire. "Yet, I want to watch, and also partake in this carnal experience."

A better response could not be had. It appears the decision has been made for him, and Jonathan cannot be any more pleased. "I shall tell my bones and muscles to mend faster, then."

"Appreciated." Cheshire kisses Jonathan.

March follows, kissing Jonathan once more before rising from the bed to dress.

Jonathan looks back to Cheshire, who has already disappeared. He was elusive even before discovering the damned masks; now, he comes and goes like a phantasm. He turns his attention back to March picking up her trousers, bracers, and boots.

"Wait," says Jonathan. "I just want to drink you in once more, before you depart."

March presses her lips together and raises an eyebrow, but her eyes give away her full heart. She waits for a moment, then picks up her linen top from the floor and goes to reclaim her swords and a small scroll from their stack of trunks. She swings her hair from side to side and runs her fingers through it; no time for braids this morning. Her long hair, hanging between the blades on her back, suits her just as equally. She returns with one of the small vials of elixir she retrieved from the Hollow, sits on the bed next to Jonathan, and holds his head up to take a small drink.

It numbs his mind. Hopefully, it will numb at least a portion of his body as well. The cold liquid surges through him, and even the once welcome chill down his body is accompanied by a thousand needle pricks.

"Thank you," says Jonathan.

"Do not thank me." A tidal wave of guilt swallows March's brief happiness. "Not for this." She rises, leaves the bottle by the bed, and straightens her harness. "You will be up and about soon." She walks to the chamber door.

"Is a step back to you." Jonathan finishes March's words from earlier.

"Damn you." She returns to the bed and kisses Jonathan once more, before leaving the chamber without a word.

The door latch clinks shut, and the air previously filled with the love songs of March and Cheshire returns to silence. Jonathan will not spend another moment confined to this bed; there is far too much to accomplish. The small moments of peace Jonathan enjoys are soon dashed at the realization of his next arduous task—dressing himself.

"Shit."

CHAPTER 5
MARY ANNE

The Duchess cups her hand over her mouth, tears forming in her eyes and running down the curve of her plump cheeks. She embraces Mary Anne in the warmest, largest of hugs, resting her chin on her shoulder and holding her tight.

Mary Anne sobs louder, echoing through the long corridor behind her. It has been ages since anyone has held her and comforted her, so she buries her face in the Duchess's shoulder and lets her tears flow.

"It is alright, my dear." The Duchess strokes the back of Mary Anne's hair, sending wave after wave of calming warmth through Mary Anne's body.

"I am worthy," Mary Anne repeats in a muffled voice.

"Of course, dear," says the Duchess.

"No." Mary Anne pulls her face away to look into the Duchess's eyes, which sparkle on the verge of tears, and sucks in quick breaths to quell the tears. "It has happened." Thick saliva cakes her mouth. "I do not know how it happened. Or why? I touched them and... and they opened. The doors to the throne room are open. I should have gone to wake you before entering, but I could not help myself."

The Duchess pulls away, tears in her own eyes, and wipes Mary Anne's cheeks with the sleeve of her robe. "Do not speak of such nonsense. Do not care or question why the doors opened. They opened. Celebrate, child. They opened for *you*." The Duchess presses her lips together in a tight smile like a doting mother. "Shall we go together now?"

Mary Anne and the Duchess race toward the throne room, smiling and laughing, as fast as the Duchess's legs will allow, holding hands like two giddy schoolgirls, Mary Anne leading the way. Grace follows at her own pace, far behind.

The servants they pass stop their chores and look on in amazement, no doubt unaccustomed to watching the Duchess enjoy herself. Or perhaps the elation in Mary Anne's heart is contagious to all around her. She laughs through her tears and tries to contain them both. Should she not? After all, this is a momentous occasion—a royal occasion.

"My dear," the Duchess huffs. "Do not dare stifle yourself. Release it. Unbridled what you believe to be true. Do not think. Feel. Embrace every emotion and allow yourself to experience everything in this moment."

"Be a queen," they say together.

Mary Anne stops, grips both of the Duchess's hands tight, and breathes deep to pull every worry and doubt from the air. She holds her breath, showing control over them, over herself, allowing her worries to fear their own suffocation. She dispels them all with one long exhalation that sends tingles through her fingers and brings her racing heart to a calm, yet eager, equilibrium. The weightless, cold rush returns to Mary Anne.

"Are you ready?" the Duchess asks.

"I am." Mary Anne stands tall and allows her lips to quiver and her legs to tremble at the anticipation. She adjusts her robe and cinches it closed. "I am."

"Prepare yourself." The Duchess cannot contain her excitement.

"From this point forward, your world will transform quite rapidly. This is momentous, not just for you but for all of Wonderland."

"What is next?" Mary Anne squeezes the Duchess's hands. "What follows?"

"The Arcana. The Grand Arcana will bestow itself upon you. I have no doubt. There is no stopping what has begun. However, we must still tread carefully."

A needle of fear pierces Mary Anne's heart. The opening of the throne room doors was a marker along her journey. She beat her hands bloody against the doors and tried her best to ignore her doubts and question her own worth. If the doors never opened for her, all would be lost. She never gave thought to the possibility her quest could move in reverse—lose everything. Could Wonderland reject her now? Even though the Duchess said the words, Mary Anne needs reassurance. She must hear it.

"Are you certain?"

"My dear, according to the Book of Queens, once the doors open, they remain open." The Duchess brings their hands up to their chests. "The Third Tenet is all but assured. We must wait for the Fourth Tenet to end the Third. Once the Grand Arcana manifests in you, your journey, our journey, will almost be at its conclusion."

"No," says Mary Anne. "Not a conclusion. A new beginning. The beginning for me, for all of Wonderland, and of a new queen's reign."

"Absolutely right, my dear. Let us not doddle any longer."

Mary Anne and the Duchess share a smile wider than the throne room doors themselves and glide the rest of the way to the throne room in blissful exhilaration, swelling with each turn of a corner into a new corridor. If this is what it will feel like to be queen, Mary Anne welcomes it, yearns for it, needs it. The Duchess lets out a small giggle as they round the corner and sees for herself the light spilling from the open throne room doors. She pats Mary Anne's hand excitedly.

Where moments ago her troubled heart knew only tears, now Mary

Anne cannot contain her laughter. How far she has come? Mary Anne remembers the first time she rounded this corner with Pat and Bill and saw Chamberlain Weiss and the Duchess waiting for her in front of the sealed doors. She was so frightened but cannot remember why; the emotion's roots run deep within her, but the reason has faded from her memory like a dream.

Now, the bright sun shines through the open doors on a brand new day. Mary Anne knew not what was in store and did not believe what the Duchess and the Chamberlain told her at first, but now an unbelievable fantasy has become her reality—her fate. A fate that comes into sharp question the moment they enter the throne room.

Every positive emotion which carried Mary Anne back leaves her body as if disappearing down a swirling drain, leaving her soul cold, dank, and hollow. The Duchess squeezes Mary Anne's hand tight to stop her in place at the threshold.

The Twins, Lysander and Uriah, stand upon the dais on both sides of the throne. Their white silk robes and silver hair glow in the morning sun. A look of smug victory curls their lips and darkens their eyes, despite the gleam within them. They pose, waiting for Mary Anne's return.

Six soldiers of Adamas, clad in armor and white tabards, with swords at their hip, wander the room caught in its wonder. Four castle servant girls wait in a line by the doors, heads lowered and hands clasped, no doubt coaxed here.

"So glad you could join us on this magnificent morning," says Uriah.

"Just in time," says Lysander. "Do you see what miracle has transpired? Wonderland has spoken."

"The doors have opened," says Uriah.

"Welcome to *our* reign," the Twins say together in a lustful, despicable growl.

CHAPTER 6

MARCH

March descends the grand stairs of the keep into an empty bailey, devoid of the scraping and clacking of armored soldiers—the silence of a graveyard. The faint smell of death drifts in the air and sends a shiver up her body despite the tepid morning air; a welcome sensation to combat the sweat running down her back. After weeks of rain, the air outside the castle is heavy, moist, and sticks to March's skin like a film on the surface of a fen. The unnatural warmth of Mirus was uncomfortable before—now it becomes intrusive.

The frames and timbers of the main gates are freshly reinforced with thicker wooden posts the size of full, aged oaks and fitted with new iron beams and crossbars courtesy of Pat and Bill's craftsmanship. Craftsmanship March must find time to question them about after her encounter with their creations in Spire Side. Like so many others, this conversation must wait for another time.

Her echoing boot steps across the stones should bring her solace. The threat of the Cult of the Mother is over thanks to the bravery of both Cheshire and Jonathan, and the sacrifices of many others. For weeks, the loyal soldiers of Mirus trained on these cobbles, called these stone walls home, slept, fellowshipped, and sought sanctuary here from the horde. Nearly every soldier, excluding the Castle Guard and the Gryphon's archers, has returned to their home to see what remains, if anyone waits for them, or if they have lost everything after the assault. The walls of the city contained the cult's rampage thanks to Cheshire's mischief, allowing the soldiers whose homes and farmsteads outside of Mirus to find fortune. However, those whose families lived in the tiers of Stonehaven were ignored by the gods, as always.

Their exodus from the castle hastened further after Mary Anne's pardon and welcome of Cheshire, Queen Slayer, who single-handedly killed hundreds of their numbers in recent weeks, not to mention the thousands more over the years. An interesting play on Mary Anne's part; March did not think her capable of reaching. Perhaps this other-worlder is not as dull as March first believed, which makes her dangerous, and makes March hate her all the more.

Before March leaves the bailey, she knocks loudly on the rear door of Dormy's wagon. Its long cast shadow gives some reprieve from the heat. A loud clatter, thumps, and muffled thuds on the other side of the door respond.

"Coming," a groggy Dormy answers, followed by another series of boxes and books falling to the floor.

While she waits, March catches the repairs Dormy has done to her wagon. The slight discoloration of filled scratches and claw marks on the door, its frame, and walls would go unnoticed to less-skilled eyes, however, March and Dormy have made many repairs over the years to erase their own presence and made much more elaborate evidence disappear. In fact, everything on the small back porch of her wagon, from the lantern, barrels, and surplus of flour sacks, is secured as if Dormy has plans to leave. She cannot blame Dormy for this decision after all she has endured.

After the clatter subsides, latches click and slide open, the wooden lock bar scrapes against the frame, and Dormy opens the door, fully dressed, eyes wide, and huffing. Most of her marmalade hair is pulled back into a thick braid, while wild wisps escape and flop around her face.

"Hello, little mouse." March runs her hand over Dormy's hair to tame the loose strands and straightens the collar of her heavy leather jacket.

"I wasn't asleep." Dormy's face lengthens and contorts to hide her yawn.

"Of course not. May I trouble you this morning?"

Dormy's eyes perk up, as do her ears, always wishing and grateful to be helpful, to be of use.

"But first, I have a question. Do you plan on a journey?"

"Sharp, you are. Yes, and at the same time, no. Since the city is, well, I won't say safer, but at least more manageable, I felt it time I returned to the Row, to my stall. I am making the preparations and will depart tomorrow."

"I am sure the townspeople have missed you and your wares."

Dormy stretches her neck and stands proudly.

"You will be careful?" asks March. "And return here at the first sign of trouble you cannot handle."

"Course I will." Dormy pulls two fat flintlock pistols, looking more like handheld blunderbusses, from under her jacket.

"I am sure of it." Dormy's indomitable smile warms March's heart. Despite their past, she, out of all their party, remains constant.

"May I ask a favor before you depart?"

"Anything."

"While I am away, I must ask you to check in on Jonathan. He is awake and still regains his land legs."

Dormy nods once doggedly, pulls the door closed behind her, and scampers toward the castle. Her trinkets and pistols hanging from her belts click rhythmically. Another clatter of wares falls from within Dormy's wagon. It surprises March the door slamming does not topple every stack within.

Her eyes drop to Dormy's gloved hand—the hand March sliced off just below her elbow, and her stomach drops. It was to save her sweet friend's life, but it does not appease her guilt, an emotion she does not feel, or allow herself to feel often. Neither has said a word about the incident to each other, and they probably never will; this is not their way. As Dormy gets farther away, March's chest tugs as if a string runs from her heart to her friend's waist.

They are all tethered. Not just to each other, but to their pasts. Invisible strings keep them in this place against their will, like marionettes trapped on a stage, ever performing. It would be easy for all of them to escape Mirus, but no matter the distance, over mountains, through forests, across seas, the strings, strong as iron chains, bind them and will always bring them back wherever they attempt to run. One day March will see them cut, no matter who she must strike down to free those she cares for. Only then will they be free, truly free, and until such a time comes, they all have their part to play, and they must act well.

The Castle Guard and archers remain dutifully positioned atop the gatehouse and the full curve of the parapets of the castle's outer wall. Below the arch of the gatehouse, one guard picks at a pile of damp wood they use for fires or when oil for the lamps runs low. The two large gate men sit on their benches, bulbous stomachs sticking out over their knees, and scratch at their necks and bare chests beneath their overalls with their massive hands and turn their heads to watch March pass between them with simple, almost juvenile, expressions.

One of the last remaining soldiers in the castle, blue-eyed and young of face, removes the new heavy lock bars and opens the door for March. Four guards stand at attention and bow their heads. Weeks prior, these same men would have thought it prudent to share an unwanted snide comment about her body or the unfounded rumors of her past. This morning, and every day for the past several weeks, they nod their heads respectfully as she passes. It should not bother her, but it is this unaccustomed treatment, so foreign, and makes her more uncomfortable than any name they dare call out or whisper behind her back.

The full brunt of dawn crests over the horizon and greets March as she steps through the gate. Beyond the walls of Mirus, the mountains, the treetops of the Queenwood, and the distant Spires of Wonderland reflect the warm glow of the sunrise against the deep-blue sky.

The Gryphon waits at the muddy edge of the road on the castle's tier and looks down into the city. March stands beside him and crosses her arms to match. The sun glints off the runic beads woven into the braids of his beard. From the heavy circles under his eyes, he has not seen sleep these previous nights; she knows them well.

"Good morrow," says March.

The Gryphon breathes in deep and exhales long. "The rain has passed and given way to clear skies. Mirus returns to normal." Words he does not know if he should speak aloud this close to the castle balance precariously at the edge of his tightening lips.

"Yet?"

"Yet, an invisible veil remains over Mirus."

Smoke rises from the chimneys of the Crest and Stonehaven. "Did you think our victory, any victory, would lift the ever-present darkness enshrouding this city? The scent of death still tickles my nose like week old fish."

"The threat is over," the Gryphon says through unmoving lips.

"The threat is never over," says March, matching the Gryphon.

"Lysander and Uriah's soldiers should arrive this afternoon." The Gryphon shifts his shoulders. "They arrive after their intended purpose, to cleanse the city of the cult, yet they still come."

"The first wave."

The comment stills the Gryphon's movements, taking in the full meaning of those three words. "Walk with me." He swings the bottom of his long coat out of the muddy road, and together they descend a stone stairway into the city, side-by-side into the Crest.

They walk in silence along the polished cobbles of the highest tier of Mirus. The soldiers tried their best to return the streets to their once pristine appearance, but blood stains the cracks and spaces between stones, like a crimson spider's web laid across the road. Shards of glass windows from shops, mansions, and manors litter the grass and streets despite the continued efforts to restore the city. Bloody hand prints line alabaster walls and columns, and bloody claw marks rip deep at oak doors.

March shivers at the sight; a curious sensation and unexpected, given she has seen and committed carnage far worse than this. At an early age, March once split a man her father *gifted* her to from groin to chest, who tried to overpower her and pin her to his bedchamber floor. His entrails, liver, stomach, and other organs splattered down upon her in a putrid, warm splash. She grabbed his exposed spine through the gaping wound to push his carcass away without blinking an eye. This is only the first thought to come to mind, and she has dealt far worse deaths to those who deserve them. Why now does she feel affected?

Since her return from the Hollow with Jonathan's elixir, the soldiers have worked tirelessly disposing of the dead left in the city. She wonders if bodies clog the Crag's narrow vein of thick black pitch—the liquefied remains of thousands of decomposed bodies. She looks back toward the castle, past the castle, to the south where plumes of dark smoke rise like false spires and fade to nothing high in the air.

"Soldiers burn the bloated corpses of the cult members and the corrupted fished from the sea in the charred remains of the harbor," says the Gryphon.

The scent from earlier becomes clear. Embers of the dead creep through the air and violate March's senses.

While the Crest bears scars, Stonehaven suffered most and took the heaviest losses. The bones of the city are strong, and Stonehaven will survive, but not unscathed. Structures will return to their former weathered states, but the ruin lies in the downcast, vacant faces of the few townspeople who brave the desolate streets—those who survived, those unafraid to tread outside their homes.

March and the Gryphon journey farther into Stonehaven, and the rhythmic clank and strikes of hammers and axes are a welcome change to the unfamiliar quiet choking the city. Lacha, alderman of Stonehaven and overseer of the Forge, manages repairs with several other smiths, woodworkers, and stonemasons. He greets March and the Gryphon with a disheartened yet determined nod as they pass. Gooseflesh ripples over her arms. Why?

She hums a tune to herself—a shanty frequently heard in Rookridge by sailors who travel to the interior of the country—in order to clear her mind and dispel the uneasy sensation while she follows close behind the Gryphon, unsympathetic to the state of Mirus, its people, or their fate. The simple notes vibrate through her body, focus her senses, and bring her sight into crystal clarity.

There.

Once the confusion of what she mistook for compassion wafts away, March discovers the true source of the all-too-familiar sensation: prickles on her skin from prying eyes. She and the Gryphon have shadows, spies for Lysander and Uriah. March turns her attention to cracks in walls, piles of mud in the street, broken fences and drains, while her true eyes search shuttered windows, cracked doors, the corners of alleyways, and under the hoods, hats, and bonnets of the townspeople they pass.

Before they reach the Row, without knowing the Gryphon's intended destination, March hastens her steps and crosses his path. Without question, he follows her up the nearest stairs to the high wooden walkways snaking above the city, boots clunking loudly as they climb.

Atop the high ways, the pointed rooftops of Stonehaven rise like jagged teeth. March and the Gryphon wait in silence and listen for any other clunks upon the stairs.

"How long have they been following us?" he asks.

"Since the Crest," says March. "Their eyes have likely been upon you since you stepped out of the castle this morning."

"I came not from the castle. I have spent these past nights in the city."

March reaches into her trouser pocket and produces the crumbled scroll. "They could have had their eyes on you any time prior to the dawn, for days. They could have seen your messenger."

"I left the missive with one of the servant girls in the castle days ago with instructions to give it to you this morning." He turns a ring on the middle finger of his right hand—his signet ring with his sigil on it.

She would expect nothing less from him, yet they can afford no mistakes, and the bags under the Gryphon's eyes are pronounced. "Your sleep deprivation hinders your senses."

"I have remained ever vigilant."

"But not rested. They are not equal."

Before she can ask, the Gryphon answers her question. "I made a strategic decision." The Gryphon glances at her sidelong. "A lie wrapped in truth. My choice will have dire unforeseen consequences for me. I cannot allow myself to be distracted by it, therefore, I remain in the city to distance myself."

What ghost haunts him? March wonders. *He speaks as if the ferryman seeks him out personally to collect his long overdue fare.*

"Nevertheless," says the Gryphon. "A new day and a new-old enemy remain. The eyes of those loyal to Lysander and Uriah will be more difficult to discover. Unlike the cult, who bore their knives proudly, townspeople can hide right under our noses. They do not brandish any form of allegiance besides the tarnished mark on their hearts."

The higher the sun continues on its circled path, the more the vibrant colors of Wonderland shrink away; the world returns to its drab grays and browns, and the blue sky pales. A pair of chirping sparrows leave their nest under the eaves of a tenement, and the Gryphon watches them flit through the air and fly out of the city until their silhouettes vanish into the distant foliage of the Queenwood. March can see in his eyes he wishes for the same thing they all do: freedom from these phantom chains.

"Do not envy them," says March.

"Pardon?"

"The birds. Do not envy them."

"How can one not envy freedom?"

"They do not fly out of joy or freedom. They fly to eat. To survive."

"Yet, they have a choice."

March and the Gryphon share a prolonged silence between them. If they were at a tavern far from Mirus, both warriors would sit at a table without a word and finish large steins of ale, mourning their own fates.

"Please, elaborate on what you mentioned earlier," the Gryphon says under his breath, turning to March.

"This is the first wave of their forces. They position their pieces carefully. An armada from Adamas sails around the Saxum cape and will approach Mirus from the south while their soldiers infiltrate the city."

The Gryphon pinches the bridge of his nose. "How long do we have?"

"Ten days. Less with a favorable wind."

The Gryphon's eyes tick side to side, playing out the scenario and answering his own questions. "Even with the harbor destroyed, at the right angle, their long guns could rain down upon the castle and city. A battalion could intercept them at the Cape. We can fortify the gardens of the castle, bringing cannons and assembling catapults and trebuchets."

"Doing any of these with the Twins in the castle will give away our hand. They will either hold the entire city for ransom and force Mary Anne and the Duchess to abdicate or destroy the city outright. They will rule over ruins as long as they rule. And whatever they destroy, they will rebuild."

"Well done," says the Gryphon. "Is anyone else aware you possess this knowledge?"

"No. I happened upon their plans by happenstance. I spotted their ships approaching Spire Side on my return trip from the Hollow. Do we bring this to the council's attention?"

"There will come a time to call their bluff, but not yet. We have ten days at best, and let us say seven at worst. We cannot afford to waste a minute more or be rash in our stratagem. This will be a long game of wits and words."

"Politics," March scoffs. "The art of lies and manipulation."

"An art form of which you are well versed."

"Naturally." Over her lifetime, March has become as masterful with her wiles as with her blades. However, these foes, Lysander and Uriah, are just as skilled in their guile and schemes, and are far more vocal—an advantage they have over March. But not Jonathan. Her shortcomings are his strengths, and the same can be said to the contrary. Though not fully healed yet, they will have need of his silver tongue.

A crisp, bright horn sounds from the main gates of the city—a signal Lysander and Uriah's troops and the turncoats of Mirus have arrived.

"The next phase of the game begins," says the Gryphon. He turns and walks away.

"Will you return to the castle?" asks March.

After the briefest of pauses, the Gryphon answers. "I will make my way there."

He lies. She knows he lies. In his small hesitation, March knows the truth.

"And you?" he asks.

"I will gain a more favorable vantage point."

The Gryphon descends the closest stairwell and disappears into the bowels of the city.

March continues along the high ways deeper and lower into Stonehaven, and the closer she gets to the Row, the crunch of horse hooves on the dirt-covered cobbles overtakes the clunk of her boots on the wooden planks. A foolish parade of men in polished armor trot into the city on horses clad in barding. Their columns fill the width of the

Long Bridge. The great serpent of soldiers on horseback slithers closer and winds up the twisting streets toward the castle. Within the hour, their number within the city will soon be in the thousands.

Every twentieth soldier carries a wide banner with the crest of Adamas sewn with thread spun from gold and silver, presenting their colors to the townspeople like a peacock. Beneath the wooden high ways, curious citizens peek out of windows from second and third floors, poke their heads from their doorways, and crowd balconies to look upon the crawling army. Their faces flush and fill with disconcerting expressions of relief and gratitude at the spectacle. Though she loathes Lysander and Uriah both, she cannot afford to belittle or underestimate their strategy and ability to put on a performance to manipulate the masses.

Their arrival could not be more fortuitous for Lysander and Uriah. Their men arrive days too late for their promised purpose, to help exterminate the cult. The Twins will craft a new narrative to fit their own plans, arriving in the city as heroes to replenish Mirus's depleted forces, and no townsperson will be the wiser. Such is the conundrum, the paradox, of war; stratagem must be kept secret, but secrets are ultimately their undoing.

CHAPTER 7

CHESHIRE

While following March, who will inevitably lead Cheshire to the Gryphon, he passes a familiar hallway—the hallway with the bookshelf and the no-longer-secret entrance to the catacombs he first used upon his return to the city. The dark tunnels were once an area of play turned to refuge and salvation as a child; now, they are lost to him. Gathered at a small wooden table brought from another area of the castle, two soldiers, one gray-haired and the second younger, Jonathan's age perhaps, sit with stretched rolls of parchment hanging off the edges, held down with several inkwells and their helmets. Cheshire leans against the corner and crosses his arms to watch this new mischief.

A thick piece of twine tied to the leg of the table stretches into the open passageway behind the bookshelf and disappears into the darkness. A few moments later, a third soldier, with a large spool of twine attached to his belt, emerges from the catacomb, lantern in hand and holding a smaller rolled parchment. They map out the twists and turns of the catacombs for their own knowledge and nefarious purposes.

The returned soldier starts to hand the scroll to the others but then spots Cheshire and tightens his grip. His eyes grow wide, his face scowls with disgust, and his lips tremble with fear.

The hairs on the back of Cheshire's neck bristle. The gray-haired soldier-turned-cartographer seated at the table looks up from his drawing, blinks several times to rest his eyes, and tries to take the scroll, confused why the third soldier does not let go of the parchment. Soon enough, he follows his gaze and discovers Cheshire, swallows, and taps the table to get the third soldier's attention. An exhilarating chill cascades down Cheshire's body, tensing every muscle when all three soldiers lock eyes with him.

Their racing heartbeats become visible in their temples and the soft area at the bottoms of their necks. Their fingers twitch, and hands inch toward the swords at their hips. Unblinking, Cheshire's smile creeps ever wider; his own heart thumps in his chest, his palms, and other parts of his body. With a quick flash of his teeth, Cheshire sends the soldiers scrambling for their swords.

"Queen Slayer," says one of them, and spits upon the floor.

"I have killed my fair share of soldiers as well, if you have not heard. Shall I add to the number this morning?"

Cheshire charges toward them, bounding from floor to wall and back again. The older soldier pushes away from the table. The other two scream. They swing, but the narrow hallway stunts their attacks; the tips of their swords catch and drag upon the stones, leaving white arches and small sparks behind them. Cheshire dodges their strikes one after another, jumping, flipping, and spinning through the air, back and forth, threading their swords like the eye of a needle. They might as well swing at nothing. Their fear overpowers their skill.

"Murderer," shouts one soldier.

"Devil," shouts the other.

Cheshire slides along the ground to get behind the soldier with the twine, grabs the slack, twirls it around the soldier's neck several times, and pulls it taut, cutting off his breath. The soldier falls to his knees, gasping for air as he tries to dig his armored fingers under the twine. Reason would have him discard his gauntlets, but panic sets in quickly as he fights for his life, eyes beginning to bulge.

The remaining two soldiers slash wild and narrow, reverting to overhead attacks to avoid their previous mistake, each clinking and sparking against the floor and walls. A miscalculated swing cuts a chunk from the table and wobbles the wide inkwell.

"Strangers," Cheshire whispers. "Trespassers. Defilers."

They grunt and scream with each attack growing wilder. Their fear subsides and gives way to hate, fueling each slash and lunge, allowing them to focus more, but not enough. Cheshire dodges every attack gracefully, spinning and ducking between them, shoving them into one another or deflecting their blades to where they glance off each other's armor plating.

"Fuck," the younger soldier shouts as he rears his head backward to escape the sword's tip ricocheting off his breastplate.

Cheshire steps between them, the hallway barely wide enough for them to walk abreast. The soldiers abandon their futile attempts at swinging in the cramped space and resort to quick and short slashes at any part of Cheshire's bare body. Cheshire kicks their wrists to block their strikes and jabs with curled knuckles at the underside of their arms —unprotected by their pauldrons—any time they leave an opening.

"You damned bastard," says the older soldier, grimacing in pain. Cheshire efficiently cut the narrow hallway in half. As long as Cheshire stays between them, the soldiers cannot swing with any actual power, and if they do, they risk hitting one another.

Cheshire catches a trusting kick from one soldier in both hands, turns it and him around with ease, and shoves him into the other soldier. They both hit the wall in a crunch of iron and steel. Their faces pound with anger. For a moment, it focused their skills, now it blinds them. Good.

"You fucking demon." The older soldier turns and swings a wild punch aimed at Cheshire's head. "How many of our brethren have you slain?"

"Thousands. Tens of thousands." Cheshire ducks under the blow and kicks the soldier back against the wall. "Hundreds of thousands."

Both soldiers push off the stones and charge Cheshire again to pin him against the opposite wall. With a hand on each of their shoulders, Cheshire leaps over them, places a foot in the middle of each of their backs and kicks sharply. The younger soldier's face hits the wall with a loud crack and he falls to the ground, unconscious. The older soldier raises his arm in the nick of time, slamming into the wall. Dazed, he falls to the ground and spits blood from his mouth.

"Monster."

"Yes. But less today than yesterday, fortunate for you." Cheshire jumps onto the table with the catacomb maps. "I was merely curious as to your work. It was you who attacked me first."

"You should be dead."

"Yet here I stand. And all the while you so blindly fought me, your compatriot has been slowly dying at your feet." Cheshire points to the third soldier, gasping, lips turning blue, neck bloody from scratching at the tightening bloody twine around his neck.

They crawl to their unconscious comrade and use the point of his sword to cut through the twine, nicking his neck, and trickling blood onto the floor. The twine pops loose one loop at a time, and once the last snaps free, the soldier gasps and croaks for breath.

"If I wished it, you would never have seen your death coming. The last of you would only have a breath to realize the others were dead before I claimed your last for my own as well. I will go about my business, and you to yours. Be a dear and spread the word to the rest of your surviving brothers-in-arms. I can easily take any of your lives at any moment, whether I best you in combat or find you while you sleep. With hundreds of thousands of soldiers from across Wonderland fallen by my hands, what chance do you think you have?"

The soldiers remain quiet and swallow audibly, knowing Cheshire speaks the truth.

"Remember this the next time you dare pull your swords on me. I am pardoned, after all. And pray I do not seek you out simply when boredom settles in."

Color returns to the choking soldier's face. "You... you will let us live?" he asks with a hoarse rasp.

Cheshire questions this decision himself. This thought sits uneasy in his stomach and crawls unnaturally across his skin.

"You wish me to change my mind?" Cheshire grins.

The soldiers scramble for their swords again.

"Do not misinterpret my words. I want you dead. All of you. Every single one. Your time will come when I determine the hour."

"Are we supposed to think you capable of mercy?" asks the gray-haired soldier.

"Mercy? Of course. But you think this mercy?" Cheshire laughs. "Oh, no. It is chance. Mercy would be me killing you quickly to keep you from suffering what is yet to come. This is my mercy."

Cheshire glances down at the detailed map, where large portions of the castle catacombs and passageways are sketched on the topmost parchment. Cheshire shifts it to the side with his toes, parchment crackling, to reveal another large sheet with sections of the Crest filled in.

"This shall not abide."

Piles of curled scrolls lie around the table and on the floor. Images of Time and the Orrery flash through Cheshire's mind, where he burned thousands of scrolls and erased Wonderland's history for all but him to recall. He wishes for a candle or a flame, of which they have none. There are other means.

"Commendable detail. You lot have certainly been busy." Cheshire picks up the large ink well between his toes and moves it to the center of the table, the center of the stacked parchments. "It must have taken quite a long time."

The gray-haired soldier's lip snarls. The other two hang their heads, knowing what follows.

Cheshire tilts his head to the gray-haired soldier. "Longer still." Cheshire flicks the inkwell with his toe and spills it out like a gushing, pulsing, open wound. The beautiful black nothingness spreads, sinks, consumes and blots out every detail upon the parchments. With a wave of his hand, he brings forth the Mask of Light and disappears before them.

The soldiers gasp, mutter prayers, and curse his name.

He did not need to but knows it will add a delicious extra element of fear to their encounter. Cheshire jumps down from the table and leaves them behind to deal with their confusion of why he left them alive. He fights every fiber of his being, screaming at him to turn back, to claim their lives, as he knows he should. They all deserve to die, but in order to take advantage of his pardon, he cannot be so brazen about his murders, leaving corpses lying about, especially in the castle. At least for now.

Back on the trail of March, who has a sizable lead thanks to the three idiots, a chill crawls up Cheshire's back, like unseen fingers. A weight presses down on his shoulders. His mother's lullaby plays in his mind again. No. Not in his mind; her voice echoes through the halls.

He turns his head to find the source. There, at the end of a long corridor, a glimpse of a woman disappearing around a corner. She wears a familiar white dress dragging behind her and has short purple hair.

Tears swell in his eyes, and he cannot catch his breath. Cheshire will not believe it, cannot believe it, but he must follow. After centuries of searching villages, towns, prisons, mines, forests, dales, mountains, and shores, he cannot believe his mother simply walks freely through the castle.

Cheshire snakes through hallway after hallway, running faster and faster. At every intersection, he catches the same glimpse of the woman rounding a distant corner. He will not, cannot, say it is her, but her dress, her hair, her voice are unmistakable, undeniable. What will he do when he catches up to her? Would it be better for it to be his mother or some random woman of the castle?

He turns the last corner and faces a short dead-end hallway with a large hanging looking-glass. Cheshire looks upon his face, his quivering lips, his red eyes, and the tears running down his cheeks he did not know were there. He wipes them away and struggles to regain control of his face.

"Did you see her?" he asks his reflection.

"Yes."

He questions if this is some phantasm or a trick of his mind, delirium, or exhaustion. It could be her wandering spirit, but to admit such a thing, he would again have to accept her death. However, if her ghost were in fact trapped here by some force, why does she appear now after weeks of him being in the castle and not before? No. It cannot be her.

His mother's soft laughter echoes somewhere in the distance behind him. His body jerks from the chill it brings. Cheshire searches the reflection in the looking-glass for any sign of movement from the hallway. His reflection searches behind him for good measure. A flash of his mother's face explodes in front of him—so close it startles him. A void takes shape in Cheshire's chest and sinks to the bottom of his stomach. This feeling, this fear, is unknown to him. For over a millennium, he fought to find his way back into Mirus, back into the castle. He hates to admit it, but one thing is becoming clear, with these halls rife with horrors, memories, and traumas: it is possible the castle is not the best place for him to be.

CHAPTER 8
JONATHAN

When the bottoms of his feet reach the stone floor, Jonathan celebrates his accomplishment with a chuckle he immediately regrets. He looks at their carefully stacked trunks in the bedchamber's corner, with his clothing and elixir. It is only a short distance, but in his condition, they may as well be placed in the Row, the market in the center of Mirus.

He braces himself on the bed and pushes off, chest, thighs, arms, and back screaming at him. Even tightening his neck to suppress his groans causes pain. Sheridan, the leader of the Cult of the Mother, and his two large followers took more than their pound of flesh from Jonathan.

Jonathan looks at his hands. A bruised imprint of one of the cult's knives lingers on his palm. He cannot remember most of his trip through the city, nor how he returned to the castle, only images of fire flash in his memory, and Sheridan's face—cut, stabbed, and sliced to the point of looking like ground meat instead of a man. His memory is full of gaps and holes; he will need to depend on others to complete the story.

This morning's tryst with March and Cheshire showed it possible to push through the pain and proved him ready to rejoin the world, which he feels left him behind. He trudges toward the trunks as if chest-deep in a muddy bog. His first labored, hobbled steps are excruciating, the next are no less arduous, but Jonathan forces himself to straighten his posture and smooth his stride. The thick mud transforms to knee-deep sand.

He witnessed Cheshire and March depart, leaving him in the cold void of their absence, but does not remember Mary Anne leaving the chamber. She left before dawn, and Jonathan has no clue of her whereabouts. Knowing keeps the shadows of his mind from creeping in and overtaking him, and their icy fingers have already clutched Jonathan's heart and at his throat. His heart races, and the muscles of his back and chest ache and tighten with every quick breath.

He grunts as he stands and reaches for his timepiece, his father's timepiece, set in a perfect circle in its chain on top of one of their trunks. He circles its crystalline face three times with his thumb. Its chain hangs over his hand and sways with the constant ticking, soothing Jonathan's mind and body, slowing his breathing and returning him some semblance of normalcy.

He collects his clothing, a pair of leather trousers and boots will suffice this day, and walks to the baths in the adjoining chamber. He steps into the hot water of the shallow pool, surrendering to its comforting heat. It relaxes his body and pulls the pain from his bruised muscles, giving him more mobility, slight as it may be. He slowly washes his face, underarms, neck, chest, ass, and cock. However, drying off is not an option in his condition.

Back in Mary Anne's bedchamber, he walks around the sheer curtains surrounding the bed until sufficiently dry enough to get dressed and pushes through the twinges to step into his trousers, which sit extremely low on his waist. Besides, whenever he encounters Cheshire or March again, one small tug is all it will take for them to free him of his constraints. The thought of his lovers causes Jonathan's cock to swell.

The bulge will help keep his trousers up while it lasts. A shirt is out of the question; his shoulders could not endure it.

He pockets his timepiece and slowly makes his way toward—toward where? The tall stone walls and the looming shadows of the high ceilings bear down on him and make Jonathan's skin itch. Images of Mary Anne, Sheridan, the Duchess, Lysander, and Uriah flash every time he blinks. He needs fresh air, as fresh as Mirus can offer, to dispel the stale air kept within the castle's lungs. Jonathan will catch up with his loves soon, but first he must clear his head.

He selects a small box of tea from his trunk he can reach without bending over and wafts it below his nose. Mugwort and sage; a strong, calming tea, perfect for this morning. His stomach catches up to the rest of his body and wakes with a growl. Before setting out to find Mary Anne, he will venture to the kitchen for a brisk cup and a much-needed meal.

Walking the length of four corridors, his trousers rub and aggravate every bruise on his legs like claws scratching against his skin. Every step becomes easier, but his boots may as well be made of wrought iron. If he remained in the bedchamber, at least he would not have needed to worry about dressing for the moment. It would not matter if he stayed without clothing if they were in the Hollow. He misses the mornings, slipping from the warmth of March in their bed and embracing the early morning chill and picturesque beauty of the valley from their balcony. The Hollow, to him, to March, and Cheshire, when he completes their trinity, is the edge of the world, where they prefer to be...lost. Though not the longest they have been away from the Mill, time inches forward in these stone halls. Jonathan has caught himself occasionally checking his timepiece to make certain of the day and time, hoping he is mistaken.

Jonathan operates on routine, the only way he can function—he woke, not thinking to look at the details as Cheshire often accuses him of. He takes his timepiece from his pocket, and his mind reels with questions when he notices the time and the day on its face. The fading color of his bruises, not deep violets and reds but rather pale yellows and greens, confirms what he fears. He should have known from the soreness in his body, the emptiness of his stomach; he misses days, not hours. There is much to discover before Jonathan can be of any use.

"Jonathan."

He thinks he hears his own name, muffled by the thoughts racing through his mind. It finds its way through the tangle and gives him a point to focus on.

"Jonathan," the calming voice of Dormy calls.

Her wares, trinkets, and pistols dangling from her belts click against each other as she approaches down the long corridor. If the sight of Dormy were not enough to lift Jonathan's spirits, she comes from the direction of the kitchen and carries a plain, yet beautiful, white porcelain teapot; a trail of steam follows her from the spout. Jonathan's mind slows, as do his breaths. The lingering sense of loneliness washes from him. This may not be what he expected, but it is what he needs—a piping cup of tea with someone he holds dear.

"You are a welcome sight," says Jonathan. He stops and leans a hand on the wall to steady himself, grateful to rest his legs for the moment.

The last time he saw Dormy, she was bloody and pale lying on the castle surgeon's cot. The poor girl was unconscious and had missed the latter part of the horde's invasion, while Jonathan was unconscious and missed her recovery. Color fills her cheeks again, and her eyes twinkle as they always have, knowing more than she lets on but willing to live in peaceful oblivion.

"Should you be up and about?" asks Dormy. "I mean, I'm glad you are up. It's the about part I was questioning, not the up. Are you ready to be about?" She wears her self-made confusion on her face.

"It was time." Jonathan enjoys a laugh despite the pain in his gut. "Thank you."

"For what?"

"For always and ever being who you are."

Before he can say another word, Dormy's smile returns and she sets to work. She bites the knob of the pot's lid with her teeth to lift it, grabs the box of tea from Jonathan, pops the lid open with her thumb, and shakes the oblong and short crushed leaves into the steaming water.

"May I help?" asks Jonathan.

"Cup," Dormy says with the lid held tightly in her teeth and turns her right hip to Jonathan. She wears a custom-made leather holster to hold a small teacup and saucer on one of her belts. When they first met, she did not carry such an amazing invention, but after a few months of knowing Jonathan, she created it for emergencies just for him should he have need.

Jonathan moves a large hanging key ring and a small pistol out of the way to untie the thin leather straps keeping the holster closed and slides the cup and saucer free, placing them together. The tickling of porcelain rain; a welcome shiver crosses Jonathan's body.

"Thank you," says Jonathan.

"Never worries." Dormy wipes a bit of dried spit from the corner of her mouth on her sleeve. "Would you like a seat? I can find a chair, or there was a small bench two hallways back."

"Thank you, but I think it wiser if I lean. I do not want to sit or stand again until I absolutely must."

Dormy stares at the teapot and moves her lips, counting the seconds. Jonathan counts the seconds as well and studies her bare fingers wrapped around the pot's handle and her gloved hand cradling its body. Even with a glove on, from the steam still rising from the spout, it should be too hot to handle. The memory hits him like a smack to the face. It would be too hot for a hand of flesh and blood, but not one of iron—Pat and Bill's miraculous engineering.

He waits and watches, counting along with her, until they reach one hundred and eighty seconds.

"What have I missed?" asks Jonathan.

Dormy inhales deeply and fills Jonathan's cup. "Well, we wiped out the rest of the cult members—drowned them in the bay. Cheshire did, and I helped. I fly an old dirigible. The city is on the mend. Pretty much all the townsfolk who came to the castle for refuge have returned to their homes. Although, from what I hear, many people are leaving or plan to leave the city altogether. It don't feel safe anymore, I suppose. Mary Anne pardoned Cheshire's crimes as Queen Slayer, and Lysander and Uriah are still in the castle. That's about the long and short of it."

Jonathan chuckles and immediately regrets his decision. What a whirlwind the world has been since last he walked the halls. "Have you seen March this morning?"

"Yes, she was on her way out of the castle."

"How is she? How did she look?" Jonathan will only believe one answer in his heart, but hearing it will again settle his agitated nerves.

"Strong," says Dormy.

Of course. Jonathan raises the cup to his lips, and welcomes the warmth on his lips. The piping hot tea shocks Jonathan's tongue and body in the best of ways and serves to relax him. The robust, fragrant aroma surrounds them and blocks out the stale air of the castle. For the briefest of fleeting moments, they find themselves back in the Hollow, however, the sight of Dormy's hand wafts the image away as quickly as the steam.

"How are you fairing?" he asks.

"Right as the rains," says Dormy with her ever-present smile—a smile like Cheshire's, which hides so much.

Jonathan must ask more specific questions. "Would you remove your jacket?"

The corners of Dormy's mouth slowly melt as she shoves the box of teas in one of her pockets, slides her right arm out of her large corduroy frock, and holds it out to Jonathan. The glove and her linen shirt conceal her arm, but a small ring of bloody dots stain her sleeve just below her elbow.

After a second drink, Jonathan asks, "May I?"

Dormy nods and holds her arm closer to Jonathan. He reaches out with his free hand and grabs her hand, pressing his thumb into her palm, then her wrist: solid, unforgiving steel, far too harsh for her gentle soul.

"Does it hurt?" he asks.

"No. I can't feel anything. Not really. But sometimes I believe I can still feel it, my own hand, just there."

"Yet it still bleeds."

"Oh. Yes." She pulls her hand from Jonathan. "The ring where Pat and Bill fastened it to my skin takes some getting used to. If I twist my arm too quickly, it tends to bleed a bit. But not much. It's lessened as the days go by. They said it would pass in the coming weeks when my body becomes more accustomed to it."

He drinks again. In all the tales Jonathan has created and words crafted into lore, he cannot find any combination to take Dormy's pain from her. "I am sorry. Truly, I am."

"Why? It wasn't you who bit me."

"No." Jonathan shakes his head and manages a single huff of laughter. He watches her move her artificial fingers back and forth, balling her hand into a fist and stretching wide. "We are a long way from home."

"This isn't the first time. We've been even farther, in fact."

"True. But not like this. Never like this."

"Do you wish we would have stayed?"

"It does not matter. The choice was made for us."

A muffled voice somewhere in the distance, little more than a hum, catches Jonathan's attention. He questions his senses at first and rubs his thumbs in his ears, but Dormy's reaction, the widening of her eyes and the perk of her ears, prove he hears more than phantoms.

"Do you hear that?" Jonathan asks Dormy.

She holds up a finger to halt any further questions. Her head tilts, her eyes lose focus, and her lips press, searching out the words Jonathan cannot hear. The garbled hum remains for a few seconds, voices beyond his comprehension, until they disappear completely, leaving only a fading ring.

"Oh, no." Dormy slides her arm back into her jacket. "I think it came from the songbirds."

As if on cue, Weiss barrels down the corridor and has to slide to a stop himself when catching sight of Jonathan.

"You." Weiss approaches swiftly, his black and white robes and long white hair billowing behind him. "Shut up and come with me. Do you ever wear a fucking shirt?"

"I can return to Mary Anne's chamber to fetch one if it would make you more comfortable."

"No. Never mind." Weiss grunts. "We have a most dire problem."

"It must be dire for you to speak with me of your own volition." Jonathan reaches the end of this cup and stares at the small floating remnants of tea leaves.

"Shut your mouth." Weiss picks at his hands through his white gloves. "I would not if this situation did not demand it."

"Let's have it, then."

"Did you not hear it? How could you not hear it? Even this deep in the castle, the songbirds are as clear as ringing crystals."

"Apparently, I took one too many blows to the head, and my senses are still recovering."

"You are useless, aren't you?"

"Tell me what it is I need to know."

"Lysander and Uriah are in the throne room," he blurts out in a whisper.

Some physical manifestation torments his bruises and wounds accompanies every emotion. The full-body sense of dread crawls across his skin like a hundred insects—tiny legs digging into his bruises.

"What of Mary Anne?" he asks.

Both Weiss's permanent look of worry, Dormy's neck and face twitches, and the pinch of her brow sets the severity of the situation.Jonathan holds Dormy's gaze and hardens his eyes—a look she knows well. Do what must be done. She nods and breaks away down another hallway, returning Jonathan's cup and saucer to its holster and keeping her wares from clanking.

Without a word, Weiss whips around and races toward the throne room, only a few corridors and a staircase away. Keeping up with his tall, spindle-like legs numbs Jonathan's own to the pain. Weiss mutters to himself, more breaths and sounds than words, and picks at his hands harder, drawing blood and staining his gloves.

"Fredrick," says Jonathan, to distract Weiss from his hands.

"Do not call me this name." Weiss does not stop but turns back to point at Jonathan and jabs a finger at him with every statement. "This is not my name. Not anymore. Gave it up. Not mine. It's the past. The past is dead." Weiss turns his attention forward again and continues to mutter under his breath. "Not my name. Dead. No. Not me. Gone"

"Weiss."

"Yes?" he answers instantly in a much calmer tone than before.

"Tell me what has happened?"

Weiss pulls the long strands of white hair from his face and tucks them behind his ears. "I do not know how this happened, but we are about to find out." He stops as they round the corner leading to the throne room to straighten his hair and robes.

Jonathan's heart drops. The throne room doors are open, and he realizes where Mary Anne has been.

Oh shit.

Wonderland has found Mary Anne worthy, and the iron guardians have indeed opened for her, allowing her one step closer to becoming queen. He should feel ecstatic, or at least some form of relief, but foreboding twists in his stomach like a snake caught in a burlap sack.

There is no time to prepare. Jonathan wanted to know what he has missed, and instead of gathering information, he throws himself into the fire. He stretches his back, shoulders, neck, and arms, stretches and clenches his fists, and puffs out his pain through long breaths. Still covered in bruises, he will show no sign of pain or weakness when he enters the throne room. He straightens his back and relaxes his face, despite his pain clawing at him.

Weiss sneers. “Let us hope your role as advisor was well chosen, and your silver tongue” — he mocks — “can save us from this.”

“I do not have a choice in the matter.”

CHAPTER 9
MARY ANNE

Her fingernails pierce her palms, drawing blood from her clenched fists, her eyes vibrate, and heat flushes Mary Anne's face with every beat of her heart—a kettle rattles inside her chest, ready to boil over and burn all those around her.

Lysander and Uriah pose at the throne—Uriah at its left, Lysander at its right—and caress the arms of the throne as if it were one of their many whores. As different as they are, they are mirror images of each other, wearing long, thick linen tunics which hang completely off one shoulder, held in place by their braided leather belts, exposing the entire left side of Uriah's body and right side of Lysander's, Several silver chains drape around their necks. They wear nothing underneath except for their boots. Their excitement of the moment is apparent in the bulge lifting the hanging fabric, purposefully positioned close to their groins.

"Guards!" the Duchess bellows, marching forcefully toward the Twins.

"How dare you?" Mary Anne follows close behind. "Remove yourself from the dais this instance."

"Why would we consider such a request?" says Lysander. "It is ours."

"Never," Mary Anne seethes. The sight, even the thought, of their disgusting hands upon her throne makes her wish death upon them. "It is mine."

"Yours? Wonderland has spoken." Uriah pushes his long silver hair over his shoulder in a dramatic sweep and motions to the servants and soldiers standing among them. "We have witnesses. The throne room doors opened upon our approach, inviting us, welcoming us into our birthright. It truly was magnificent."

"Prophetic," says Lysander.

"Inevitable," says Uriah.

"I saw it." A soldier with orange stubble and a scar across his nose steps forward. "It is as my lords describe."

"I witnessed it as well." Another soldier, with dull green hair, stands beside him.

"Ay," the rest of their soldiers say, forming a line to the right of the dais.

"You lie. You lie with every vile breath!" Mary Anne shouts.

"If you still doubt us, take the words of your own." Lysander leans on the arm of the throne and looks toward the castle servant girls, beckoning them. They approach Mary Anne and the Duchess with their heads bowed low, backs turned to the Twins.

"Speak," the Duchess spits out in an angered whisper. "Make sense of this."

A girl with deep-yellow curls poking out of her kerchief says, "We weren't here when the doors opened."

"Their soldiers came and asked us to accompany them," another servant says.

"Did they force you?" asks Mary Anne.

"No. They asked politely but insistent," the orange-haired servant continues. "When we arrived, they and the other soldiers were already in the throne room."

"We did not want to cross the threshold of the throne room at first," says a servant with long dark-blue hair.

How can this be happening?

Mary Anne forces her hands open and looks down at the blood from the crescent-shaped wounds. After all this time, the throne was hers, is hers. Wonderland chose her, proved her worthy, and now these two, these lying snakes, mean to steal it from her.

"Have these men threatened you in any way?" the Duchess asks the servants loudly. "You must be truthful. We shall protect you against any threat they have levied against any of you."

The servants shake their heads, eyes telling Mary Anne and the Duchess some part of them wishes the opposite were true.

"We wish it were so, ma'am." A mousy servant with red hair steps forward. "It is as they say. There was no one here except for them when we showed up."

Twelve castle guards arrive at the threshold of the door and let loose a bevy of various expletives, and gasps punctuate the crunch of their armor. The Duchess raises a hand, and they form a line behind her and Mary Anne. Mary Anne expects the soldiers loyal to Lysander and Uriah to reach for their swords, but they stand confident and calm, never looking in their direction.

"Cheats." Mary Anne pushes her way through the servants, voice deep and resonant. "The doors opened for me, for the future queen of Wonderland. Not you, you viper's brood."

"How can such lies spew from such a delicate face?" asks Lysander.

"She was delicate when we first saw her," says Uriah. "It would have been sweet to savor such an innocent face when we fucked you. The pinched brow. Biting your lip. Delicious. There is something different about you now, perhaps darker, more brass."

"More to my liking," says Lysander. "Perhaps now she will look up at us with hungry eyes when we fuck her," says Lysander.

"No one is fucking me, you putrid piles of horseshit." Mary Anne's deep shout echoes through the cavernous chamber. "You will step down and leave the throne room immediately or you will be forced out."

The Castle Guard step forward and take their place in front of Mary Anne and the Duchess, hands on their swords, while the servants run from the chamber. Lysander and Uriah's soldiers form a line in front of the dais, ready to defend their lords. The Twins take pleasure in the rise they bring out of Mary Anne and chuckle darkly, glancing at each other, ignoring her threat altogether.

"You dare threaten violence against us?" Lysander asks. "Wonderland's rightful rulers?"

"You are not!" Mary Anne shouts.

"Mary Anne," says Uriah, "the more lies you speak, the deeper the hole you may find yourself."

"You threaten us?" the Duchess snaps.

"It was merely a cautionary warning," says Uriah. "It is you who speak out against the throne, against the blood of Wonderland. The penalty for such action, such treason, is, well..."

"Treason." The Duchess scoffs. "This nonsense, this charade, ends here and now with us. Your treacherous lies will not make it out of the—"

"Just speak," a nasal, distant, disembodied man's voice says. "Say it, quick."

"Fine," says another man's voice.

Someone is in the tower using the pipe announcement system, speaking to the city through the stone birds spread throughout Mirus. She recognizes these voices. How does she know them? The realization comes too late; Lysander and Uriah's men—the two scoundrels she and Jonathan encountered in the Rookwood.

"Attention, Mirus. It is with an overjoyed heart we can announce the return of Wonderland's rightful heirs," one voice says.

Mary Anne's heart thunders to the point she feels she might explode. Even if the realization came earlier, there is nothing anyone present could have done. The tower is half a castle away, and they would need to leave the throne room to Lysander and Uriah.

"The heirs of the Kings, Lysander and Uriah, are welcomed home and now sit upon the throne of Mirus. Celebrate, for you do not have one king, but two. Rejoice in the streets. You are welcome into the castle to bear witness to this holy and joyous event."

At first, Mary Anne tries to ignore the flashes of foul deaths she can imagine upon the Twins, but the more she looks upon their smug faces, the quicker she embraces the hatred and welcomes every thought. Victims of the guillotine, where their heads flop into bloody baskets. Jonathan runs them both through the gut with his long sword, pinning them to the wall. Throwing them from the Long Bridge and watching them break and splatter amongst the stones at the bottom of the ravine. Tying them to posts at the top of the gatehouse, dousing them with oil, and letting the city watch them burn. She forces herself to blink to erase the images from her head, images she has never wished on anyone.

"There you have it," says Lysander. "You heard the truth ring through the air and spread across the city for every citizen of Mirus to hear."

"Your truth," says Mary Anne.

"Which is still the truth," says Lysander. "By all means, spread yours as well. Say what you will to the masses. See if they believe you."

"Look at her." Uriah leans forward and rubs his fingertips and thumb together as if balling up the last, smallest piece of decency he possesses. "Your face conceals nothing, does it? The murderous intent in your eyes and the twitch of your lip amuse me."

"They will never believe you," says Mary Anne. She tries to push her way through the Castle Guard, but a hand grips hers. At first she thinks it is the Duchess, but Jonathan's soothing voice becomes a beacon in this darkness.

"There is nothing we can do at this moment," he says.

Mary Anne was so focused on the Twins she did not hear him approach. His muscles twitch from the pain he must be in. He should be in bed, but thank every god in Wonderland he is here with her now. She squeezes Jonathan's hand, and he returns the gesture. The burning heat of her skin subsides when she looks into his sparkling gaze in the false light of the throne room.

It's not fair. She dares not say her thoughts out loud, though the tears welling in her eyes speak volumes. *It's not fair.* From the gentle furrow of his brow, she knows Jonathan understands.

He winks at her then turns his attention to the Twins. "A word."

"Just one?" asks Lysander. "It would seem you have already overstepped your allotment."

"Where is the harm in allowing us a closer, civil audience without the menagerie of soldiers between us?" Jonathan asks. "This is not war."

"Yet," Mary Anne says under her breath. The Twins tread into dangerous waters without considering the ramifications of this stunt.

"Let them approach." Uriah waves to their soldiers casually, and they create a row to their left.

"Go," says Mary Anne. She leads Jonathan down the center of the throne room, the Duchess following at their heels, and the Castle Guard assembles in a row opposite the soldiers of Adamas.

She has heard Jonathan, March, and even the Duchess make mention of a game, like chess, but much crueler. For the first time, walking between opposing soldiers, staring up at Lysander and Uriah, Mary Anne comes to terms with what the Book of Queens spoke of: a piece, a pawn yet to become queen, on a chessboard. This may be a game to some, but the consequences for all are quite real.

"What are you going to tell them?" Mary Anne asks Jonathan.

"Me? Nothing," Jonathan whispers. "They need to hear your voice."

"What?" Mary Anne says without moving her lips, worry scrunching her face.

"They cannot harm you," Jonathan continues. "Not here, not now. Do not worry about the production of the surrounding soldiers. This is all for show. Make your words count."

An immense pressure bears down on her shoulders and her stomach. She does not possess Jonathan's silver tongue. This single moment will define all of their futures, the future of Wonderland, and her life.

"What can I say to make a difference?" she asks.

"Words. The right words can spark rebellion, topple kings and queens, liberate, manipulate, trap even the most cunning, and reshape the world. Words are stronger than any steel ever crafted from the heat of a forge, and in the right hands and mind, they are the most devastating of weapons."

"I do not know what to say." Mary Anne swallows audibly as they approach the dais.

"Speak from the heart." Jonathan squeezes her hand.

His strength, his unfaltering faith in her, fuels her determination. Mary Anne lets go of his hand and steps in front of Jonathan and the Duchess, inches from the dais, inches from the throne, inches from her destiny. What would Jonathan do? There is no way she can convince them to step down willingly, so her words must have another purpose. The Twins may come from the line of kings but they are more correctly the spawn of Narcissus—ego personified. She does not need to work up some lies to shame them when the truth is weapon enough.

"You have no right." Mary Anne speaks low enough to keep her words from the others in the throne room.

"We have every right, stupid girl." Uriah steps to the front of the dais. "We are the last heirs, the rightful heirs, descendants of the kings of old."

"The throne is ours by birthright and blood," says Lysander. "Queens were nothing more than usurpers."

"Perhaps it was time," Mary Anne whispers. "If what you say is true, why have the throne room doors remained shut for you both?"

"Spin whatever tale you wish," adds Jonathan. "We know the truth. As do you."

Mary Anne steps closer to the dais, facing off against Uriah. "You had to wait for them to open—to open for me, for a queen whom

Wonderland chose. You swooped in and took credit for a feat you could never achieve."

The Twins' expressions remain frozen, hiding their thoughts behind them, in sharp contrast to their expressive arrogance earlier.

Words are powerful indeed.

"Believe what you want," says Lysander. "The fact of the matter is we are here, and you are" — he looks down his nose at her — "beneath us."

"Not to mention, the people have heard it for themselves," adds Uriah, his obnoxious arrogance returning. "Those who are loyal to our blood and Wonderland's history will rally to us. There is little you can do."

"The army of Mirus—"

"The army of Mirus," Lysander cuts Mary Anne off, "is all but decimated after the battle—"

"Slaughter," Uriah interjects.

"After the slaughter by the Cult of the Mother," says Lysander. "Our numbers and our will are greater."

"Face it, little girl," says Uriah. "You are new to this game. We have played all our lives. It does not matter how we win. We win because we are better."

"You believe this to be over, but this has only just begun." Mary Anne's voice and body tremble with anger. Waves of heat pulse across her face with every heartbeat.

"Quite right," says Lysander. "You are welcome to join us in our bedchamber this evening to celebrate." The smug asshole speaks as though victory already rests in their hands.

"Never," says Jonathan, surprising Mary Anne. Out of the corner of her eye, his jaw clenches and flexes despite his relaxed body.

A crowd of servants and guards gather at the throne room doors, unsure if they should enter but decide they will watch this conflict. They must have heard the announcement. Of course, they heard the announcement. The entire city heard it. But they do not know everything.

There is more. They have mentioned nothing about the Book of Queens or the Tenets. According to the Book of Queens, opening the throne room was only the Second Tenet. This marks the beginning of Mary Anne's true journey. The Twins make no mention of the Grand Arcana, the true power of Wonderland. Perhaps it is because they do not know about it or they cannot possess it. Upon Mary Anne's arrival, the Duchess said only the queen could wield such power; Lysander, Uriah, and the kings could not. If she can harness this power, these men will stand no chance.

"You have not won," says Mary Anne. "And you will not win."

Uriah leans closer. "We will take everything from you," he says in a dark whisper. "The only reason we do not slice the throats of you and your compatriots here and now is because we know the long game."

"But make no mistake," says Lysander, "when your usefulness is done, we will kill all of you." He glances at the Duchess. "Including you."

How dare they threaten her? How dare they threaten Jonathan? Mary Anne must be careful of her words. Too much honesty will give her intentions away. "Play your game. You have never played against me before. You will find me not just an equal, but a superior opponent."

"A woman." Lysander sneers. "How quaint and laughable."

"Enough of this," says Lysander. "You waste our time with this droll nonsense."

Three quick pistol shots ring out in the distance. Mary Anne wonders if the townspeople fight against each other already, but she is not aware of anyone in the city, be they loyal to Mirus or Adamas, who possess pistols except Dormy. The half-grin at the corner of Jonathan's lips let Mary Anne know she is correct in her assumption.

"You are right," says Jonathan. "We did."

"Attention, Mirus." Dormy's voice resonates through the songbirds. "The Duchess, who has watched over Mirus for years, and Mary Anne, your future benevolent queen, defend and challenge the claim to the throne from the usurpers Lysander and Uriah. Treachery is afoot. Those who support the queendom, come to the castle to make your voices known."

The crowd at the door cheer and applaud.

Lysander laughs. "What is this?"

"Words have power," says Mary Anne. "You have your truth. I have mine. Yet, only one can be correct, and the world will know soon enough. The people and Wonderland will decide, and I believe you already know who Wonderland has spoken for."

"Clever little cunt," says Uriah. "This could have been peaceful. However, if it is a civil brawl you wish to have, so be it. Not the plan we had hoped for, but we can adjust. You and yours will not survive what is to come."

"Thank you," Jonathan says loud enough for all to hear. He strides back toward the crowd at the door. What was two dozen now sounds like the buzz of hundreds cramming the corridor outside the throne room. "Ladies and gentlemen, the Duchess, Mary Anne, future queen of Wonderland, and the ignoble, forgive me, the noble twins Lysander and Uriah have resolved to settle this challenge peacefully."

Mary Anne does not turn to watch Jonathan perform his own type of magic, able to snare the hearts and minds of all he speaks to with his enigmatic charm. Instead, she stares at the faces of the Twins. Their masks of peace and contentment remain in place, but their eyes stretch with rage.

"The throne of Wonderland has sat empty long enough," Jonathan continues, "but now we are closer to having this sacred seat occupied than ever before. Go out and spread the word to the city. Let no one raise arms against one another. Both parties will come to terms."

"Yes." The Duchess joins in her grand fashion, sweeping arms and dramatic hand gestures. "Wonderland is strong. Mirus is strong. You have proven it these past few harrowing days and nights. We will endure and see this challenge through as many others before us." She turns back to the Twins. "Do you agree?"

The hushed murmur of the crowd falls to deafening silence. Lysander and Uriah share a brief side-glance with each other.

"We have an accord," says Uriah. "This matter will be settled in less than two weeks' time, and Wonderland will have its rightful rulers."

Rulers. Mary Anne will not allow them the last word and turns to the crowd. "And until such time, out of mutual respect and to preserve the sanctity of this hallowed hall, we have all agreed to leave the throne room unoccupied until the final decision has been made."

If Mary Anne cannot lay claim to the throne room, which she has suffered for, neither will they. "You have your truth," Mary Anne whispers. "I have mine."

"After you." The Duchess motions to the door. "Will you gentleman please lead us from the chamber?"

While the Twins may have thought this heated encounter would come to an end in swords and fists, Mary Anne, Jonathan, and the Duchess have dealt a blow they did not expect to their weakness: their pride and vanity. Surely, they could contest Mary Anne's words and start a brawl here in the throne room, but then they become the aggressors and reveal themselves to be the villains they are. Eventually and reluctantly, the Twins agree and step from the dais.

"All together, as a sign of solidarity," Uriah says before his boot hits the floor.

"Of course," says Mary Anne.

Uriah steps between Jonathan and Mary Anne, and Lysander between Mary Anne and the Duchess, and they all stare at the door in front of them, not glancing at each other in the slightest. At the far end of the throne room, the crowd watches in whispered anticipation.

"If you will not lead," Mary Anne whispers, "I shall."

Those simple words are enough to spur Lysander and Uriah into motion, walking as slowly as running molasses toward the door. It does not take a mind reader to know they all share the same thought: they all fear any of them will turn and bolt back to the throne, but Lysander and Uriah could not sink so low while an audience watches, and neither can Mary Anne. Her morning began with euphoria, then defeat, and now she walks, head held high, triumphant, from the throne room, though not the outcome she wanted nor expected.

This experience has drained all emotions from her, save for hate. Hate is enough. Hate is warm, like a stoked fire. She recalls the images of their deaths that flashed in her mind previously and lets them linger, enjoying them perhaps longer than she should or at least longer than the woman she was before would.

"You will die for this, bitch," Lysander whispers without moving his lips.

"In a most horrible way," Uriah adds. "But not before we take everything from you, as we promised."

The crowd parts as they reach the throne room doors. Mary Anne stops and ushers Lysander and Uriah through, keeping up appearances and letting the double meaning of her words strike true. "You first."

CHAPTER 10

MARCH

Standing about the city, the Gryphon descended into the city, gooseflesh tickles the back of March's neck again. Another pair of eyes watches her from somewhere close. The sweet aroma of leather and earth grows stronger and wraps around her. She glances over her shoulder at the pointed rooftop, feeling Cheshire's warmth upon her back. Regardless of the reason he followed her into the city, she is glad of his company, her dark guardian angel.

"Your pardon," she mocks, "allows you to walk the streets freely. There is no need for you to hide beneath your masks anymore."

"Old habits."

An off-key tone in Cheshire's voice piques March's concern. "Something troubles you."

"I fought three soldiers in the castle this morning. I fought them. I did not kill them."

"How uncharacteristic of you? Perhaps you are coming down with a touch of something." March wonders if this will last, if this is strategic, or something more. "Or perhaps you lacked the necessary energy after our time together this morning."

"Hardly," says Cheshire. "It boggles me. It is this place."

Before they can leave Cheshire's hidden lips, she recognizes the truth in his words. Mirus, the last place any of them aspire to be, changes them all, no matter how hard they fight against it. It happens every time she and Jonathan would unfortunately find themselves in Mirus.

"I have not felt myself of late either. Only when I am with you and Jonathan, away from the world, do I remember and embrace myself fully."

"I will not lose myself here." Cheshire's voice drops quivers in the wind.

"You will never be able to lose yourself, because Jonathan and I will always be here to find you."

"You both are my tether to this world," he whispers.

"As are you." She stays facing out to the city and reaches a hand behind her to find his warm body and the hard muscles of his stomach—like running her hand against the cobbles on a summer's day.

Cheshire presses against her, trapping her hand between them. His unseen hands grab her waist, and he lays his forehead against the back of her hair, missing his warm breath on her neck, concealed by the mask. March slides her hand down between them, expecting to find his short, tattered trousers, but instead, to her pleasure, grabs full hold of his hard, warm shaft. She squeezes, and Cheshire squeezes her arms just as tightly. Back in the Hollow, she would take him here without question, but this damned city and all its constraints vexes March's every instinct.

"Perhaps we should all stop denying who we are for the sake of Mary Anne and this place," says March.

Cheshire pushes his hips against March, his cock sliding back and forth through her grip. His fingers slide into the back of her trousers and gingerly trace the curve of her backside and run the valley between.

March's stomach clenches, and she smiles at the gentle tickle of his touch. "I have need of you."

"I am well aware. Tempting as you are, I know you have other intentions at this moment. All it would take is a shadow, and I could whisk us back into the castle. No, somewhere else, somewhere deep in the Queenwood, where no one could hear us."

"If only we could, dear heart."

"You just suggested we not fight our urges."

"Urges, yes. We will ravage each other and Jonathan again soon enough, but for now..."

"Something else draws your attention, as it does mine."

March tilts her head to the Long Bridge. "Lysander and Uriah's numbers will soon outnumber our own; another battle looms."

Cheshire scoffs and continues to trace March's backside. "You realize I have returned to the city for my own reasons, none of them concerning Mary Anne or the fucking throne. I will let these factions tear each other apart with fire and neighbor-stained steel."

"Of course," says March. "I do not wish for you to give up your endeavors. However, I believe you would find it most difficult to complete your quest if someone beat you to the destruction of the city before you reach its end."

"Explain," says Cheshire after a brief pause.

"Time ticks down. Their armada will arrive in half a fortnight. I wager a storm of cannon fire raining down upon the city does not coincide with your plans." Her fingers squeeze and dance upon Cheshire's cock as if playing with the keys of an organ. They stand together, enjoying their intensifying connection as March sways forward and back with every slow thrust of Cheshire. His muffled breaths become quick and deep.

"What do you ask of me?" Cheshire whispers through animalistic breaths.

"Old habits," says March. "I wish nothing more than to unleash you upon the city. While you are about your business, would you mind taking as many of their men off the board as you can?" March cannot see it, but she can hear the grin in his deep, mischievous chuckle.

"Not to worry." His cock pushes through her grip to his base and back again. "I shall be the demon they believe me to be, the demon you want me to be."

"Yes," she whispers. "I am thankful the thousands of cult members you killed have not quenched your thirst."

Cheshire thrusts slower and harder into March's hand. "I am insatiable."

March releases her hold on Cheshire. The sensation of Cheshire's fingers from his other hand caress her neck, the underside of her breasts, and down her stomach, sliding in the front of her loose trousers. Her stomach spasms at his gentle touch, not wanting him to stop. March reaches down and taps the wet tip of Cheshire's head but pulls away for fear she will not be able to stop, finally spinning around to face him, and though invisible, she knows exactly where to meet his eyes.

"By the by, I was followed this morning. Would you be my darling shadow, find them, and dispatch them in whatever way entertains you best?"

"Any who looked upon you with ill intent will never see the sunset of this day. I ask one thing in return. the direction of the Gryphon."

It makes sense now why the Gryphon stayed clear of the castle's interior. She does not need to ask, nor will she, but the lie the Gryphon spoke of was to Cheshire, and now he distances himself the best he can. Whatever bitterness festers between them will remain with them. The Gryphon, mighty general of Wonderland's armies, fears her lover; rightfully so. Any who challenge him or look at him cross end up food for the ravens and foxes.

"Down the stairs." March points to the east. "He did not cross under the high way, so you may find him in that direction."

"Thank you." Cheshire's growl fills the air in front of her.

The heat from his touch fades from her skin, and so does he—gone with the pitiful breeze. She raises her hand to her nose to breathe in his intoxicating scent once more, feel his warmth, and licks her finger to savor Cheshire's sweet taste. It is difficult, nigh impossible, to deny the unbreakable animalistic hold he has over her and Jonathan, but she must, damn it.

"I need to fucking kill someone."

Farther down the high ways, closer to the Row, the crescendo of the procession of horses and soldiers passing underneath drowns out the clunks of March's boots. Large horse-drawn carts, painted pure white, break up the monotonous lines of soldiers like beads woven along the length of a long braid of hair. Red chests with iron banding fill the back of each cart; their lids hang open purposefully to allow the mounds of gold, silver, and gemstones within to sparkle in the sun. Adamas, the gilded city of Wonderland, has come to Mirus's aid. Or rather, to buy the soul and loyalty of the townspeople—whoever is willing to sell for an empty promise.

The citizens of Mirus, who were not previously enthralled by the shining appearance of the soldiers, are now enraptured by the sheer spectacle of wealth carried through their streets like farmers weary after their harvest. Lysander and Uriah win the fight before the first blow is struck.

If only the townspeople could see through the facade. The white paint, freshly applied in the last few days, covers aged wood, bent nails, and loose bolts. Mud covers and cakes to the white wheels, and what does not stick, flings onto the wagon. The treasures contained within each chest were stolen from Mirus long ago. So long ago, in fact, the townspeople scarcely remember this currency originated from their home. Their shapes are unmistakable, each denomination a different phase of the moon—full golden circles, silver crescents, and copper half circles.

Two unfamiliar men's voices squabble briefly, squawking out of a stone songbird sitting on a tenement's eave to her right, and echoes through every other throughout Mirus. "Attention, Mirus."

"What fresh hell is this?"

The voices announce Lysander and Uriah's claim to the throne. The rhythmic trotting below becomes chaotic and dissonant. Soldiers cheer, snapping the reins of their horses, and speed toward the castle as fast as the twisting streets of Mirus will allow.

"I leave the castle for less than an hour and it all falls to shit."

She searches around for any glimpse of the Gryphon or sound from Cheshire, but their feud carries them elsewhere, deeper into the city.

March turns from the Row and races through the high ways back toward the castle, the thump of her boots rivaling the horses. The dark stone and shingle roofs of stores and tenements rush by in a blur beneath like a raging river. The pointed roofs of taller buildings crest up out of the corner of her eye like waves. She sails above the winding twists and turns of the streets of Stonehaven and will reach the castle before Lysander and Uriah's soldiers. With their current foothold in the castle, after this proclamation, their men cannot be permitted to enter to further strengthen their grip on the throat of the city.

She descends the stairs into the Crest. The joyous, celebrating faces of the sycophant rich loyal to Lysander and Uriah turn March's stomach. The soldiers have not reached this tier of the city, yet the rich hang out of their windows, wait on their balconies and terraces, or gather behind their gates and fences.

Without warning, three pistol shots ring out clear as temple bells through the songbirds followed by Dormy's soft yet forceful voice. She issues a challenge to Lysander and Uriah for all to hear.

"Clever girl."

"Those who support the queendom, come to the castle to make your voices known," Dormy finishes.

Though proud of Dormy, this call to action will have unforeseen consequences; both sides will crowd the castle gates in an inevitably volatile gathering.

March reaches the tier of the castle; its looming wall reflects the sun. A wall which once meant protection and safety from threats outside. Now, the monsters already lie in wait within. The soldier, the young blue-haired man from earlier, opens the small door hidden in the gates for March, who skids to a stop once in the gatehouse.

Before any of the other guards can form the questions, the confusion of their pinched and curled faces makes it clear. March grabs the door before it can latch and locks eyes with the guard—his face twitches. "Before these gates shut, I must send you through them. Take off your armor, now."

The soldier does so without hesitation. Two others join in unbuckling the leather straps of his pauldrons, gorget, breastplate, and greaves.

"I have a command for you, but not as a soldier. As a soldier, you are a target. Most of our forces have returned to their homes in Stonehaven and beyond the city wall. We must get word to them. Tell them to remain ready, but do not act rashly. They must carry their swords but not wear their armor. And if they have a sword not of the Castle Guard or Mirusian army, it would be better. If they do not have one, buy, barter, or steal one."

The soldier's armor clanks to the stones as it falls. He stands ready, wrinkled trousers, tunic, and boots.

"You still look like a soldier. Lose the tunic."

The guard fumbles with the thin leather straps tying it together up the center. March takes a dagger from her thigh and slices them in a swing. Caught off guard, the young man stammers, trying to understand, trying to speak.

March grabs several long pieces of semi-dried wood from the pile against the wall and rubs her hands on the large leather animal hide they sit upon. She hands them to the guards and takes the remaining dirt from her hands and rubs it on the soldier's face, chest, back, arms, and hands. March takes his tunic from him and lays it on the ground, placing his scabbard, sword, and several pieces of wood on top of them, then ties the bundle together by the sleeves. One of the other guards picks it up and hands it to his newly disheveled brother-in-arms.

"Carry it over your shoulder," says March. "Look down as you walk.

Do not run. Fight only as a last resort. A busted lip or black eye is not a reason to start a full city riot."

The soldier steps through the door, and before he descends into the Crest, he turns back to March and says simply, "Thank you."

For what? Potentially sending him to his death? He is inexperienced, trusts her, and fought valiantly against the cult. There are other soldiers who trusted her before and died under her command willingly—idiots.

"Lock the gates," March commands as loud as a cannon blast. "Now."

One soldier lowers four lock bars onto the small door. Two others twist a giant crank to lower thicker lock bars from the side walls into place. One of them nearly covers the width of the door entirely. The two large gate men rock forward, hands pushing off their knees to rise from their benches and lumber to the gates. Their unnatural height allows them both to reach up to the curve of the gatehouse and grasp giant handles. They pull down a new, reinforced portcullis. Chains rattle and gears clank within the stone walls until the sharp iron teeth of the portcullis bite into the earth.

March runs from beneath the gatehouse into the bailey to find the archers, castle guards, and soldiers atop the parapets awaiting her command.

"No one of Adamas or loyal to Lysander and Uriah are to enter those gates," she shouts.

Across the bailey, the Doorman waits at the main doors to the keep, wringing his hands. Despite his commitment to his duty, uncertainty and fear are clear on his face, even from a distance.

"Gather the Duchess and the others," March shouts to him. "Ask them to meet in the council chamber at once."

He nods frantically and runs into the castle, not knowing if he should leave the door open or close it.

An archer from above lifts his helmet's visor. "Is this an invasion?" he asks in a gruff voice. "Should we strike down any who try to breach?"

As much as March wishes to say yes, any public death would cause the uprising Lysander and Uriah wait for. The invasion has already happened under their noses while they worried about threats. This is the long breath the world takes before the skies break open and unleash a torrent of rain, shake the ground with thunder, and blind with lightning.

"No," she says. "We cannot risk it. Not yet." This time, they cannot eliminate their enemies. The fight against the cult was simple—kill them by any means necessary, fire, blade, or arrow. This battle will prove much more complex. "Let me convene with the others and I will have a better answer for you. Not one of them enters. And someone alert me as soon as the Gryphon returns."

The soldiers bang their fists against their breastplate, the large gate men look on blankly and sit back on their benches, and the archers disappear from the backside of the gatehouse to take position facing the city.

The approaching thunder of galloping horses' hooves upon the cobbles of the Crest stop March's brisk walk to the keep. She turns back and runs the curve of the wall, climbs the wooded stairway at the far end of the bailey, and crosses the back to the top of the gatehouse as the polished armor and waving pendants come into view. The horses slow and clop to a stop surrounding the gates.

"Open the gates." The unmistakable voice of the turncoat Red Knight calls out from behind a silver visor, trimmed with red accents.

The murderous temptation March felt earlier vibrates at the back of her eyes. She sets her foot on the parapet and looks down upon the disgraced Red Knight. Twelve archers take their place beside her, six on each side, arrows drawn, but bows slack for the moment.

"The castle is closed today," says March. "Much to discuss—far too important for the likes of you—before we can entertain your party."

"We heard the call through the air," the Red Knight says. "I assume your feeble ears heard it as well. Open the gates for the army of our new lords and kings." His slime-covered, grating voice seeps out from between the space in his visor, adding a metallic tinge to his already irritating voice.

"We heard it." March rests her forearm on her raised knee. "And I heard what followed. Did you not?" She taps her temple with her middle finger. "Or has the loss of your eye affected your hearing as well?"

"You dare speak down to me?" The Red Knight removes his helmet to reveal a brown leather eye patch with a red cross covering his missing eye.

"I speak to you in the matter fitting your new role: the bitch of Lysander and Uriah." March grins. "Traitorous, opportunistic wretch. Careful how you speak to me before I claim your other eye."

"My lords will hear of this, and you shall suffer dearly."

"I am sure." March laughs, angering the Red Knight further.

"Open the gates!" the Red Knight shouts.

The cacophony of the soldiers' armor, their mutters, and mumbles, and the anxious clack of horse hooves fill the air. Townspeople who heeded Dormy's call rise from the stairways through the Crest, spooking the horses and crowding the street further. Soldiers and citizens exchange words, curses, and threats, tensions cloaking the air as bodies fill the street.

"We will not stand for this," the Red Knight shouts, "especially by some whore parading around, pretending to have power, exposing her body for all to see, when we all know you are just some strumpet plaything kept around to entertain the men."

The growing crowd of soldiers chuckle, making lewd kissing and sucking noises, slurps, and moans. They think themselves clever. They are children, and March has heard it all before.

The archers' breaths become heavier through their nose, pinging against the inside of their helmets. A different sound than those of the soldiers of Lysander and Uriah. Do they take offense at their words?

She brings her foot down from the parapet and stretches, revealing slightly more of her under breast. They shift uncomfortably in their saddles, small cocks trapped in place. March has their attention, as she expects and wants—the reason she selected this ensemble today. March endures and enjoys their taunts and attempts to goad her, insult her; part of her misses them. A constant, though negative, is still a constant.

"Whore? Strumpet? Plaything?" She raises her right hand, studying their armor. The archers draw and aim their arrows at the Red Knight, with deadly precision. "Yet I still hold more power than you. You thirst for it, demand it like a child, sell your soul for it, while I have possessed it all my life."

"Our lords will hear of this," the Red Knight says again, trying to conceal the tremble of fear and anger in his voice.

"You have said this once already," says March. "Not to worry. I am on my way inside the castle to discuss important matters. Though I doubt I shall remember to bring you up."

"We will not stand for this!" the Red Knight shouts.

"Sit. Lie down. Die for all I care, but you will wait." Even though the archers are feet from her, she speaks loud enough for the audience below to hear. "Until I return, they remain outside the gates. If any try to breach our defenses, consider it an act of aggression against the city. Oh, and the weak point of their armor is at the top of the gorget, the bend of the elbows, and the slit in their visors—too wide to offer any real protection, especially from arrows at such close range."

March leaves the wall while the Red Knight and other soldiers still shout crude and lustful obscenities. Running across the cobbles of the bailey to the keep, March wonders why the safety of the city falls to her and hers, only feeling disdain for this mound of earth and its people. Yet there are men who fight for her, who have, dare she say it, respect for her, for whom she must be responsible. Little do they know, March does not care what fate befalls them. In the end, Jonathan, Cheshire, and Dormy are what matters, and she will sacrifice any and every one until she sets foot back in the grassy meadow of the Hollow with them.

CHAPTER 11

CHESHIRE

Cheshire walks unseen through the smaller side streets and alleys, where shrinking puddles remain after the storms. Sparkling, filled cracks in the dark cobbles, hidden in shadows between tenements, reflect the blue sky above. Thick, heavy-tread mud cakes over walkways, mostly dried, except for areas closest to spouts and in deeper shadows. Footsteps crack and reveal the unnaturally dark moist mud underneath, probably mixed with blood. Among the many footprints in the mire, he searches for those specific to the Gryphon, wide, abnormally long, and deep.

The back alleys keep Cheshire away from the procession of soldiers. If he still had access to the stocks of oil he used to raze the harbor, he could make quick work of them all in one spectacular winding pyre the length of the city streets. If time allowed, he could find more; stores must be replenished by now. However, there would bound to be one or two idiot soldiers who would run screaming into an old tenement or storefront while on fire and set the city itself ablaze. Cheshire cannot risk such stupidity with his mother still unaccounted for, but it is an idea worthy to save for later nonetheless.

The hunt for the Gryphon proves more difficult than Cheshire first thought, considering his towering stature. Finally, in a narrow alley, Cheshire catches a glimpse of boot prints in the deeper mud, matching those of the Gryphon's boots—only three steps in a broken line, nothing more. His steps and remnants of mud, being a different color and consistency, should continue on the stones and dirt of the city street, but his trail is gone without a trace. Regardless, Cheshire stretches his shoulders, heart racing; the hunt is on, and now Cheshire has a direction.

Down another side street, he discovers another set of boot prints; three again. Following the steps like arrows, several streets over, Cheshire crouches near a third set; two this time, no, three again—the last pressed in the shallowest bit of cracked mud.

Once is chance, twice is luck, three times is conspiracy. What game has Cheshire missed? He raises his eyes and searches the walls, finding the smallest scrape of mud upon a low windowsill, gutters above it, and smudges along the walls and crates. The damned Gryphon plays the game too well and leaves enough crumbs to entice and whet Cheshire's thirst for revenge. The gutters run the length of the walls, where uneven bricks jutting out serve as grips, and small boxes, puddles left from the rain, and emptied chamber pots are used to conceal more steps.

Cheshire lowers himself to the ground, face almost touching the mud, and inspects the boot prints.

"Oh, fuck you."

The weight distribution of the steps is wrong, all wrong. The heel should be the deepest part of the impression, especially for someone of the Gryphon's height, but here the front of these boot prints press harder into the mud—the sign of someone intentionally walking backward. Walking backward to lead Cheshire in the wrong fucking direction.

Cheshire runs back to the second set, spooking horses as he slides unseen between them on the crowded streets, and then returns to the first set he stumbled upon. Every boot print matches, weight contrary, planted purposefully. A well thought-out play by the Gryphon.

He resumes his search in the opposite direction, passing through the never-ending line of freshly bathed soldiers on horseback, wagons, and men and women of Mirus, dirty from boot to bonnet, covered with dust, ash, and small specks of wood from the ongoing repairs, appearing more like those who dwell in the Boroughs.

In the shadows of the winding high ways, two men, out of place, one tall and thin and the other shorter and portly, lean back against one of the support beams and catch Cheshire's attention. They face opposite directions and do not risk glancing at each other, as if to appear as strangers to others. Amateurs. They both wear indistinguishable, yet ill-fitting, clothing from the workers of Stonehaven—brown leather, linen, and corduroys. Their clean faces and hands give them away though; either they are not taking part in the city's restoration and avoiding all dirt and soot wafting through the air, or they have recently arrived and stolen their wardrobe. The thin man tries to waft something invisible away from his face and scrunches his nose. These two reek of the pampered ilk of Adamas.

"I lost her," the thinner of the men says, trying not to move his mouth.

"I did too," the shorter man says. "Few streets back."

Their failure at subtlety makes them even more conspicuous. Cheshire stands feet in front of his soon-to-be victims and listens as they discuss their failure.

Cheshire fiddles with the end of his mother's sash, twirling it in hand while thinking of how to dispatch them. Since the moment Cheshire discovered the Mask of Light and the Mask of Shadow, he learned to use them as he fought to survive, but he has yet to discover their limits without the pressure of death, and the Ace looming over him. The thought of his old adversary, who has yet to resurface since the events in the bailey, brings a different homesick ache to his chest. The constant threat of death has defined his life since his tenth year.

Until this moment, Cheshire took for granted the power of the mask; even when fully clothed, the mask took this into consideration. The Mask of Shadows allows him to bring others with him through any shade he chooses. What are the limits of the Mask of Light?

"The lords said we should not return to the castle without a report. How are we going to give a report when we have lost her on our first assignment?" asks the thin man.

These two believe they had a chance tailing March—a laughable notion. She would plunge her blades deep into them, killing them with a single stroke. It would be a mercy for these men to die at her hands. Cheshire has no mercy to give them.

"Well, if we found her, I'd fuck her here in the back alley, give her a proper go," the short man says.

"As long as you're willing to share." The thin man laughs—the last laugh to ever pass his lips.

"I swear, the whores here don't compare to the ones we have up north."

The hairs on the back of Cheshire's neck bristle, and a pulsating heat overtakes his body. To follow her earned them death. To speak of her earns them suffering. Cheshire picks up a small stone from between the cobbles and holds it in front of their faces, waving it back and forth. They see nothing. Cheshire touches the building opposite of where they stand, pressing hard against the brick. No reaction from the soon-to-be dead men. Therefore, it stands to reason the building remains while the pebble turned invisible with him.

Too large, perhaps. Somewhere in between. He wonders if March was invisible at his touch.

On the other side of the alley, a length of dirty rope hangs from an old hook next to piles of cut boards and a table covered with old hammers and chisels. How he would love to take his time with these two, but he should first find out if these idiots act alone or with others. Cheshire takes the rope and the longest chisel in hand and walks in front of the men—no reaction.

Perfect.

He circles behind the men and the support post and swings the rope to build up momentum, which whooshes through the air.

"You hear that?" asks the thinner man, perking up.

Before the short man can respond, Cheshire whips the rope around their necks and post, yanks hard, and slams the back of their heads against the wood. In the seconds of disorientation, Cheshire tightens the rope, twists it, and shoves the chisel in between the taut coil as a handle. With every turn the rope tightens, constricting the men's air. They panic, gasp for breath, and scratch at their throats, able to touch what binds them but unable to see, to comprehend.

Earlier, Cheshire nearly took the life of the soldier in the castle the same way yet left him alive. These two will pay for his mistake.

"Help!" gasps the thinner man, struggling and losing his footing in the wet muck below the highway.

"Do not speak another word," Cheshire whispers beside them.

"What is this? What is this?" The short man swings and kicks at nothing.

"I am Death," says Cheshire. "And I have come to collect."

"Oh, shit, no." The thin man reaches out, fruitlessly, as if trying to grab the walls around him, too far from his reach. "Gods above, help us. Save us," he gasps.

"Demons," the other says.

"I am a force of nature. I hold the life of every soul in my hand, and they live by my temperance."

Their fingers find the gaps between the rope and the support post and pull. Cheshire feels the strain on the rope and turns the chisel end over end, tighter and tighter, until their words stop and their breaths amount to little more than death rattles.

"Care to make a deal with Death?" whispers Cheshire. "A deal can always be struck, if you are willing to pay the price?"

Both men nod frantically, slobber spewing from their mouths. Their feet slip and dance in the mud as if they stood upon the gallows. Blood covers their fingertips from digging into their necks.

"Whoever kills the other shall be spared. This is my deal. Act quickly before your breath or my patience wears out."

Their hesitation lasts less than a second. The short man elbows the thinner man in the face. *Crack*. The thin man swings his fist back into his partner's groin then returns the elbow to the face. *Crack*.

Cheshire continues slowly turning the chisel as their scuffle intensifies. They punch and kick feebly at each other. Standing side-by-side hinders their attacks.

"I grow bored," says Cheshire, twisting harder. The rope, the beam, or perhaps the men's necks, begin to creak and pop.

The thin man cries out with what little breath he possesses and slams his boney elbow into the neck of his partner. Over and over again, he hits at the short man, who tries to fend off the blows with his hands. The ropes leave their necks stretched and unable to be protected. The thin man has longer arms, longer reach, which gives him greater speed behind his strikes.

"Please," the short man begs through his broken jaw and teeth. But the thin man does not relent. The short man catches the other's arm, and with his strength, bends it backward against his own neck, breaking it at the elbow. *Snap*. The thin man's wail of pain is little more than a rasped breath.

The short man takes inspiration from his partner and thrusts elbow after elbow to the thin man's neck. With a broken arm, his comrade can do little to defend himself. *Crack*. *Crack*. *Crack*. *Crack*. As Cheshire tightens and reaches the limits of the rope, the final blow is struck, breaking the man's neck.

Crack.

The thin man's arms fall to his side, lifeless, his head bobs, and his feet slip out from under him, skidding and leaving small trails in the mud.

"Well done, servant." The temptation to kill the second man grows within Cheshire like creeping vines. Not yet. Cheshire loosens the rope, and the short man falls to the ground, gasping, crying, and retching over the cobbles. The thin man collapses, joints at odd angles, like a broken and discarded doll.

"This is the first life you have taken," says Cheshire.

The man shakes his head, coughing up blood, and feebly tries to crawl away, bloody fingers digging into the spaces between the stones. It is too late for him. Cheshire gleefully straddles the man's back and wraps the rope around his neck again like reins.

"You said you would let me live," the man croaks.

"I said you would be spared this fate," says Cheshire, tightening the coil around the man's neck. "I never said I was finished with you."

"No, please."

"The woman you followed. She is mine, and I am hers. She is someone I hold most dear. A lover who deals death as well as I. Following her was enough to seal your fate, but the vile, foul way you spoke of her is beyond reprehensible and why you must die. Do give my regards to the ferryman."

"I... I am sorry. I didn't know. Forgiveness, please. Mercy," the man pleads. "Death makes deals, yes? Can one life be traded for another? We were not alone. There are others sent out to follow her."

How advantageous—the information he wanted given willingly.

"Three. There were three others. Five of us in total, at least for this morning. The others planned to regroup behind an old tenement some city blocks from here."

"Take me to them."

Cheshire yanks on the rope and brings the short man up to his knees, then his feet. Cheshire jumps on the man's back and wraps his arms around his neck, tightening the rope. The man yelps with fear, his knees buckle, and the air smells of piss.

"On your way," Cheshire whispers in the man's ear.

The short man limps through back alleyways, bearing Cheshire on his back, stumbling and slipping every few paces. They pass an open window, where a woman hangs a sack of potatoes from a hook near the windowsill. She takes no notice of the bloody man or his passenger. Farther they pass an older man enjoying milk of the poppy, slumped near a cask full of water, without reaction. Farther still, three men from the Forge sit on a wide bench on break from repairs, and none of them take notice, at least visually. Blacksmiths raise their heads, hearing the short man's wheezing, but are unable to find its source. If not for the loud clatter of soldiers and horses, the damned man would draw the attention of the entire city.

"Tell me truthfully, what precisely were your orders?" asks Cheshire.

"Nothing. Just watch. Follow the woman," the man huffs. "See who she talks to and report back to my lords."

"Why do Lysander and Uriah care who she speaks to?"

"I don't know. I don't know. I don't know."

"What else were you asked?"

"If the opportunity presents itself, request she come back to meet with my lords in private."

"Why would they make such a request?"

"They have something planned."

"What a waste of a breath and time you are. Your lords must be sick of you and hold no value to your life. To follow her is to bring death upon yourself. Unfortunately for you, I found you first." Cheshire tugs on the rope around the man's neck. "Another question. Have you, by chance, seen the Gryphon in the city?"

"Earlier, yes. He walked with the woman for a bit, but we lost them both."

"Where were you when you lost them?"

The man stammers, trying to recall. "We were approaching a cross way. There was a tri-level building across from a fruit vendor, then buildings with arched doors at their corners instead of their faces."

Cheshire knows the area and the exact spot of which the man speaks. Another staircase to the high ways rises behind the tri-level tenement, hidden from view. Cheshire could not find any footprints from the Gryphon because he took back to the sky. Once this lot of prying eyes are dead, Cheshire will resume his hunt.

After several turns through city streets, they approach a small recess of a tall timbered tenement draped in shadow. Three men, dressed as the other two were and just as clean-faced, lean against the walls. One with slicked-back hair puffs on a small pipe, another digs dirt out from underneath his nails, and the last taps his hands nervously in his crossed arms. In their attempt to appear inconspicuous, they fail miserably. If Cheshire happened upon them without his guide, he would have killed them for the simple fact of looking suspicious.

The short man stands before them and waits for a reaction from his partners, thinking they will come to his aid. He holds his hands up and waves them, but they pay no mind because they do not see him. The man with the pipe perks his ears and shifts his eyes side to side hearing the faintest footfalls.

"What spell have you bewitched me with?" the short man asks. "Here they are, just as I said."

The man with a pipe chokes and coughs out smoke. "What was that?"

"What did you say?" the man with crossed arms asks the others. "Witchcraft?"

"Nothing," the others say, looking around nervously. "Don't talk of witches. Not in this place."

Their collective heartbeat pulses through the air—the beautiful rhythm of fear. The one cleaning his nails draws a long dagger from within his coat, while the other two stand and search the roofs and peer out to the street.

"I'm here," the short man pleads. "Help me."

"Who the fuck said that?" The man with the dagger swings it in different directions erratically, pointing at nothing.

"Where are you?" the man with the pipe screams. "Show yourself, you damn demon."

"Fuck this," she slick man says. "This is not what I signed up for."

"Stand your fucking ground and fight."

"Fight what?"

"What in all the hells?" The short man whimpers. "What have you done to me?"

"Never you mind," Cheshire whispers in his ear. "If you wish for me to release you, I ask only one more thing."

"Name it," the short man whispers back, on the verge of tears.

"Kill them."

CHAPTER 12
MARY ANNE

She wants Lysander and Uriah dead, impaled on every sword of the Castle Guard until they resemble bloody pin cushions instead of men. They are not men, but deceitful beasts.

The Duchess speeds Mary Anne, Jonathan, and the Chamberlain away from the throne room, where guards of Mirus and soldiers of Adamas remain positioned, to the council chamber. Their heels and boots click and clack heavily across the stone floor. The Duchess mentions something about how they must gather in private to collect their thoughts, something about calmer heads prevailing, all muffled by the pounding of Mary Anne's heart in her ears. Her mind reels out of control—a locomotive barreling down its track, fire burning, smoke billowing, body shaking.

All Mary Anne had to do was sit, the throne hers for the taking, and wait for someone, call someone, anyone, be they servant or guard to bear witness. Instead, like a child, she ran to the Duchess for validation, acceptance, and acknowledgment. Mary Anne wasted precious time trying to find the Duchess when she could have ordered any servant to fetch her.

Jonathan might have been the correct course of action after all, but could she leave her bedchamber once there? With the adrenaline and excitement coursing through her body, the temptation to take Jonathan and have him all to herself may have been too great, wanting him, waking him, giving herself to him. Where she sought validation through the Duchess emotionally, she would have received it from Jonathan physically.

Her stomach aches, twisting in knots, punishing her for her choice. No matter what choice she made, the same outcome would have come to pass. The vile Twins would have reached the throne room and waited. Mary Anne must question how long were they there? Did they happen upon the throne room, or do they constantly test the doors? This is not a coincidence, but conspiracy.

Their deaths would be a simple matter. The thought plays in her mind over and over again, like a skipping record on a victrola. Inside the castle, the Twins are outnumbered. She could have screamed, commanded the Castle Guard to come to her aid, or ordered them to slay the brothers. On the other hand, the soldiers loyal to the Twins still in the keep would descend upon the throne room, and many would lose their lives in the struggle against them for Mary Anne. Acceptable losses, if it meant the deaths of the arrogant scoundrels. Commanding their deaths should have been the first thing she did before the crowd assembled.

Jonathan reaches down and takes her wrist and slides down to take her hand, loosening her grip. His heat matches her own. Her fingers intertwine with his, and she looks into his eyes—beautiful, determined, yet haunting. Her eyes drop to his shirtless body, where they would feast upon his physique, but the bruises pull her back from her thoughts to the present. She made the only logical choice. Jonathan is in no condition to fight. The Gryphon is nowhere to be found. March is elsewhere, probably indulging in more adulterous activity, when Mary Anne has need of her swords.

Should and *would* play no part in the present. What matters most is what comes next, how they plan, how they win, how the Twins pay, and how they will die.

"Wait." The Duchess stops their caravan, turning on her heel. "We act too rashly. Mary Anne, return to your chamber and dress for the day, for the coming events. Carter, escort her. Weiss, in Lady Audrianna's stead, assembles a small group of the Castle Guard to post outside of the council chamber. Reconvene in ten minutes' time."

They move as one down the hallway, and without acknowledgment, at the next intersection, the parties separate to follow their intended paths. Mary Anne remains silent still until she enters her chamber and flings open one of her dozens of wardrobes. She releases an unbridled scream, beginning first with clenched teeth and ending with her mouth agape, cheeks and jaw in pain, and her body shaking.

To her shock and surprise, Jonathan stands behind her and wraps his massive arms around her. She can feel his warm breath upon her ear and neck. The heat of his body, and the solid form of his muscles, permeates her thin robe with ease, pressing against her back. He holds her until the beat of her heart, not losing intensity, transforms from anger and desire. He steps away, and the colder air between them makes the divide all-the-more clear.

"You would normally ask if I am harmed," says Mary Anne.

"There are times words fail, and action is the more appropriate course," says Jonathan. "I apologize for not wearing a shirt or asking for your permission."

"You never need to ask my permission. And I prefer you without your shirt," says Mary Anne. She unties her robe and allows it to slide from her shoulders and pool on the floor at her feet. She slowly turns to face Jonathan, bare, chest heaving, ripples running over and tightening her skin. The words leave Mary Anne's mouth before she can stop them. "I prefer you wearing nothing at all."

Jonathan stands toe to toe with her, the look in his eyes so innocent, but does he not know the effect he has upon her senses? Her reason? "Within these walls, we have spent much of our time without our clothing. However, wearing nothing would not be suitable for the council, where we must make haste to return."

Mary Anne cannot help but feel small as Jonathan walks to his trunks to collect his frayed blue longcoat. Foolish of her to present herself in such a way to Jonathan when the others wait for them, but she could not resist. And Jonathan, ever the gentleman, never looked below her eyes.

"Later," Mary Anne half jests.

"If you wish."

It is more than a wish. It is a deep and unquenchable yearning. Jonathan is correct. These past few weeks, they have spent many nights and afternoons in their bedchamber without clothing, for Mary Anne to enjoy his body, but while he fucks March, Cheshire fucks him, or he watches Cheshire and March. Being a spectator is no longer enough for Mary Anne. She should think of the matter at hand, but her mind always returns to Jonathan.

Mary Anne pushes dresses and gowns aside to select the dress she altered days ago, with the sides completely removed, showing the unbroken line of her skin from shoulder to foot. The freedom, especially now, empowers her. She clasps her silver belt around her waist; the metal circles cold against her hips.

While slipping on her tall boots, a frock Mary Anne has not noticed before catches her eye. At the side of her wardrobe, crammed behind gowns with full flounce and slit sleeves, a red longcoat peeks out. She never thought to look for anything else besides gowns in her wardrobes.

Mary Anne runs her hand along the sleeve and pulls it from its hiding spot. A heavy brocade longcoat hangs before her, made to resemble an exquisitely designed patchwork of crimsons with rich golden thread and decorative embellishments, similar in color to the dress she wears.

"Jonathan," she calls, breaking his concentration before he dons his blue longcoat with the least amount of pain. She holds the new coat up for him, and he graciously accepts.

He walks to her and turns his back, wincing as his broad shoulders pinch together, and waits. Mary Anne guides his hands through the sleeves and slides the longcoat up, mesmerized by his flexed arms, shoulders, and back.

He turns to present himself to her for her approval. The longcoat hugs and fits his body as if meant for him. It hangs open, revealing his chest and the muscles of his stomach like his other coat, but the cut of the tailoring hugs his body and makes Jonathan appear even more dashing and debonair than before, which Mary Anne did not think possible.

Jonathan holds out his hand for Mary Anne. "Shall we?"

She takes his hand and squeezes it as they leave their bed chamber. His grip matches hers, heartbeats joining in their palm. Jonathan feels it as well. Mary Anne can see it in his eyes. He does not let go. She knows he will never let go, no matter what follows.

CHAPTER 13

CHESHIRE

The short man sits against a wall of the tenement, blood gushing from a deep stab wound, wheezing, legs wide, slumped over and clutching his stomach, clinging to his last few seconds of life. The color drains from his face and hands as the blood pools and spreads under his body. His three other compatriots lie dead in corners of the alcove. The short man managed to kill two of the three, suffering his mortal wound. He snapped the neck of one while still invisible, and a nearby stone, fallen from the tenement's wall, ended the second's life with a quick bash to the head, but not before he plunged the dagger deep into the short man. Cheshire dispatched the third, burying the stem of the pipe deep into its owner's eye.

Cheshire picks up the dagger from the ground and kneels in front of the dying man, still unable to be seen. "You managed better than I expected."

"I did as you asked," the short man says, barely a whisper. "You... you said you would let me live. I gave you three lives. Give me mine."

"Silly mortal. You took two. I claimed the third."

"But you said you would let me live."

Crack! Cheshire strikes the man across the face. "I said I would release you. And I am. How dare you insinuate I would lie? I am Death. I am the only truth."

The man sobs, feeling the approach of his end. While he cries, every time his stomach constricts, more blood pours out of his wound. No matter how much he feebly presses against his stomach with both hands, crimson rivers flow from between his fingers.

"What are you?" he asks.

Cheshire waves his hand in front of his face and wipes away the Mask of Light as if made of smoke, returning it to his glove.

The man raises his head and looks upon Cheshire's face for the first time.

"You're a child."

"No. I am not. I have not been for quite a long time."

The man looks into Cheshire's eyes, lip quivering. "I do not care what you are. I do not want to die."

"Little to do about it now." Cheshire grins.

"Please, please do not leave me alone, here at the end. I... I am frightened."

"What is the matter? No whores for you to surround yourself with?" Cheshire grabs the man's jaw and digs his fingers into his skin. "You called my love a whore, remember? I do."

The man tries to speak, to apologize, but Cheshire crushes his jaw. He twirls the dagger in the other hand and drives it straight into the ground through the man's crotch. A new flow of blood pools between his legs. The man screams, body spasming, but can only release weak, panting rasps.

Cheshire waves his hand over his face, summoning the Mask of Light, disappearing from the man's sight.

"Die alone," says Cheshire, as he leaves the whimpering man.

He walks into the street and stretches his back, rejuvenated and refreshed. Fuck the pardon; Cheshire will play along when it suits him and play the devil when it does not. His next target must be the Gryphon, who, in the past, has proven to be quite the adversary, even though Cheshire has proven his skill in strategy equal to, if not superior to, the disgraced general. The scars of the city prove it.

Out of the corner of his eye, at the far end of an alleyway visible for split seconds at a time between the river of horses and soldiers, Cheshire notices the woman he glimpsed in the castle. His stomach drops again. The gray hood she wears obscures her face, but the short locks of rich lavender are unmistakable.

"What lunacy is this? I am not free from these apparitions even if I leave the castle?" Cheshire's body tenses, wanting, needing to give chase. Would he catch up to this woman, or would it be another instance of the castle corridors where the phantasm is always out of reach?

A stone songbird above him snaps him from his thoughts. It squawks out some ridiculous, but intriguing, news as he climbs and claws his way up the tallest nearby tenement. The voices sound familiar. It tickles him. How wondrous. The matters of the throne do not interest Cheshire, unless they are detrimental to those he cares most for—Jonathan, March, and Dormy—but this lovely, timely spark of chaos gives him what he needs.

He does not know where the Gryphon *is* currently, but thanks to the idiots who made the proclamation, Cheshire knows where the Gryphon *will* be. Despite the Gryphon's best attempts to avoid the castle, avoid Cheshire, and conceal himself somewhere in the city, the news hanging in the air will propel him back to the castle. Cheshire needs only intercept him before he reaches the gates.

He pulls several nails from loosened shingles then leaps from rooftop to chimney to eave to cupola toward the castle with the same ease and grace as when he flies through the trees. Each moment of weightlessness soaring between structures, the air rushing around his bare body like a rock in the stream, tickles the pit of his stomach, and renews his spirit even further. It reminds him of his first nights in the capital.

The Mask of Light keeps the wind from his face except for the small wisps cascading through its eyeholes. It will prove most valuable while sneaking up on the Gryphon. Not to mention the added benefit of not drawing unneeded attention to himself—a naked man jumping overhead with his cock flapping between his legs or, at this point, hard as steel from the anticipation, would call attention from any onlooker across Stonehaven.

If the Gryphon wishes to reach the castle before the crawling army beneath, the high ways are the quickest route. Cheshire sprints across the long spines and up the slopes of slanted roofs, muted clacks of shingles underfoot, and climbs higher into Mirus, racing toward the castle. The vast high ways above the city stretch out like branches over Stonehaven, and four stairways, the roots of the wooden network, begin where Stonehaven meets the Crest. Cheshire races to the path nearest the center of the complex—the closest to the castle's gates. He climbs the top of a metal spire on top of one temple of the Suicide King in Stonehaven. From this perch, he can see the high ways as if looking down on a map and searches every direction, looking for a sign, wondering if he missed his opportunity. After all, the Gryphon's stride is nearly triple Cheshire's when walking, let alone running.

The Gryphon finally rises into view far to the north. To confound Cheshire, he must have alternated using the high ways and streets while leaving his broken backward trail. He runs with a slight limp as fast as his aged legs will carry him. His long gray hair flows behind him like a horse's mane at full gait. Cheshire leaps across the spines of rooftops to close the gap between him and his quarry. He must move faster to match the Gryphon's speed.

When he reaches the side of the high way the Gryphon runs, Cheshire pries a long board from the edge of the roof where he waits.

Five seconds.

He slides it through the triangle supports of the high way's railings, keeping hold in order for it to remain invisible, and locks it in place in the opposite railing in order to topple the Gryphon.

Four seconds.

The Gryphon runs with the determined speed of a hunter pursuing its prey.

Three seconds.

Goose flesh covers Cheshire's body.

Two seconds.

The second the Gryphon's boots should have caught the board and sent him crashing to the planks of the walkway, he leaps over it.

How? How did he see it?! Cheshire screams in his head.

"Now is not the time, you impudent child," the Gryphon calls behind him without breaking stride.

Cheshire looks back to the bare spot of the building where he pulled the plank. The Gryphon's keen eyes must have seen it pull away from the structure before it broke free and became invisible. Coursing heat from his head to his feet strips him of the euphoric high he felt after his much-needed triumph dealing with Lysander and Uriah's spies.

"You will account for me!" Cheshire roars. "Liar! Falsifier!" He gives chase, running on the rails of the pathways, barely wider than his foot. Already found out, Cheshire pushes his legs to their limits to catch up with the Gryphon, disregarding any noise he makes in his pursuit. They near the high way's end where they will descend into the Crest. Cheshire has little time to act and less to think.

To catch the Gryphon is not enough; Cheshire must get ahead of him to stop him before he reaches the street. The quick pats of his feet on the rails soon are overtaken by the heavy clomps of the Gryphon's boots and the horses beneath. Right before Cheshire runs side-by-side with him, Cheshire leaps across to the opposite rail and throws a handful of nails at the Gryphon's face.

Before his plan went to shit, he planned to flick them onto the wooden planks as a distraction for the Gryphon, allowing Cheshire an opening; perhaps only a singular but powerful knee to the jaw will bring the Gryphon down. The nails will do minor damage to his face, but the Gryphon will need to blink, and in the second they provide, Cheshire will be victorious.

However, the nails betray him. The moment they leave his hand, they reappear in the real world and give away his position. The Gryphon's haunted yellow eyes spot them in flight and trace them back to Cheshire.

The Gryphon grabs the side of his coat, longer than he is tall, and flaps it wildly at Cheshire with the fury of his namesake's wings. The thick whipping fabric knocks the nails from the air and sweeps over Cheshire's body, giving form to the invisible. Lunging forward, the Gryphon reaches out with his free hand and grabs at Cheshire—his fingernails scrape against the chin of the mask. In order to escape, Cheshire falls backward off the rail and catches himself, clinging to the cross bracing beneath. The Gryphon huffs and descends the stairs into the Crest to travel up toward the castle, not giving Cheshire a second thought.

Cheshire's blood turns to fire. It feels as if his face may blister and combust at any moment. He crawls topside again, but by then the Gryphon is gone, disappeared into a mob rising from Stonehaven, headed to the castle as well.

The crunch of the soldiers and horses below stifles any insult or curse Cheshire would scream into the wind. If the Gryphon will not face him in the city, he will have no choice but to answer for his actions inside the castle walls.

Cheshire gives chase again, not to catch the Gryphon but to make certain he enters the castle first. Lysander and Uriah's troops have already reached the gate, which will slow but not stop his entrance. The streets of the Crest clog with mounted soldiers in polished armor and the people of Stonehaven.

Unsatisfied, frustrated, Cheshire gives in to his dark, yet entertaining, urges. He drops from the high ways and slips a dagger from an unsuspecting soldier's belt and runs along the street to the east, jumping and stabbing at the insides of random soldiers' thighs, unprotected from their armor. The stabs are quick and wounds deep. There are not enough surgeons in the city to save them, nor is there enough time to fight their way out of the crushing crowd. Soldiers scream and pull on their reins. Horses rear up, adding to the confusion. The screams, the clatter, the chaos from behind feeds Cheshire and drives him forward. Seventeen lives he claimed in quick succession in the span of a few seconds.

Cheshire climbs the stone stairways, leaping upward using the heads and shoulders of townspeople like stones in a river, to reach the highest tier of the Crest. He rounds the curved wall the castle sits on and stops at the back of the large stately manor house with a blue roof belonging to March's mother. In the wall, opposite the tall fence lined with Juniper trees, he presses the precise stones in order and a doorway opens with a soft exhale to the catacombs under the city.

Gripping the dagger tight, Cheshire prepares for any Mirusian soldiers still foolish enough to map out his hidden world. The stagnant breath of the castle soon replaces the cool rush of air from the catacombs. Pardon or no, he will not forget or deny who he is, the person this city made him. He will embrace the division, being both loved and alone, prince and exile, son and slayer. He will smile in the sunlight as the pardoned hero for the masses and grin in the shadows as he decimates his enemies, claiming the lives of all who stand in his way, no matter which side they fight for. And it shall feel magnificent.

CHAPTER 14
JONATHAN

Silence fills the council chamber—the sort between the initial cannon blast from a ship far out at sea and the constrictive, pensive, impending boom when it finds and destroys its mark.

The Duchess sinks into the back of her chair at the head of the long oak table, tapping her fingers. Jonathan studies Mary Anne across the table, seated at the Duchess's right hand. Once, a timid young woman who sat in her chair with perfect posture, hands clasped in her lap, trying to conceal her worry, now in her place, a determined woman leans back in her chair, matching the Duchess, with an unnerving pinch of confidence upon her brow—one hand resting on the table, the other rubbing at her mouth, eyes unfocused and overtaken by a multitude of thoughts.

Jonathan sits to the Duchess's left with an empty chair next to him, waiting for March. Everyone's eyes search the room, not catching anyone's gaze, as if seeking an answer, waiting for it to appear like some phantasm's whisper.

Weiss, seated next to Mary Anne, picks at the cloth of his gloves with muted *plunks*. The Duchess pushes out each breath while the rapping of her fingers on the table keeps a second hand's pace. Seconds become minutes. Jonathan fears the minutes will become hours. Silence is not a place Jonathan fancies.

With so much space, his mind races with thoughts of what may be, might be, could be. The long council table running the length of the chamber mocks his own far away in the Hollow. This one sits empty and lifeless, except for the red fabric spread across the table from end to end. The sound of Jonathan's own breathing overwhelms his ears. The length of the table should be covered with tea services, woven doilies, silver trays overflowing with pastries, fallen leaves from the sprawling oak above, candles, and wisps of steam rising from the spout of every teapot. This is not Jonathan's table, not the Hollow, not his home.

The iron clink of the chamber door's latch behind Jonathan is the first sound beyond the breath and taps at the table, quickly followed by the scent of linseed oil, old parchment, citron, and vanilla, snapping Jonathan back from the depths, filling his lungs and his heart. March sits beside Jonathan, and his heart jumps to his throat. She sets her harness and swords by the side of her chair between them. The chasm in his chest makes it seem as though months have passed since he has fully looked upon her radiance and confidence, though it has been a few hours at most. She hides her emotions far better than Jonathan, keeping her steely expression, chest heaving with each breath. The smooth, soft area below her neck betrays her racing heartbeat.

She looks his red coat up and down and rolls her eyes. Her hand reaches for his under the table, and out of sight, they squeeze and hold onto each other tightly as if they shall never see each other again, treating every moment as if it is their first and their last. Every time Jonathan lays eyes upon her, he falls in love all over again, the same with Cheshire.

Out of the corner of Jonathan's eye, Mary Anne stares at their shared moment, brow furrowed and nose flaring. March squeezes Jonathan's hand all the more.

The door swings open, violently this time, as the Gryphon enters, causing all at the table except Jonathan and March to jolt from the noise. He swiftly closes it behind him, waiting for the iron latch to click into place. The Gryphon's longcoat rustles as he walks around the table behind them all, pulls the heavy chair out next to Weiss, and drops onto the seat, his weary expression clear to all.

Jonathan looks to March for answers.

Cheshire, her raised eyebrows say.

"Enough of this." Mary Anne breaks the silence.

Jonathan is unsure if she means their silence, the waiting, or of his connection to March, since Mary Anne still does not take her eyes from them. The Duchess's eyes shift to Mary Anne as if waiting for her to speak.

"Nothing?" asks Mary Anne. "We walked the entire way from the throne room to the council chambers in silence. Does no one have anything of substance to say? News? A plan?"

"We tread carefully," says the Duchess, shifting in her chair. "Whatever stratagem we design, we must take into account the—"

"No," says Mary Anne. "Enough treading carefully. The throne room doors are open. I will not allow these two treacherous swines to rob me of what is to be mine when I am so close. We have three of Wonderland's most skilled warriors in this room. We could kill Lysander and Uriah here, now, in the castle and be done with it."

Her answer, the spike in her tone, and the sharpness of her words take everyone by surprise—all but March.

"You say *we* as if you would swing the sword," says March. "You would risk our lives so easily with no knowledge of these men and of what they are capable."

"Oh, but I am quite certain you have full knowledge and are well accustomed to their skills and what they are capable of, having experienced it yourself," Mary Anne says pointedly, glancing back and forth between March and Jonathan.

It begins.

March releases Jonathan's hand and softly lays it on the hilt of one of her swords. Jonathan looks to March to break her attention from Mary Anne, but she does not meet his gaze. Every possible way to kill Mary Anne dances in the pink shimmer of her eyes.

"March has yet to face them in combat," says Jonathan, trying to dispel the sparking cannon fuse in the room, but it does little. Jonathan studies March's face for a hint of this new animosity, but she remains stone. On the other hand, Mary Anne raises her eyebrow as if victorious over March in some game unknown to him.

"This will get us nowhere," says the Duchess, snapping everyone in the chamber from one point of tension back to the other. "Gryphon, Weiss, Lady Audrianna, Carter, what say you?"

Silence—enough to suffocate the room.

"I believe Mary Anne to be correct," says Jonathan. "We must move swiftly, but with caution. Since our arrival in Mirus, the divide between the citizens has become increasingly clear. A great number still see Lysander and Uriah as the rightful heirs. I have no doubt the number grows substantially with the arrival of their army."

"And their wealth," says March. "They bring in chests of gold, silver, copper, and jewels by the wagon."

"There is no way to truly tell what part of the city remains loyal to the crown or to them," says Jonathan.

Mary Anne squirms uncomfortably in her chair. "Which is why we... you must strike first before we are overtaken."

"The first volley has already happened," says the Gryphon. "The entire city heard their proclamation."

"But Dormy challenged it," says Mary Anne.

"Yes." Jonathan straightens in his chair. "But both will only widen the chasm. Lysander and Uriah do not have a foothold in the castle and the city. They have it in their coiled fists."

"What is the saying?" asks Mary Anne. "Cut off the head of the snake and the tail will perish with it."

"A nice try, but we found this to be false with the Cult of the Mother." Jonathan holds up his bruised forearm. "I killed Sheridan, but the horde continued."

"I agree with Jonathan," says March, "and though I hate to admit it, Mary Anne speaks the truth, though she may not have all the details she requires."

"Go on," says Mary Anne. "Educate me."

"With pleasure," says March. "Unfortunately, this snake possesses two heads. This snake's bite, the venomous lies spewed by the Twins, is far worse than the infection spread by the cult. This poison has eaten away at the city little by little for centuries and will grow stronger in the coming days. The Twins' presence threatens everything. The disheartened and despondent people of Mirus are ripe for the picking, susceptible to influence, and easy to sway."

"Killing them now would only make them martyrs," says Jonathan.

"Now or later, would the result not be the same?" Mary Anne sits forward in her chair and places both hands on the table. "They will always be martyrs no matter when they die. The question we must ask is how we handle the aftermath."

The Gryphon raises his eyes and looks at March. She shakes her head. She knows something—something of use.

"We will find the battle we face more difficult than the cult," says Jonathan.

"What can be more dangerous than a mindless, blood-thirsty horde?" asks Mary Anne.

"An easily manipulated blood-thirsty horde who can reason, plot, and lie," says Jonathan.

Mary Anne leans back in her chair, more on her mind, more on her lips, but she holds them both behind the disappointment in her eyes. This explains the Duchess's silence. She knows Jonathan will be more than the voice of reason; he is the voice Mary Anne will not, cannot, argue against.

"This battle will be fought, won, or lost on many fronts," Jonathan continues. "First, the people of Mirus. Duchess, you must help with the citizens of Mirus, play the political side none of us are experienced enough with. Mary Anne, you cannot have a queendom without subjects. The time for hiding within the castle has ended. It is time you are with the people. And I shall be with you."

"Carter is correct," the Duchess chimes in, calmer than before, as if this were her plan all along. "The throne room doors are open, but Wonderland will still decide if you progress. Your fate is still in the hands of the people of Wonderland. They are Wonderland. You must be deemed worthy of the Third Tenet before progressing to the Fourth."

"And you must reach the Fourth Tenet," March relents. "No pressure. But it would prove beneficial to have the power of the Grand Arcana on our side against the Twins and their army."

"Lady Audrianna speaks wisely." The Duchess leans forward, confidence growing.

"And I will aid where I can in translating the book," says March, "since I fear some of your teachings have not been translated correctly."

Weiss gasps. "I beg your pardon."

"You are welcome." March ignores Weiss. "And in between those times, I will focus my efforts on Lysander and Uriah, if the Gryphon will take back the mantle and lead the soldiers of Mirus."

"Of course." The Gryphon inhales deeply, breathing in renewed purpose.

"Of course," Mary Anne repeats.

"No," says Jonathan. His disagreement takes March aback. "No, this is not a simple divide-and-conquer scenario. What worked before will not work now. We are smarter than the Twins and more skilled, but only when together. They know us and will try to separate us, divide us."

Jonathan must keep Mary Anne close. But he would also have March remain by his side than with the likes of the Twins. However, she has her own agenda. He will hold on to her as long as he can without impeding her way.

"At least you, Mary Anne, and myself," says Jonathan to March. His eye half-winks to add, *and possibly Cheshire, to keep him from trouble.*

"Unrealistic," says March.

"Now, more than ever, it is imperative we think and move as one. The strength of the Twins comes from their unity. There is never a time one is without the other." Jonathan grabs March's hand.

"Would it not benefit us to put a wedge in between them?" asks Mary Anne.

"Where is our time better spent?" asks Jonathan. "Trying to divide a relationship that began in the womb or work toward making ours just as formidable?"

"Your trio has proven just as fearsome," says Mary Anne.

The air leaves the room. Not by name, but Mary Anne mentions Cheshire. Jonathan and March wait for a reaction from the Duchess.

"If I am to be queen, if we are all to survive, will we not need everyone?" Mary Anne continues. "Your trio is no longer a secret, and neither are your combined skills. I witnessed you three face, defeat, and slaughter dozens upon dozens of brigands and mercenaries. Jonathan, you said all of us. Cheshire is pardoned. Do you not think, out of gratitude, he would help us on this occasion?"

Still, the Duchess gives no reaction to the proposal, eyes focused on a scratch she repeats on the tabletop.

While Mary Anne's request is simple, not altogether wrong, and comes from a place of innocence, she does not understand Cheshire. Neither Jonathan nor March fully understand him either, to be honest. He is a force of nature Jonathan and March can tame at times, while at others they have learned to weather and ride the storm.

Jonathan looks to March. "Would you like to ask him, dear heart?"

March chuckles and shakes her head. "You have much to learn, Mary Anne. And little time to do so."

A clatter outside the council chambers catches their attention. The door swings open and slams against the stone wall behind it. Lysander and Uriah enter like lords of the manor, still wearing their white robes draped loosely on their bodies, smug looks upon their faces, and brandishing their weapons for all to see.

Jonathan cannot be sure if they have come to parlay, to fight, or both. Whatever is to happen next, his earlier thought holds true. It begins.

CHAPTER 15
MARCH

March expected them to show up, just not so soon. Lysander rests his massive longsword over his shoulder, and Uriah carries his silver glaive over his opposite shoulder and wears his brown and black whip draped around his body. She does not turn to face them—it would only add to their theatrics if she showed them the slightest bit of attention. March positions her head and softens her gaze to see the Gryphon to her left, Mary Anne across, Jonathan next to her, and the glint of her swords' hilts sparkling in the bottle of her eyes.

"Pardon the interruption," says Lysander.

"Intrusion," says March.

"We were uninformed there was a council meeting," Lysander continues.

The Duchess stands and pounds her first on the table. A deep thud punctuates her words. "How dare you show your faces?"

Mary Anne, impatient, unaccustomed to these types of interactions, pushes away from the table and stands, seething. "Leave these chambers at once."

Jonathan and the Gryphon stand to join the others, Weiss sneaks behind his chair, and March remains in her seat.

"Was this a private affair?" Uriah moves his long hair behind his ears. "Did we interrupt a meeting of conspirators? I should hope not." He sits several seats down from March in the middle of the long table, while Lysander prowls the long way around to the other side and sits opposite his brother. "What will the people of Mirus think? Not an hour after our ascension to the throne we are already plotted against?" They rest their weapons on the table with loud clangs.

With the Twins out of the way, March turns her head slightly to see behind her. Four soldiers of Adamas in their polished armor and white tabards scuffle with the four castle guards outside of the chamber, iron scraping, clanking, and sliding against each other.

"Hold," the Gryphon bellows.

The Castle Guard stops moving, locking and trapping the arms and bodies of the soldiers, blocking them from pushing through the entryway. Lysander holds up a hand, and the soldiers of Adamas stop struggling. Both sets of men stand at attention, crowding the door. Clinking and dull clacks continue sporadically as they shove each other.

March turns her head back to the table to keep the Twins within the edge of her sight. The rest return to their seats with loud screeching and scratching of the heavy chair legs.

"Mary Anne," says Uriah, "thank you for showing us proper respect and standing as we entered the chamber. As it should be. You should become accustomed to it. We promise to treat you fairly."

"Until you ask us not to," says Lysander.

"Do you believe your words affect me?" Mary Anne rises again and moves to the head of the table to stand next to the Duchess. "The sight of you repulses me. Do not confuse revulsion with fear or anger. I have faced many men like you in my lifetime. It does not matter where I am. You are all the same."

March cannot help but smirk. Mary Anne's determination surprises her—disgusts her. A glimpse, a shard, of a possible future queen glimmers in Mary Anne. A shard is not enough to cut, but it is enough to get the lot of them killed.

"You have faced no men like us before." Lysander leans back in his chair, running his fingers along the full ridge of his blade.

"This is not why we have come," says Uriah. "The time for banter and debate has come to an end."

"Why did you, then?" asks Mary Anne.

"To reach the end of this ridiculous situation." Uriah chuckles. "Rather than unneeded bloodshed, while we are in the privacy of these council chambers, our father's council chambers, we recommend a peaceful and civil relinquishment of the castle."

"And city," says Lysander.

Uriah circles his finger around one knot on the wooden table, taking time and sucking the air from the room. "All we ask is for you to acquiesce to our request, and we can move past this nonsense."

The contrast of their voices grate at March's ears. Uriah's voice paints smoothly, like the skilled strokes of an artist's brush. Every word, and almost syllable, from Lysander strikes like a smith's hammer. And then there is the obnoxiously proper and over-articulated voice of Mary Anne.

"Never," Mary Anne and the Duchess say simultaneously.

"We will not entertain such an absurd and idiotic idea," says Mary Anne.

"Wait," March tells her, then finally turns her attention to the Twins. "Have you convinced yourselves we would believe you come bearing tidings of diplomacy while you fondle your weapons?"

"True." Lysander tings the tip of his nail on his sword. "We could kill every one of you in this room, here and now."

"You could try," says March.

"And you will fail in your attempt," adds Jonathan.

The Twins chuckle, humoring their words. "We are not

unreasonable," says Uriah. "We do not expect an answer at this moment. We shall allow a fortnight for your final decision."

Always a deception with them. They give Mary Anne two weeks to decide, meanwhile their ships sail to Mirus and will arrive before the time given. Fortunately, from what March can see in their faces, they are unaware she knows of their strategy. The Gryphon's eyes wait for March's. She finds them and blinks slowly instead of nodding.

"A fortnight, during which you expect us to cohabitate peacefully in the city and the castle?" the Duchess asks mockingly.

"In two weeks' time," says Lysander, "we will expect your answer."

"And what if the answer is unchanged?" Mary Anne centers herself at the head of the table. The Duchess pushes back to allow her room. "Since the throne room opened for me, and not your repulsive ilk."

"You have your version of the truth," says Lysander.

"We have our version of the truth," says Uriah.

"And the one, rightful truth will come to light," says Mary Anne. "It always does."

Not always. Secrets keep them all alive.

The Duchess pushes her chair forward for Mary Anne to sit, and she does so without noticing, arms spreading wide on the table, while she takes her place by her side.

"I have entertained this pointless conversation long enough," says Mary Anne. "You have until sunset for you and your men to vacate the castle."

"Your option seems very one sided," said Lysander. "We try to reason with you, and you act rashly."

Underneath the table, March taps her finger on the top of Jonathan's hand, preparing him.

"We take their offer," says March.

Everyone turns their attention to her, wide-eyed, waiting for more information on this unexpected answer.

"As wise as you are delicious." Lysander's eyes tick up and down from March's lips to her chest.

"Out of the question," Mary Anne snaps.

"We will take their offer." March's eyes, not her words, quiet Mary Anne. She leans back in her chair and huffs. "Because in less than two weeks' time, half by my estimate, the armada of Adamas will reach our shores."

"What armada?" asks the Duchess.

"Forty ships at least, by my count. Sloops, galleons, man-of-wars."

Until this moment, Lysander and Uriah have moved and shifted in their chairs, making themselves comfortable, marking their territory like mongrels. After March's admission, both pause in time for the smallest measure of a second—passed unseen by the others around the table except for the Gryphon, but long enough to give March a moment of blissful satisfaction.

"No retort?" March asks. "And do not waste the air in the room and try to deny it or speak of *your truth*. They sail around the eastern coast of Wonderland even now and will approach from the south."

"This is why you so graciously give us two weeks," says Jonathan. "Give us a false sense of peace for the time being, and when the city faces the unexpected threat of cannon fire, you believe we will have no choice but to surrender."

The Twins lock eyes and shrug their shoulders then turn back to the others.

"We appreciate your thoroughness, Audrianna," says Uriah. "No point in hiding behind pleasantries, then."

Lysander leans forward and rests his massive arm on the table with a thud. "You will surrender the capital to us, or we will rain fire down upon Mirus and everyone in it."

"You would dare destroy the capital city, all of its people, in your quest for the throne?" asks Mary Anne.

"Without hesitation," says Lysander, "and with a smile on our faces. We have little need for the people of this city. Once crowned, the new capital of Wonderland will be Adamas. We will have no need for a city of ruins."

"Do you see why this is a futile endeavor, child?" Uriah asks Mary Anne. "You have done the heavy lifting for us. Why do you think we agreed to help against the cult in return for refuge in the castle? It was not out of fear, but patience, waiting for the throne room doors to open. And you have no witnesses to say it was you who opened it, while our soldiers and your servants saw us enter the throne room first."

"It does not matter." Mary Anne spits her words. "You will never truly possess the power of Wonderland. You will not have the Grand Arcana."

Lysander scoffs. "Our line ruled long before the dependency of the Arcana. We have no need for tricks and magic. The promise of this power complicates the world. It does not solve its problems. We have no need of it."

"I will solve this world's problems," says Mary Anne. "Starting with you."

Uriah's fingers play with the long silver chains around his neck. "Have you asked yourself, does Wonderland actually need saving? Is this some thought of your own?" He glances at the Duchess. "Or has someone else placed this thought into your head?"

"Enough," the Duchess bellows. "We are finished with your lies and half-truths. Mary Anne and all around this table will save this city and all of Wonderland."

"You see, the reason we will be victorious," Uriah continues. "While you fight and spend your time and efforts to *save* the city, we are content and more than willing to sacrifice it all in order to rule the entire country. Can you say the same?"

The air, so thick with tension they may as well all be submerged under water, the pressure squeezes their heads and presses on their chests. Each breath and heartbeat of all in the chamber is palpable. The air pulses. Eyes dart back and forth to each other at the table.

"Don't touch me," one soldier whispers behind them. No one else hears his words but March.

The white of Mary Anne's eyes becomes visible around the crystal blue in them. The question Lysander and Uriah pose is hypothetical, but they wait for a response or some form or retaliation.

March takes a long breath through her nose. A familiar aroma drifts through the thick air of the chamber—leather and earth. The scent finds Jonathan a moment later, and he perks up in his seat, eyes scanning the room.

March looks behind her at the chamber door, which has remained open since Lysander's and Uriah's entrance. The guard who spoke rubs at his legs, parted wide enough for someone smaller to slide through.

At the opposite end of the chamber, at the far end of the table, the red fabric running down its length shifts and bunches.

Hells. March clutches Jonathan's hand. Their hearts jump together, thankful and fearful. *What, or rather who, better to cut the tension?*

Cheshire appears, waving his hand across his face, moving the air as if he controlled the curtain of reality itself. He sits cross-legged on the opposite head of the table, eyes wide, eyes burning. No matter how many webs of deceit or strategies Lysander and Uriah create, one thing they cannot account for is the chaos Cheshire brings with him.

CHAPTER 16
CHESHIRE

A palpable heat radiates in waves off Cheshire's skin, changing the temperature in the chamber. The hair on the back of his neck stands on end, every muscle in his body flexes and twitches, and his eyes grow so wide they strain, never blinking, burrowing into the abyss where the Duchess's soul should be. Everyone in the periphery of his sight vibrates, blurred by his hate.

He sits upon the table, elbows on his knees, and he holds his hands in front of this face, fingertips pressed against each other. The Duchess holds her composure for appearances' sake, but Cheshire knows and relishes her look of masked terror—the tightening and small twitch of the aged muscles of her neck, the quick flair of her nostrils, fingers digging into the table so not to tremble, the wrinkles around her lips pulling in as she tightens her mouth.

It has been over a thousand years since he stared clearly into the eyes of his mother's abductor, a woman she trusted. Her face has been the all consuming thought filling him with ten lifespans of hate. The reason this city, this world, will burn.

In the infirmary days ago, when Jonathan was returned to the castle, it would have been a simple task to kill the Duchess had Cheshire not listened to Mary Anne. On the other hand, if he had not listened to Mary Anne, the castle would have been overrun by the cult. Tensions were at their peak then, everyone pulled in too many directions at once. Cheshire could not savor the surprise.

The first time he looked into her eyes was the infirmary. It was then she learned for certain he had returned to Mirus, and her fate was all but sealed. If not for Jonathan lying unconscious on the cot before him, he would have allowed the darkness to swallow him whole, hearing his mother's last words in her failing voice echoing in his mind, and ripped the Duchess's face from her skull, muscle, sinew, and all in an instant. It took every ounce of restraint, every ounce of love he had for Jonathan to turn his back on her.

On the top of the gatehouse, when pardoned by Mary Anne, he did not turn his head to the Duchess. He wanted her to worry, to question his next action, to fear what he might do. Taking her life in front of a crowd would be a fitting end for her, but it was not the time, nor would he want to bring such attention to a woman who deserves to die alone.

Cheshire has grand plans to destroy Mirus to torment the Duchess before her death, but opportunities continue to present themselves. The gatehouse, the infirmary, even when he snuck aboard her carriage to enter the city and the castle, he could have throttled her before they entered, approached the Long Bridge to Mirus, yet he stayed his hands. The sole reason she, and the villainous Gryphon seated to her right, remain alive is for the secrets and the answers they keep. One of them knows the location of his mother, and if it takes until their dying breaths and screams of agony to divulge the truth, so be it.

The Duchess last locked eyes with Cheshire when he was in his tenth year—tears streaming down his cheeks, bottom lip quivering, fidgeting with his mother's shawl around his neck, concerned about her failing health. After a thousand years, the Duchess still hides behind her sick painted smile. After a thousand years, Cheshire wonders what the Duchess thinks of the man, of the monster, she created.

Presently, some of the menagerie seated at the table may complicate matters. Mary Anne poses no threat. He will snap her neck, spinning it around to see the back of her chair before she dies. Then Jonathan will be free from her grasp and the magic keeping him bound to her, to this city. All it will take is one swift kick to the head to bash and crack the Chamberlain's skull against the wall, blood splattering his white hair.

Contrary, the Gryphon and the Twins will pose the most inconvenience. The Gryphon, with his misplaced honor, will defend the Duchess and Mary Anne. Lysander and Uriah have no love for the Duchess. They would be glad to allow Cheshire past and rip her jaw from her face. They will, however, undoubtedly attack, seeing him as an eventual thorn in their side.

At the first movement of Cheshire's hand, everyone at the table clenches; all but March. She blinks slowly and shifts her attention toward him, shimmering eyes through swaying strands of vibrant pink hair. She wants him, wills him, to do it. The air in the room ceases to move, waiting for Cheshire to act. He swings his finger back and forth like a sharpened pendulum from Lysander, to Uriah, to the Gryphon, to Mary Anne, the Duchess, then Jonathan and March. He winks at his loves, and after several passes, his finger finally ends where it must, aiming at the chest of the Duchess and her vile heart.

The Duchess's eyes grow wide, unblinking at Cheshire. The Gryphon scowls, and the lines of his face dig deep. Lysander and Uriah slowly turn their heads to face him while their fingers creep toward the handles of their weapons. Mary Anne's eyes twitch. Weiss grabs hold of the back of his chair. March reaches for the swords at her side. The Gryphon shifts, slowly reaching for the sword at his side. Jonathan balls his fists. A single grain of sand teeters on the edge of a mountain cliff, ready to fall and start an avalanche to destroy everything before it.

In half a heartbeat, Chesire lunges forward, sprinting down the length of the table with silent footfalls toward the Duchess, unable to help himself. He must put this gathering to the test.

Lysander, on his left, attacks first, swinging his longsword wildly, meant to cleave Cheshire in twain just above his waist. Cheshire ducks under as the Gryphon swings upward with his sword and deflects Lysander's strike into the air. Uriah takes hold of his glaive and unfurls his whip—a coiled serpent ready to strike.

Half a table away, the Duchess's eyes grow wider, staring at Cheshire from behind her scowl, neck shaking. The Chamberlain runs and cowers in the chamber's corner.

Uriah takes aim and plunges his glaive toward Cheshire's legs. He leaps up just as March, with remarkable speed, pulls both her swords and brings them down on the glaive's handle, pinning it to the table.

The soldiers of Adamas clash with the Castle Guard, trying to subdue them, holding them to the wall with their bodies or shoving themselves into the doorway, jamming their entrance.

Almost there. Mary Anne foolishly steps in front of the Duchess with arms wide to shield her, as if Cheshire would hesitate taking her life. She thinks the pardon she gave grants her immunity or some sort of protection. It grants her time until her usefulness has run out. If she wishes for it to expire this moment, Cheshire will gladly abide.

Jonathan catches the *crack* of Uriah's whip out of the air, wrapping it around his bruised forearm to prevent a deadly strike. The opportunistic miscreant took his chance and aimed for Mary Anne. Cheshire slides under the taut, braided leather, riding the bunched red fabric, closing in on his quarry. So close. He can smell their fear, almost feel their breaths, and it brings joy to his heart.

Lysander kicks the Gryphon's chair as he tries to rise, knocking him off balance and allowing Lysander room for another wide slash of his sword at the head of Cheshire. The Gryphon stabs his sword into the table to block Lysander with a loud *clang.*

March swings her swords upward to slice through Uriah's taut whip to free Jonathan, but he releases the tension in time for the blades to pop the loose slack into the air. He recalls it with a flick of his wrist while he reaches back with his glaive, ready for another attack.

Lysander elbows the Gryphon in the shoulder and sweeps his longsword overhead, nearly decapitating him, slicing through the back of his chair, igniting sparks across the stone wall.

The Gryphon prepares to block Lysander. March prepares to swing at Lysander and Uriah.

"*Cheshire.*" His mother's voice hits his ear like the ring of an anvil, as clear as if she were standing at the side of the table next to Jonathan.

What devilry is this?

"*Cheshire,*" she calls again. He loses his breath as if submerged in icy waters. The Duchess is almost in arm's reach. He could rip through Mary Anne and be at the Duchess's throat in less than a second.

Jonathan turns and grabs the tall back to the heavy oak chair and swings it overhead. At the apex of its arc, as all blades descend and converge on the middle of the table at Cheshire, he looks toward where he heard his mother's voice but meets Jonathan's eyes instead—a pleading, worried look swirls in the two pools.

Can Cheshire reach the Duchess? Yes. Will he be able to enjoy her death? Not here. Not now.

In the time it takes the Duchess to blink for the first time, Cheshire thinks of seventeen ways this scenario will play out, and each time someone he cares for or himself pays the price at the hands of Lysander and Uriah. Jonathan and March will be drawn into a fight, not theirs. Cheshire will not risk them.

Cheshire squints. *Fine.*

He wipes his right hand over his face, summoning the Mask of Light, disappearing, and jumping to the floor just as Jonathan brings his chair down with his mighty arms on the table.

CRASH.

The blow comes down hard and brutal. It blocks every blade and cracks the council table in half.

"*Cheshire.*" His mother's voice calls to him, from the hall this time.

Why?

He slides between the scuffling soldiers' legs and sprints from the council chambers. Cheshire's head pounds with pulses of heat—the temptation, the call, to stay and finish his work, but his mother's voice, this unnatural yet familiar siren's call, does not just tug at his heart, it pulls him like a carriage and horses free of its rider. He remembers himself. No matter how much he craves for the Duchess's death, he yearns even greater for his mother's life, and he must leave the Duchess behind to uncover the root cause of this apparition haunting him; so be it.

CHAPTER 17
JONATHAN

C*RASH.*

The massive chair smashes down onto the table, obliterating it. It was all Jonathan could think of, having forgotten his own sword in Mary Anne's bedchamber. A lump grows in his throat, and time holds its breath, freezing everyone in place. The only reason Jonathan knows time moves on is the ticking of his timepiece in his trousers' pocket.

When the pieces crumble to the floor, in the midst of the short-lived chaos, Cheshire is gone. Or is he? With the Mask of Light, Cheshire could still lurk in the corners of the room or stand right next to Jonathan. No, he would be able to smell his love if he were near. Jonathan hopes for all involved, Cheshire has indeed fled far away for the time being.

Blood from old bruises trickles down Jonathan's arm from the tendrils of Uriah's whip, and his back and arms scream in pain. Fortunately, without enough room for Uriah to wind the coil to its full extension, it does not wield the pain and destruction it is capable of. A fresh wound and another scar. At least Jonathan was able to absorb the crack before it reached Mary Anne. Treacherous fuck.

Uriah recoils his whip and wraps it around his body. March, the Gryphon, and Uriah slide their weapons from the rubble, ready to continue the fight, the point of each blade directed at someone at the table. Breaths are deep and long, and Jonathan's heartbeat thunders in his ears. He needs his elixir, which he also left in Mary Anne's bedchamber.

"Enough," says Mary Anne, unwavering in voice.

"Hold," the Gryphon commands the Castle Guard. They pull away, this time slipping into the council chamber to keep the Twins' soldiers out.

The tension in the room, thick and heavy as the opium rooms in the Garden, does not release its hold on anyone. All surrounding the table, or what remains of it, look into each other's eyes, waiting, questioning if the fight continues. There are no tempered heads at the table at the moment to prevail, so a strategic one speaks to end this fray before it begins anew.

The bottom of one of March's eyes raises to tell Jonathan, *we need time.*

She knows, as does Jonathan, the only way to move forward is to concede for now and meet some uneasy truce for the time being.

A quick half-blink tells her, *agreed.*

"We accept your offer," says March. "Two weeks. Or rather, until your ships arrive."

"How dare you?" Mary Anne shouts at March. "You do not have the authority—"

"We accept." The Duchess steps from behind Mary Anne and tugs at the bottom of her bodice to straighten it.

The tension lessens but never dissipates.

"At the end of which time," says Mary Anne, unwillingly conceding, "the rightful ruler of Wonderland will sit on the throne."

"Indeed," the Twins say together.

"Until then," says Jonathan, "no harm will come to anyone at this table from another's hand, their soldiers, or the townspeople of Mirus."

"Surely, you cannot suggest we would be held accountable for the actions of the thousands of townspeople, citizens of Mirus, who take action into their own hands?" asks Uriah.

"Of course we do," says Mary Anne.

"I see. Will you account for your bastard, then?" asks Uriah.

The word tenses Jonathan's arm, wanting to leap across the table and break Uriah's jaw. March's eyes twitch beneath her pink hair. Uriah goads them, wanting another attack.

"Cheshire is a rogue," says Jonathan. "We could sooner tame the seas than command him."

"Yet, he shares your bed," says Uriah.

"And in those years, neither March nor I have ever had any sway over his intentions or actions," says Jonathan.

This is not entirely true. They have delayed him on occasion but never stopped him. Cheshire and his personal agenda and hatred for the Duchess will pose a severe complication to matters. After what Cheshire revealed to him and March—the Duchess being responsible for the disappearance of his mother—Jonathan wishes beyond all might he can bring some peace to his lover. Although, to Cheshire, this peace means the death of the Duchess, which Jonathan cannot allow. Not now. He, March, and Cheshire, on three separate paths, strands of fate woven together until the end of the world, find themselves diverging, fraying. He will delay his love as much as he can until Mary Anne sits on the throne and, gods willing, decides to return home.

"Do you not claim him?" Lysander asks.

"Of course we do, and we will defend him to the death." His stomach falls. The Duchess must know by now of their relationship, but to say it out loud in front of her is brave or foolish. It does not matter. Regardless of the consequences, he will never deny Cheshire or what he means to him and March—the third piece of their soul to make them complete.

"Then, any life taken will be repaid in kind tenfold," says Uriah. "Blood for blood. And retribution will be swift."

Jonathan sees the path the Twins put them on. "So if one of yours is struck down—"

"We will claim ten," says Lysander.

March twists her swords ever so slightly in air, still pointed at Lysander and Uriah. "And if we follow suit and claim one hundred of your men?"

"We will claim one thousand," says Uriah. "The city streets will cascade with blood. A beautiful crimson fountain."

"And when will this cycle end?" asks Mary Anne.

"When you relinquish the throne," says Uriah. "Do so now, and not one life will be lost. The longer you wait, the more you risk innocents will be lost because of your pride. Unless you treat us and ours courteously and with the respect due to us."

Jonathan can see the words bubbling at Mary Anne's lips. They deserve no respect and will be given none—only tolerance for now.

"We shall spread the word," says Jonathan. "As we expect you to do the same."

"Of course," the Twins say together.

After a stretch of silence, Lysander pokes at the inside of his cheek with his tongue and finally lowers his sword from the Gryphon's direction. "On another matter, what of our men?"

"What about them?" asks the Duchess.

"They are here in the capital, after all," says Lysander. "They shall require accommodation in—"

"How dare you even ask after you threaten us?" Mary Anne snaps.

"This is your hospitality?" asks Uriah.

"In the city." Jonathan cuts him short. "Not the castle."

"Do you expect our soldiers, who journeyed across country, field, and mountain to aid Mirus in their time of need, to return to their camps in the wood?" asks Lysander.

Jonathan smiles. "Let us call a spade a spade. Your soldiers arrived, encamped outside the city, before the cult ever presented a problem, and did not enter the city until the threat was over."

"To coincide with the ships soon to be in our harbor," March adds, "which you could not have sent word to and have them arrive in time to help with the infestation. They were here at both of your behests, lying in wait to take the city long before the throne room doors opened."

The Twins look upon Jonathan and March, both impressed and annoyed.

"Your men are free to remain in the city," Jonathan continues. "There happens to be a surplus of empty apartments and houses at the moment from those who lost their lives these past days and nights. Your men can take temporary lodging in them under the condition they attend to the repairs. A simple request as opposed to paying rent and taxes. And since you both have been so generous with the number of soldiers you have provided, those who do not find lodging must return to the Queenwood. No encampments or tents spread throughout the city. I believe we all want Mirus to return to some form of normalcy. Would you not agree?"

"Agreed on all parts," says Uriah. "And our current company and yours have unlimited access to the castle and the city. If one of our party leaves, they may return without question."

"Not unlimited," says Mary Anne. "Until this matter is concluded, the throne room is off limits to either party." Words difficult for her to speak by the twitching of her lip. Frustration builds in her eyes, having come so close but needing to let go and step back for the good of everyone.

"We shall accept these terms for the time being," says Uriah, "with the caveat, they may be renegotiated if needed and a new solution must be reached."

"Fine," says Mary Anne.

Lysander saunters around the debris of the table. "As entertaining as this gathering has been, we shall leave you to conclude it. This has been quite enlightening." He and Uriah push their way through the Castle

Guard to leave the chamber, their soldiers in tow, heading into the castle.

There is nothing else to say. Mary Anne stares daggers at March for defying her. The Gryphon, distracted, scans the corners of the chamber for Cheshire. March checks the condition of her blades. Weiss stands and straightens his robes, hair, and spectacles. The Duchess puts her hand on Mary Anne's shoulder, but there is a slight wince at her touch.

What a wondrous predicament. Jonathan looks down at the giant wooden shards and splinters of the table between them all. The red fabric that ran at the center of the table along its length winds and curves like a river of blood, a portent of events to come. When they must be at their most unified, strongest together, all Jonathan sees are cracks and divides waiting to widen.

CHAPTER 18

MARY ANNE

Mary Anne can still feel the heat pulsing in her face as she, Jonathan, and March start the long trek to their bedchamber. Jonathan, walking with perfect posture, leads their trio, March, head tilted and thumbs hooked on her suspenders, saunters a step behind him, and Mary Anne brings up the rear, watching them.

It is not enough for the Twins to flaunt their cocksure and self-proclaimed superiority, March parades her body and familiarity with Jonathan at every turn. Can Mary Anne not be in control of one aspect of her life without the interference of others? March believes herself better than Mary Anne, even though her indiscretions go unnoticed. Jonathan is the only constant she has in her life, and Mary Anne is through being held at arm's length. Jonathan mutters words beginning with the letter L to himself, lost in his own world.

Mary Anne is soon to be the most powerful being in all of Wonderland, and yet she lets others have control over her life, her destiny. She will control what she can, where she can, and who she can, until one day soon everything will be within her power.

She grabs March by her upper arm to turn her around. The second March spins around, eyes wide and twitching, a dagger from her thigh points at the soft underside of Mary Anne's jaw. March looks over her shoulder to watch Jonathan continue to walk, consumed by his thoughts, then turns back to Mary Anne.

"Touch me again without my permission," whispers March, "and the only reign you need worry about is your blood and organs as they splatter upon the stones when I split your gullet."

"I am finished with the likes of people who attempt to lord their power over me: Lysander, Uriah, you."

March steps closer. "You dare include my name among theirs?"

"Why not?" Mary Anne, tired of March's threats, releases her and steps back. "You belong with them. You have already fucked them. I assume more than the first time I saw you on your knees with their cocks in your mouth. How many times have you let them have their way with you? How many times have you lied to Jonathan? And now, in the council, you volunteer to focus your efforts on Lysander and Uriah. Is this your plan? To keep them busy, fuck them until they are completely distracted? I should let you do it. But I know in your heart it would destroy Jonathan. He deserves better."

"Your heart?" March sneers. "And you are better?"

"I am. I am better than Lysander, better than Uriah, and I am most certainly better for Jonathan than some unfaithful tart. You offer to help me then hold a dagger to my throat. Untrustworthy to the core. You obviously have no problem being shared, so unless you want me to speak the truth to Jonathan and let him know what an adulteress you are, it is now you who will share."

"You believe I would share Jonathan with you?"

"If you do not want me to take him completely for myself, yes."

No sign of remorse or shame crosses March's face. She twirls her dagger in her fingers and sheathes it on her thigh. Her eyes linger, the last thing to turn from Mary Anne as she walks after Jonathan, who has long disappeared down the corridors.

Threats or being ignored—Mary Anne cannot decide which is worse. Does March believe Mary Anne will not expose her deeds to Jonathan? This is not how she thought this day, this walk, this impromptu discussion would end, but she will rescue Jonathan from her clutches.

Mary Anne walks side-by-side with March. "You have no power over me. Remember this."

"Power is an illusion." March does not so much as glance toward Mary Anne.

"Power is absolute. Power is control."

"Allow me to prove you wrong."

Grace holds the bedchamber door open for them when they return. Inside, Jonathan sits on their bed, longcoat folded over the headboard, trousers around his ankles, grimacing as he tries to remove his boots, cock half-hard already.

March walks toward the bed, removes her swords from her back, and lets her suspenders fall off her shoulders. Her loose trousers fall, revealing almost half of her backside. She lays her swords by the bed, unties her linen top at the same time as she kicks off her boots, and lets her trousers fall to the floor. She stands bare in front of Jonathan, and he embraces her, wraps his arms around her waist, and kisses her tenderly. His arms were around Mary Anne not so long ago. It should be her.

After their lips part, March whispers something to Jonathan, lays him back on the bed, and walks back to Mary Anne, who waits by the chamber door. March slams the door shut, almost hitting Grace, and pulls Mary Anne by the wrist toward the bed.

What is happening? Wait. Now? This is not what Mary Anne expected. So soon? Her heartbeat thumps in her throat.

They stop at Jonathan's feet, in-between his legs, trousers still around his boots. March unclips Mary Anne's silver belt with a single flick of her finger, and the fabric of her dress pulls away from her body, startling

Mary Anne momentarily. March pulls the dress over Mary Anne's head, leaving both women bare, standing in front of each other, standing in front of Jonathan. Mary Anne swallows, fighting the urge to look down at March's body, and cannot help but move her hands to cover herself.

March scoffs, leaves Mary Anne to remove her boots, climbs onto the bed, and straddles Jonathan's head while facing Mary Anne. She spreads her knees and lowers herself until Jonathan's tongue jumps up to greet her. His wide arms wrap around her thighs and pull her ever harder onto his face. Her eyes soften and flicker at the touch of his tongue.

Jonathan's cock grows to its beautiful full length, bouncing, flexing, pulsing. The muscles of his stomach and chest tighten as he laps harder at March. She leans forward and takes his shaft in hand and points it straight up in the air, and with the other hand points to the floor for Mary Anne to kneel between Jonathan's legs.

At any other moment, any other time, Mary Anne would explode at the thought of being ordered or controlled, yet her body moves of its own accord. She falls to her knees, breathing heavy—no choice but to surrender in the moment. With a finger, March commanded Mary Anne to her knees, and she obeyed. In the hallway, during their confrontation, Mary Anne thought she had the upper hand; she was mistaken. Does it matter, after all, in the moment? Just like the throne room this morning, it may prove wise to submit slightly, give up something in order to gain everything—in this case, Jonathan.

Mary Anne straddles Jonathan's boots, held prisoner by his trousers, and moves closer, sliding her hands along his thighs. His thick muscles harden at her touch, sliding her hands higher up his legs.

Oh, my God.

The dreams of Mary Anne's first time with Jonathan did not begin this way. They started simpler, with a kiss, looking longingly into each other's eyes, alone with him.

March leans forward to kiss Jonathan's glistening tip, all the while his face remains buried in her. She takes him into her mouth, pleasing him slowly. He moans softly, and his legs squirm and tighten in Mary Anne's hands.

Even though March's mouth conceals half of it, Mary Anne dare not take her eyes from Jonathan's cock. She has seen it before, always when occupied with March or Cheshire, or March and Cheshire, in unimaginable positions, but this time she is not across the bed or concealed in shadow.

As she slides her hands farther up his legs toward his crotch, she moves her body closer, resting her arms on his legs. She rubs her face along his thighs, taking in his scent, his heat, intoxicating her senses like the strongest wine. Jonathan's muffled moans from between March's legs vibrate his entire body. Mary Anne drinks in his glistening shaft, wet from March's mouth, with her eyes, mouth watering, jaw tingling.

March continues to pleasure him, head rising and falling, moaning from Jonathan's own brand of magic—a magic Mary Anne craves as well. Mary Anne moves her head closer, heart pounding, while March takes more and more of Jonathan in her mouth, yet there is still room for Mary Anne. She draws closer to his shaft, so close she can feel her breath bounce from it back to her face.

Her moment of worship ends abruptly as March grabs the back of Mary Anne's head and pulls it forward, smashing her face against his balls and his cock. After the surprise dwindles, March releases her grip, and Mary Anne keeps her face against him, rubbing her face against him, his heat, then extends her tongue ever so slowly to the base of his shaft. An exquisite amalgam of salt, sweat, and his teas find a home on Mary Anne's tastebuds. She wants to devour him whole. Hesitantly, she licks at his balls, moving them around with her tongue and nose. Jonathan's moans increase, pushing Mary Anne to take them into her mouth ravenously and licking up his shaft.

March still selfishly has the head and half of Jonathan's cock in her mouth, refusing to release it. She locks eyes with Mary Anne as she glides her tongue up its length; the look in her eye is one of victory.

Mary Anne's tongue takes long swathes along Jonathan's cock, slow and deliberate, not breaking eye contact with March, until March finally sits back and presses on Jonathan's chest as her body quivers. Mary Anne takes hold of his cock before it falls to his stomach, feeling how truly hard he is. Hypnotized by the grandeur of Jonathan, she did not realize she had been touching herself with her other hand until her body and stomach twitch.

She gazes at Jonathan's length and head, pulsating, leaking, glistening in the palm of her hand. Mary Anne raises herself on her knees and finally takes him into her mouth and tastes him fully. The tang hits her jaw like a welcome hammer on an anvil. She moans, not moving, wanting to savor this moment. Again, her body moves on its own, knowing her desires. She bobs up and down, taking more and more. The slow and steady pace becomes a flurry of haste, feeling him swell in her mouth. She looks up past the slab of muscle before her, where she wishes to see Jonathan's eyes gaze back at her, his tender smile beaming brightly as she pleases him.

Instead, his tongue ravages March, whose own muscles tense and relax quicker than before. Even in victory, March keeps his eyes and mouth from Mary Anne purposefully. Mary Anne wants to taste his lips, look into his eyes, while... while he makes love to her.

March shakes the bed as she climaxes, holding her breath, until she erupts into a long and quivering moan.

Mary Anne's breaths become quick, butterflies fill her stomach, her vision blurs, and unseen fingers massage the back of her head.

She dare not look away from the climax she will claim for herself soon enough, at the hands and mouth of Jonathan. Unexpectedly, he reaches down and caresses Mary Anne's cheek and runs his fingers through her hair. Her heart jumps. His touch, of his own accord, ignites a second fire in her, warming her body and bringing tears to her eyes, never having touched her in such a tender way. Her fingers have never thrummed so hard or fast against her body. Jonathan puts pressure on the back of her head and pumps his hips up into her mouth.

Mary Anne releases noises she has never uttered in her life. Her stomach sucks in, legs shake, muscles twitch, and her body gives in to the euphoric explosion. She moans and squeaks, mouth agape, while Jonathan continues to pump faster. Her body melts as if sculpted from wax to cover Jonathan's body of marble.

March reaches down and pulls Mary Anne's head from Jonathan, and with a glance orders Mary Anne onto the bed. Breathing hard, Mary Anne obeys and lies on her back next to Jonathan.

They both rise. March lifts Mary Anne's knees, pushes them back onto the bed, and lowers herself so close, her heat pulsing against Mary Anne's. The shock steals every word and question from Mary Anne, though she can barely form a thought, as Jonathan kneels behind March. He looks down, cock in hand, and glides its tip back and forth, across both Mary Anne and March, teasing their sensitivity.

It is happening, Mary Anne thinks to herself, feeling the weight of Jonathan upon her, preparing for the sharp pain and long pleasure she felt while wearing the rings. But it does not come.

March inhales and holds her breath as Jonathan takes hold of her hips and pushes into her. Again, Mary Anne feels cheated, until she realizes with March seated on top of her, she can feel the length of Jonathan's cock rub against her. Every thrust rocks the bed, and though he chose March, Mary Anne shares each pump from him. She forces her legs to widen and presses her hips upward, balls slapping against her, hoping, wishing Jonathan will slide from March and find her.

Though this fantasy does not happen, the sensation from every thrust from Jonathan ripples through her body. Mary Anne wants to see him, touch him, but March's body blocks her view. Mary Anne reaches out and grips at the sheets of her bed, twisting them, trying to find something to hold on to as her mind reels, trapped physically and emotionally in the ecstasy of Jonathan. She grabs her own breasts, hoping Jonathan will reach out and take them in his hands.

The harder and longer Jonathan thrusts and pulses, the more March lowers her body onto Mary Anne, her breast inches from her face. Their moans rival each other. Mary Anne tries not to look, but March has other plans: she grabs Mary Anne's head and presses it to her breast, her nipple at her lips. Mary Anne closes her mouth at first, but the euphoria humming in her body craves physical connection, takes control, and parts her lips, taking March's nipple in her mouth. Never in her life did Mary Anne think she would be in this predicament, in this position, but she cannot control herself. She sucks and plays with March's nipple with her tongue as ravenous as Jonathan slides against her.

March reaches down, moving Mary Anne's hand away, and takes her breast in hand, pinching at her nipple, driving Mary Anne to bite down on March. She does not want this; yet she does. If this is what it takes to have Jonathan for the time being, then so be it.

Mary Anne's body quakes, as does March's. Butterflies fill her stomach, ready to explode and flutter through the rest of her body. Jonathan moans louder and bears down on both of them. She is ready. He pulls March back to sit up, slides from her, and pushes his cock between them. Mary Anne looks down to watch his beautiful head appear and disappear between her and March's pressed bodies.

Unable to hold back any longer, Mary Anne releases the butterflies caged in her stomach and climaxes with a scream she did not know she possessed. Jonathan turns March's head back to kiss her as she climaxes, swallowing her moan. The heat between the three of them burns deep in Mary Anne's body, still twitching as Jonathan relentlessly rubs against her sensitivity. The high crashes down, and Mary Anne's eyes almost fall to black from her quick breaths.

Jonathan pulses and grows against her. Both he and March look down as he climaxes, unable to stop moving, and sprays ribbon after ribbon over Mary Anne's body from her stomach, across her chest, to her face.

His body jolts, bucks, and shakes until he has no more to give. Mary Anne reaches down to touch his swollen head, but March pushes them off and they collapse next to Mary Anne, March's body blocking Jonathan from her, and her leg hooked over his waist—both forgetting Mary Anne is present.

This moment should have been special. March robbed her of it, willfully souring her victory to prove a point dancing dangerously close to the edge of Mary Anne's patience and resolve. She feels a sick swirl in her stomach, tawdry, dirty. Why? She did not know what to expect, included yet still an outsider, and grateful it happened despite the hollow feeling in the pit of her stomach.

Her head is a blur. She rises and walks to the baths to wash. This was everything she wanted, yet it is not how she planned it. This is not how she dreamt of it. This is not what it was supposed to be. In the end, it does not matter now. It is too late to go back.

Part II

CHAPTER 19

CHESHIRE

Cheshire does not sleep during the night, though he should have returned to March and Jonathan, but it is of little consequence. Why must he always find himself in the in between? The Gryphon has returned to the castle. The Duchess knows of the certainty of his presence, and her fate and will take precautions to prevent Cheshire from getting close to her again. His mother's voice—her counterfeit voice—pulled him from the council chamber and lures him still through endless corridors and stairways, always glimpsing the back of her dress and hood, never her face.

His pursuit ends rounding a corner into the tall front corridor of the castle with a ceiling like the bone ribs and spine of a leviathan. At its end, the Doorman waits, dutifully standing at attention, even with no sign anyone passed this way before Cheshire.

Curiosity becomes spite and gives way to anger. This is not his mother but rather some phantom, an apparition, a wraith from the underworld sent to drive him out of his wits. He will find out the hand who conjured and controls this woman.

Well past twilight, he returns to a lower floor of the castle and stares at a blank brick wall where an arched door once stood—his mother's bedchamber. The proper bed chamber for the queen, a woman, or anyone, rather than the garish room in which Mary Anne resides. His mother's chamber has been erased from existence, sealed off and filled with stones, by order of the Duchess. This was the last place he saw her, health fading, skin pale, yet still with a powerful voice. His stomach tightens, his chest aches, and the tears flow again. The closer Cheshire gets to uncovering the riddle of his mother's disappearance, the deeper her absence affects him. For a thousand years out in the mountains, fields, and wilds, his mother was somewhere he hoped to find, a thought, albeit a far-off fantasy. Here in the castle, his emotions continue to flood back to him like a damn breaking over and over again, no matter how much he tries to repair it. He is close; she is closer.

Revisiting this spot will not provide any more clues; there is nothing here for him, nothing left of his mother. His mind drifts to another area of the castle he has avoided, and he travels deeper into the lower levels, traveling down two staircases and winding corridors until he reaches another unassuming door in a lonely hallway. His door, or rather, the pathway to reach his childhood bedchamber.

Inside, the larger chamber appears untouched by time, used as storage over the years. Undisturbed layers of dust cover the stone floor, and dingy linens cover stacked furniture and also collect centuries of dust, showing no sign anyone has been here perhaps since he left the castle. Not even the Duchess knew where he slept and where his mother kept him away for good measure.

Oak corners and legs peek out from beneath their shrouds. Old books, vases, and wooden crates stack higher than the furniture and carve out thin paths as if through the northern mountains. His heartbeat engulfs his body as he retraces the steps his mother would take to visit him in his chamber, and the way he would take to explore the castle while everyone else slept, all the while placing each foot on the edge of the hanging linens and the claw and orbed feet of wardrobes and tables, to keep from leaving a single footprint. After several turns and ducking under a stack of precariously placed crates cantilevering over the path, Cheshire comes face to face with a large painting, double his height, leaning against the wall. The painting depicts a picturesque landscape—a simple dirt road bordered with a lush, vibrant forest on both sides, their canopies forming a perfect arch, and at its center, the road ends in a vibrant sunset of bright ambers, blues, and pinks.

Cheshire recalls his mother's words. "A world unto yourself." She gave him the world, unseen and undisturbed by all else save for him and her, their own private queendom inside the castle, throughout the city and country. The temptation to wipe the dust from the painting to reveal its vibrancy moves his hand, but he retracts it in a clenched first. No one can know he was here.

The painting slides as easily as it did all those years ago to reveal a simple wooden door, much taller in Cheshire's memory. Why does he pause? He twists the ends of his mother's sash in his fingers. He can murder countless men, yet a simple door causes his hands and legs to tremble. Cheshire prides himself on his memory and the ability to recall a thousand years of memories, but some he left behind this door when he was forced to flee from the city.

Cheshire contemplates returning on a different day, another time. The door will always be here. Is it better to remain blissfully ignorant and believe a lie or confront the harsh truth? The place sews the seeds of doubt in his heart, but he refuses to let them take root.

The door creaks open, and a cold, stale air seeps out, held captive. Where the rest of the castle shows evidence of changes and redecoration, his chambers remain untouched, except by his hand, long ago in his tenth year. In one corner, his small wooden bed, sheets flung askew and draped on the ground. In another, a large round-top chest containing old toys and books sits with its mouth agape, a short wardrobe for his clothing, a small oval looking-glass, and last, three small mannequins, as tall as he was then, lean off center. The remnants of chipped, painted eyes and mouths he added adorn their otherwise blank faces. Cheshire could not bear to have them without some sort of expression. Two wear pristine, yet faded, black jackets with braided epaulettes and braiding across the chest and stomach to connect their toggle closures, and gray trousers.

The third mannequin stands bare, because its jacket lies hidden in the room behind the tall looking-glasses—the clothing Cheshire ran from the castle in. Over the years as he grew, he removed the sleeves and cropped the jacket, too small for him, refusing to part with it—his only remembrance of the life he had. In order to repair his trousers, he would take the excess material from his jacket or stolen leather scraps to patch holes and add panels to make them larger to fit his growing body.

He sits on the bed and crosses his legs, as he would every night, waiting for his mother. No matter what castle or city business must be done, his mother never missed a chance to tell him sweet dreams and tuck him into bed. At least until her health began to wane. His eyes grow heavy—the strain and pull of his emotions catch up to him. It would be simple to curl up, rest, and drift off to a place where the genuine memories of his mother meet him, the hazy moment between waking and dreaming.

As his body relaxes, succumbing to his weary thoughts, a memory as smooth as smoke appears in front of him. His mother sits on his bed next to him. Her face appears as clear as summer's day; a smile to make the sun jealous, her cheeks to match the dawn, and sparkling lavender eyes to make the moon blush. Cheshire's chest heaves with each breath.

"Good night, sweetheart," she says.

It comes without warning. He weeps out loud, not carying who hears him, if anyone could hear him this deep in the castle. His stomach spasms, his heart rises to this throat, and snot runs from his nose, to match the seemingly never-ending stream of tears.

"Why do you cry?" she asks in a voice sweeter than any tune or song of Wonderland.

"I miss you," Cheshire sniffles. He is in his tenth year again, smaller, looking up at his mother, yet thinks with the thoughts of the present. "What if I do not see you tomorrow?"

She runs her fingers through his hair. Cheshire can almost feel them. "What if? What would my brave adventurer do?" she asks, tugging at his playfulness.

Cheshire stands on his bed, determined. "I would search the world for you. And I will find you. I will."

"Of course you will." His mother pats the bed, and Cheshire kneels next to her. She cups his face tenderly. "So much life in you. You will outlive Wonderland itself."

She moves closer to kiss his forehead, but as quickly as the vision appeared, it fades again into the darkness of his bedchamber, leaving him alone, unable to feel the touch of her lips. Cheshire wipes his nose on his forearm and slows his sporadic breaths. *What could have been?* The life he and his mother could have had; the Duchess robbed them both.

Unable to think about sleeping, he kneels in front of the oval looking-glass, through the grime, to meet his reflection and regain his bearings. "Back to the matter at hand. To our purpose."

"What do we know?" his reflection asks.

"In every chamber, closet, trunk, or spare room I have searched, no trace of my mother can be found."

"Then reason would have it, her belongings" — even his reflection has a hard time speaking the words — "are gone. Do you believe the Duchess would keep any hint of her near?"

"I did not believe. I wished."

"Why did you come here? Nothing of hers is here."

"I am."

His reflection joins in the sobering silence.

"I... I wanted to feel her."

"We have. Now we must continue on."

Cheshire's reflection speaks the truth, but a question scratches at the back of his mind, and he will not be able to focus on the Gryphon until he has answers, and nothing vexes Cheshire more than not knowing.

"Wait. This was different." Though hesitant at first, Cheshire finds himself grateful for the realization this visit brings. "This—she—is memory, not illusion."

The apparition haunting Cheshire keeps her distance—always at a distance, teasing him as if playing a cruel game. Were he face to face with the true vision of his mother, she would leave him with the sensation of a warm embrace. The other woman who takes her form leaves him with an unsettled feeling crawling on his skin.

"Why not here?" asks his reflection. She should make herself known the closer she is to a place meaningful to her—her chambers, his chambers, but nothing.

Cheshire hears its disembodied voice—whether distant or clear as day, depending... depending on what? Oft times he catches mere glimpses of her walking through the castle corridors, running away and never toward him. This last time, appearing clearer than before, she led Cheshire toward the front doors of the keep.

"I am asking the wrong question. The who or what matters not—it is the why. There is reason and purpose for all things."

The manifestation appeared clearest to him in the streets of Stonehaven, with her face still hidden from view. This is not coincidence. The farther he is from the castle, the closer she appears and the closer he is to the truth. Cheshire knows all-too-well the bricks and mortar of the castle hold only centuries of lies. This specter wants him to give chase, to follow her to a predetermined location.

He questions if this is another deception of the Gryphon or Duchess to lead him into a trap or remove him from the keep, but both are too superstitions to dabble in sorcery or witchcraft, the most base uses of the Arcana. Something or someone else calls and uses the image of his mother as bait. It is clear he will not find his answers in the castle.

Cheshire leaves his bedchamber with one last glance before shutting the door and sliding the painting back into place, making sure its edge aligns with the dust on the floor, and returns three levels up, nearing the front doors to the keep.

"Cheshire," the disembodied voice calls again, proving his theory.

Dawn nears, and Cheshire approaches the Doorman seated on a tall stool, nodding off, head bobbing and eyes fighting against the call of sleep. He startles and jumps to his feet as Cheshire approaches. Confused, half-asleep, and half-terrified, the Doorman does not know whether to reach for the door handle or run.

"Calm yourself," says Cheshire. "I have not come to kill you. This day."

The Doorman reaches for the handle with a shaking hand and opens the door quickly, not taking his eyes from Cheshire. Beads of sweat slide down his temples, and his lips twitch erratically.

"If I wanted you dead, I would have waited until you fell asleep then opened the door you are so duty bound to and slammed your head in it again and again until it resembled more than spilled jam and loose wine skin."

Cheshire crosses the threshold into the pre-dawn air and walks confidently toward the main gates across the bailey, with the Castle Guard and the Gryphon's archers atop the gatehouse gazing down at him. Torches reflect and flicker in their iron helmets and the hate they must bear toward him. He could have used either of the masks in his possession to leave the castle grounds, but why not put this pardon to the test? If they attack, what better way to start his morning than stretching and claiming several more lives?

"Cheshire," the woman's voice calls again, louder.

"I will find you, witch," he mutters to himself.

To his left, the lanterns within Dormy's wagon burn bright and the shadows moving past them catch Cheshire's eye. She toils at her work at all hours—ever diligent. Stomach growling, he pays her a visit, and as always when he reaches the back step of her wagon, the sound of muffled scuffling from the other side of the door greets him. Before he can reach for the handle, the door pulls open wide enough for Dormy's arm to stretch out with a small burlap sack, swaying back and forth in her hand. From the bulges within, Cheshire would say at least a pair of apples, a small loaf of bread, and a large wedge of cheese. Her eyes peer at him through the door. He knows what she has been up to and will not interrupt or make his suspicions known. All of those close to him are entitled to their secrets. Cheshire takes the sack and bows his head. Dormy slams the wagon door.

"Cheshire," the voice calls a third time, and becomes more annoying each time. As much as he wants to find the Gryphon, this voice must be dealt with first, or at least simultaneously.

Cheshire digs through the sack and discovers he was correct, and finds a few fresh plums thrown in as well. He bites into one, and the juice drips down his body. Six guards in all stand at the ready, hands poised at their swords when Cheshire approaches the arch of the gatehouse. The two large, bulbous gate men stare down at him from their benches. He has not looked upon them or been this near since his arrival in Mirus, hidden in the Duchess's wagon. Their eyes, beady, dark, and hollow, follow him, ticking as he moves. Darkness understands darkness, and there is something uncertain behind their glossy expressions.

The guards open the door within the gates without a word from Cheshire, happy to be rid of him.

"Good riddance," a guard says as Cheshire steps through the door.

"Oh," says Cheshire, "you will allow me back in when I return." He has no need for them, because he can enter the castle from any of the tunnels in Mirus. The guards grow too bold in their comfort.

"Not likely," says another guard.

"You have family in the city, yes?" Cheshire asks them with a smile.

The color in their cheeks fade.

"I thought so. Keep this in your simple minds. It would be wiser for you to keep me in the castle rather than loose in the city. Who knows what I might do?"

"Are you not pardoned for your crimes?" one guard stutters, confidence lost.

"I am. Savior of the people and all. Do not make me change my ways."

"Yes, sir," one guard says uneasily, and shuts the door behind him.

"Sir?" Cheshire jests. "What has this world come to?" With a wave of his hands he disappears from sight and descends into the Crest to follow the voice beckoning him, find the person who controls it, and kill them —simple work for the morning.

CHAPTER 20
JONATHAN

Early next morning, before the sun crests over the horizon, the sky mixes with shades of blues, purples, pinks, and oranges. Small clouds circle the mountain peaks surrounding Mirus, and their small snow caps glitter as if the mountains themselves cry at the dawn.

Jonathan and March lean against the inner curve of the castle wall of the bailey near the gatehouse, waiting. Jonathan counts the cobblestones and finds patterns, connecting paths, and images hidden within the mundane. March, stoic, arms crossed, one boot resting on the wall, leans on Jonathan's shoulder and puffs at a loose strand of pink hair in front of her face. He rests his chin on the top of her head and breathes her in; her spirit fills his. They both have a tip of a finger hooked inside of each other's trousers, tenderly moving it back and forth to feel each other's skin.

Perfect. Almost perfect.

They have not seen Cheshire since his appearance in the council chamber. Jonathan assumed he would join them during the night but hopes he and March will see their lover this day. Not just his body, but his soul, yearning for their missing piece to complete them.

On the other side of the gatehouse, a dozen guards mill about with four of the Gryphon's trained archers. They converse with each other in a low rumble, poke at their armor, kick at pebbles, and a stray laugh escapes their group every so often.

Across the bailey, the Doorman opens the main doors to the keep and bows at the waist. Even from this distance, Mary Anne appears with more confidence in her posture and in her walk. Her face lights up like the lanterns at dusk when she spots him. Her maroon gown and long gray traveling cloak flow behind her as she strides toward them.

"This should go well," says March.

"It will," says Jonathan. "We have overcome worse. Far worse."

"Us I trust in. It is everyone else I do not. And need I remind you, this will be Mary Anne's second time in the city since her arrival."

"I predict it will go as well as the first."

"When Lysander and Uriah confronted us, rekindled the division of the townspeople, and incited a riot?"

"Precisely." Jonathan kisses the top of March's head.

"At least you are realistic about it." She turns her head up and gives him a small kiss on the lips.

Jonathan tries to recall their first confrontation in the market. Mary Anne met them after arriving in Mirus separately with the Duchess. The Red Knight, a scoundrel, escorted her into the Row in the royal palanquin, and soon after Lysander and Uriah strode in on horseback. It feels like ages ago. Jonathan wonders if Mary Anne realizes how long it truly has been since her arrival in Wonderland.

"Morning." Mary Anne greets them warmly, stopping with a bounce in her step.

March walks between them toward the gates and motions to the soldiers and archers to head out before them.

"Morning," says Jonathan. "You look lovely this morning."

"Are you prepared?" March asks.

"As prepared as one can be, I suppose." Mary Anne keeps herself from fidgeting with the edge of her cloak. "You look dashing this morning. You are not wearing the red coat today?"

Jonathan looks down at this worn leather trousers and open linen shirt, held mostly closed by the leather strap from the scabbard on his back. "Thank you. No, I fear the tailoring is cut too tight in the shoulders if a fight breaks out. And I would not want to ruin your gift. I can wear it again when we return to the castle."

"Or, perhaps wear nothing," she says, blushing. Thoughts of their time together last night swim in her eyes. "I see March continues to wear a wardrobe to *impress* as well."

She speaks of March's trousers, the small linen wrap around her chest, and her braces. The two could not look more opposed. Jonathan cannot recall the last time he saw March in a gown or anything fancier than linen, cotton, and leather—and he is perfectly content with her contentment.

March's fingertips tap at the pommels of the swords at her hips.

"Shall we?" Jonathan offers his arm, to which Mary Anne takes hold without hesitation.

By the time they step through the door, the soldiers and archers have already disappeared, scouting ahead.

Far down the curve of the castle's outer wall, the Gryphon waits, leaning against the white stones. Jonathan cannot be sure March or Mary Anne take notice, but he will not bring attention to their protector. Once the gate door closes behind them all, the Gryphon nods and disappears into another part of the Crest.

March stops in the middle of the road before they reach their first staircase into the Crest. Her head turns one way, then the other, pink hair brushing against her back in the wind, studying the dirt.

"Blood."

Jonathan tries to discover what she sees in the hundreds of hoof and boot prints dug into the ground and finally finds the splotches where the tans and browns of the earth take on a darker hue, as if cast in shadow.

"Spilled yesterday," March continues.

"I do not recall any news, and the Twins did not mention it," says Jonathan.

"What happened, then?" asks Mary Anne.

March turns back to meet Jonathan's eyes. "This is where Lysander and Uriah's soldiers gathered upon their arrival, crammed together. It is not uncommon for soldiers or their horses to sustain cuts or injuries maneuvering in such tight quarters."

Her eyes let him know this is not the whole truth. The glint in them says, *Cheshire.*

Up to his mischief already. Cheshire cannot be controlled, but he can be distracted. Jonathan and March will need to work toward keeping their lover at bay, occupying his energies with other activities to keep the bloodshed to a minimum.

March leads on, farther into the Crest, keeping several steps ahead of Jonathan and Mary Anne, ever vigilant, with a weather eye on every street they enter from the long stairways connecting them. Additional Mirusian soldiers on patrol nod out of respect as they pass. After each encounter, she rolls her neck or shoulders, uncomfortable, as if to ward off unseen hands.

Mary Anne, on the other hand, marvels at the wonders of the city she missed previously, unable to keep any question to herself. She asks about the intricacies and richness of the Crest, the stark design differences and appearances of structures and citizens when they cross into Stonehaven, and the architecture and culture of both. Jonathan tries his best to answer while counting every stair they travel.

Most citizens in the Crest peek from their window, balcony, or porch and study Mary Anne with intrigue from a distance, viewing her as either a feral animal or the enemy, keeping their distance out of apprehension, or disdain, their allegiance plastered plainly on their face. If they have any supporters in the Crest, Jonathan cannot be sure, but wagers the majority, if not all, of the wealthy side with the Twins.

They reach their first kind face when they cross into Stonehaven.

"Bless you, miss," a woman in a worn apron and bonnet says. She leaves the woman she travels with, wipes her hands on her apron, and tentatively holds her hands out. Mary Anne takes them in hers, and the woman inhales, tears welling up in her soft amber eyes. "Thank you for your strength, miss." She slips her fingers from Mary Anne's grasp and continues down the winding road back to her companion, hand clutched to her chest.

On a lower tier of Stonehaven, a man and woman spit at their feet from across the street. A wonderful difference between the Crest and Stonehaven. In the Crest, the self-proclaimed elite will ignore and turn their noses up at what they disapprove of. Townspeople of Stonehaven have no quarrel making their opinions known. Jonathan prefers the second; spit in the face is better than a knife in the back.

Farther down still, two young girls with saffron hair, in long linen dresses and kerchiefs, whisper and giggle to each other behind cupped hands before they decide to run up to Mary Anne.

"Are you her?" the shorter of the two asks. They cannot be further along than their tenth year and cannot keep themselves from staring at Mary Anne's hair.

"Are you the queen to be?" the other asks.

"I believe I am," Mary Anne says, bending to their level.

"You're quite pretty," the taller girl says.

Mary Anne blushes and laughs. "Thank you. As are both of you."

"Thank you, miss."

"You don't call her a miss," says the shorter girl.

"Well, what am I supposed to call her?"

"Your Queen, Majesty, or Royal High person."

"Highness is the word," says Mary Anne. "I am none of these yet. For now, you can call me Mary Anne."

"Mary Anne," both girls say together.

They continue to converse, and Mary Anne's ease and confidence become ever more apparent. The frightened girl of the Rookwood is gone, and in her place, a woman capable of becoming queen. Other townspeople stop and watch their interaction, at first with quizzical, unsure expressions, which slowly change as they observe Mary Anne with the girls.

While they chat, Jonathan surveys the few shops along the streets and the windows of the tenements above. Dozens of unfamiliar faces look down upon him—the soldiers of Lysander and Uriah. A horse tied to a post reveals each apartment they have taken over, and fittingly the streets near them smell of horseshit.

From the corner of his eye, March waits by the next staircase. Her attention travels up and down the street, stairs, and up to the sky, looking for a sign.

Jonathan places his hand on Mary Anne's shoulder to let her know they must press onward.

"Since you have been so kind to me," says Mary Anne, "even after I am queen, you two, just you two, can still call me Mary Anne."

"Truly?" the shorter girl says.

"Yes. It was very nice meeting you both. I hope to see you again."

"Likewise," the taller girl says. The girls, unable to contain their excitement, skip down the street hand-in-hand.

"What do you hear?" he asks March, joining her across the street.

"It is what I do not hear which troubles me. You saw as well as I the soldiers spying on us from the windows like an unkindness of ravens hidden in the shadows of the canopy. I would half-expect them to be out in the street making their presence known. Yet, they do not." She turns to Mary Anne. "Were Lysander and Uriah in the castle when you left?"

"I do not believe so," says Mary Anne. "I purposefully passed by their chamber with several of the Castle Guard. Their door was an ajar, and it was unoccupied, except for half a dozen naked women crammed on their beds, bed, rather. They pushed them together to create one."

"They have a head start on us," says March. "I rose before the dawn to try to intercept them. Their soldiers remain in their quarters because their masters are in the city."

"Is that not contrary thinking?" asks Mary Anne.

"A large enough assembly or patrol of soldiers invites suspicion," says March. "Incites rebellion. They will hold true to their words until it suits them. If one of their men falls, their retribution will be swift. They will avoid a brawl until one of the Mirusian soldiers starts it. They believe they have already won."

Jonathan admires how March's mind works, able to think of dozens, if not hundreds, of possibilities in an instance, just like Cheshire. He, on the other hand, relies on his instincts. He is the amalgam of both March and Cheshire—she, calculated and strategic, moving only when necessary, looking ahead to the outcomes, while Cheshire acts out of impulse with just as much strategy, without a thought toward the consequences. Jonathan acts out of impulse but has no choice but to think of the ramification of his action and the cause and effect each will have.

A young man with light blue hair, an open tunic, and a worn sword at his hip runs up the stairs to meet their party. He bows his head toward Mary Anne then turns his back to whisper to March. She gives no thanks or acknowledgment before he returns down the same stairway. A twinge in March's eyes reveals her plan, and Jonathan's heart aches; she means to separate from them.

"Where are you taking Mary Anne?" she asks.

"To the Row." He addresses Mary Anne. "I saw the way you spoke to each of the townspeople: personable, relatable, dare I say influential. This is where your strength lies. The Row will give you the chance to speak with many of the citizens individually while others watch on."

"I am ready for the task," says Mary Anne.

Jonathan glances to March. "I take it you will venture somewhere else?"

"What? No." Mary Anne disagrees. "No, we are to remain together. Is this not what Jonathan suggested in the council meeting?"

"You have twelve soldiers following a street behind you. Not to mention four of the Gryphon's archers, less inconspicuous, trailing on the rooftops. You will be fine."

Mary Anne looks back to spot them.

"Do not draw attention to them," Jonathan whispers.

"To answer your question, dear heart," says March. "While Mary Anne may excel on a smaller scale, Lysander and Uriah prefer to draw crowds. And the largest open area in the city, outside of the castle, is..."

"The Quadrangle," they say together.

"Which the soldier confirmed. Fortune favors us, for the moment. At least this way I can keep them in one place, and you need not fear a confrontation with them if we part ways now."

"What soldier?" asks Mary Anne.

March cocks an eyebrow. "The one who delivered the information to me moments ago."

"I thought him some random townsperson you might have some arrangement with. He was handsome in face and body."

"We can see where your mind is at," says March.

"Agreed," says Jonathan. "With you in the Quadrangle, if something should arise, I trust in you to reach us first."

March turns and walks down the curve of the street to take another stairway. "I shall meet you back at the castle."

Jonathan watches her until she descends the next stairway. He and Mary Anne walk on speckled sunlight shining through the branches overhanging the stairs. Jonathan has not left the city since his tryst with Cheshire in the grotto. It was a glorious time with this lover, surrounded by rocks and streams opposed to stone and iron. Somewhere by the sea. Once this threat is quelled, Mary Anne and, by extension, he will be able to travel outside the city walls. Jonathan wants to visit the sea with his loves, somewhere far away from Mirus, and feel the brine upon the wind.

They continue their path down to the Row, taking stairways to lead them to the eastern entrance of the market, far from the Quadrangle. The streets are emptier than Jonathan assumed. To be expected. It will take time for it to resume back to its normal bustling activities.

"Jonathan?" Mary Anne breaks his thought with a pensive look in her eyes, something brewing behind them.

He imagines it is a question or comment about their own threesome with March. She has been massaging the muscles of his arm firmer than usual while they walk. Jonathan wondered when she would bring up the topic—probably wondering why he and March left the bed so early this morning without rousing her. Jonathan blushes, never broaching the subject of sex with Mary Anne before.

"Do you ever question March?" she asks.

The question, though predictable, takes Jonathan by surprise.

"What do you mean?"

The question hides behind her lips, unsure if she wants to continue.

"What's said is said. You will not offend me. But I think it wise you ask this while she is not present."

"When you are apart, do you ever question her activities or the company she keeps? March spent countless days and nights with hundreds of soldiers while training them. She is brazen with all sorts of men. The way she dresses invites scandal, rumors, and wandering eyes. Even now, she ventures off to meet Lysander and Uriah. Do her whereabouts or actions ever invade your thoughts? Do you ever *question* her?"

He understands. Mary Anne's feelings have blossomed, especially after their own tryst yesterday, and she finally puts words to, dare he say it, the jealousy she has felt for quite some time.

"Once, many, many years ago, I happened upon the ruins of an old manor in the middle of the forest near Ilex, desolate, dilapidated, forgotten. Nature reclaimed it long before I stumbled upon it, stones overgrown with creeping ivy and ferns. Most may have thought it a natural rock outcropping, but the remnants of an arched stone doorway and straight lines of what once was a chimney gave away its secret. There were charred bits of wood, long petrified. Signs of a fire. I explored and found a set of crumbling stairs leading to a lower chamber filled with the stones from ceilings and walls caved in from above. Little sunlight made it below, and little grew there because of it. Except for a solitary lily among the stones. Its beauty thrived despite its solitude and surroundings. One's initial thought might be to question how the lily could grow in such conditions. But to question it would undermine its strength and purpose. It was not my place to know why or how it came to be. I was meant to cherish its wonder and appreciate having stumbled upon it at all. We are all products of our upbringing—you, March, Cheshire, and myself. All different, all uniquely different, flaws included. I would have it no other way."

After a long stretch of silence, Mary Anne asks, "What happened to the lily?"

Jonathan knows she speaks of the analogy of the flower, but he gives a different answer with the same meaning. He smiles as wide as the crescent moon on an autumn's night. "She followed me, and walks with me still—bare skin, swords, and all. My flower of steel."

Mary Anne loosens her grip on his arm while they make their way down the last few tiers to the Row, but Jonathan lays his hand on hers and rubs it with his thumb. It is little comfort, but he did not intend to push Mary Anne away in the slightest. After all, the day before, they crossed a line there is no returning from.

CHAPTER 21

MARCH

The street gradually becomes more crowded the closer March draws to the Quadrangle from the east, and no doubt every other entrance will look the same. Reminiscent of her first visit, men and women crowd and crush themselves to glimpse upon the Twins, though not this crowded before. This time, she will not traverse the rooftops to gain a better vantage point, instead pushing and sliding her way through the crowd, searching above their heads for any sign of Lysander and Uriah. The platform at the center of the square with the pillories, where she would expect to find them, to stand a head above everyone else in the crowd, is filled with more onlookers. Their sight line allows March to follow their focus to the Far Side Tavern on the southern face of the Quadrangle.

Murmurs from the crowd eventually reach her ears, telling of the Twins inside the tavern since before the dawn of sunrise, welcoming loyal townspeople and paying handsomely to have a drink with anyone who sits with them. There is no need for the people of Mirus to riot if Lysander and Uriah feel they have the upper hand. Soldiers in the city, ships soon to be in the harbor, and Lysander and Uriah in the townspeople's thoughts and hearts. All they need to do is bide their time.

March could force her way through the crowd, but whispers of her presence will travel faster than she can, and the Twins will know she approaches before she makes it halfway through the square. She pushes her way back out of the crowd until it thins and climbs the closest set of stairs to the next tier of Stonehaven and the rear door of the distillery attached to the tavern—a solid oak door with iron bands and a large padlock. With no windows to speak of, the crowd remain at the bar below and leave this section of the city empty for now.

She unsheathes her sword, about to slide it through the shackle and body of the lock when she hears the crunch of boots behind her. She swings her sword out and holds the point of her blade at the unlucky person who dares to follow her—the young soldier with blue hair.

He throws his hands in the air. "I'm sorry. I did not mean to startle you."

March guffaws. "Not possible." She turns back to the lock and slips her blade through the shackle.

"Do you need help?" He persists after she does not answer. "Are you certain? You could use my sword, so as not to damage yours."

"Mirusian steel is too wide, forged for even the most unskilled soldier to hack at their enemies, like an apprentice butcher at the block, not for more delicate tasks."

"How about a dagger?" The soldier pulls the blade from his belt.

"You are quite incessant."

"I believe you mean persistent."

"No. I do not." March sheathes her sword, takes the dagger, and in one swift pop, breaks the shackle from the lock.

"Besides, we are not unskilled," the soldier says. "Not anymore. You made sure of it."

She flops the dagger in his hand handle first. "Job is done. Off with you."

"I did as you commanded. Sent word to as many soldiers as I could find and asked them to do the same. And any new brothers I come across I continue to spread the word."

"Stop," says March, prying open the door. "Continue now and all you do is make yourself a target. Let the word spread naturally."

"Understood. By the way, my name is—"

The loud, deep clang of the door cuts off the soldier's words. Like all the others, March does not care to learn the names of the dead.

"Fuck me," March says with a chuckle.

The sweet smell of whiskey and rum fills the distillery and overtakes her senses. The door leads to a stairway to her left and a network of suspended walkways above what must be two casks—larger than any March has ever seen, equal to twenty tons or more. They sit upright instead of on their sides, twenty feet tall. Other apparatuses, coils, distillers, and smaller stacked casks line the walls of the large room. The proprietors of Far Side brew their own spirits, and from the aroma, the liquors are not the best of quality. How can they be at this quantity? But from her recollection, what it lacks in flavor, it makes up for with its potency.

March turns a large crank attached to a thick chain and pulls up a large bucket from the center of the closest cask, drizzling beautiful, sweet amber-brown drops as it rises. It would be rude not to sample the draft while here. She locks the crank, takes the bucket in hand, and takes a mighty swig. She releases the bucket and lets it swing back and forth as she swishes the whiskey from side to side in her mouth. The notes of smoke and vanilla overpower all else; not bad, but not good either. She will partake of her stock and wash the taste from her mouth when she returns to the castle.

Down the stairs and through the middle aisle of wooden giants, she reaches a preparation area with large tables, tools for repairing casks and steins, and buckets for collecting leftover liquor. Raucous laughter and cheers from the tavern wait on the other side of a door beyond the tables. March peers through the dingy circular window in the door, much like a ship's porthole.

As much as March does not want to speak to them, let alone lay eyes on Lysander and Uriah, in order to survive, they all must do things they do not want to do. The door bumps against a large man blocking its curved path when March pushes it open. Through the small sliver of face March can see through the opening of the door, this man is not someone she recognizes. He shuffles to the side enough to allow March to slide through, staring down at her chest all the while.

"Oh, shit," he mutters when his eyes rise to meet her face.

Men and women pack the door to Far Side as if they were fleeing a fire in reverse. Their necks crane and bend to see around others to look upon the Twins. Women tired of their mundane lives fawn over them because of their purposefully brooding and dark nature and find pleasure in being fucked, used, choked, and abused by them, blinded by their empty promises. Men who can no longer bring joy to their women watch and try to imitate their arrogance, mannerisms, and their use of women —poorly. March sees it most in the men of the Crest, too consumed by their wealth and status to care about others.

The breath of others fogs the already grimy windows as they press their faces against the square panes. The tavern owner flaps a small rag at them, fearing they will crack the glass.

March questions why she fights for this city. Let the cannon fire rain down and destroy it all. Those who are intelligent enough will see it coming and escape, while fate will take those marked to die, those loyal to Lysander and Uriah. *Respectless idiots.*

Before March can close the door behind her, Uriah calls out.

"Look who decided to join us."

At the center of the mob, a dozen women surround him and his brother—flowers from the Garden, a few castle servants, and general townsfolk clamoring to be near them. A flower straddles each of their laps, leaning back against their chests.

"Come and clash a cup of wine," says Uriah.

Lysander pulls his hand from beneath the dress of the flower on his lap, waves a hand, and dismisses the other women sitting across the table, including his and his brother's rider.

An older man with small spectacles, a man of Stonehaven, lingers by Uriah's side momentarily and hands him a small glass orb. March cannot make out the contents, but it resembles those used by the fire brigade to douse fires in the city. Once Uriah tucks the orb into his robes, concealing it as March approaches, the man nervously pushes his way out of the tavern.

Reluctantly, March shoves her way through the crowd, pushing shoulder, head, and full bodies out of her way, like noxious, slovenly cornstalks in a packed field ready for harvest. The laughter turns to a rippling cacophony of under-breath gasps, scoffs, jeers, and lustful and lewd sounds, drawing attention away from the Twins. When March reaches the table, she flips an empty chair around and straddles it to sit, resting her arms on the worn back.

"Wine?" she asks. "Rather delicate for the likes of you two. Especially in the morning."

"We celebrate," says Lysander. "Join us."

"Celebrate the way you like." March looks over her shoulder at the bar. "Rum. An unopened bottle." She hopes it is better than the whiskey she tasted earlier. The glass bottle slinks and sloshes, passed hand-by-hand by several patrons, from the bar to their table.

"I knew there was a reason I liked you," says Uriah. "Several, actually." His eyes fall to her breasts and then lower, summoning some power to see through the table at her open legs.

March dusts the top rim and neck, pops the cork, and takes several gulps. The taste is not all together smooth or pleasant, and perhaps a bit too much sugar, but it will suffice. She keeps them waiting until she finishes a quarter of the bottle.

"Several, indeed," says Lysander.

She sets the bottle down on the table with a loud *clunk* and keeps hold of its neck. "If you must be lascivious, at least be original."

"Is this what you tell your men?" asks Lysander.

"My men think nothing like you two." March smirks and wipes at her lips with the back of her hand. "And I need not tell them anything."

While the Twins blather on with sex-laden compliments, March's soft gaze inspects the crowd in the tavern, recognizing a good deal of townspeople from Stonehaven, a few prominent men from the Crest, wearing hooded cloaks to disguise themselves and blend in with the rabble, and former soldiers of Mirus—traitors all. Less than two dozen out of more than a hundred are unknown to March: soldiers from Adamas. She expected more of a presence, but without them, there is more room for eager and susceptible ears. The turncoat Red Knight is nowhere to be found, no doubt occupied with an errand from his new masters, playing at their ball sacks like bags of gold.

"To what honor must we raise a cup for you to grace us with your presence?" Uriah circles the top of his goblet with a wet finger.

"Enemies close and all," says March, taking another drink.

"Oh, come now. Must we be enemies?" Uriah slides his finger in and out of his goblet.

"Do you really wish to showcase your ignorance to everyone present?" she asks.

"Here to spy, little strumpet?" Lysander says in a low growl.

"To spy would mean there is some hidden information or agenda to be uncovered," says March. "You have nothing to hide, after all. Your thoughts are as clear to me as the windows of this tavern, however filthy. Therefore, there is nothing to uncover and, hence, no need to spy." She takes another long drink.

A suppressed chuckle from somewhere near the door wafts through the air. Uriah's eyes harden, and Lysander sucks at his teeth. The crowd waits, unfamiliar with anyone willing to challenge the Twins publicly.

"Please, continue," says March. "I come to partake in drink and listen. What were you discussing before I barged in?"

"Nothing much at all," says Uriah. "We speak of changes we plan to make to the city, listening to the concerns and needs of the people, and promises of abundance for all."

The crowd cheers as if rehearsed.

"But while we have you here," Uriah continues, "seventeen of our men died outside the castle walls when they arrived. What do you know about this? And I believe five more of our men were found slain across Stonehaven. It would be a shame if first blood was drawn by such carelessness on your part."

"Nothing," March answers with a half-truth, knowing she asked Cheshire to be the instrument of their murders but not the means or method of their deaths. "I was there, atop the gatehouse. No shot was fired, nor order given to attack. Whatever fate became of your men is at their own hands."

Uriah keeps his hand in his robe, turning the glass orb. Lysander squints at March, studying her, not in his usual lewd manner.

"We would like to offer you a gift," says Lysander.

"I want nothing you offer."

"Do not be so sure," Lysander says under his breath, lips at the rim of his wine goblet.

"Fancy a straddle as well?" A sickening, velvet voice behind March interrupts them.

The poor insult is barely laughable, yet for some strange reason, its familiarity, like all the other insults she endured the day prior, gives her a sense of solace. These past weeks spending her time as general, trainer, tutor have won the respect of most of Mirus. After years of self-imposed exile, escape, peace, while rumors fly around Wonderland on the wings of birds, it feels odd, contrary to be treated in such a way by anyone except Jonathan and Cheshire. A fire ignites within her—a song needing to be sung.

"Careful," Uriah tells the man.

March laughs within, holding her face as smooth as marble. She stretches her arms behind her head, arching her back and revealing more of the underside of her breasts. The men in the tavern mutter and whisper while women scoff and sneer. Although, there are several women among the crowd who whisper and try to cover their smiles but do not avert their eyes.

"Come on, now," says the man. "Only one side of the tavern gets a show?"

"She has killed for less," Uriah warns.

"What? We all know the sordid tales of March. Runaway. Fighter. Whore. Turn around so we all can have a proper show." The man laughs. "Or do you only perform for those as rich as the brothers?"

Odd how March has missed these days. She takes her bottle in hand, steps onto the chair, and then on top of the table. She chugs from the bottle, raising it high above her head. Her fingers rub against the bottle as she drinks and examines its heft and weight of the thick glass—quality. The body of the bottle is thinner, not by much, but enough.

Other men in Far Side join in with their own encouragement, whoops, and whistles—an all-too-familiar tune. She finds the man: a neighbor of her mother's—tall, broad shoulders, tailored coat and neck ruffle. March has known him and his lingering gaze since she was young and still resided with her parents.

"Come now," the man says, "price is no object. You should know what I can offer. Or if you would rather, I can arrange a more private showing back at my manor, where you can stop your teasing."

"The public has never deterred me," says March, finishing the bottle.

"Finally." The man pushes through the crowd to take his place at the edge of the table, licking at his lips like a glutton at a feast, looking up at March.

The cacophony of the crowd crescendos. Her steel at her hips kept silent in their scabbards beg, cry out, to sing. The overcrowded tavern poses a challenge, but March's aim and accuracy can pin a falling needle to a wall through its eye. She can easily skewer this pig of a man through the neck, chest, or eye without endangering anyone else, though most deserve the same end.

A simple melody will suffice. She squats on the table and rests her forearms on her knees, mimicking how Cheshire would often perch. The man moves closer. The overabundance of perfume mixed with his sour breath invades her space.

"You know how long I have waited for the chance to have you?" the man says with a grin. He stretches his neck forward to peer down the cleavage of her linen top. As most do, he does not look her in the eyes. If he did, he would see her true intention, and his death, waiting in their reflection.

Crack. March slams the bottle down onto the table, taking all by surprise. All except the Twins. It breaks halfway down the body, leaving its neck a strong handle, and the jagged points left on the body, a beautiful instrument. Before the small shards of glass *tinkle* and *ping* off the table or stone floor, March thrusts the broken, sharp end of the bottle into the man's face.

Shards stab deep into his forehead, eyes, cheeks, and chin—a perfect bloody circle. The man screams through a clenched jaw, held shut by the thick shards of glass piercing below his bottom row of teeth. He reaches to dislodge it but is too late. March stands quickly, hooks her boot behind the man's neck, and with a sudden jerk and twist, slams his face, bottle and all, onto the table. A loud *crack* fills the silence. The glass held together and embedded itself deeper into the man's head. The crack was the sound of the man's skull cracking into pieces. He twitches and claws at the table for a moment before sliding down to the floor, gurgling his last breath before dying.

March looks down at Lysander and Uriah, of course unfazed by the death at their feet. The Twins sit motionless as snakes, looking up at her with expressions she did not expect. It sends an unearthly chill up her body. After years of enduring their lustful gazes and advances, they look up at her with a strange sense of pride.

"You are welcome," Uriah mouths.

Fuck.

This was their gift? March steps down from the table, shoves the dead body out of the way with her boot, and straddles the chair again. The crowd shifts and slides backward like ripples in a pond in order to put as much space between them and her as possible, which is not much. Whispers spread out of the tavern and to the masses outside. Men and women try to hide their grunts and hisses as they press back against each other, pushing their way out of the door and widening the space between the table and the crowd further.

"Let no one forget," says Lysander. "March is the greatest sword in all of Wonderland."

It is odd and unnerving to hear these words from the Twins, though she knows why they are spoken. She holds up her hand, and within seconds, a new trembling bottle of rum slides into it.

"Well played," she says under her breath.

The Twins publicly acknowledge this title, her rightfully earned title, because they intend to take the mantle from her publicly, adding to their celebrity. They can try.

And the gift given to her was not a death, not exactly, but rather the reaction of the crowd—a sense she long missed since returning to Mirus weeks ago. While fighting and defending, she earned the respect of the city. However, respect is not what she seeks, wants or cares for; it is fear. This is the uneasy feeling she carries with her.

"You see," says Lysander, "we can be civil."

To almost anyone else, a brutal death would not be accompanied by the word *civil*, but in the world she, Jonathan, Cheshire, and the Twins inhabit, a quick kill is as civil as one can get.

"We need not be at odds," says Uriah. "Not completely. Our quarrel with the usurper Mary Anne has little to do with you, with the exception you stand in our way. It can be different. There are other gifts we can give."

"No."

"Are you sure?" Uriah asks with an arrogant half-grin. Not his usual lustful gaze, like his brother. He plots. His eyes hold information, a secret, some small parcel enough to pique March's curiosity, and she hates him even more for it.

This is a conversation for another time. A new whisper wafts into the tavern with mentions of a festival, and the Twins look away from March for the first time and to each other with the slightest twinge of irritation about their eyes.

She opens her bottle and drinks again. The Gryphon believes the battle to come will be one of politics and words instead of blades and blood. March knows better. She is well versed in Wonderland's histories. No matter the conversations had, they all end in bloodshed. Perfect, for March is well equipped to handle either situation but prefers her blades to speak, no, to sing for her, as it should be. After all, in the end, she would much rather embrace the frigid grip of being feared than respected.

CHAPTER 22

MARY ANNE

His answer took Mary Anne off guard. It was beautiful and heartbreaking all in the same breath. She squeezes Jonathan's arm tighter as they walk down a zig-zag stairway, drawing closer to the Row. Her lips twitch with the words clawing at them, hesitant to continue, but she must.

"Does she tell you what she does?"

"When she needs. And I do the same."

"Do you not find this bothersome?"

"Do you recall our first trip to Rookridge?"

"Of course." Mary Anne remembers a blurred memory, as if someone smudged a painting before it dried. She remembers the two highwaymen they encountered, Jonathan fighting them off, and a lingering sensation of being frightened on the journey, but not the *reason* she was frightened.

"I did not inform March of every detail, nor did she ask. We enjoy the mystery."

"Mystery, perhaps, but what of secrets?"

"Secrets are, at times, a necessity." Jonathan rubs Mary Anne's hand on his upper arm.

"Do you not see secrets as dangerous?"

"They can be. Although from my experiences, the truth can have far worse consequences."

They descend farther into the city, and Jonathan's gaze remains ever vigilant, searching the path ahead of them.

Mary Anne's heart aches at his damned honor, his innocence, and pure naivety. Or is it willful ignorance? How could he not see, sense, or feel March's infidelity when she flaunts herself in front of every man she comes across? Jonathan would only feel the kindness of her embrace, the loyalty and warmth of her heart, and the heat of her body. She hopes last night will not change their dynamic but instead draw them closer. They were inches away from fucking last night, at March's behest, no less. So quick to give him away to spare her own indiscretions.

Jonathan's attention is somewhere else, brow pinched. They drop from the last step of the stairway onto the next street of Stonehaven. Her stomach drops as if there were one more unexpected step when she sees the cause of his distress.

Despite the efforts of the Mirusian soldiers to repair the city, this street of Stonehaven still bears deep gashes, blood stains on stone and wood, broken windows, and doors with markings as if they have been gnawed upon. What horrors did the citizens of Stonehaven face while Mary Anne was secure in the castle? This must be where the horde grew in number, uncontrolled, ripping at doors, tearing at families, and stealing countless lives before ascending to the castle. The higher tiers of Stonehaven and the Crest still have their share of scars, but nothing like this. This street, and who knows how many others, remains an open wound.

"I had no idea," Mary Anne says under her breath.

"It was worse," says Jonathan. "Far worse. The sun reveals the aftermath in a silent city, but the clouded days and pounding rain transfigured Mirus into a misshapen maze of nightmares given form from our darkest thoughts."

Mary Anne leans her head on Jonathan's shoulder. The image of his battered body carried in the Gryphon's arms flashes in her mind. For the first time, she entertains the merit of keeping secrets. She does not know what he endured, nor how she would handle knowing what happened.

Ahead of them, Alderman Lacha sets the wide oak door to a tenement into its half-barrel iron hinges by himself. He survived the ordeal. His trunk-like arms handle it as easily as Mary Anne would a serving tray. Faded scratches cover his chest and arms underneath his apron.

"Good morrow. What is the condition of the rest of Stonehaven?" asks Jonathan.

"Are there more streets like this?" asks Mary Anne.

Lacha wipes sweat from his forehead but leaves a swath of dirt in its place. His silence speaks volumes. The door clunks into place. He opens and shuts it, assuring his work, before turning to Mary Anne. The bags under his eyes bear the weight of countless hours of toil and work.

"Ask what you will of us," says Mary Anne, "and you shall have it."

"So easy, is it?" Lacha's face twists. "Repairs are simple," he says with his deep gravel of a voice. "We from the Forge—those of us who are left—have worked through the nights to bring some comfort during the restoration of the city."

"Your work is commendable," says Mary Anne.

"Spoken like someone who has no clue of what took place here." Lacha lifts a post wider than Jonathan and sets it in place as a support for a section of the second story of the building, jutting out over the street. He takes a large iron hammer from his belt and swings at the post, knocking it into place inch by inch.

Mary Anne looks down the curve of the street, where three other smiths, along with soldiers of Mirus, replace shutters and remove broken doors.

"I do not know what to say."

"Say nothing," says Lacha. "What words could you offer any of my people to bring them any modicum of relief?" Lacha continues to swing at the post until it stands upright. "What we need, you could never give us." He hooks the hammer back in its loop and scoops up a pile of wood scraps from the previous tenement support beam.

His words take hold of Mary Anne's heart. Has she failed the people before her reign has started? What must she do to win them over when she loses the support of the city leaders? Instead of answers, more questions bombard Mary Anne. What did she expect, after all? Lacha speaks true. Countless soldiers and innocent townspeople lost their lives while Mary Anne cowered within the castle.

She reluctantly thinks of what March told her during their time of capture in the dungeon. Mary Anne cannot wait for someone to save her. Act as if no one is coming, because in this instance, there is no one else. The beacon of hope for this city must be her, a lighthouse to cut through the darkness of the treacherous and uncertain waters they brave. Winning the throne will be a game of politics, but handing out food and supplies to those in need, while necessary, will not be enough. In order to be victorious, she must be willing to get her hands dirty.

Mary Anne unclasps her cloak and drapes it over Jonathan's arm. She pushes up her sleeves to her elbows, as far as her cuffs will allow, and stoops to pick up the thinner pieces of timber fallen from Lacha's arms.

Lacha looks down at her, eyebrow raised. "What do you think you are doing?"

"Saying nothing."

Lacha huffs through his nose, mustache whiskers vibrating, and nods for her and Jonathan to follow him, leading them around the curve of the street to a gigantic pile of posts, broken door frames, smashed planters, and broken chairs and dressers. Soldiers load the debris into lines of carts and ferry them off to the eastern side of the city.

Mary Anne drops her armfuls into one cart with space and shoves them in so they will not fall out.

Mary Anne hisses through her teeth. A thick splinter jabs into her thumb just below the bend and exits above it just below the skin, keeping her thumb from bending. There is no blood, but her hands and arms are covered with lines of dirt from the wood.

"May I?" asks Jonathan.

Mary Anne offers her hand, thinking he will pluck the splinter out with his fingers, and braces for the pain. Instead, he holds her hand up to his mouth. His soft lips wrap around her thumb. His teeth pinch and bite at her skin. If there is any pain to be felt, the butterflies in her stomach block it out. His lips part and suck as if kissing her. The strength of the grip he has on her wrist, the power of his mouth devouring her hand, and the press of his tongue on her skin sends the butterflies fluttering between her legs. He acts as if he has done this hundreds of times before, which he probably has, but to Mary Anne, this is the most sensual act she has ever felt, including their time the previous night. This is an intimate moment shared between the two of them for the first time.

Her fingers caress Jonathan's cheek, not wanting him to stop, but eventually he pries the splinter loose and spits it into a cart. He examines the groove left in her thumb. Mary Anne cannot look away from his protective expression and his full lips.

"Are you harmed?" he jests. A question Jonathan has needed to ask frequently during their time together.

"No," Mary Anne says in a breathy whimper. In her mind, she imagined Jonathan asked if she wanted him to stop. Jonathan releases her hand, and while it falls back through the air to her side, Mary Anne forces herself to let go of the pressure building in her body. She inhales deeply, blinks, then pretends they did not just have an affair in her mind in the middle of a street of Stonehaven. "Thank you."

"Of course." Jonathan turns as if nothing happened—nothing, yet everything. He takes larger pieces of timber from approaching soldiers and stacks them in the wagon.

Mary Anne, brimming with tension in her body, follows his example. At first, the soldiers approach her hesitantly, out of surprise more than fear, not expecting her to take part in the reconstruction. She greets them and lifts the planks and pieces she can carry from their arms and places them in the carts. More soldiers approach, and Mary Anne continues to be of what use she can to lighten their load. It is nowhere near enough, but she is compelled to act.

Half the afternoon passes when Lacha finally says, "Enough of this, for now." He pats a soldier on his back to send the line of carts away. Soldiers lift the carts and wheel their caravan down the street, clacking against the stones and timbers clunking.

"I can do more." Mary Anne's eagerness gets the better of her. "I can."

"Ay," says Lacha. "We will see, now won't we?"

Mary Anne nods in agreement, determined to prove her worth yet again. This time not because she needs to gain his approval for her own worth but because Lacha and the other townspeople need to see she is capable, she is strong, and she is powerful.

"Where will the soldiers dispose of the refuse?" Jonathan asks Lacha.

He combs through his beard with his giant fingers. "Every spare scrap of wood, no matter how small, will help rebuild the harbor. When we get back around to it. As you can see, more pressing matters take our attention." He lowers his eyes to Mary Anne. "Where were the both of you off to?"

"The Row," says Mary Anne. "I have spent far too much time in the castle. I must be among my people."

"On with you, then."

On a day bound to create more questions, she will at least have the answer to one. She calls to Lacha as he walks away. "Alderman Lacha. What you said previously about what you need, I can never give you. What do you need?"

The towering blacksmith looks over his shoulder at her. "Perhaps 'never' was too strong a word. Rather, let me say, what we need would be near impossible."

"I do not believe in the word. To believe in it gives it power. What do you need?"

"What we need," says Lacha. "What we all need, is for our home to be placed, like it once was, where innocents need not die for others' gain. And mark my words, as long as the throne continues to be fought over, innocent blood will continue to be spilled."

With those final heavy words, Lacha continues with his work, turning the corner between buildings, off to repair the lives of more Mirusians.

Mary Anne keeps hold of Jonathan's arm while they descend the last two tiers to the Row. The wide canvases above, hanging motionless between buildings, offer reprieve from the sun and bathe the market in a soft orange glow. The market bustles with commerce, though not at the level Mary Anne remembers from her previous visit. Women, men, and families of Mirus peruse the Row, some with their child in hand tagging along, and shop from grocers, butchers, furniture dealers, and pawnbrokers to replenish lost necessities, as well as the irreplaceable.

Without Mary Anne's traveling cloak and hood, her hair stands out among the crowd like a dark bead in a jar of multicolored glass. The townspeople continue their shopping but cannot hide their curiosity, their worry, their indifference, and from a few, their animosity.

"What is this despondence in their faces?" Mary Anne whispers to Jonathan. She noticed this on the young girls and the other townspeople she encountered earlier. Their smiles, while trying to be genuine, hide something else.

"This morning? Guilt, I would wager," says Jonathan. "They feel the unsettling paradox of feeling grateful to have survived and also the guilt of living while those dearest to them do not."

"How do you lift such a weight?"

"When you speak to them, do not think of what you need to tell them. Start with what they need to hear. Lysander and Uriah treat them as pieces in a game. This is where you will differ from them."

Right.

"Hello, everyone." Mary Anne wastes no time. Lysander and Uriah have a head start, and there is no need to dawdle. Only a few townspeople closest to Mary Anne slow down but do not stop. "May I please have a word?"

"May I?" Jonathan asks.

With a nod from Mary Anne, he scales a pair of large crates stacked at the corner of a tanner's shop, holds onto a rusted gutter, and leans into the street.

"Good day, people of Mirus." Jonathan's sweet tone carries over the crowd. If not his words, his eyes win them over. Everyone in earshot stops and looks up at him with reverence and fondness, as if he himself were the sun breaking through the gloom. "I am glad to see you all. I know these past days have been harrowing." Jonathan holds open his shirt with one hand to reveal his bruises.

Some townspeople cover their mouths, some avert their eyes, while others gasp.

"Make no mistake, the events of the Cult of the Mother touched us all. No one escaped without injury of some kind, and we will all bear scars in remembrance."

The crowd draws to him like moths to a lantern, entranced, caught in his spell.

"I did not come to speak with you about the past. I come to bring you your future. Someone accompanies me, to whom it is my greatest honor to introduce."

Jonathan jumps down from the crates, stands toe to toe with Mary Anne, and wraps his hands around her waist. "May I?"

"Of course."

He takes firm hold of her and lifts her onto the crates as if she weighed nothing more than a doll to him. The sweeping motion causes Mary Anne's stomach to drop, but she steadies herself, as Jonathan did. Her heart thunders. What once was a handful of townspeople now numbers in the hundreds—their eyes full of questions and doubt. She looks down into Jonathan's sparkling blue eyes and finds the focus and strength she needs.

"Good day. My name is Mary Anne Elizabeth. You do not know me. I arrived in your city a stranger from a distant land. I wish nothing more than to know you better. With your blessing, I humbly ask..."

Many in the crowd lower their heads or roll their eyes. Jonathan was correct. Familiar with the game, perhaps they expect the same treatment, the same tactics Lysander and Uriah use on their followers.

"I have not come to talk of riches, promises, or thrones, but to give my condolences. I choose to focus on all of you. The Cult of the Mother struck Mirus a crippling blow. What you lost can never be replaced, and I will not pretend otherwise. The scars upon this city will be lasting, but we will endure."

"Are you going to tell us 'Mirus is strong'?" a voice from the crowd scoffs.

"Do you need to be told?" Mary Anne asks forcefully. "I will not speak platitudes to you and waste your time. Look upon Jonathan Carter, the strongest and bravest man I know; a man you know, physically, in spirit, and in heart. He laid unconscious for days, healing from his injuries, yet here he is among you again, against all odds, helping to repair this city. I have learned from his guidance and kindness and... like him, Mirus needs to heal. You must heal."

The air shifts in the Row. The townspeople look to one another, questioning if they can trust her words.

"The city will have four official days for mourning," she continues, not knowing if this is a custom in Wonderland or not. "Do what must be done. Do what you need to do. Ask for help from each other, from me. You will have it if it is within my power. After those four days, we will hold a grand city-wide festival to remember the lives of those here, to celebrate those who have traveled on without us, and the future of a resilient Mirus. Not because Mirus is strong. Because *you* are strong."

The Row falls silent except for a few hushed comments. Whatever they are, Mary Anne cannot hear them over her own heartbeat. The townspeople wear their expressions clearly, still curious, untrusting, and questioning. Each one teeters on the edge of a decision to change all of their futures.

"Carter's boy." An older gentleman with a white beard and soft rose-colored eyes steps forward. He scratches his balding head. "You believe her? Do you follow her?"

"Mary Anne does not need my endorsement. Do not allow my belief to sway you. Think of yourselves and your families. She has come to Mirus, and the throne room has opened for her. I was there to witness it, regardless of what others claim. Wonderland has made its choice. Therefore, so have I."

The smattering of whispers grows to conversation and their dull eyes brighten. The weight does not lift from the shoulders of the townspeople, but it grows the smallest bit lighter.

Jonathan's words were true, mostly, and also masterfully played. He convinced them with his silver tongue without them being the wiser. Her advisor, her support, her lover.

He holds his arms out to catch her, suggesting she drop into them. Mary Anne swallows and jumps from the crates into his waiting arms. He cradles her in his muscles, his face inches from hers. She can feel his sweet breath upon her face. He sets her down, without a second thought, as a gentleman should. Mary Anne wishes the moment lasted longer and was sealed with a kiss. How can they be so physical with each other yet the simplest affection, what she craves most, has yet to happen?

"Do you believe it was a good idea?" asks Mary Anne.

"The festival? It was an idea." He winks. "I dare not pass judgment on it while it is still in its infancy. Either way, I shall be by your side to see it through to fruition."

They continue toward the west side of the Row, away from the Quadrangle, where townspeople, man, woman, and child alike, greet Mary Anne with smiles; not out of courtesy, but revealing their hopes.

"I beg your pardon." An elderly woman who sits next to the entrance of Barlow's Bakery and Flower Shop, plump of face, blushed cheeks, and eyes glossed over calls to them. "Spare a moment for a blind woman?" Her voice cuts through the crowd.

"Hello," says Mary Anne.

The woman smiles, and the beautiful, deep wrinkles of her face read clear, like the marked paths of her adventures on the map of her life. "Good day, young woman." She reaches out and finds Mary Anne's hand and squeezes it. "And if I am not mistaken, did I hear Carter's boy accompanying you?"

"You did, ma'am," says Jonathan. "I am glad to know you are still here, Henrietta. Mary Anne, this is Henrietta Barlow. Her—"

"I can tell her who I am on my own," Henrietta says with an involuntary shake of her jaw and a wave of her hand.

"Please do," says Mary Anne.

"My family has owned our business for generations. Generations long before me, before Stonehaven was Stonehaven and we were all Mirus. My great grandsons and great granddaughters mind the shop now. While I sit out here and enjoy the twilight."

"It is only dusk, Mrs. Barlow," says Jonathan, with a joking grin.

"You know damned well I mean my years, not the time of day." She laughs and beckons Jonathan forward. He kneels and takes her hand.

"It is good to know you are still here, as well," she tells him. "And tell your father Theophilius to visit once in a while. It seems as though I have not seen him for an age."

"Thank you," says Jonathan, after a slight stutter.

The gentle admiration in Henrietta's face captivates Mary Anne. She cannot see Jonathan, yet she tilts her head toward him and dotes upon him as if he were a member of her own family returned after a long trip abroad. The people of Briarwell looked upon him with the same esteem, as did the townspeople in the Row.

"Is there anything we can do for you?" Mary Anne asks.

"I did not call you over to ask you for anything," says Henrietta. "I needed to tell you something. These eyes failed me long ago, but my ears are sharp as iron. I heard you speaking to the crowd." Her hand tightens in Mary Anne's. "I have lived a long and fruitful life, and been in this city all my years, during the Age of Kings and the Age of Queens. I needed you to know you lifted my spirit this day. It has been years since I have heard hope and determination like yours."

Mary Anne's chest grows heavy, and she inhales deeply to keep tears within.

"I heard you from afar. You brought up a memory I have not thought of in years. You reminded me of Queen Dinah, the first beloved Queen of Wonderland. And may I say, never believe a disparaging word anyone says against her. Her light brought this city, this world, back to life."

Mary Anne swallows the knot in her throat and cannot stop the tears from flowing down her cheeks. She may not have known what answers she sought this day but learned the answers she needed to know.

"I hear her in you, young woman," says Henrietta. "The trouble with Wonderland is its people have a tendency to forget. Use your light to remind everyone."

"I will," says Mary Anne, the knot quickly rising again.

"Oh, dear, I did not mean to make you cry."

"On the contrary, you have brought such joy to my heart. Thank you."

"Tears can accompany joy. A good thing to remember. You walk a path few have been successful at." Henrietta gives Mary Anne's hand a good shake before letting go of her and Jonathan. "Off with you now. You've wasted enough time with an old woman."

"Never," says Mary Anne.

"Off with you," says Henrietta. "You have much to do."

"Henrietta, if I may, could—"

"Oh, take what you want and stop blathering. Just promise you will return so I can hear your voice, so much like your father's, one more time before I leave this world."

"I shall." Jonathan plucks a large white rose from a table next to Henrietta, its bloom larger than his palm, and offers it to Mary Anne. "For you. Its real name is a mouthful, but they are known in the common tongue as Ever-Last Roses. If you were to pluck a flower from a bush, it would reappear within a day's time, and the flower, even when cut, will never wither."

"It is the most beautiful flower I have ever seen." Mary Anne swallows her tears but lets her joy show proudly in her eyes. "Jonathan, you have brought such happiness into my life..." Mary Anne wants to express her love to him—he must know it on some level, otherwise, why would he touch her so? But her heart stops the words from forming. This is not the time. Though she will cherish this tender gesture forever, this moment is not about her, but the people of Mirus. "It is time I shared the same happiness with everyone else."

After a long and eventful afternoon, dusk approaches, and Mary Anne and Jonathan climb the twisting stairs out of the Row.

"How do you feel?" asks Jonathan as they cross out of Stonehaven.

"Lighter than air," says Mary Anne, twirling her rose in hand. "I feared the start, but after spending the day in the city, I know this is where I must be. To look upon the faces of children, Lacha, Henrietta, you, and everyone else we encountered was pure magic. I have never felt so inspired in my life."

Her heart thunders in her chest again. Today she has seen the possibilities. Jonathan bore witness to what she is capable of, and she feels as if she can accomplish anything.

"Thank you."

Enough waiting. With March occupied with her other consorts, Mary Anne will harness this new found vigor and claim a kiss from Jonathan before they reach the castle. She turns to embrace Jonathan, ready to give her heart, but he is gone, disappeared into the late afternoon air. He walked not two stairs behind her a moment ago; she is sure of it.

"Jonathan? Jonathan?"

The Gryphon's archers hear her call and climb down from the roofs of Stonehaven to surround her in a protective circle, arrows in hand at their bows.

"To the castle," one of the archers commands.

"Wait, what of Jonathan?"

"We will return to search for him, but we must ensure your safe return."

Mary Anne clenches her teeth, jaw throbbing. Every ounce of cumulated happiness from the day falls from her like a tin pail of water, slashed along its bottom. She does not want to leave him but knows the archers speak the truth. Following them, she glances repeatedly over her shoulder for Jonathan. He could not simply vanish. Jonathan would never abandon her. There is foul play here.

CHAPTER 23

JONATHAN

Jonathan panics for only a moment as the hand comes from behind him and covers his mouth. If not for the unmistakable scent of Cheshire, he would have grabbed his unknown assailant by the head, snapped their neck, and thrown them down the stairway.

"Do not say a word," Cheshire whispers in Jonathan's ear as he rubs his hand over his shoulder and down his chest. Jonathan's eyes flutter at his touch, cock fighting against the leather of his trousers.

Mary Anne searches for him, curious, lost, unable to see Jonathan, mere stairs behind her, looking through him like a pane of glass.

"Jonathan?" she calls.

What devilry is this? Jonathan looks to his chest and can see Cheshire's muscled arm. How is this trick possible? He turns his head and falls into the purple glints behind one of Cheshire's damned masks, and the question flits from this mind.

"Jonathan?" she asks for him again, louder, worry filling her voice.

He does not want to see her in such a state, clutching at her neck and breaths quickening.

"Shhhhhh," Cheshire whispers into Jonathan's ear, pulling his shirt open, and reaches around to shove his hand down the front of Jonathan's pants.

Jonathan's muscles contract at the sensitive touch, breathing heavy through his nose, mouth still held shut by Cheshire's tight grip.

The archers descend and escort Mary Anne up the stairs and back to the castle. She glances over her shoulder every few steps, looking back for him. Little does she know he was always here with her.

"Do not fret over her," says Cheshire. "The archers will make sure she returns to the castle."

Jonathan pulls away from Cheshire to the opposite side of the stairs and his lover vanishes as the last touch of his fingers leaves Jonathan's skin.

"I cannot see you," says Jonathan.

"Yes."

"But I could when you held me."

"Yes."

"Make sense of this."

Cheshire's hand rubs up Jonathan's chest, and his lover becomes visible again, standing in front of him. "I have learned wondrous things. Just as powers of the Mask of Shadows extend to those I touch, the Mask of Light has similar properties, rendering those I keep in contact with invisible to the eye. Though not as potent a power. There are limits I find. And you shall help me explore them." Cheshire unlaces the front of Jonathan's trousers.

The same tickle rises up Jonathan's stomach and descends between his thighs, obeying Cheshire's silent command to harden for him.

"I have experimented with handheld objects, a spy from Lysander and Uriah of smaller frame before I killed him." Cheshire wraps his hand around the base of Jonathan's cock. "But I need someone larger." Cheshire rubs his other hand across Jonathan's chest, pinching at his nipples.

Jonathan should return to Mary Anne, but the temptation, the literal pull, of Cheshire is far too great. He reaches down and squeezes Cheshire's cock, already hard and twitching.

"I can see you," says Jonathan, "yet I cannot look upon your face."

"I can take the mask off." The mischievous, truthful grin is apparent in Cheshire's voice. "I have no quarrel taking you here and now in the open air for all to see."

Jonathan chuckles uncomfortably to hide his own temptation. He knows Cheshire would, and Jonathan has half a mind to let him—more than half. If they were in the Hollow, there would have been no conversation at all. Once Cheshire touched Jonathan, they would both be lost to time, indulging their every need as the sun and moon bear witness on their circled paths.

Cheshire possesses an otherworldly, hypnotic, feral attraction in every fiber of his being, and radiates it from every muscle, grin, and wink. His body is heat. His scent twinges at the back of Jonathan's jaw like a tart, watery apple. He possesses his own undeniable gravity. His presence, or the hope of his arrival, leaves Jonathan and March waiting at the edge of a frozen moment in time, lost between heartbeats waiting, yearning for him to spark the next.

Jonathan swoops Cheshire up in both arms and lifts him at the level of his chest, staring through the holes of the mask, swimming in Cheshire's purple tide. He kisses each of the beautiful muscles of Cheshire's stomach. The head of Cheshire's cock brushes against Jonathan's cheek the lower he kisses until he can tease no longer and takes Cheshire into his mouth. Jonathan carries Cheshire down the stairs, curling him up and down, taking more and more of his lover into his mouth.

Cheshire runs his fingers deep through Jonathan's hair with the arm wrapped around his shoulder, in long strokes to match Jonathan's mouth. Taking up the width of the stairs, Jonathan turns them sideways to make way for a gentleman traveling to the next tier and a woman traveling down. Both quicken their pace, eyes darting in all directions, hearing the muffled moans and breaths of Jonathan and the hisses of Cheshire through gritted teeth.

They laugh at the oblivious passers-by, but Jonathan keeps Cheshire in his mouth, teasing the ridge and the underside of his head, making Cheshire squirm and buck in his arms. Jonathan steps off the bottom stair back into the Row, forgetting for a moment how close they were. Jonathan moves to the side of the stairs, in front of a wide window of a baker's shop. Dozens of townspeople go about their errands and shopping, unaware of the affair happening feet, and for some travelers inches from them. Jonathan's lips start to slip from Cheshire's cock, but his lover grabs the back of his head and thrusts full and deep. The muffled, choking grunt Jonathan releases catches the attention of at least half a dozen townspeople. They pause for a moment, startled, then move on.

A couple walking arm and arm stop in front of Jonathan and Cheshire, unknowingly looking through them at the sale the baker has in the last few hours of operation. They chat and comment about loaves of bread and biscuits while Cheshire thrusts harder into Jonathan's mouth, until his taut stomach smashes against Jonathan's nose, and his cock fills his throat. Jonathan holds his breath, holds in Cheshire, until the couple leaves. He coughs out a breath and sucks back in a mouth full of spit. Cheshire thrusts fully again and again, and Jonathan relishes each pulse deep within his throat.

Is this the freedom Cheshire feels: to be unseen by all? How easy it would be to slip away from the world. This rapturous moment of freedom takes Jonathan by surprise, and he craves it and Cheshire more and wonders if the power of this mask would extend to three?

"Let me down," says Cheshire, insistently.

Jonathan, catching his breath, follows Cheshire's line of sight. The Gryphon walks head and shoulders taller than anyone else farther down the market. He slips to the ground from Jonathan's arms, but Jonathan catches hold of his wrist. If he lets Cheshire go completely, he will vanish, not to mention the untold chaos Cheshire will bring to the city.

"Release me," Cheshire says, cold, stern, body stiff—a sharp contrast to his loving demeanor moments earlier.

Jonathan knows the command was a courtesy. Cheshire can slip from his grasp with little more than a turn of his wrist. As much as Jonathan wishes he could, he has never been able to hold on to Cheshire, by physical force at least, no matter their size difference.

He pulls Cheshire close. "No," says Jonathan. He must deter Cheshire for the time being. "Stay. Fuck me. Here. Now."

Cheshire squints at him from behind his mask, puzzled perhaps, or weighing his options. Fortunately, as much as Jonathan cannot resist Cheshire's pull, the same can be said for his love.

"You started this," Jonathan smirks. "Finish it." Another word does not need to be said.

Jonathan finds himself at the fury of Cheshire, unlacing his trousers enough to pull them down to his knees. His cock breathes a healthy breath from the Row after being confined and cramped, trying to escape. A thought Jonathan never believed would cross his mind—the excitement and the rush of the dank air of the Row to his bare ass and bobbing cock.

Cheshire kneels in front of him and snarls, the mask keeping Cheshire's beautiful face from Jonathan, as well as Jonathan's shaft away from Cheshire. His frustration tightens his muscles, veins becoming clear on his shoulders and neck, and pushes his desire into frenzy. He stands, turns Jonathan around, and pushes him against the baker's window.

Jonathan's chest and face lay against the cold glass. He can feel the wet thickness of Cheshire slide between his ass, teasing, throbbing. Jonathan pushes his hips back.

"Yes," Jonathan pants.

Cheshire pushes his entire length in; hot, solid, pulsating with a single thrust. Bursts of his hot breath puff out and fog the window. The confused bearded baker within tries to wipe the fog away with a rag from his belt and cannot fathom where it comes from or why it persists.

Despite the dozens more townspeople walking behind them, shopping in front of them, this special moment is known only to Cheshire and Jonathan, in the middle of the city yet a world away. As Cheshire slowly pushes and pulls in and out, Jonathan gasps, stomach flexing, and revels in the glorious sensation of their union, and the unexpected freedom it brings.

CHAPTER 24
CHESHIRE

Cheshire taps on the scabbard Jonathan wears on his back, and his love pulls it over his shoulder with his left hand, about to let it fall to the ground.

"Do not let it go," says Cheshire.

Jonathan nods, taking longer than usual to comprehend it will reappear if he drops it. Understandable, considering his mind and body are otherwise consumed and distracted.

These limitations will not hinder Cheshire; as long as Cheshire stays in Jonathan, his arms are free. He yanks at Jonathan's shirt, slipping it from his right arm, across his body, until it dangles from his left wrist. Jonathan's back is a sculpture's dream–a tapered waist expanding to broad, muscled shoulders. In this position, Jonathan's shoulders pinch, and Cheshire runs his fingers down the deep grooves between the muscles. Jonathan's half-laughs half-moans bring Cheshire to rake his nails down Jonathan's back to his full, round ass.

Cheshire takes extraordinary pleasure watching himself slide in and out, hips moving back and forth, while Jonathan's ass flexes. Jonathan inhales every time Cheshire pulls from him, as if trying to regain the breath Cheshire steals, and each exhale fogs the glass of the baker's window with every thrust. He takes hold of Jonathan's waist and thrusts harder, faster. The moans Jonathan tries and fails to suppress come quicker, and his head rocks back and forth.

At first, Cheshire thought himself cross at Jonathan's obvious attempt to keep him from the Gryphon, but the bewildered reflections of the townspeople in the glass awaken something more feral inside. He thrusts even harder into Jonathan than before with their audience, similar to when Pat and Bill were with them. Now, the rough, rhythmic slapping of the skin draws curious looks. Jonathan's mouth becomes parched with each quick pant. The window of the baker's shop rattles at their love.

Curious townspeople crowd around the noises. Unwillingly, Cheshire slows his stride, wrapping his arms around Jonathan, kissing and licking at his back, swirling his hips to keep Jonathan's body shaking. Eventually, the crowd disperses, and Cheshire side steps with Jonathan to the small section of brick wall between the window and the stairway—a sturdier grip for Jonathan. Once Jonathan takes hold, Cheshire begins again, hammering into Jonathan, assuring he takes the full length given but not slapping against him nearly as hard to draw another crowd.

Cheshire teases and toys with Jonathan, removing his hands from Jonathan's waist and slowly pulling his cock out to where just his head lingers precariously within his lover. If he were to slip out, Jonathan, bare ass and all, would become visible to the world.

"No, no, no, no," Jonathan whispers, and pushes his hips backward, taking in Cheshire again. "Do not leave me."

This time, Jonathan bites the fullness of his bottom lip, and Cheshire's own legs shake. He stands still, his hot breath rising through his mask. Jonathan looks back, curious why Cheshire stops. A cocked head to the side is the only sign Jonathan needs. He braces himself on the wall and pushes his hips back and forward, fucking himself on Cheshire as he stands firm in the streets of Mirus. Cheshire's free hands push up his back roughly and grab handfuls of Jonathan's hair.

Jonathan becomes insatiable, speeding up, and slowing down, without an end in sight. Cheshire reaches around and finds the tip of Jonathan's cock, dripping wet, and raises his hand to Jonathan's mouth. His tongue greets Cheshire's fingers eagerly, taking them into his mouth. He pulls his fingers from Jonathan's lips, to his brief disappointment, and takes the fullness of his cock in his grasp. Jonathan whimpers and drives himself back onto Cheshire and forward into his clenched grip.

Almost too much to bear, Cheshire feels the end nearing and drags his teeth along Jonathan's back and bites at the muscles without bruises.

"Yes, yes, yes," Cheshire hisses. He leaves Jonathan's hair and reaches around to Jonathan's chest as he swells, grows, and climaxes within his love. Warmth envelopes both of them. Cheshire's body vibrates, stomach muscles spasming, ass clenching, laying his head on Jonathan's back.

Cheshire stops moving, but Jonathan does not, nearing his own climax. However, Cheshire will not let such a sweet reward be wasted on the streets of Mirus. He pulls from Jonathan, who gasps when Cheshire leaves his body, and turns him around, keeping a hand on Jonathan at all times, lest he reappear. The mask will not allow Cheshire to taste his love, so he turns away to face the street, takes hold of Jonathan's cock and guides it to his own ass, awaiting the stiff, wondrous ache.

Jonathan keeps hold of his sword and shirt in his left hand and wraps his thick right arm around Cheshire's body and pulls him back against him. Cheshire welcomes him in a single thrust, legs about to buckle. Jonathan lifts Cheshire from the air, arm wrapped tightly around him, and repays the hard thrusts into his love. Cheshire leans his head back on Jonathan's shoulder, body at the mercy of Jonathan's surge. Dancing at the precipice already, taking everything Jonathan has to give as passers-by stare through them, Jonathan climaxes, biting at Cheshire's ear.

Cheshire's eyes flutter back, feeling the hot breaths in his ears, and welcoming Jonathan's warmth into his body. Both stay motionless, except for their breaths and heartbeats gently swaying them back and forth. Jonathan kisses the side and back of Cheshire's neck while continuing to pulse within him. Cheshire wants nothing more than to feel Jonathan's lips against his own.

Once Jonathan releases Cheshire from his embrace, Cheshire slides Jonathan's trousers up to his waist and tucks his still-swollen cock inside, securing it for good measure. More than the fantastical adventure they both shared, Jonathan's smile washes Cheshire in a warm glow in the fading light of dusk, as if some angelic figure shines down upon him, if he believed in such things.

"I am sorry I kept you," says Jonathan.

"I am yours to keep," says Cheshire.

Damn it. Cheshire leads Jonathan by the hand up the stairs, where they first encountered each other. With no one in sight at either end, top, or bottom, Cheshire wipes his hand over his face, dismissing the Mask of Light back into his glove. Their simultaneous reemergence into the physical world startles Jonathan, who looks around, more concerned with Cheshire's exposure than his own.

Before he says a word, Cheshire jumps and wraps his arms around Jonathan's neck, kissing him firmly, slowly. Jonathan wraps his right arm around Cheshire's waist to keep him in the air once more. Cheshire's head swirls, able to fall asleep in Jonathan's arms immediately. There is no telling how long they were lost in their embrace. The last light of dusk has been replaced with the work of the lamplighters. He could accompany Jonathan back to the castle and share the night with Jonathan and March. It would fill his cup after so much turmoil has sloshed its contents free.

"Ahem." A woman with a large basket of groceries waits on the stairs below them.

They look at her, lips still pressed together, and cannot help but laugh. This woman, who sought food for her husband or family, comes across a fully naked Cheshire, feet dangling, in the arms of a half-naked Jonathan.

"Pardon us," says Jonathan, ever the gentleman, without lowering Cheshire to the ground. They have been caught in worse predicaments.

The joyous feeling filling inside Cheshire slips away. As the woman passes, Cheshire notices the same hooded figure impersonating his mother. The night and lantern glow conceal her face, but the cloak is the same.

The woman passes, huffing and grumbling. She should at least chuckle at the awkward show she stumbled upon.

Cheshire looks into Jonathan's eyes, catching the twilight. His smile fades.

"Do not stop smiling," says Cheshire.

"How can I not?" Jonathan kisses Cheshire gently on the lips. "I see in your eyes you are about to leave once more."

"It is my nature."

A pit forms in Cheshire's stomach. The tepid night air creeps between them as Jonathan lowers Cheshire to the steps.

He looks to the bottom of the stairs again. The woman has moved to the other side of the street, yet still waits, face unseen.

"Do you see her?" Cheshire asks Jonathan.

"The woman in the cloak? Yes."

If Jonathan can see her, she is not some illusion or ghost. The answer, this confirmation, gives Cheshire a wave of relief he did not know he needed. Until now, Cheshire believed this woman to be a figment of his own exhaustion or a spirit to torment him—a shadow of the past. This is proof she is neither, she is real, and therefore she can be caught to pay for the pain she has caused.

Cheshire rests the side of his head on Jonathan's chest, keeping his eyes on the woman. "Every step away," says Cheshire.

"Is a step back to you." Jonathan runs his fingers through his lavender hair. He will not ask any more questions. This is not their way.

With a final kiss, Cheshire takes a step back and waves his gloved hand over his face again, summoning the Mask of Light onto his face and vanishing before Jonathan. The focus of his eyes shifts, trying to find Cheshire again, chest heavy with breaths. Is this how Jonathan and March always look when he leaves?

Cheshire cannot remember a time when he looked Jonathan or March in the eyes before departing. His custom is always to disappear before they notice him gone. He always thought it a fun, mischievous game, but now he realizes why it has become a habit. Seeing the twinkle fade from Jonathan's eyes and his smile shrink into pressed lips cracks Cheshire's already broken heart.

He turns and walks down the stairs, leaving Jonathan, unable to bear his expression. A crushing weight presses down on Cheshire's chest. He fights against the muscles of his face, biting and twisting his lips to quell any tears from forming. He turns back, unlike him, and watches Jonathan trudge up the stairs and vanish when he crosses into the next tier of Stonehaven.

Below, the woman has disappeared from the street. Cheshire will not sleep until he finds her, and if not her, then the Gryphon. One, no, both will suffer for leaving him no choice but to leave his loves without him tonight, and instead share a bed with Mary Anne. This all must end soon, Cheshire will see to it. One way or another.

CHAPTER 25
MARCH

By the time the lamplighters climb their rickety ladders to bring a warm glow to the streets of Stonehaven at the fading light, the masses in the Quadrangle dwindle, leaving only the few patrons who sit and drink themselves into oblivion within the Far Side Tavern. Seven empty bottles of rum crowd March's side of the table to the Twins' four bottles of wine. March, Lysander, and Uriah hold their liquor better than any other soul passed out against the walls, in chairs, under tables, and on the bar.

Lysander and Uriah did not converse or rile the crowd; their presence was enough to empower the townspeople to discuss a "new Mirus," and "a return to Mirus," without the need to divulge any part of their plan. Throughout the afternoon of silence and drinking, they briefly exchanged glances—facial twitches and subtle movements to let March know they have their own unspoken language, as she and Jonathan do.

March has learned enough for one night, the depth of the Twins' influence, and pushes away from the table, fingertips buzzing from the drink, but nothing more.

"Considering the amount of rum you put away, shall we accompany you back to the castle?" Uriah asks, finishing the last drop from his goblet, showing no signs of his own drunkenness except a red hue in his face and the slightest of slurs.

"Your chivalry knows no bounds." March flips her chair around, pushes it under the table, and walks into the night. "I will manage."

The wooden legs of the Twins' chairs scrape and knock against the wooden floor, the iron of their weapons scrape against the table, and their boots soon crunch the dirt behind March. They catch up and walk at her sides—a set of mismatched bookends—and continue to mask their inebriation, or try to at least. The slight wobble of their shadows on the ground from the moonlight or the loose swing of their arms give them away.

It is disappointing and disgusting they all have the same destination. She could find some reason, any reason, to venture into the city to separate from them but feels it unwise to allow them to reach the castle before her. March leaves their words hanging in the air, putting several paces between them, tired of smelling their alcohol-laden breath.

"There is no need for warriors the likes of us to be at odds," says Lysander. "There is much we can offer each other—even greater gifts."

"Such gifts," says Uriah, the slight slur in his words rearing its head. "Gifts no one else in all of Wonder could give to you."

"There is nothing you two can offer I would ever want." The tips of March's fingers tingle again, not from the alcohol but from the need to reach for her blades. If she drew them, there is a chance she could defeat the Twins in their current condition, but finds little amusement and satisfaction in defeating them in the night? She will defeat them with their wits and with an audience.

"Are you sure?" Uriah asks again with long, annoying, drawn-out vowels, more persistent than he asked in the tavern.

Townspeople, still about their business at this late hour, stop at the sight of the three walking in the city together, watching with wide eyes.

Lysander hums a deep off-tune shanty, filling the quiet night as they draw closer to the Crest and the castle.

"How can we gain your trust?" asks Uriah.

March laughs deep in her stomach at the suggestion, the assumption, the gall these two possess. "Trust? You fucking idiots. With our sordid history, you expect me to trust a word out of your mouths? Any dealings we had are finished."

"Precisely what we wish to discuss with you," says Uriah. "We guarantee you will be unable to refuse the gift we have especially for you."

Something more than lust churns in their minds, behind their eyes, yet entertaining the Twins is like entering a cistern contaminated with pig shit. In order to find out what they plot, she must tolerate and wade into their filth.

"No," says March, expecting her rejection to quicken their steps, but the uneven sound of their footsteps comes to a stop. *Fuck*. She left a hook for them, and they returned one of their own, enough to pique March's suspicions. If she turns to talk with them, they win this match. *Not this night.*

Their game continues until they reach the border of the Crest, where the Twins slowly catch up to March and stop again and again trying to bait her, laughing, thinking it amusing or playful, but to March it only serves to increase her nausea.

"Before we reach the castle," Lysander calls after her, "we would have a word with you."

"You have had far too many."

"You will give us occasion," Lysander snaps.

March stops, fingernails tapping, dancing, on the round ball of her pummel, tempting her. The castle waits two tiers above, and all she needs to do is motion with her head when they reach the gatehouse, and the archers would rain down iron-tipped arrows on her enemies. Such a sweet song it would make—the high piercing notes of the arrows and bolts cutting through the air.

"I will give you nothing," says March.

When they reach the castle's tier, the guards atop the parapets click and give a sharp whistle to signal March's return, and the door in the gate opens before she can reach it. It no longer creaks after Pat and Bill's reinforcements; it slides with the heft of a vault door.

The guards' armor clenches and clangs at the sight of Lysander and Uriah trailing March through the door, ready to protest. A side glance from March orders them to stand down and seal the door behind them with a loud *thunk*. She turns to face them for the first time when they reach the center of the bailey.

"We knew you would warm up to us," says Uriah, beginning again, before she can turn away from them. "Wait. We have one particular gift. One we know you will be most eager to accept."

"And you still have not told me what you two expect in exchange for such a gift?"

"Terms can be discussed at a later time," says Uriah. "First, allow us the chance to tell you what it is. Make no mistake, you are Wonderland's prize, and we do want to fuck you more than any woman in this world or the next." Uriah's tone shifts. "But, in truth, we know full and well we shall never have you; not yet, anyway. You have made it quite clear. We simply keep up the facade to grate at your skin. We do thoroughly enjoy the rise we can elicit from you."

Is this game, honesty or strategy? Either way, their bodies betray their words, cocks fighting against the thick fabric of their robes. Lysander squeezes at his bulge as if to relieve pressure. Uriah stands, too pompous for his own good, allowing his robe to sway with his, as if it would have any effect on March.

"No sexual reciprocity needed, but you will want—" Lysander's response is cut short, and both his and Uriah's attention move over

March's shoulders, to someone behind her, heels clacking on the cobblestones.

She knows the quick rhythm of the gait too well, and dread weighs heavily in March's chest. The Twins walk past her. She glances over her shoulder to see her mother, Bronwen, approaching, walking between Lysander and Uriah.

"Hello, daughter." Bronwen winces at March then calls back to the Twins. "I shall join you in your bedchamber, presently."

"As you wish," they say together.

"Of course, you are fucking them."

"Do not speak so crass to me." Bronwen tightens the fur collar of her robe.

"I speak how I like."

"Not to your mother."

"If you ever deserved such a moniker, I have yet to witness it in all my days."

A soldier, not of Mirus, runs past as they converse and catches up with Lysander and Uriah at the top of the stairs to the keep. March must consider Bronwen is nothing more than a distraction on the Twins' part to make sure March does not hear their conspiracy. March squints, peering past Bronwen as she continues to speak rubbish of family, to read the soldier's lips, but Lysander and Uriah position him with his back turned, glancing every so often to let her know they still play the game.

"Besides," Bronwen continues, "someone in this family must have standards and the good sense to continue our legacy."

"Legacy?" Bile churns in March's stomach. "You think they will give you a child?"

"They understand excellent breeding. After all, they wanted you above all others."

"And you believe they will settle for you."

Bronwen laughs. "I have already enjoyed the company of both brothers several times."

"As have most of the women of the Garden, half the Crest, and more than a handful of servants from the castle, and every brothel in Wonderland. What wonderful company to count yourself among."

"I know you already had your own arrangement with them, under my roof, no less. Why not give in, surrender to their desires, their lusts, and all will be well? You already had a taste. Enjoy the entire banquet."

"You know nothing."

Bronwen's smug expression slowly melts. "You understand nothing."

"I understand all too well." March waves her hands in the air between them like trying to dispel some noxious odor. "This conversation is done. When are you returning to your home?"

"Our home."

"Your home."

"This night," says Bronwen, "after I have had my fill of the brothers."

March points past her at the Twins entering the keep as the soldier crosses the bailey toward her to return to the city. If March can rid herself of Bronwen, she still has a chance to question him.

"They wait for you. Off with you," says March. Bronwen remains steadfast, adding to March's vexation. "Why have you journeyed out of the castle when what you obviously want *waits* for you inside?"

"Because I required a much-needed word with my daught... with you," Bronwen corrects herself. "These next few days will be dangerous."

"I am well aware."

"You should reconsider Lysander and Uriah's offer."

"What offer?"

"To be with them, give yourself to them, give them what they want, and you will be safe. You shall be protected."

The skin on March's face and arms burn. "Only you would suggest I sleep with two men who you have already fucked and plan to fuck shortly. Then again, you always had a predilection for younger men."

"I did what I had to do, and enjoyed every moment, to keep myself safe."

"And there's the rub." March's fingers curl toward the handle of her swords. "Why am I even entertaining this conversation? You never, once in your life, have thought about my safety. This is about you. It has always been about you. And this is yet one more attempt in a long line to pawn me to Lysander and Uriah, hoping it will gain you favor with them."

Bronwen's response is a knowing squint, accepting all accusations proudly. "Now, I suggest you accompany me to their bedchamber."

"No words have been invented to describe the hate I bear for thee," March says in Old Prodigium, the original language of Wonderland. Less than a handful can read it and far less recall how to speak it.

"How formal. You do remember your education. I feared the two scoundrels you choose to bunk with might have affected your wits along with your senses and taste," Bronwen replies in the same tongue. "See, our family has—"

"Another mention of family and I will slice your throat before another false and foul word leaves your mouth. You will bleed out here on the cobbles, and every soldier and guard will watch the life leave your body as I stand over you and wait for you to die."

March wishes for any noise to fill the empty bailey—crickets, wind rustling through the canopy of distant trees, or the songs of nightingales or nightjars—but the gentle sounds of nature cannot break through the harsh stone of the city. The pops and crackles of the torches from atop the wall, the slight shift of steel armor against chain mail, and her mother's breaths, intentionally provoke March.

The soldier approaches, less than ten paces away.

"Go join them. Now. While I allow you to walk away," March says slowly to make her intention clear.

Bronwen opens the top of her robe, revealing her cleavage shoved up by a tight corset beneath, and flaps the end of it, turning away and walking back to the keep.

The moment Bronwen turns her back, the soldier passes, and March swoops her leg behind the soldier, kicking his foot out from under him.

He cannot catch his misstep, foot hooking behind the other, and falls to the ground with a crunch. She pulls one of her swords, enjoying its hums as it breaks free and breathes, flips the soldier to his back with her foot, and holds the point of her blade to his throat.

The soldier stretches his neck and tries to crawl back. "You cannot kill me," he says. "We have a pact."

"Look around you." Archers, members of the Castle Guard, and the soldiers near the gate watch with eager anticipation. "Do you think anyone present will help you? I will puncture both your lungs before you can utter your first scream. And no one will find your body. Rest assured, your meager absence will not affect our agreement in the slightest. What did you tell them? I shall ask once."

With a shaking jaw, the soldier holds nothing back. "I told my lords five bodies were found, men of Adamas."

"When?"

"This morning. Killed the day prior from the look of it."

"Anything more? You stood with them for quite a while."

"They ordered me to do so."

"Ordered you." March huffs. "And then they told you to tell me everything when I stopped you."

"Yes."

Lysander and Uriah anticipated her actions, unable to control their arrogance, wanting to prove their intelligence and their assumed victory. It does not matter to them whether March is aware of their small moves within the city when she already knows their larger plays to come.

She waves the soldier away with her sword before sheathing it. As he scrambles for the door, the thought crosses her mind to kill him or keep him confined to the castle, but the damage has already been done. Both sides will pay a heavy toll for allowing Cheshire to operate unchecked, but in a game of strategy, the best way to combat a loaded deck is a wild card—her wild card.

CHAPTER 26

MARY ANNE

Mary Anne's fork clinks against her plate of cabbage, roasted potatoes, and mutton, barely picked at as she sits alone at dinner. The lonely candelabra of seven candles at the center of the table adds to her isolation in the dark dining hall without windows. Her only company, the rose Jonathan gave her, rests next to her plate. The dozens of empty seats around the table compound the acidic worry churning in her stomach, stealing her appetite. Earlier, the Duchess tried, barely tried, to comfort her, assuring Mary Anne Jonathan would return safely, and Mary Anne wants to believe her. But the last time Jonathan left the castle, the Gryphon brought him back in his arms.

After what must be an hour of sitting alone, rearranging the food on her plate, Grace opens the large door at the far end of the chamber and waits for a response from Mary Anne.

"What do you want?" Mary Anne shouts, out of frustration. So consumed with thoughts of Jonathan, Mary Anne forgot Grace is incapable of responding. Her lips move to apologize but stop; queens do not apologize. It does not stop the swell of guilt. Mary Anne rises from the table, takes her rose, and meets Grace at the door, head bowed, not proud of her words. "Lead on."

Grace leads Mary Anne into a new, unexplored chamber of the castle. From its many round couches, ferns, and picturesque paintings nearly reaching the height of the lofty ceilings, it appears this room's purpose is for entertaining a great number of people. Many corners of the castle remain a mystery to Mary Anne. Since her arrival, there has been little time for leisurely activities, let alone sightseeing. Grace closes the door, and Mary Anne selects a plush mauve chaise to sit on while she waits in the expansive room, though she does not know what she waits for. She taps her heel against the smooth marble floor, still on edge, wondering, hoping Jonathan will come through the door unscathed and whisk her away back to their bedchamber. Though he would try to explain what happened, it would not matter. Having him back next to her, being in his arms, will be apology enough.

The door swings open and, to Mary Anne's disappointment, Bill steers a trolley or tea cart of sorts, back wheels larger than the front, with a long linen cloth draped over it. Whatever the cloth conceals, it is not a tea service. Weiss follows, and the Duchess rounds out their number and utters something to Grace, which Mary Anne cannot make out, before ushering her from the room. The door shuts, but not before Mary Anne catches a glimpse of at least four guards.

The Duchess waits a moment before spinning to face Mary Anne with her small painted smile, and as she approaches, Mary Anne questions whether the Duchess took the pause to collect her thoughts or stuff them away until she can focus on them during a secluded solitude. Perhaps the events of these past weeks weigh on her as much as everyone else, even though she chooses not to reveal it to the others.

Bill parks the trolley in front of Mary Anne, and Weiss removes the long white cloth carefully, before throwing it onto another nearby couch. Four unassuming, ordinary, everyday objects lie separately on a small silver tray—an old necklace, whose chain and locket are covered with a thin layer of patina, a polished opal stone, the bottom half of what appears to be a broken scepter, and finally, a bent copper broach.

The bottom of the Duchess's large gown swings like a bell when she stops at the trolley. Her hands float through the air like feathers caught in a breeze and beckon Mary Anne to rise. She takes her place with everyone surrounding the trolley—the Duchess opposite her, Weiss to her right, and Bill to her left. From one of his many leather pockets on his many belts, Bill produces a jagged cut, but extraordinarily beautiful, polished red gem and places it in the middle of the four peculiar objects.

"Do you think—"

The Duchess cuts off Mary Anne by holding up a single finger before she has a chance to discuss Jonathan.

"We must focus on more pressing matters. We hope this day to be a turning point for you, Mary Anne," says the Duchess. "Thank you for meeting us here, off the beaten path, as some would say. With Lysander and Uriah and their men prowling the corridors, it is of the utmost importance we continue our work without their intrusion. Therefore, we will meet in a different location every day. Your handmaiden will bring you to us."

"But will the guards not give away our location?" asks Mary Anne.

"They would, if I had not stationed twelve other sets around the castle on different levels, and four pairs ordered to walk as if they have somewhere important to be. I also informed your handmaiden to stand outside other doors throughout our meetings to mislead them."

"Masterfully clever," says Weiss.

"Indeed," says Mary Anne.

"To the task at hand. Take a close look, dear." The Duchess waves her hands over each of the objects on the trolley. "These artifacts are a piece of Wonderlandian history."

"They are lovely," says Mary Anne. Beautiful as they are, all pale in comparison to the ruby gem at the center of the table. Glints of light move along its sharp edges, almost as if it is alive.

"Each once belonged to a previous queen of Wonderland," the Duchess says. "As with the relics in the reliquary, imbued with the Arcana of the Old Ones, perhaps some remnant of the queens' power remains in these simple trinkets. Perhaps they can serve as a spark or kindling to awaken the dormant power within you."

Mary Anne reaches down and picks up the opal first, handling it with care, and rubs its smooth surface with her fingers. Weiss stares unblinking at Mary Anne, Bill looks around the chamber and blinks slowly as if bored with the situation, but the Duchess does not take her eyes from the gem on the trolley.

Nothing.

After a few turns of the stone, Mary Anne returns the opal to its tray and picks up the broken scepter—the base of what she assumes is its golden handle. It ends abruptly with a jagged crack. She has not the slightest clue what to do with any of these objects. Mary Anne holds the handle aloft and gently swings it back and forth.

Nothing.

Mary Anne holds the necklace in her hand and examines it, searching for a hidden detail, which is not there, and imagines the center of the ruby glowing like a heartbeat. She holds the necklace closer to the gem.

Nothing.

"Should I feel something?" Mary Anne asks, setting down the necklace.

"Do you feel anything?" asks Weiss.

"I do not know what I am supposed to feel."

"We do not know," says the Duchess. "Only the queen knows. We can only dream."

"This is ridiculous." Instead of reaching for the broach, Mary Anne grabs the gem and holds it out in her palm between their quartet.

Weiss pulls at the tips of his thumbs. Bill raises his eyes, finally showing interest. The Duchess squints and spins the ring on her finger.

Mary Anne studies each point and slanted face of the ruby. Surely, it would summon some feeling within her chest, her stomach, or the faintest of tingling in her body. Nothing. She does not bother putting the gemstone back on the trolley and instead hands it to Bill.

A tingling does take over the back of Mary Anne's head and sinks to her stomach—shame. One moment, the overwhelming pride of being proven worthy by Wonderland surged through her. The next, the nauseous drop of feeling insignificant once more. How can she pass a test if no one knows the correct answer or outcome? They describe the Arcana as if it were the blood and breath of Wonderland, coursing through the land and air, giving life to the world. How can she begin to imagine how to *summon* such power or know what it might feel like?

"No," Mary Anne says sharply. "I have made it this far. Wonderland chose me. I am worthy. I am ready." She snatches the gem back from Bill. "I have passed the First and Second Tenet. The only obstacle keeping me from becoming queen, *to be a queen,* is the vague ending of the Third and unlocking the Fourth, and yet no one can tell me what it will feel like, what I should feel, or how it will manifest."

"Precisely," Weiss says, wiping his spectacles with the long end of his sleeve.

"How did it affect the previous queens? When did they gain access to the Arcana in relation to when the throne room doors opened?"

"I wish I could give you a certain answer," says the Duchess.

"Give me *any* answer." Mary Anne points the ruby at the Duchess. "I need every possible piece of information, from the Book of Queens, any other tome available, or conversations with the elders or the alderman. I must have everything."

The Duchess takes the gem from Mary Anne and weighs it in her hand. "The answer I can give is the answer you do not want to hear. They were all different. It happened at different times for them, some quicker than others. It all is relative. In the past we have brought in Wonderland's most revered soothsayers and seekers to read bones, the portent of rune stones, and interpret the stars. There is no way for us to know."

"At least tell me what they could do," Mary Anne pleads. The further she journeys down this path, each answer is met with three more riddles. As the Duchess inhales, Mary Anne speaks for her. "Allow me to guess. It was different for them all?"

"It was," says Bill, taking the gem back from the Duchess and returning it to the pocket on his belt. "But the one thing they all had in common—their power was unmatched."

"Not so unmatched they could prevent their own murders." The words escape Mary Anne before she can catch them.

"You speak of matters you do not understand," says the Duchess.

"Tell me. Show me. I have wandered these halls and found no trace, painting, or portrait of the past queens, and all I have to go off is a book in a dead language. Who were they? What powers did they possess? What did they accomplish? How did they die? And before you say they were different, give me each of their examples, then."

A hush of Mary Anne's creation fills the room. It is awkward for no one but her. The others soften their gaze, each looking a different direction, recalling a memory perhaps.

"The next time we meet, we will go over the Fourth Tenet in detail," says the Duchess. "We have not spoken of it because it can be quite overwhelming. You are making your way through the Third Tenet, and are nearly through; the throne room doors are proof of it. Now, more than ever, we must prepare you for the last leg of your journey."

With the Twins in the castle, there is no guarantee how soon they will all convene again. Mary Anne will look to March to help translate the book. Despite their disagreements, their goals align for now.

"I thank you," says Mary Anne. "But I will not wait until our next meeting. Tell me something. I am tired of crumbs."

The Duchess waves her hand, and Weiss and Bill, with the trolley, make their way toward the door. Mary Anne expects the Duchess to sit with her, as they have many times before. Instead, the Duchess takes hold of one of her free hands and rubs the top with her thumbs. She waits for the door to close behind them.

"My dear. The chapters over the Fourth Tenet speak of the queen's ultimate authority in Wonderland."

"Yes?"

The Duchess's expression, or lack thereof, puts Mary Anne on edge. "I cannot put it any simpler. The queen has ultimate authority in and over Wonderland. Whatever she decrees does not just become law, it becomes the fabric of reality if she wishes it to be. If you commanded the flowers to bloom in winter, they would follow your command. If a mountain stood in your way, it would fall before you. At any point, if you want the entirety of Wonderland's people to kneel to you, you only need to speak the words and it will be done."

Mary Anne pulls her hand from the Duchess, at first fearing bad news, but this information is far more terrifying. The word impossible rears its head in Mary Anne's mind again, and goosebumps cover her arms, uncertain if it is from fear or exhilaration. She believed ultimate authority meant sovereignty, not dominion. It all becomes clear to Mary Anne.

"This is the reason Lysander and Uriah fight to keep a queen from the throne."

"Indeed," says the Duchess.

"Why have none of the previous queens not dealt with them before?"

"Balance." The Duchess leads Mary Anne toward the door. "Any queen who killed the last heirs of the kings of Wonderland would soon find the country in open rebellion."

"But would she not have the power to stop the people?"

"Stop them, how exactly? Bend them to her will? Kill them? Imprison them? The prior queens have been both benevolent and not. A queen must rule with a precarious balance of respect and love for her subjects, and a healthy dose of fear from those who would dare challenge her reign. Though the queen possesses the power, she must know when it is wise to use it."

"Balance," Mary Anne repeats. "To have such power, a queen must have equal amounts of restraint."

"More," says the Duchess. "There are more stipulations in the Book of Queens. Ultimate authority does not mean unlimited power. We will go over them soon."

Mary Anne does not have the answers she sought, but an answer nonetheless. No wonder the Duchess and Weiss were vague about the Fourth Tenet. Had Mary Anne heard this weeks ago, before witnessing the few instances of magic in the world, she would never have believed it.

"Tomorrow evening, I shall spend the day in the city, and upon my return Grace will guide me to our next location." Mary Anne collects her flower from the chaise before they leave the chamber.

"Agreed. And while you are about the city, Weiss and I shall begin planning this festival of yours. It shall be an event to remember, taking up every street in Mirus. Everyone will celebrate, and we shall host some of Mirus's elite here in the castle. It shall be glorious."

With Jonathan unaccounted for, she did not think to mention it, but of course the news reached the Duchess's ears long before Mary Anne returned to the castle. The Duchess pats the top of Mary Anne's hand before opening the door.

"Off with you. Dream of being the queen you need to be; the queen we all need you to be."

When she returns to her bedchamber, a single candle in one of the many standing candelabras nears its end, casting dancing shadows on Jonathan and March asleep in each other's embrace, legs and arms intertwined, with no worry or concern for Mary Anne. She should feel relief; her faith and trust in Jonathan well placed, but to return to their bed without her, with March no less, coiled around him instead of seeking Mary Anne out to let her know of his return, rips at her heart.

She twirls her flower in hand before setting it on the small table next to her bed.

Mary Anne undresses, drops her gown to the floor, and sits on the edge of the bed untying her boots, all the while feeling Jonathan and March shift, hearing their slow, heavy breaths answer each other.

She slides into bed, keeping distance between them, as the candle dwindles to nothing, leaving them together yet apart in the darkness. Her eyes adjust, and Jonathan's form, his broad shoulders sloping down to his buttocks, becomes visible, more detailed, washed in the grays and blues of the night.

Unable to keep away, Mary Anne lies behind Jonathan, forming to the shape of his body and taking in his warmth. His face nestles in March's pink hair. Even in sleep, she keeps his lips from her. Mary Anne rests her head against his back and rubs her nose and lips against his relaxed muscles and, hesitantly, risks sliding her left arm over and down his body, taking his soft cock in her hand, squeezing it tenderly.

Lost somewhere in the middle of a dream, Jonathan reaches back and drapes his arm over Mary Anne, fingers brushing against her hip before his arm falls limp and heavy upon her body. Any ill feelings Mary Anne may harbor melt away from her body with Jonathan's warmth, as does her heart. Jonathan touches her, holds her of his own accord without coaxing or interference from March. Perhaps he did enjoy their meeting of the flesh the day before and holds some place for her, however small. No matter; Mary Anne will accept it and watch it blossom, like the flower, the beautiful flower, he gave her. A gesture not to be ignored, either. As Mary Anne drifts to sleep holding Jonathan, he holding her, and her time with the Duchess this evening, endless possibilities and desires which once were distant dreams take shape and manifest themselves in the palm of her hand.

CHAPTER 27
JONATHAN

The crashing slam of the bedchamber door against the wall rips Jonathan from his peaceful slumber, heart racing, eyes foggy. Mary Anne gasps as she wakes. March rolls from the bed and grabs the sword she keeps beside it. The Duchess, dressed in her morning robe and hair pulled back in a braid, out of breath herself, waits for them, hand still pressed against the door.

"The castle walls," she says through heavy breaths. "Immediately," before running out.

Mary Anne stumbles, trying to step into a gown.

"Forgive me," says Jonathan, handing Mary Anne her open-sided gown and silver belt. "There is no time."

Jonathan catches his trousers, tossed by March. She slips into her own trousers and whips her heavy gray longcoat overhead, slipping it onto her arms, and picks up her shoulder harness and swords as she bolts from the bedchamber. Jonathan and Mary Anne follow, still trying to shake the sleep from their eyes and the dream fog from their mind, running down four hallways before Jonathan realizes he still carries his trousers in hand. It is not until he nears the main corridor of the keep he can hobble into them, jumping on one leg then the other, leaving them unlaced, hanging low on his waist.

The Duchess is the first to disappear into the bright white of dawn through the doors held open by the Doorman, then March, with Jonathan and Mary Anne following close behind. Jonathan blinks and squints to focus and gain his bearings in the sudden shift of dark to light. The Duchess remains at the top of the stairs and waves them forward.

None of them took the time or even thought of their boots. Their bare feet slap against the stones of the bailey as they run to the eastern stairs. With one hand, Jonathan keeps his trousers held up to his waist and with the other takes Mary Anne's hand for her to keep pace. Once they reach the tall wooden stairway, Mary Anne's hand slips from his, and she leans against the rails and catches her breath.

"Go on," she says. "I will catch up."

Jonathan looks up the center of the spiraling stairs. High above, March's hand grips the rail in rhythm as she climbs almost to the top. "Forgive me, once more," he tells Mary Anne, swooping her up in his arms and racing up the stairs, taking three at a time until they reach the top of the castle wall, and finally sets her down.

Castle guards fly by to meet March and Dormy at the mounted spyglass above the gatehouse. The long brass cylinders shine in the waking dawn. Dormy holds it in position while March peers through it, turning and focusing one of the many rings. She pulls away and her pressed lips let Jonathan know the game is on, and the Twins have made the first move.

Jonathan nestles his face into the brass eyepiece and his lashes flick against the glass. Far in the distance, the hazy details come into focus on the spine of a rooftop in the middle of Stonehaven, between the Forge and the eastern end of the Row. The sun crests over the mountains, lowering its beams onto the city, where the trickles of blood discoloring the shingled roofs become apparent.

A tall, bloody pike, at least seven feet in length, holds up a naked body like a macabre weather vane or scarecrow, arms and legs limp and splayed. The pike's shaft enters between the body's legs, not centered, probably through the soft bit between thigh and balls, and out of the gaping wound where a head should be. The ragged flesh peels back from the muscle—not a clean cut. This man was made to suffer.

"There are nine more," says Dormy.

"Nine more what?" asks Mary Anne.

"Ten in total?" asks Jonathan. "Show me."

Dormy swivels and repositions the spyglass to each body by memory. Every one in the same or worse condition as the last: arms snapped off at the elbow, bowels spill out on thatch and shingle and already provide for the ravens. The last, far to the west, is only a torso, with stumps for arms and legs, pierced sideways through the ribs.

Mary Anne ushers Jonathan back to look through the spyglass. She squints, scratches her face, and jerks back when the body comes into focus. She clasps her hand to her mouth and narrows her eyes repeatedly, trying to make sense of what she has seen.

"Cheshire," says Mary Anne in a disdainful half-snarl.

"He may be the cause, but he is not the culprit," says March.

"This is not his way. These bodies are on display for all to see." Jonathan pinches the bridge of his nose and turns to one of the nearby guards. "Are Lysander and Uriah still in the castle?"

"Yes," the guard answers. "They left and returned before dawn."

"We need to tie fucking bells around their necks," says March.

"I have some," says Dormy.

March tucks the wild hairs at Dormy's temples and takes hold of the spyglass again to examine the bodies further. "They held true to their word."

"Explain," says Mary Anne.

March huffs. "A soldier of Lysander and Uriah informed me five bodies were discovered two days ago. This is their retribution, as promised."

"So we must pay for Cheshire's misdeeds? Can he not control himself for a day, an hour, or any amount of time?" Mary Anne snaps. "Why would he do this?"

"Because I told him to do so," says March. "I told him before we convened in the council chambers."

Dormy hides in the spyglass, and Jonathan hangs his head. He would bring the brim of his hat down if he remembered it.

"Do you realize what you have done?"

"First, yes," says March. "Second, understand I do not answer to you. I am not one of your servants for you to bark or command for your pampered needs."

Mary Anne's chest rises and falls with increasingly deep breaths the more March speaks. "Do not speak to me as if I am weak. I am not weak."

"Those who have to say what they are, or shout it, are never what they claim to be. If you must say it aloud, it must not be true."

"Enough." Mary Anne seethes. "We must reconvene and plan our next move."

Jonathan stands between both women. "I fear there is no time. The longer we leave this incident unattended, the quicker the poison of Lysander and Uriah will spread through the townspeople. The gruesome spectacle of these bodies will stir up further dissension amongst the people. They will want to respond. Those who are brave enough will respond, and we cannot have innocents becoming murderers."

"Send March," says Mary Anne. "They are her *responsibility*, after all. Go out as you are. I am sure she can easily stop them once and for all."

Dormy takes the collar of her oversized coat and pulls it over her head.

March, not the least bit bothered, says, "I can put a stop to this with the tip of my blade through your temple. Then all our problems are done."

"Not all of them," mutters Jonathan.

"Jonathan," says Mary Anne.

"Apologies."

"Mine, at least," says March. "But I shall go and return before midday."

"No," says Jonathan. Disagreeing with March sets a foil taste in his mouth, yet it must be done.

Her head ticks toward him. The slightest movement, but Jonathan knows she is taken aback by his unexpected opposition, being of like mind at all times.

"In this instance, I believe a calmer head and sly words will prevail." He winks at March. "We need not add any more to the body count and risk upsetting the already precariously lopsided weighted scales. Besides, March's place is better suited in the keep, closer to Lysander and Uriah."

"Closer, indeed," Mary Anne says under her breath.

"Speak again," says March.

"I shall go with you, Jonathan," Mary Anne protests. "My place must be in the city, among the people. I told them I would be there for them, but how can I do so if I am confined to the castle? What if I command you not to go?"

"You are not queen yet," says March, standing side by side with Jonathan.

Jonathan touches Mary Anne's cheek. "I must make sure it is safe enough for you first."

March returns to the spyglass. "The bodies are what Lysander and Uriah want us, us specifically, to see. If their goal was to divide the people, they would place the corpses in places of prominence: the Forge, the Row, the Long Bridge, at the foot of the castle. They mean to draw us, and perhaps you, Mary Anne, out into the city. If the people revolt, a stray blade to your side is easily hidden and justifiable."

"Well said," says Jonathan.

"They bait us," says Mary Anne. "They bait you while they sit in comfort within our walls. What if it is a trap?"

"Do not worry," says Jonathan. "It most definitely is a trap. And we will not know its intent if we do not trigger it. They made their move, and now we must make ours. One cannot move without the other, and we hang in a stalemate until their armada arrives."

"What of the Gryphon?" asks Mary Anne. "Where is he? Can he not go in your stead?"

Jonathan and March share a knowing glance and know he has not returned to the castle. Little does he know Cheshire is in the city as well, or perhaps he does and stays at a distance in order to keep the fighting, at least Cheshire's, far from the castle. As much as he may not want to admit it, they have met their equal in each other as far as stratagem.

"He is just there," says Dormy, pointing into the city. "With several soldiers. They remove the bodies from the pikes. Oh, now he's gone."

"Thank goodness," says Mary Anne.

"There you have it." Jonathan kisses March on the forehead. "The Gryphon attends to the fallen. Perhaps you can aid Mary Anne in her lessons for the time being while I am away, and we can all reconvene at midday."

Both March and Mary Anne have no retort, at least expressed out loud. They know this is another task in need of immediate attention, and besides Weiss, March is the only one to help translate the Old Prodigium in her book. If Mary Anne can draw closer to the Arcana, the entire game is over, every player wiped from the board. History may yet repeat itself. The thought of which fills Jonathan's cup with a sense of sweet relief and bitter dread, creating a foul mixture.

Without the time to return to Mary Anne's bedchamber, Jonathan sizes the boots of a guard two positions to the right. "Soldier, sir, would you mind terribly if I borrowed your boots so I do not have to travel back into the keep?"

"Yes, sir," the soldier answers, not quite certain.

"I shall return them to you, I promise," says Jonathan.

"Or fashion me with a new pair?" the soldier asks.

"Done," March answers.

The soldier obliges, among the call of other soldiers asking in jest if Jonathan wants anything of theirs to receive it new in return, and steps on his right heel and slides the boot off and then the other, and hands both to Jonathan.

"It is settled, then." Jonathan steps into each and pulls them up by the cuff—a little loose, but a close fit.

"Not quite." March presents a small vial of Jonathan's elixir from her pocket.

His heart exhales. He would be nothing without March. She uncorks the vial, holding it in her mouth and hands it to Jonathan while she laces his trousers, tugging at his hips, leaving them sitting low on his body. Jonathan closes his eyes, tilts his head back, taking this moment for himself, and drinks the cold liquid. It slides over his tongue and coats his throat and relaxes his shoulders he did not realize were tensed.

"Will you not take a sword?" asks Mary Anne. "Any guard can offer you theirs."

"The weapon I need this day is not a sword yet is just as sharp."

After leaving the castle grounds, Jonathan slips his hands into his trouser pockets, with his elixir, and walks into the Crest and onto the high ways. The severity of the situation should require Jonathan to act with further haste, but sprinting through the city will only invite more suspicion and attention.

Far to the east and west, the sun shimmers along armor on rooftops. Groups of six soldiers quickly work together at each site to slide the dead off the pikes to dispose of the bodies. Four men carefully remove the body and two soldiers work at removing the pike driven into the wood. The odd one or two vomit onto the thatch or shingles when the bodies slosh blood onto them or unexpectedly spill more entrails onto their arms. The soldiers carry the bodies to the edge of the two-or-three-story tenements, mouth something below, to other waiting soldiers perhaps, drop the bodies out of sight, and climb their way down.

Jonathan passes from the Crest into Stonehaven, and the shouts of the townspeople grow in number the farther down he travels: gasps, shouts of anger, heated arguments, and the weeping of those who worry their loved ones are gone. They wail for fathers, husbands, and sons.

Once Jonathan reaches the Row, he hears three familiar voices addressing a growing crowd. Below, the Red Knight, out of his armor, and the two buffoons who continue to plague Jonathan's path, Morgan and Bartholomew, or whatever their names are, stand on large crates of vegetables in the middle of the busy market street like barkers, spewing their lies and hate to the gathering masses.

"Do you see?" the Red Knight shouts. "Do you see what this woman, the false queen, you put your faith in, has wrought upon this city?"

His two stooges punctuate everything the Red Knight says, with "Yea," "False," "Cruel," or "Devil," to provoke the heightened emotions of the townspeople.

"Though our lords are challenged, they seek a peaceful and diplomatic resolution to this conflict," the Red Knight continues. "She chooses violence. Violence against the innocent."

"Why would she do this?" Bartholomew asks.

"Because she does not have your best interest at heart." The Red Knight sweeps his arm out across the crowd, pointing at various townspeople. "She cares only for her own prosperity and not yours."

"Liar," a woman shouts from the back of the crowd, and throws a head of lettuce toward him. Others who support Mary Anne pick up rocks from the ground and look for other objects to throw. A nearby grocer at his stall holds up a small crate of potatoes for townspeople to grab.

"Am I?" The Red Knight clutches his chest, his poor act apparent. Though his heart is filled with deceit, lying out loud is not among his few skills. "We come to you with words, not armed. We come to you with words, while she comes to you with blood. Look to the sky. Is this not proof enough?"

The pelting begins, potatoes fly through the crowd, and Jonathan cannot help but laugh. Potatoes fly overhead. The Red Knight blocks the projectiles with his forearms, Morgan takes a potato to the back of the head and yelps, and Bartholomew catches a small spud and prepares to throw it back. The Red Knight catches his arm—theatrics, every moment.

"Those who were ruthlessly, savagely slain through the night did not belong to your number; they were our men. Our loyal men, ripped apart, dismembered, and shamefully hung, bodies desecrated by the soldiers of Mirus! We will not submit to their fear-mongering or threats."

What?

This must be false, more theatre, or some deception. With their severed heads, and without clothing, there would be no way to identify the dead. If they are from Mirus, it would take at least a day for their loved ones to realize they were missing.

Tensions rise. Those loyal to Lysander and Uriah peppered among the crowd make themselves known, and the crowd turns on itself, shoving, cursing, and punching. To quell the growing fire in the market, Jonathan doubles back toward a stairway one tier higher in order to circle around people to get to the rear of the mob to say his piece and pull their attention from the Red Knight.

Back on the ground, in the shade and shadows between buildings, Jonathan heads for the nearest alleyway—a long, narrow stone arched between buildings with shops above. The sound of the outraged townspeople grows louder as he nears the other end. However, a group of large men, as tall and as broad as Jonathan, block the exit, clear from their posture they waited for him. They wear basic corduroy and leather pants and linen shirts, while others wear wool or leather jerkins and tunics. Jonathan counts the silhouettes of their heads, blurred by the backlight—thirteen, a baker's dozen.

"Difficult to hear the speech from this deep in the alley, gentleman," says Jonathan.

These are not men of Mirus or Adamas, nor are they soldiers; they are fighters, brawlers, specifically sent for, bought, and brought here by the Twins to handle the work their soldiers cannot. They knew. Jonathan wonders if this is coincidence or if there are several other alleys with groups of hired muscle waiting. Jonathan's muscles have loosened, though not completely recovered, but are more than ready to be exercised and put these men to the test and beat the bloody shit out of them.

Jonathan stretches his arms out, measuring the distance. Three feet from fingertip to wall on both sides; wide enough for his swings but also room enough for these men to maneuver around him. He will need to restrain the power of his punches to not kill these men, to abide by their agreement and not add more fuel to the pyre. He rolls his shoulders, stretches his fingers, clenches his fists, and a wave of tightening muscles ripple up his arms, across his shoulder, chest, and torso. Pain lingers slightly from his previous wounds, but he will manage.

He exhales and relaxes his body, poised. "Let's have it, then."

CHAPTER 28

CHESHIRE

Unbeknownst to the specter, the moon looks after Cheshire—a surrogate mother—granting him her soft light to chase this false figure through the streets. If this charlatan believes she can hide in the shadows, the circled orb of his guardian will see her revealed, however elusive.

She dips and turns corners, cloak whipping behind her, then reappears at the end of different alleys, at the top of stairways, or in the middle of streets where the lights from the lanterns silhouette her figure, turning the city he knows into a damned maze. Cheshire climbs rooftops and eaves for a better vantage point to lay eyes upon her, but with a blink, she disappears and appears somewhere else.

His eyes weigh heavy but pushing through exhaustion has become second nature to Cheshire after a thousand years dodging the Ace. Even the moon prepares herself for slumber behind the mountains. In the dim light, a group of six of soldiers of Lysander and Uriah scurry through the streets carrying large, blood-stained burlap sacks like rats ferrying food away to their holes. Blood drops trickle from the poorly concealed dead body and catch the moonlight, shimmering as they fall.

Killing a handful or more soldiers would give him the additional surge of adrenaline he needs. The specter will still continue to appear after he dispatches them. If he is no closer to the Gryphon or the specter by dawn, Cheshire will go on a spree to release his frustration.

Another tier lower in Stonehaven, a different group of six soldiers from Adamas walk the streets suspiciously, without the body but with its blood on their hands. They do not see Cheshire, hidden in the shadow of a narrow alley of two tenements. He waits for the sixth soldier in the group to pass. Though they wear helmets, Cheshire has learned how to reach under their edges, grab at the jaw, twist, and deliver a quick snap of the neck. Sudden deaths are not his favorite, preferring them to linger, but he will make an exception for this soldier.

From the shadow, his footsteps fall silent on the dirt and keep in time with his prey. Within arms distance, Cheshire reaches for the soldier's neck, but as his fingertips graze the steel curve, the woman reappears on the opposite side of the street, less than ten paces away, as if she passed through the wall of the mercer's shop behind her. The shadow of the heavy gray hood she wears obscures the details of her face, but the smallest lock of lavender hair hangs from the unnatural darkness. Not quite the abyss compared to under the Ace's hood, but there is nothing natural about this woman.

Two soldiers turn their heads to look at her, none the least bit startled, as if she stood there the entire time. Perhaps she did, and Cheshire is the one giving more agency to this ghost than he should. Contrariwise, perhaps he ought to treat this woman as more of a threat than he has.

Cheshire stops and turns to face her, letting the soldiers grow distant in his vision. He makes it a point not to blink. He will not allow her to vanish. The woman's cloak, draped closed, hides all detail of her. The hairs on the back of his neck bristle. His heart beats in his face. He charges at the woman masquerading as his mother, but when he reaches her, she vanishes, and Cheshire's palms slam against the brick wall behind her. His nails scrape into the dewy stone into clenched fists.

She appears a block away along the curve of the street. He would think he imagines her, if not for the soldiers and Jonathan being able to see her as well. He is not yet past the point of exhaustion where he cannot tell what is real. It takes at least a week for the hallucinations to set in.

"I tire of this game," he says to the figure, not loud enough for her to hear but sure she knows his mind. "I have others to play."

The woman raises an arm, revealing a light gray gown beneath her cloak, and points somewhere over Cheshire's head. What new hell is this? Will he turn to see nothing, and then turn back for this apparition to be inches from his face? He does not want to heed her signal, yet his curiosity itches at the back of his mind. If this is indeed a ruse, and she closes the gap between them, all the better. He will finally be able to lay hands upon her.

He shifts his eyes first, as he always does, and keeps her figure in the corner of his eye. Nothing. Whatever she points at is farther still. Cheshire breathes deep, braces himself, and cranes his neck.

"By all the devils in every hell."

The woman points far to the west, almost hidden by the curve of the city. Silhouettes of soldiers carefully trek across the rooftops of the temple and tenements toward a headless body skewered upon an iron bar—the bodies Lysander and Uriah's men carried throughout the night.

Even at this distance, the armor of Mirusian soldiers is unmistakable. And among their number, the silhouette of the Gryphon, towering above them, stalking carefully along the thatched roof. Cheshire snaps his head back to an empty street—the woman is gone. Fine with him; his hunt has suffered from his divided attention. Perhaps the specter knows this and is why she pointed out the Gryphon to him. A question for another time.

With silent grace, Cheshire scales the side of the tenement—hands and feet finding impossible grips on shutters, shifted planks of wood, eaves, and corner stones—until he reaches the top of the city. Rooftops jut out of the city like tombstones in a neglected, overgrown graveyard.

The dawn catches several more out-of-place, misshapen bodies. Eyes ticking from side to side, he discovers ten. Groups of Mirusian soldiers attend to each headless body, but Cheshire keeps his attention on the Gryphon. Cheshire leaps across the gap of an alley and runs down the spines, edges, and slopes of Stonehaven.

An epiphany sends a chill down Cheshire's bare body. He hates to think of the Gryphon as his equal, but he must give credit to the noble tactician that once inhabited the disgraced mind. Cheshire has spent most of his life being pursued by the Ace, soldiers, guards, archers, and the Gryphon. He can use this to his advantage. Cheshire perches several buildings and a street away from the Gryphon and balances perfectly at the end of the spine of a long wooden beam. His mother's shawl around his neck waves in the dull breeze. He stands perfectly still, waits, and watches.

The old general senses the hunt and Cheshire's gaze burrowing a hole through his back. He turns, long gray hair swinging, and his yellow eyes travel the distance and pierce Cheshire as if his adversary stood feet away. Their lock could not be broken if the city burned around them.

Cheshire shifts his weight to his right foot, and the Gryphon shifts to his left, mirroring Cheshire, preparing. The old man's eagle-eyed vision is noteworthy. Cheshire raises his left arm straight out to his side, and the Gryphon mirrors again. His long gray hair falls as he shifts his shoulders. If the Gryphon doubts Cheshire's intentions, he would not play the game.

His heart races, body tingling, alive with the anticipation of this confrontation. Outside the false safety of Mirus's walls, he fought the Ace as constant as the faces of the moon. He does not miss being pursued, but rather the challenge of a worthy opponent. And with the Ace's whereabouts unknown for the time being, he will make one of the Gryphon again. Outside these walls he is prey; inside he is a predator, the predator. He is a killer. This is what the city made him, and he must embrace his nature again.

Cheshire darts his eyes to the right, a street higher in Stonehaven, where another group of soldiers pull another headless body from its spike. They glance toward Cheshire while they work, but none of the Mirusian soldiers see Cheshire as an immediate threat because of Lysander and Uriah's presence. He turns back to the Gryphon, who stares back from beneath his pinched brow. Cheshire's grin lets the Gryphon know he means to stack each soldier's head down the iron spike, in one ear and out the other. The Gryphon shakes his head—a true warning. Cheshire has his undivided attention.

"Yes," Cheshire whispers.

The instant Cheshire bolts for the soldiers, the Gryphon soars through the air toward him, covering great distances with every bound, his longcoat and hair flapping behind him like the wings of his namesake. Cheshire slides down the steep truss of the tenement to an old enclosed bridge passing over the street connecting the third level of the building he runs on to the first level of the tenement on the higher tier. By the time Cheshire climbs to the top, the Gryphon reaches the same roof. Cheshire waits on the edge of the wooden beam, putting himself halfway between the Gryphon and the bridge, poised to run at the soldiers on the adjoining rooftop to his right.

"Finally decided to show your face, liar." Cheshire laughs. "Coward."

A twitch takes over the Gryphon's right eye. The second insult, albeit true, cuts worse.

"You will not harm them." The Gryphon's voice bellows across the shingles.

"I believe I shall. You may keep me from plunging them onto the spike, but a push will suffice. A fall from this height will kill them if they fall correctly. Those lucky enough to survive, I will attend to thereafter."

"You will do no such thing."

"Stop me."

Four steps are all Cheshire manages to take before the Gryphon swoops down, grabs him by the forearm, lifts him off his feet, and grabs Cheshire's throat with his free hand. Not hard enough to throttle him but enough to keep him in place, airway pinched. Cheshire bats at the Gryphon's gauntlet with his free arm and kicks his feet, reaching out with his toes to scratch at the Gryphon's face.

"Falsifier," says Cheshire. "Dishonorable."

The Gryphon tightens his hold on Cheshire's throat. "You do not know of what you speak."

"Disgrace." The heartbeat in Cheshire's head intensifies, not from exhilaration, but from the lack of air.

"You will stop talking one way or another. All I need to do is keep you here, immobile, until our work is done. Then I will deposit you back inside the castle. Be grateful if I do not place you in the oubliette where you found me."

The audacity the Gryphon possesses, continuing his ruse, fuels each of Cheshire's kicks, wilder, fiercer, landing blows on the Gryphon's chest and chin. He grimaces, but none faze him.

Cheshire wraps his legs around the Gryphon's outstretched arm, feigns struggling, but braces himself in the process. The Gryphon lifts his arm high into the air, as if Cheshire weighs nothing, and brings him down onto the wooden shingles with his full weight behind him, taking a knee to hold Cheshire in place on the higher part of the roof's slope.

The blow dazes Cheshire, despite tucking his head, and steals the air from his lungs. A small sacrifice in the grand tapestry of what is to come. After all, the Gryphon has slammed Cheshire through the floors of the harbor and choked him to unconsciousness. He knew the Gryphon would not hesitate to incapacitate him.

"Yield," the Gryphon commands.

Cheshire's legs fall from the Gryphon's arm and fight for a foothold among the shingles. Cheshire's eyes grow wide, fighting for breath, to free himself from the Gryphon's gauntlet, his time limited.

"Yield."

Cheshire reaches for the Gryphon's face frantically—his fingers stretching and bending, ready to claw at his weathered cheeks, unable to reach. He mouths once more, slowly for the Gryphon to understand. "Please."

The Gryphon does not release his hold but pulls Cheshire to a sitting position, bringing them face to face. The hot breaths from his nose bear down on Cheshire's brow.

"Yield."

"Thank you," Cheshire mouths. He plants his feet, toes curling, digs into the shingles, pushes all of his weight forward, and shoves the Gryphon backward.

The Gryphon realizes his error too late; his hands are useless, kneeling in an awkward position over Cheshire, with nothing behind them but open air and the bridge three stories below where Cheshire made sure to be caught. Unwilling to release Cheshire, and unable to stop their momentum, they fall from the side of the tenement and tumble through the air.

A calculated risk, Cheshire prepares to take the full brunt of the impact, but the Gryphon twists in the air and wraps his arms around Cheshire, shielding him, the moment before they slam through the roof of the bridge. Old timbers, beams, and supports snap and rain down with them. The addition to Cheshire's weight knocks the air from the Gryphon. He gasps like some unfortunate soul risen from the dead, exhumed from the soil for the first time in a hundred years.

A large section of the roof collapsed under their weight. The posts bearing the weight of the sections around the hole creak and groan from the stress.

Cheshire flops free, reclaiming his own breath through the dust filled air. "Make up your mind," Cheshire rasps. "Do you wish me dead or alive?"

The Gryphon cannot yet speak. He shakes his head, wincing in pain, sucking in every bit of air and coughing it out. A fallen post pins the gauntlet of the Gryphon's right hand. Cheshire picks up a large, pointed chunk of fallen beam and brings it down on the Gryphon's trapped arm. Before the point can pierce his muscles, the Gryphon swings his free arm wildly and smacks Cheshire away into the wall of the bridge. The posts groan louder, the bridge creaks, and dust rains down on them.

The moment he hits the wall, Cheshire pushes off, jumping for the Gryphon again before he can free himself. The Gryphon slips his hand from his gauntlet and backhands Cheshire away to the other side of the bridge into another of the splintered posts. As Cheshire predicted.

Instead of aiming for the Gryphon, Cheshire kicks at the post. *Crack.* The posts of the roof buckle and snap. First one side of the bridge, and then the other crumble down with it. Cheshire rolls out of the way to escape the falling debris as the hole grows wider, beams and posts clattering to the floor of the bridge with loud, resounding clunks and knocks.

They fall to the floor, but not onto the Gryphon. On the opposite side of the growing pile, the Gryphon, on hands and knees, catches his breath, his scowl filled with a thousand curses.

Cheshire roars, picks up a small piece of timber, and lobs it at the Gryphon's head, which he deflects. "Must I bring the entire fucking city down upon you?"

"It will require much more to keep me from my duties, young one." The Gryphon rises to his feet, cracking his back, and clutching his left shoulder with his gauntlet-less hand, exposing a wide circular ring on his middle finger.

To Cheshire, the mention of duty slides from the Gryphon's mouth like bile. He charges, runs up the piled debris, and leaps. With his bare hand, the Gryphon snatches Cheshire by the throat once more and slams him to the ground. The stone floor of the bridge is less forgiving than the wooden shingles. He fights against the grip, pulling at each of the

Gryphon's fingers, all the while pressing his thumb against the ring until it leaves an indentation.

"You will listen to me, ungrateful brat," says the Gryphon, leaving Cheshire space to breathe and speak this time.

"I will. I will have the truth from you if it costs me my life."

"Do not be so rash or naïve."

Cheshire reaches up to claw at the Gryphon's face again. This time, the Gryphon kneels on Cheshire's torso to keep him in place.

"Damn you," Cheshire shouts.

"Shut your mouth and listen to what I must tell you."

"Nothing should cross your lips except the truth and an explanation for your lies."

"Another time." The Gryphon tightens his grip again. "You will hear me. You have cost me a great deal of time. After removing the bodies from the roofs of Stonehaven, my next task was to search the alleyways near the rally currently happening near the Row."

"What does this have to do with—"

"Shut up. Groups of Lysander and Uriah's men lie in wait, apart from the rally, at what I can presume is at each of the nearest entrances to the Market. They mean to make an example."

Cheshire continues to struggle in vain.

"My place is on the rooftops," the Gryphon continues, "and since you have cost me so much time, your place must now be in the alleyways of the Stonehaven." Before Cheshire can utter another rebuttal, the Gryphon cuts him short. "You will do this because my spies tell me young Carter left the castle and heads toward the market."

An odd burning contradiction fills Cheshire's chest. He loses the will to fight the Gryphon. Instead, a growing rage fills him, aimed toward any who would dare lay a hand on Jonathan. His love can best two dozen men at least—Cheshire has seen it with his own eyes—but images of Jonathan's bruises flash in his mind. Regardless of his strength and skill, he must wonder if Jonathan has healed enough. But all this may be for naught; this, too, can be false.

"Is this another one of your tricks?" asks Cheshire. "Your lies."

The Gryphon releases his hold on Cheshire and takes a step back. "We will have our reckoning. Your relentless nature will see to it. However, whatever is between us does not involve Carter. The question you must ask yourself is: are you willing to sacrifice him for me?"

"You know the answer before you ask the question." Cheshire gets to his feet and rubs his thumb with his fingertips, examining the design—the same as the wax seal from March's scroll. "Damn you. Damn you to every level of hell there is, and may every foul curse fall upon your head."

"I shall pay for my deeds in due time." The Gryphon lowers his head. "However, this is not it. And you waste what little time Carter has."

The burning contradiction rises to Cheshire's face, flooding it with heat and bringing him to tears. For what reason he does not know. "I hate you," Cheshire says simply, before leaping from the open wound of the bridge to the street below and running toward the Row. "I hate you."

CHAPTER 29
JONATHAN

The first man rushes forward with a wild swing to the side of Jonathan's head. He blocks it with his coiled arm and immediately jabs the man in the face. The man stumbles back, bends over, and spits out copious amounts of blood and several broken and whole teeth. The second and third men dart forward to box Jonathan in on the sides. He prepares for an attack, but it is the fourth man who rushes him and punches for Jonathan's face. As soon as Jonathan raises his hands to block, the second and third men land blow after blow to his ribs.

Jonathan kicks to the side, snapping the second's knee backward, sending him to the ground howling like a mongrel. His position is quickly taken up by the fifth and sixth men. Jonathan takes the breath of an opening and grabs at the belt of the third man—smaller than the others—at his left side, pulls him off his feet, and swings him at the fourth man, slamming them both into the fifth and sixth with such force their bones rattle as they collide with the curve of the wall. The fourth man falls unconscious on top of the others. Two immobilized for the moment, writhing—eleven more to go.

Damn it.

The opening does not last long. The seventh, eighth, ninth, and tenth shove Jonathan and pin him against the wall. Jonathan covers his face and absorbs blow after blow. The men attempt to pry his arms away from the shield he has made around his head, but they are not strong enough. The eleventh man tries to thrust a kick at Jonathan's legs through his partners.

Barrage after barrage continues on Jonathan's arms, torso, and back. Each punch and kick sends a shock of pain instantly through his body like a boulder dropped into a still lake. Each nerve catches fire. He breathes it out with heavy breaths through gritted teeth. Jonathan stomps on the eleventh man's foot, cracking several bones, causing him to yelp, and the sudden noise causes the surrounding others to wince. Jonathan elbows the eighth man, to his right, in the cheek. *Crack.* He ducks under a jab to his face and swings wildly upward, catching the jaw of the seventh man. The ninth opens his mouth to scream, perhaps to intimidate. Jonathan reaches into his mouth with four fingers, grips the bottom of his jaw, and slams the man to the ground. From this lower position, Jonathan rises with a knee to the tenth man's gut, knocking the wind from him, doubling him over.

The twelfth and thirteenth run in and catch Jonathan off balance with two forceful blows to the back. The pain from the strikes would be enough to take Jonathan down, if not for the areas already being numb from previous blows. They keep at the same spots. He should have worn a shirt, since his previous bruises have almost completely faded but still draw his attackers' attention, leaving him vulnerable. On second thought, these bruises do not make him vulnerable, but rather give his attackers targets. They believe this is where Jonathan would be weakest and, therefore, he can predict where most of them will strike. Thankfully, they pull focus from his trouser pockets and his elixir.

Jonathan realizes he cannot afford to pull his punches any longer. Besides the man with the broken leg, the other twelve are still capable of fighting. He must take the fight out of them. They will not die, but they will break.

He thrusts the heel of his boot into the stomach of the eleventh man, who staggers back to the opposite wall, arms outstretched to catch himself. Before he can move, Jonathan pins the man's wrist against the wall, and with his lunging momentum, punches his upper arm, cracking the bone against the stones. *CRACK.* The man grips his arm, wailing in pain.

A hand grabs Jonathan's left shoulder. He turns and punches the third man in the face. Jonathan can feel his nose shatter and concave against his knuckles. The fifth and ninth man aim for the bruises on Jonathan's sides. He steps back to evade and, with both hands in tight fists, crosses his arms high, swinging them down and back-handing both in the face. They spin on their way to the ground.

In this tight space, he cannot maneuver as he can in the open. Jonathan must keep moving, ending their attacks before they begin. The twelfth man shoulders Jonathan in the stomach, but he flexes just in time to absorb the blow.

The seventh, one of the larger men, reaches for Jonathan's neck with both hands, but Jonathan pushes his arms up between them, circles around them, hooking them under, trapping them. The man struggles, but Jonathan will not let go. He suffers several blows to his sides and shoulders, but his determination will not allow Jonathan to let go. The look of horror on the man's face is short-lived. Jonathan grounds himself and, with a solid jerk upward, snaps both of the seventh man's arms below the elbow, bending them backward. He roars out in short bursts of pain, staring at the four bloody points of bone stabbing out of his flesh. Jonathan finally releases him, and he staggers back in disbelief at his dangling, useless arms. He will never regain full use of them again.

Such a sight gives pause to the other men. The seventh man collapses backward, trying to catch himself on his arms, and screaming in pain again when his arms bend at odd angles against the ground.

The others charge Jonathan all at once, swarming him like beetles on a carcass. They deliver blow after blow, and he can feel their knuckles dig into his skin. With such close quarters, their strikes lose power, but also limit Jonathan's swings. He fights relentlessly, delivering a full blow to the sternum of the third man, the tip of his elbow to the throat of the tenth, a punch inside of the right thigh of the thirteenth, and slamming a fist down on the toes of the fourth. He slowly wears them down, but not accustomed to showing any restraint, the fight drags on too long for Jonathan's present condition. If he could only let loose, this fight would be over in a matter of seconds, giving his body the reprieve it needs.

"No! Stop!"

Over the scuffling of feet on stone, grunts, and cries of pain, one man shrieks deeper in the alley. The others stop their assault and back away. Jonathan keeps his guard up and turns to look at what or who he has to thank.

Of course.

Cheshire, wearing the Mask of Shadows, holds the sixth man by the back of his leather tunic and dangles him through one of the cast shadows on the wall. His lower-half kneels and disappears into the right wall, while his head and shoulders reemerge through another cast shadow from their group on the left wall.

"What the fuck is this? What the fuck is this?" the sixth man cries, unsure of what to think, looking at his backside across the alleyway.

"What devilry is this? By the gods. Demon." The men mutter around Jonathan.

"The mere thought of attacking him would have been enough to kill you," says Cheshire. "But you touched him. You hurt him. Now your deaths are demanded, and you will not go peacefully."

Before Jonathan can say a word, Cheshire legs go of the man's tunic. Jonathan half-believed the man would continue to fall through. He could not have been more wrong. The shadow splits the man in half like the sharpest butcher's cleaver. His body and arms slump twitching to the stones, leaving a wide bloody streak against the wall. His head and shoulders fall to the ground like a sack of grain, managing one more cry before his eyes glaze over and his life pours from him with his blood.

The wonder and danger of these masks in Cheshire's possession sinks into Jonathan's marrow. He banished the cult into the shadows. Jonathan himself experienced it, passing through the dark with his love. But it only works as long as Cheshire keeps hold. With the power Cheshire possesses, he truly does play with the people of Mirus, able to wipe them all from the earth in an instant if he so wished.

The remaining men stand dumbstruck. The wrong decision. Cheshire reaches through the shadow on the wall and grasps the back of the twelfth man's hair, pulling him back to the wall. The others cower to the opposite side of the alley. Cheshire pulls the man's head through the shadow up to his neck, some twenty feet away. The shadows of the men cast from the sun at the entryway of the alley scramble into different shades and lines along the wall, but the one shadow Cheshire holds captive in his sight remains constant: Jonathan's.

"No," says Jonathan. "We cannot kill..." Jonathan shouts in a whisper.

Cheshire tilts his head at an odd angle. The sunlight catches the crests of lavender in his eyes. Jonathan can see his grin without seeing his face. There is no stopping him. The man continues to scream. The others curse and clump together.

"Fuck." Jonathan winks at Cheshire. "Make it quick. And silent."

Jonathan takes part in Cheshire's game and steps to the side. His shadow slips down the wall, severing the twelfth man's head and his scream with a silent, clean cut. His body crumples to the floor, and Cheshire pulls the head away from the wall and holds it up to show the men. He waves his left hand over his face, removing his mask, and tosses the severed head at the feet of the other men.

Jonathan takes advantage of their shock, clenching his fists, thankful to Cheshire releasing the restraints he set on himself. They will pay for it later, but for now, he turns and punches the head of the eighth man with all his strength. It rebounds off the stone, and Jonathan catches his head with a second punch, slamming it against the wall, cracking the man's skull.

Cheshire appears like a wraith in the middle of them, wraps his arms around the head of the fifth man, and with a smile to rival the crest of the moon, twists the man's head around with a quick snap, and then leaps over to the first man still holding his bloody mouth, and kicks him toward Jonathan.

Jonathan punches the third man, blood gushing from his broken nose, twice more in the chest, *thoom, thoom*, cracking and caving his ribs in on his vital organs.

The men are reluctant to fight Cheshire, whether it be because they believe the tales, especially after his work with the shadows, or perhaps they are unprepared to engage in a fight with a fully naked man.

Jonathan catches the first man by the throat, flips him overhead, and slams him down onto the second man, who is still nursing his broken leg. While bent over, Cheshire slides his sweaty body across Jonathan's back, pulls an unseen dagger from the belt of the thirteenth man, and in quick succession stabs it up through the soft part of his lower jaw, high into his skull, slashes the throat of the ninth, clear to his spine, and shoves it down into the skull of the fourth, twisting it to crack the skull for good measure.

Jonathan stomps on the second man's pelvis, smashing it, quickly followed by his head to stop the screams. With a swift and powerful jerk of his leg, he kicks the first man's head into the wall. It bounces off the stones, and he falls limp.

The final two remain. Cheshire climbs Jonathan's back and leaps off to knee the tenth man in the middle of the back, sending him skidding across the ground. Jonathan sweeps the legs of the eleventh man. His chin clacks against the stones. Jonathan takes hold of the man's ankle and drags him deeper into the alley toward Cheshire. The man fights against him, fingernails bending backwards and breaking, but Jonathan's grip is too great. He takes hold of his ankle with both hands. Cheshire jumps up and lands with both knees in the middle of the man's back. As he screams, Cheshire flips the tenth man over as Jonathan swings the eleventh man overhead and brings him down on his partner.

Their screams end when their bodies collide, knocking the air from them. They gasp and wheeze.

"Again," says Cheshire.

Jonathan obeys, swinging the eleventh man over his back like a sack of flour and brings him down on the tenth again. *Crack*. And again. *Crack*. With each additional swing, the sounds become increasingly wet, like two bloody pieces of meat on a butcher's block. When the heads of both men are little more than skin sacks of shattered bones and their chests resemble smashed bread, blood soaking through their linen, Jonathan finally stops, letting the broken leg slip from his fingers.

Jonathan huffs, head throbbing, and body burning—the pain finally catches up with him. He takes in the blood circle around him, more sacks of flesh and splintered bone than men. He walks to each of the thirteen men to make sure none still breathe, wondering how they will hide this. Thankfully, the raucous noise of the crowd overpowered the screams.

"Oh, wait," says Cheshire. "We almost missed one."

The man whose arms snapped and bent back at the elbow plays dead, but the thundering heartbeat in his neck betrays him. Cheshire sits on the ground, puts both his feet on the man's shoulders, and reaches down, grabbing the underside of his jaw. He lowers himself down, eye to eye. "What made you think you could touch him, leave a mark on him, and not reap what you sow? Are you ready to welcome death?"

"Please," the man mumbles through his pressed mouth, spitting out blood.

"I am your death, and for your crimes, I have come to collect." Cheshire stretches his legs and pulls the man's jaw toward his body.

"Wait," shouts Jonathan.

Cheshire growls in frustration.

"Just for a moment."

Cheshire releases the tension. Jonathan kneels next to the man and grabs him by the throat, digging the tips of his fingers deep into the sides of his neck.

"I require a single answer to a single question."

The man gags and chokes, his windpipe crushed between Jonathan's fingers. He tries to bat away Jonathan's grip with his arms, but they flop around out of his control, eyes wincing, wide with pain, fighting for his life.

"Darling, would you mind?" Jonathan asks.

Cheshire crouches over the man, grabs both his wrists, twists his forearms around, skin spinning at the elbow, and forces them to touch the man's shoulders. He nearly goes into shock from the pain—eyes rolling back, body spasming, mouth agape, lips turning a pale blue. Once the fight leaves him, Cheshire takes hold of the man's jaw again.

"You do not have my permission to die... yet," says Jonathan. He loosens the grip on the man's throat.

He gasps, deep and loud.

"Answer my question," says Jonathan in a soothing tone.

"Will you let me live?"

"No. I am afraid the only choice you have left is a quick death at my hand or a slow, painful one at his." Jonathan glances up at Cheshire.

"Please," the man begs, tears streaming down the side of his face.

"Answer the question." Jonathan tightens his grip momentarily. "The dead bodies displayed on the rooftops. Were they truly men of Adamas, or were they Mirusian?"

"Mirusian," the man says through his tears. "It repaid the blood spilt of our men."

Jonathan shakes his head. "Devils."

"Have your answer?" Cheshire asks

"Yes, but—"

Cheshire gives the man's head a quick jerk, pulling his skull from his spine. The body falls slack.

"I had another question," says Jonathan.

"You said you needed one answer for one question."

"Yes, but an answer can spark another question."

"What is your question?"

"Why did they do it? Why not just kill townspeople and make it known?"

"Do you not see the bigger picture? Without their heads, their identities remain a mystery. The Twins pose dead Mirusians as their own to bait the people, blaming you, and giving them reason to continue the bloodshed, justly, with no one the wiser."

His lover speaks the truth; he always does. Jonathan took the bait. Now thirteen more men lie dead at his hands. Blood to be repaid. Perhaps this would have turned out different had March come in his stead. Jonathan flicks at the tip of his fingers with the tip of his thumb. Before he succumbs to the downward spiral of thoughts, the shimmer of Cheshire's eyes and his grin anchor him.

"I have missed killing with you," says Cheshire, a breath away.

Jonathan breathes heavily and laughs. "In honesty, watching the way your body moves, it does make you undeniably irresistible. It is the intense look in your eyes, the way you defy logic with every sensually dark movement and flex of your body, and your damned smile."

"I can tell by the bulge pushing your loose trousers away from your body." Cheshire places his tongue on the side of his upper lip.

"As ravenous as you make me, we are not fucking here among the dead."

"It does not need to be here."

Jonathan must tread carefully. He cannot withstand Cheshire's pull, which is how he ended up being fucked against a bakery window the day prior. But once they begin, there is no stopping, and as much as his body calls, it must be another time.

"Perhaps later. You can collect both March and I."

"Agreed," says Cheshire without a second thought.

An image of March dancing through the alley, blades shining and spinning, flashes in Jonathan's mind. He squeezes the bulge in his pants and shakes the thought from head. He must focus. "We must get rid of the bodies."

"Fine." Cheshire stands, cock hard as stone, pointing at Jonathan's face, causing his jaw to tingle.

"Have I told you I prefer this new look of yours?" Jonathan stands, the head of his cock pointing out the top of his trousers.

Cheshire taps it with his finger, temptation swimming in his eyes. He kisses it and pushes it back into Jonathan's low waistline. "Off with you," says Cheshire.

"What of the bodies?"

"Yes, yes, the bodies." Cheshire stands and licks Jonathan's lips. "I shall take care of them." Cheshire tilts his head to the side, measuring the slain man's head with his hands. "I believe I may have a use for them. Do not ask for what."

"But I should assume your plan will come at a cost to us."

"Most definitely," says Cheshire. "But later."

Jonathan wishes he could say anything to change Cheshire's mind, but by now his love has come up with at least twenty ways to use these bodies to fuel the chaos within the city to his own whims. There is no way, therefore, there is no reason to speak. He kisses Cheshire on the forehead before he swipes his left hand over his face and summons the Mask of Shadows.

"Go," says Cheshire, his voice hollow behind the mask.

Jonathan looks at his hands, splattered with blood halfway up his forearms, and drops speckling his torso and face, probably. Not the best appearance to stand in to address a crowd about not being violent. He walks back up the zig-zagging alleyway and finds a bucket filled with rain water outside a back door. He hides his hands in his trouser pockets, feeling the cold touch of his elixir. The caress of the vial on his skin calms his racing heartbeat.

He climbs the closest set of stairs to the high ways above Stonehaven and, at the top, takes a sip of his elixir for good measure. The walk back to the castle gives Jonathan time to think and prepare for whatever Cheshire has planned. For Cheshire, 'later' can mean an hour, a day, or a week. Time has no meaning to him the way it does Jonathan, counting every step, fighting not to count every minute of a millennium, wondering when his timepiece will tick its last.

CHAPTER 30

MARY ANNE

Mary Anne does not acknowledge Grace when she enters the bedchamber and finds March laying her longcoat, trousers, and swords on one of their trunks. Apparently, she has no plans to dress anytime soon, and walks to the bath door connected to Mary Anne's room.

"Come along," says March, speaking to Mary Anne as if she were a child.

Mary Anne cautiously waits by the door, flashing back to the first time she saw March without clothing. She laid on Jonathan's couch as March walked by with such confidence—the same unwavering confidence she has today.

"You really do not understand this world," March says. "Fine, stay there and spend the rest of the day with soiled feet."

Not wanting to give March the satisfaction, Mary Anne lifts her foot. Even though the servants and Pat and Bill keep the castle tidy, the bottoms of her feet are caked with layers of dust and dirt from the corridors, the courtyard outside, and the castle wall, appearing more like the paws of some woodland beast. It would have been prudent to all of them to wear boots, but the Duchess spoke with such haste, none gave thought to it.

Reluctantly, Mary Anne joins March in the baths, not ready to undress yet. The warmth of the long bath fills the large white and gray marble chamber, and the steam rises from the water, still except for the ripples made by March already sitting at the bath's edge. Mary Anne sits a distance away, for fear some thought of drowning her lingers in March's mind. She lowers her feet into the hot water and the soothing heat travels up her body. She rubs her feet together under the surface, then grabs a smooth clump of gray-green soap, smelling of mint and rosemary, on a nearby tray and scrubs at the bottom of her feet and between her toes.

Out of the corner of her eye, she watches March methodically and slowly wash, almost as if her mind has sunken beneath the water. She does not say a word the entire time until she extends each leg from the water to inspect her work, water trickling down her calf and thigh. Mary Anne cannot help herself from stealing glances at March's body; not out of envy, but curiosity. She truly has the most unique body of any woman Mary Anne has ever encountered, though Mary Anne has seen few women without their clothing. Without a word, March leaves Mary Anne alone to steep in the baths. The water around her feet turns a murky gray and brown. Her mind drifts to March's comment from earlier, her jab. She said 'this world' and not 'the world' as if there were another for Mary Anne to understand. What an odd choice of words.

She rises from the water, taps her feet dry on a course-fibered mat and returns to her bedchamber. Across the room, March rummages through one of her trunks, pulls another pair of trousers, and collects the suspenders from the pair she wore the day before. Mary Anne opens a wardrobe, using the door as a makeshift divider to separate her from March as they dress. Perhaps it is a habit, since they spend many nights naked, laying near each other, but always divided by Jonathan. Why does the daytime and the fact they are upright make it feel any different? Silly, really, since two nights ago, March's body was rubbing against Mary Anne's, her breast was in her mouth, without a word of protest.

Mary Anne unties her silver belt, lifts her gown over her head, and hangs it on a small iron hook inside the wardrobe door. The door slams shut as soon as she moves her hand away, startling Mary Anne. She covers her breasts and crotch out of habit. March leans, arms crossed, against the adjoining wardrobe. Her trousers hang low on her hips, suspenders hanging loosely at her sides, revealing the lines of her muscles disappearing below the belt line and traveling down between her thighs. A fresh, thin, light-beige linen hangs from her hand—another wrap for her chest.

"Your confidence and your modesty are quite selective, are they not?" March makes a sucking sound with her tongue and teeth.

"I beg your pardon."

Marsh chuckles under her breath, tying the linen wrap around her, securing a belt connected to a smaller band around her thigh, holding five daggers, and slips on her back harness with swords, metal clinking. She grabs the Book of Queens from the table near the bed, gives Mary Anne a side-eyed glance, and heads toward the door.

"Are we not supposed to study? Is this not the reason we are together?"

"We are, but not here. Quite enough happens in this chamber, and I doubt you will be able to concentrate. I shall meet you in Weiss's study. Hurry along and do not keep us waiting."

Mary Anne feels a shiver of spite crawl up her skin again—no better fuel or motivator. She pulls another gown of layered lilac and burgundy silks from the wardrobe and lays it on the bed. After a quick inspection, Mary Anne makes quick work of the seams, pulling and ripping here and there, removing several layers until the neck of the gown plunges to a deep v. She removes the bodice, and the sleeves sway freely from the shoulders to the cuff at the wrists, leaving her arms bare. She slips the transformed gown on and finishes by slipping on her dark-brown boots and the silver chain belt to keep her gown to her body.

With a last check in the looking glass, Mary Anne marvels at her creation. The drape of the neck falls below her navel. Her previous gown she grew fond of only had open sides. Mary Anne is no longer sure if March meant her previous jab as an insult or a challenge. Far more of her body shows—no more than March's—and why should she not own her body, her confidence?

Mary Anne leaves her bedchamber, with Grace following close behind, and heads toward the Chamberlain's study. The gown straightens her posture, as it should be, head held high, shoulders back, and chin up. As she walks through castle corridors, a small rush of wind brushes over her bare hips like water around a stone in the middle of a river, and now it tickles her torso and slides beneath the hanging fabric, caressing her sides and under breast. Perhaps this is the reason Cheshire struts through the castle without clothes, Jonathan always without a shirt, and March in her particular garb. The sensation is exhilarating, quickening her heart in a new, exciting rhythm—freedom.

"Return to my chambers," she tells Grace without looking back. "Take every garment from my wardrobes and alter them. They need to be at least half of what they are." Mary Anne will not hide behind the storybook image or puffed shoulders, or drooping cape sleeves, or the twelve layers of heavy damasks, brocades, and taffetas. "Off with you."

The clacks of Grace's shoes grow distant behind her. At first Grace served as a needed guide for her, leading her through the massive labyrinthian castle. Mary Anne does not need to be escorted any longer. After all, Grace can rest her feet and stay where needed: Mary Anne's chambers.

March waits, leaning against the dark wooden post doorframe to the study door, the Book of Queens tucked under her arm, and Dormy by her side, examining the stonework of the ceilings. Mary Anne stops in front of the door and waits for a moment but realizes March will never open the door for her, and does so herself.

Inside the Chamberlain's study, several loose pages of parchment shift and hiss along the floor in his wake. The Chamberlain tinks at his three hour glasses with a gloved finger. Stacks of books and parchments around his study create a precarious forest all to himself. The sheer amount of books and pages absorb any ambient sound in the study. Even March's boot falls and Mary Anne's breath seem muffled.

"Hello," says Mary Anne.

Parchments slide and fall off the table from the Chamberlain's erratic arm movement, startled by the greeting.

"You are late." The Chamberlain straightens the few pages left on the table, looking at his own pocket watch, and flips the hourglass over again.

"I cannot be late, because you were not expecting me," says Mary Anne, sitting in one of four hard leather wingback chairs facing the center of the study.

"Words spread in this castle faster than any foot can travel," says the Chamberlain.

March crosses in front of Mary Anne and sits in the chair to her right. The Chamberlain joins them, pushing fallen pages with every step like autumn leaves on the forest floor, and sits in the chair opposite Mary Anne, tossing the end of his robe over his lap. Dormy explores and loses herself within the stacks of the room.

"Where shall we—"

"The Fourth Tenet," Mary Anne cuts him short.

"Yes." The Chamberlain holds his hand to March for the Book of Queens.

"No, no," says March. "You are so wise, you do not need it." The spine crackles and snaps as she opens it and the ends of its dark cover thump onto the arms of the chair. "Proceed."

For a moment, Mary Anne believes March is actually on her side.

Weiss squints and takes his spectacles from his face to wipe them clean with a small handkerchief from the inside pocket of his robe.

"As you are aware, the Six Tenets fall under three separate categories. The first two are your Education."

Mary Anne watches March pull at the fabric and metal tabs sticking out of the sides of the book, keeping up with the Chamberlain.

"The Third and Fourth deal with the Manifestation of the Arcana. The fifth and sixth take place at your Coronation."

"Yes, I have heard this before," says Mary Anne.

"The Fourth Tenet"—Weiss sighs—"specifically discusses the powers granted to the queen by the Grand Arcana."

March flips a chunk of pages in hand, finds the chapter, and follows along with her finger.

The Chamberlain continues, the tips of his fingers pressed together. "The powers gifted to the previous queens of Wonderland have varied from queen to queen. No real documentation accounts for what or how this happens."

"'The Grand Arcana'," March reads, finger skimming over a long paragraph of runes, "'a power without measure flows through Wonderland. Palpable, living, connecting all things.'"

"Yes, we are well aware." The Chamberlain scrunches his nose, annoyed at March's ability to read the old text. "I have informed her of it myself."

"There are several pages missing." She taps at the pointed edges of torn parchment protruding from the middle of the book. "There are several pages missing throughout the book."

Dormy scuttles to March's side, nose almost touching the book, and running her finger along the jagged edges. March flips to the front of the book and the first missing page for Dormy to inspect as well. Her head jerks from side-to-side, taking in the details, and then disappears back into the stacks.

"Time has such an effect on books." The Chamberlain gestures to this study. "Do you think these pages of loose parchment are blank? No. I scavenge and hold the record to prevent any knowledge from being lost, to the best of my ability. And some things fall through the hands of time. I may not know everything, but I assure you, it is almost all here in this chamber. And I guarantee everything of note still resides in The Book of Queens. You shall see there are many repaired and reattached pages."

March leans the open book to Mary Anne to show her the evidence of a page torn in half and mended with some sort of glue. She continues to read. "'The queen has ultimate authority, ultimate power in Wonderland. The Grand Arcana flows through Wonderland and thus will flow through her, granting her power over all.'"

"But what *is* this power?" asks Mary Anne.

"It is difficult to explain." The Chamberlain rises from his seat and paces through the stacks of parchment and books.

March sneers at the Chamberlain, flips several pages, searching. "'The gifts bestowed by the Grand Arcana derive from the Divine, The Old Ones, seven ancient gods, the First of Wonderland.'"

"Yes." The Chamberlain waves her off.

"'Mind, Balance, Form, Life, Death, Nature, and Time,'" March continues.

"Together in harmony." The Chamberlain appears from behind a stack to make a grand sweeping entrance.

"No." March laughs. "You have the wrong translation."

The Chamberlain clutches his chest. "How dare you? I have studied and translated the Book of Queens more than anyone. I have more knowledge than anyone, save for the Duchess, on the subject."

"What a paradox knowledge is, true knowledge. The more you possess, the more you realize you do not have."

The Chamberlain, grumbling, rushes to March's right side to follow her finger placement. Mary Anne rises and hurries to March's left side.

"This symbol following the names of the Old Ones, here."

"Yes, the symbol for harmony. A queen shall possess all powers in harmony," says Weiss.

There is so much more still for Mary Anne to learn, an insurmountable amount of knowledge. She has heard mention of the Old Ones, but not their purpose or positions. By their names, they appear to be elemental or ethereal beings—gods, even. Do their monikers dictate what they held dominion over?

"No," says March. "This is not the symbol for harmony." March knows better than most, not just because of her knowledge of the old tongue, but because Cheshire traces it upon her and Jonathan's skin when they lie together. " Turned on its side, as it is scribed here, it is the symbol for discord. Nowhere on this page or the ones prior does it say a queen shall inherit all the powers of the Old Ones. It does not read 'together in harmony.' It reads, 'together discord.'"

"What does it mean?" asks Mary Anne.

The Chamberlain stutters again, stands, and adjusts the collar of his robes. "It can be simply interpreted as separate or apart. Thinking of the past, the queens only possessed one genuine power of the Old Ones. Therefore—"

"You have witnessed it?"

"Yes," he says, somber in tone, no flourish or grandeur. "There are few alive who have, I would wager. The queens used their powers sparingly at best."

"Balance," says Mary Anne.

"Precisely." The Chamberlain adjusts his spectacles and walks among the stacks again.

"Continue," Mary Anne prompts March. "Please."

"'A queen's word is law under the Grand Arcana and therefore is incontrovertible.'" March flips a page. "'A queen cannot alter or negate her own decrees once spoken and is bound by the Grand Arcana in mind and the physical.'" Unlike the other pages, the runes on these past two are written large and sit in the middle of empty parchment.

March flips back two pages to where the jagged edges of the missing pages peek out and rubs her hand on something invisible on the opposite blank page, then traces a symbol on it, then traces it again backward. Disconcerting to Mary Anne.

March flips back to where she was and continues to read. One phrase to each page. "'The body becomes the vessel. Words and gestures are its conduits.'"

Flip.

"'Queens have the ability to make any decree regarding the land and its inhabitants, and can only decree what is known.'"

Flip.

"'The decree of a queen cannot overrule the decree of another.'"

Flip.

"'The power of the Grand Arcana is limitless within Wonderland.'"

March turns the next few pages, all blank, until she reaches a page with a large rune on it. Mary Anne does not know the rune but knows its meaning. The previous chapters each began with a rune similar in size. She knows this to be the beginning of the section for the Fifth Tenet.

"You see. A list of stipulations for the Fourth Tenet," the Chamberlain says proudly.

"Nothing more?" Mary Anne follows the Chamberlain through the stacks. "This is the information I was promised? Intriguing, yes, but vague, even more so. A list is all the book provides. No instructions? No history?"

"No. Why can you not let it happen naturally, as the others did?"

Mary Anne's annoyance at the twittering Chamberlain stokes into anger by his purposeful apathy and avoidance. "Because five days from today," Mary Anne shouts, rising, and backing the Chamberlain against one of the stacks, "our enemy will be upon us with a force we cannot match and lay siege to Mirus. I must find a way or force this to happen in order to save the fucking city, and by extension, the entire country, and you have no more to offer."

"No. Why do you think I have been so obtuse? I despise not knowing." He looks over Mary Anne's shoulder to March. "And I despise those who pretend to know more than I, all the more."

"Pretend?" Mary Anne snaps. "You hate those who know more than you."

The Chamberlain turns and disappears deeper into his study.

"You coward," she calls after him. "I am glad I chose Jonathan as my advisor instead of you, despite your obvious attempts to sway me. He has done more for me than you ever can."

Thump.

March closes the book, tucks it under her arm, and walks to the door, Dormy in tow. "Come along, Mary Anne."

At first, Mary Anne turns to unleash the anger she should direct at the Chamberlain, but a simple side glance from March tells Mary Anne there is more to be said. She follows March out of the study and slams the door behind her, leaving the Chamberlain to his cowardice. The muffled sound of toppling books and papers rain on the other side of the door, followed by the Chamberlain's pathetic scream.

Mary Anne catches up with March, temples pounding.

"I bear no love for you," says March, "But you must accomplish this task, and we want the same thing in the end. At this moment, we are aligned, and therefore, if you question my trustworthiness, your assumption is wrongly placed. I know you must succeed."

"Thank you."

March says a word in the Old Prodigium tongue.

"What word do you speak?"

"You saw me trace my finger on the blank page."

"Yes. Your face told a different story."

"Indeed. Time may claim pages, but nothing is gone forever. If one looks hard enough, and knows where to look, there are always traces. Even though several pages are missing, they leave ghosts, impressions on the parchment, after years of sitting closed."

"At first I thought it nothing, then observing the confusion Weiss had with the rune for 'discord,' flipping it. I traced it the right way round."

"It said?"

"One word." March's tone lowers. "Weiss uses the word stipulations. Wrong on all accounts. Some who pose as educated, like Weiss, are dangerous in their mistranslation. The ghost rune was clear once it could be seen again. It read, simply, 'Warning.'"

"Warning?" Mary Anne loses the heat of anger from her face and a cold flushes her cheeks.

"The book is purposefully, frustratingly, written vaguely. If you want answers, we can continue to read, yes, but you must also speak to someone who was around the previous queens, and you are acquainted with two of them."

"The Gryphon and the Duchess."

"I am done with this for the day." March drops the heavy book into Mary Anne's arms.

"Where are you going?"

"About my business. So should you be." March does not look back, Dormy following. They turn down the nearest corridor and disappear from sight.

A churning fills Mary Anne's stomach, as if suddenly set upon by a bug or illness. Never have the Duchess or Chamberlain made any mention of warnings or precautions along this journey, and those they have come from outside threats, not this close. *Nevertheless, to wield such power, warnings would be necessary, justified,* Mary Anne reasons to herself.

Mary Anne will trust March and use her knowledge as long as she has need, and will summon the Arcana even if she must force it, unsure what such a task entails. While March and Jonathan are off, she will seek the Gryphon and the Duchess for answers owed. The churning feeling sticks with Mary Anne as she orders every servant she happens upon to find the Duchess and the Gryphon and report back with their location. The Chamberlain may take Mary Anne for a fool, but she knows full well the meaning of discord, and the book does not say the powers of a queen will bring harmony, and does not mean separate or sunder. Discord is conflict.

An odd idea takes form. The Duchess hopefully works on preparations for the festival, Weiss is useless, and the Gryphon is unaccounted for presently. Yet Mary Anne wants, needs, answers. There are two others available with knowledge of the past, albeit skewed, but a half-truth is better than no truth at all.

Mary Anne changes directions against reason, following her gut, and finds a servant girl. "Take me to the bedchamber of Lysander and Uriah."

Blush overtakes the servant's face and she leads Mary Anne to a completely different wing of the castle, far from her bedchamber and the throne room. As they reach the end of a long corridor, with a large pair of oak doors, similar to those of the Duchess's chamber, Bronwen slips from inside, tightening her robe, and walking past Mary Anne without acknowledgement.

Inside, a grand chamber, smaller than Mary Anne's, houses similar columns and candelabras around the perimeter. The thick aroma of heavy perfumes and sex waft through the chamber like an opium den. At its center, one massive bed created by pushing two together, with no less than twelve women, all nude, writhing over each other like a den of vipers, waiting. Some belong to the Garden, women of business, who have elected to remain in the company of Lysander and Uriah. Others Mary Anne recognizes as servant girls from the castle, to her disappointment. At least twenty trays and carts surround the room with lavish spreads of fruits, meats, breads, and libations; no need for the women to leave.

"Have you come to join us?" asks a yellow-haired girl, kneeling on the bed.

"Heavens no," Mary Anne sneers. "Where are they?"

Another young girl with blue hair kneels next to the previous, fingers running down the middle of the yellow-haired girl's chest. The rest of the women lay across each other and casually watch the conversation.

The yellow-haired girl finally speaks up. "They mentioned something about the bailey, and working up a sweat before returning to us."

Mary Anne leaves, unable to take the odor any longer. She will find them, find her answers, no matter where she must follow them. If the Duchess, Weiss, and the Gryphon will not tell her, she will descend into whatever level of hell to get what she needs. After all, after making a deal with Cheshire, the devil himself, as far as she is concerned, Lysander and Uriah are mere children.

CHAPTER 31
MARCH

Hearing scuttlebutt among the servant girls that Lysander and Uriah uncharacteristically wait in the bailey, March makes her way outside the keep with Brynjar and Flynn at her back, Absolom and Seamus on her hips, and a belt of daggers on each thigh. As the Doorman opens the main doors for her, she can hear the song of iron and steel and the loud crack of a whip resonating across the cobbles. A crowded circle of soldiers, both Mirusian and Adamasite, forms at the center of the bailey—a crude mix of men in full armor, some in their linen tunics, and others bare chested.

At its center, Lysander and Uriah engage in a sparring session with each other—fearsome to behold and a force to be reckoned with. They wear half-robes over their trousers, held in place by braided leather belts, exposing Lysander's left shoulder and Uriah's right. Lysander, with a grounded stance, swings his long sword with such force it is almost as if he summons the winds with every strike. A heavy whoosh accompanies every attack, creating his own hurricane around him. Where Lysander may summon the wind, Uriah is wind personified. His half-robe and long hair swing and flow with every dodge and attack. His whip in constant motion behind him—a serpent ready to strike. He leaps through the air, thrusting his glaive at his brother's neck. They laugh as they spar, knowing each strike could be a killing blow. Preening Peacocks.

The expressions of the soldiers are a mix of poorly concealed worry from those of Mirus and smug pride from those of Adamas as the fight continues. On the far side of the circle, the soldier with light-blue hair spots March atop the step of the keep, pushes his way through the crowd, and runs the circumference of the circle to her.

Fuck.

"Afternoon," the soldier says, stopping several steps below her. "Have you come to watch?"

"No," says March, not breaking her eyes away from Lysander and Uriah.

"Have you come to challenge, then?"

"No."

"You appear prepared for it." The soldier points to her assortment of weapons.

"This is what I wear when I go to market to buy groceries."

The soldier's eyes grow wide. "I would be fearful to see what you have when you are prepared for battle."

March walks past him down the stairs, studying every movement, stance, and tell of the Twins.

"Are you sure you will not fight them?" the soldier asks, following at her heels. "It would be a great sight to bear witness to. We could learn so much more than what you taught us in training."

"Stop," says March. "There is one piece of wisdom I did not impart to all of you while you were under my command. Would you like to know what it is?"

"Of course."

"This air of goodness and kindness about you—kill it."

"What?"

"Kill it before it gets you killed."

"You think kindness is weakness."

"It is a liability, especially in battle."

"A rather bleak outlook on the world." The soldier keeps in step with her, remaining by her side. "My name is Jack, by-the-by."

"Just because you tell me your name does not mean I will care for your death any more than any other soldier who has died under my command. Because you feel some misplaced camaraderie with me, do not think I will go out of my way to save you."

"Why, then, do you fight for us?"

She leaves him on the steps without an answer. Instead, she whispers to herself, "I do not fight for you. I fight for us," imagining the faces of Jonathan, Cheshire, and Dormy.

The raucous cheers grow louder as March approaches and the stinging high notes of well-crafted steel ring in her ears. The crowd parts for her. At least the soldiers of Mirus, while those of Adamas stay planted, as if walking around them is an insult. Water flows around stones in a river and never gives them a second thought. And as time goes by, they wear to nothing.

By the time March emerges into the eye of the storm, Lysander and Uriah stand in a respite, sweat covering their bodies.

"Thank you for gracing us with your presence," says Uriah, with heavy breaths.

"A wonder your presence is within the castle, while your men handle your dirty work," says March. "Should you not be out in the city with your soldiers? Then again, doing so would make keeping up appearances and keeping your hands clean difficult."

"Care for a dance?" Uriah asks.

"Not with the likes of you."

"It is inevitable," says Lysander. "It is bound to happen, eventually. You know this as well as we do."

"Is this to the death, then?" she asks.

"Why are you in such a hurry?" Uriah rests his glaive over his shoulder. "Besides, we have yet to finish our conversation."

"I will say again, there is nothing I want from you."

"One match," says Lysander. "Purely for demonstration. So our soldiers can bear witness to the greatest sword in all of Wonderland." He speaks without a hint of mockery, as before.

The Adamas soldiers in the crowd scoff and laugh, which quickly turn to arguments with the soldiers of Mirus.

Uriah raises a hand. "Enough. Give respect where it is due."

Their comments make her blood boil. March does not need to proclaim her ability. She knows the atrocities she has committed. However, the Twins continue to shout her accolades at any chance with the underlying pretense of defeating her later to claim victory. They will try and they will fail.

They approach her at the center of the circle, out of earshot of the soldiers. "Let us make this interesting," says Lysander. "For every strike we land, we will take the life of a soldier of Mirus. For every strike you land, you can claim the life of one of our soldiers."

"I will not play at your games," says March.

"Or we could just turn on your unsuspecting soldiers now and slaughter them before you," says Lysander.

"As I walk away."

"You would turn your back on your soldiers?" Uriah smirks.

"They are not mine."

"Who else's would they be? The Gryphon is nowhere to be found," says Lysander.

"You know well he is out in the city cleaning up your mess."

"Our mess?" Lysander says louder for the crowd to hear. "The men who were slaughtered were, are, soldiers of Adamas, loyal men, who did not deserve to have their bodies mutilated thus by your soldiers. According to our agreement, blood will repay blood."

"Would you like to pick the twenty from the soldiers around who will serve as payment?" Uriah asks. "Or shall we?"

The air changes and grows heavy within. Every soldier in the bailey, both Mirusian and Adamasite, keep their hands hovering above the hilt of their swords; their eyes twitch and quiver. Swallows become audible in the silence consuming the circle of men. One wrong word will fuel yet another brawl and stain the cobbles with blood once more.

March unsheathes Brynjar and Flynn from her back; the long *slink* their steel makes exiting the leather begins a song she does not want to sing, but will enjoy hearing none-the-less. She knows they will not risk harming her, for now at least, and this gives her an opportunity to experience their fighting style first hand.

The men erupt in murmurs, shouts, and cheers, disrupting the quiet before the overture. With shit-eating grins, the Twins take position and create a triangle with March within the circle of soldiers. Lysander swings his longsword in a wide arc overhead and holds it straight out to his right. Uriah twirls his glaive overhead with his left hand and commands his whip to spin along the ground, stirring up dirt with his right.

March sighs. "A quick dance."

The swiftness and ferocity of her attacks take the Twins by surprise. They may expect a simple demonstration, but March has other intentions, swiping at Uriah's throat as he spins his glaive around his neck for its blade to deflect hers. March follows through with her second blade and knocks the glaive off balance, off of his shoulder. Uriah catches its long shaft when it falls to the level of his hand, as if beckoning it. His eyes dart to her right. March spins and blocks a forceful thrust from Lysander's longsword. Uriah dodges as well.

She steps behind Lysander and swats at his open back with the flat side of her sword. He ducks before she can make contact and, at the same time, dodges the wide swing of Uriah's glaive. March kicks at the shaft, stopping it dead on its arc. Dull vibrations run up her leg. She much prefers the high vibrations of steel on steel.

March puts herself between them again to test a theory, lunging at Uriah with one blade and then the other. He wields his whip as good as any shield, coiling it in midair to block her blades.

"Would now be a good time to speak to you about our gift?" asks Uriah.

"Again with this shit?" March ducks below Lysander's swing. Her hair follows in its wake. She looks up. His eyes dart to his brother, and both strike simultaneously. It happens again and again. They fight together, but they must coordinate and signal to each other. Perhaps she will suffer their conversation. "What could you possibly possess to interest me?"

Uriah stabs at her foot while Lysander brings his longsword down from overhead. March lifts her foot and rolls out of the way, her steel clanging against the stones. She stops, blows the hair from her face, returns Brynjar and Flynn to her back, and wakes Absolom and Seamus from her hips, made of wider, thicker steel.

The brothers look at each other; another signal. Lysander kneels, and Uriah steps on his brother's trunk of a thigh and leaps at March, glaive poised to spear her midsection. She flips Seamus in hand, blade down, and prepares to launch it at Uriah still hanging in the air, or so she wants him to believe. His reactions are near as fast as hers, stabbing the tip of his glaive into the cracks between the cobbles to stop his momentum and placing both feet against its shaft.

"Revenge," Uriah says with a smile.

"Down," Lysander shouts.

Uriah slides down the shaft and brings it with him to the ground, ducking under another impressively wide swing from Lysander's longsword.

"You offer me what I am already skilled at?" asks March, sliding back to avoid the strike. "Such a waste of breath."

Lysander strikes twice more, positioning March between them, keeping his massive blade moving. This is his strength. Even if he slows,

Lysander allows the momentum of his steel to guide his body, making this bear of a man as fluid as a serpent.

Uriah's whip *cracks* close to March's head. It echoes across the stones and rings in her ear. The Twins hold an advantage in their distance ranged attacks. Uriah's glaive and whip and Lysander's longsword can reach March anywhere in the circle. The farther she distances herself, the more risk she puts herself in. They know this, she knows this, and they want her to move in close to continue their damned conversation; so be it.

March charges Uriah, delivering strike after strike, never stopping, aiming for his head, legs, torso, arms, hands, and back.

"Not so much offering you a what." He blocks them all with the spinning shaft of his glaive. "But a who and how." His eyes squint and glance behind her.

Uriah does not move, and March is too close to him for Lysander to strike with his sword. She sidesteps and lowers herself to the ground, spinning and swiping both blades just above the cobbles. March narrowly avoids the blunt force of Lysander's shoulder to her back. Her blades cause both to misstep for the first time. Uriah blocks Lysander the instant before they collide, and both skid along the ground.

The crowd of soldiers fills with a mixture of chuckles and gasps. The Twins scan their audience, hiding their anger behind false laughs, turning the match back into an exhibition. Uriah and Lysander grip their weapons tight, veins bulging from their forearms to their shoulders. They are not used to hearing laughter directed at them.

Despite their many victories over the years, for their strength and skill, they have a weakness able to be exploited. They must signal one another before each attack to make sure the other prepares and evades, fighting together yet separate. March, Jonathan, and Cheshire, on the other hand, move as one, feeling the air and pulse between them, never needing to warn the other. They are one.

This song bores March, and before they can strike again, she stands and stops their attacks with two words. "Who? How?" she asks in a sardonic melody.

Lysander tenses his arms and chest, still affected by the slightest of ridicule. It is Uriah who steps forward to meet March, whip slack and using the glaive like a walking stick, its pointed steel hilt clanking and chipping the stones.

"Who indeed? None other than your dearest mother," he says.

The mention of Bronwen, not even by name, is enough to set March's skin to crawl and her body to tense. The fact March must breathe the same air in the city as her brings an acrid taste to her mouth.

The crowd grows silent, except for the shifting of weight, leather, and armor rubbing against each other, and the chaotic rhythm of breaths.

"Enough for this day," Lysander shouts. "Off with you."

Their men slowly leave by the door in the gate, thinning the crowd. The soldiers of Mirus remain until March nods, giving them permission to disperse, some to the keep and others to the city. The light-blue-haired soldier is the last to leave. March stares at him until he becomes uncomfortable, and he joins his brethren in the city, looking back over his shoulder before walking through the gates.

"What of Bronwen? Is she not part of your alliance?" asks March, freely since they are alone.

"Her influence is needed, surely," says Lysander. "But let us be honest. There is only one of her line that interests us."

"Back to this old song." March wants to walk away, but her curiosity gets the better of her.

"A different tune," says Uriah. "We want to give you the means to exact your revenge upon her."

"If I wanted revenge, I would have simply cut her throat in the night long ago."

"Yet she still affects you," says Uriah.

"And you have yet to take her life," says Lysander.

"Because you wish for more." Uriah chuckles. "For some, death is too simple when suffering is owed. You know this."

March does not give a thought to Bronwen when away from Mirus, whether she is in the Hollow or adventuring in any other part of the country. However, she is the cause, the architect of the terrors which plague March's dreams and paralyze her in the night and the day. March killed her father years ago but did not take the life of her mother. Deep down, she knows her mother needs to suffer.

"What if we gave you the means to end her influence in the city?" asks Uriah. "It is easier to return from the dead than to resurrect a tarnished reputation."

"How many knew of your parents' dealings?" asks Uriah.

The civility in their voices puts March on edge.

"Warmongering?" March asks, purposefully deflecting the path they want to lead her down—a path she does not want to travel—yet they must have a reason to reach its end.

"Warmongering to be sure," says Lysander. "However, we speak of their dealing and treatment of you."

A chill runs up her entire body as if plunged into the northern waters in midwinter. She holds her remarks; this is the time to listen.

"We know what they have done to you," says Uriah, his sincerity troubling. "I dare say we are the only men still living who made arrangements with your parents."

"Still a matter easily remedied," says March.

"Your parents were monsters, but they were also business people." Uriah holds his glaive in the crook of his arm and slowly coils his whip in hand. "They tracked every coin, which means, whether or not their dealings were legitimate, when money or other precious commodities changed hands, they kept records."

"Expose her," says Lysander. "Lay her sins bare before the city for all to see."

March hates the idea of agreeing with these two, but what they suggest is unlikely to have any effect.

"Your gift, though suspect, would have no merit." March weighs her swords in hand, considering sheathing them. "I, too, have my own reputation."

"A reputation which began because of your mother and your father," says Lysander. "Did it not?"

Half-truths are the Twins' native tongue. After she left Mirus, her mother allowed rumors to start, but it was March who made sure they spread, perhaps hoping they would in some way harm Bronwen's spotless reputation—the shining, respectable alderman of the Crest and her daughter, the whore.

"What if we told you we still have *the* document?" Uriah squints, with disconcerting sincerity. "Proof they promised you to us, penned by your father and signed with the quickest quill stroke of your mother, accompanied by the wax seal of your family crest. If such an artifact were to circulate through the city, it would be damning. I find the written word cuts deeper and is far more difficult to deny."

If they, in fact, have this in their possession, it could indeed be her mother's undoing. She was of age by the time her mother promised her to Lysander and Uriah. However, there were hundreds of times and years beforehand. The people of Mirus, or anyone of any self-respect for that matter, put up with a certain amount of vile actions, whether they accept, agree, or simply ignore them. However, in the case of children, there can be no remorse and no redemption. The masses will turn, and those who try to defend those actions will be dealt with just as swiftly.

March sheathes her swords. "If I were to believe you, what would this cost me?"

"You have not listened from the beginning," says Uriah. "This is a gift."

"Oh, I have heard you clearly, and you speak as if I do not know your own reputation or what you two truly desire."

Uriah chuckles. "Your mind is a wonder in and of itself—sharper than any blade forged in this age, the last, or any yet to come. Which makes you all the more alluring. Can you blame us for attempting a different tactic? We intend to give you this gift with no obligation."

"But for such a rare and priceless item, should an opportunity arise"—Lysander speaks vaguely yet pointed—"where our paths align, however momentarily, we ask you consider your choices."

What game of chess do the Twins play at? Before this encounter, March thought they saw her as only the prize. While this may still be true, now they see her as a player in their game; a game she does not wish to play.

"Produce the scroll," says March. "By end of day."

"Of course," they say together in an unsettling moment of honesty. "You shall have it."

Before March can respond, Mary Anne's irritating voice cuts their conversation short, calling from the top of the stairs to the keep. "May I have a moment?" she asks of Lysander and Uriah, approaching quickly.

"Of course," says Uriah, in a higher mocking tone, the register, the facade March knows him well for.

"I went to your chambers in search of you, but the servants, or women, said I would find you here." Mary Anne straightens her posture.

"And here we stand," says Uriah.

"I would like to have a conversation with you. Your presence is requested for a game of croquet at dusk," Mary Anne tells them. "Refusal is not an option."

"Nor would we," says Lysander. "The last match we played with you was one to remember."

The color washes from Mary Anne's face.

"We shall meet you on the court after we bathe and change," says Uriah, who then turns to March. "And as for where we left off in our conversation, we can continue there if you care to join the game."

"Fine," says March.

The Twins walk toward the keep with their arrogant swagger, weapons over their shoulders. Mary Anne stares at March with an upturned nose and disgust in her eyes, eyebrow cocked to let March know all Mary Anne thinks she knows.

Mary Anne follows March back to the keep, until she walks in stride with her, chest up, and an air of superiority about her

"I see nothing has changed," Mary Anne says under her breath.

Mary Anne will believe what she will either way, and there are larger problems to contend with than Mary Anne's assumptions, therefore March will give her no explanation.

"Before we part ways," March calls to the Twins. "There is one unresolved matter.." The unanswered question scratched at the back of her mind, while they attempted to distract her with the talk of Bronwen.

The Twins turn around before they reach the doors of the keep.

"Oh." Uriah snaps his fingers, feigning remembrance. "The blood to be repaid for our mutilated brothers. Not something you need worry about. It has already been handled."

CHAPTER 32
CHESHIRE

Snap.

After disposing of the bodies, washing his hands, and returning to Stonehaven, Cheshire breaks the neck of the first Mirusian soldier he crosses and leaves the body limp in the shadows of an alley jutting off from the Row. With the Mask of Light, the fool never saw his fate waiting right in front of him. He paid the price for the Gryphon's defiance, as will others he crosses paths with, regardless of their allegiance. This chaos spreading across Stonehaven, chaos not of Cheshire's doing, overshadows his own work and irritates him to no end.

The Gryphon used Cheshire's love and dedication for Jonathan as a weapon against him; a mistake he will soon regret. Cheshire has pieced together his plan but misses one key component, and until he finds it, it would be unwise to confront the Gryphon. What worked before will not work again, and he cannot afford to give the Gryphon any more tactical knowledge. He wipes his hand over his face and banishes the Mask of Light back into his glove.

"Cheshire," the voice calls out. Louder than before. The figure of the woman impersonating his mother stands at the far end of the alleyway near a stack of discarded crates.

"Can I have no peace from you?"

"Cheshire," the woman says again. The accuracy of her mimic sends icy fingers down Cheshire's body. She sounds like his mother with a slight unnatural echo in her voice.

"Damn it all. You have made a grave mistake appearing now. Though you helped to point out the Gryphon, it is you who has my undivided attention now."

The woman beckons him with a soft hand. He must admit she wants him to follow her, but chasing after her on foot would be a waste of time and effort. If she wants him, she shall have him. He waves his left hand over his face, summoning the Mask of Shadows, and jumps into a sliver of a shadow cast by a nearby awning and bursts through the cast shadow of the crates sending broken pieces of old wood and straw stuffing skidding across the stones.

For once, the woman steps back defensively, but not surprised. He plays her game, blinking intentionally to allow her to disappear and reappear farther away. Cheshire jumps through the shadows of nearby barrels, awnings, and townspeople, chasing the apparition deeper into Stonehaven. She appears to learn as well. The first three times she waits for Cheshire to reappear feet from her before disappearing, but by the fourth, she already widens their gap before he fully exits a shadow.

They head east through the streets, alleys, dead ends unable to confine them, and the rooftops of Stonehaven. The woman finally changes direction to the north, toward the Boroughs, when they reach the southern side of the Forge.

The bellowing, pulsing flames from forges breathing like dragons give ample shadows for Cheshire to dart through. Shadows are as dark gossamer curtains to him as he passes through them, one after the other, in quick succession.

For a moment, Cheshire believes he has lost sight of the woman, expecting her to reappear somewhere far down the curve of the street. Instead, she appears at the end of another alley to the left of Cheshire at the edge of the stone stairs leading down to the Boroughs themselves. The mastermind behind this deception is still unclear, but it makes sense now why this apparition has become more bold the lower Cheshire travels in the city. Whatever or whoever is behind this resides in the lowest level, often the forgotten tier, of Mirus.

Cheshire does not rely on the shadows anymore, recalling the mask into his glove. When he blinks, the woman does not disappear, but instead descends the stairs slowly. Cheshire leaps from his perch and follows, townspeople gasping as he crosses the street, careful not to lose sight of the woman.

They pass townspeople from Stonehaven climbing the stairs and servants from the Crest with wrapped packages and their hoods pulled far over their faces; attempts to hide their identities and purchases from the Crooked Market, the only reason anyone from above would make the trek down to the Boroughs. Some stare at Cheshire's face quizzically, worried, while others stare at his cock, not used to seeing a man walk casually through the streets with nothing but a thin shawl wrapped around his neck. They can do as they wish, stare as they wish. Cheshire's priority is the hooded figure bobbing down the long stairway until they reach the soft earth of the Boroughs.

The woman evades him casually, turning through the labyrinth of broken wooden shanties and makeshift shacks. Still, she does not attempt to lose Cheshire, just lure him. He closes the gap between them before they reach the crowds of the Crooked Market. As they approach the wide pillars of the Long Bridge over the Boroughs, the woman turns a sharp corner quicker than before, ducking behind the large stone structure. Cheshire, cautious, runs to catch up, turns the corner, and stops dead in his tracks less than five feet from the woman who faces him without fear. Even at this distance, her face cannot be seen.

"Have we had enough, then?" Cheshire goads her. "Is this all? No grand reveal? No soldiers lying in wait? I am rather offended, actually. I expected more."

The woman remains silent and points to the south.

Cheshire clicks his teeth. "I tire of these games. I have followed you this far and I will have my answers now."

No response.

"Or I shall leave. I have humored you long enough. I know you are not my mother, but you should suffer for the effrontery you possess to imitate her. Knowing now you are not her, but some conjuring, I can choose to ignore you. Call my name as many times as you like, scream it from the rooftops. I will not hear them and will not heed them once I leave here, of this you can be certain. You can play this game alone for the rest of eternity."

The woman tilts her head and her lavender hair falls from behind the shadow of the hood. Still, she mocks him, mocks his mother. Cheshire pounces for the woman and grabs hold of her cloak for the first time below the clasp, keeping it closed below her neck. Her eyes hide deep in the hood's shadow, but a smile creeps wide at the shadow's edge—a smile his mother would never possess.

His hands begin to prick and itch as if a thousand insects bite his palms. He releases his hold to find a white powdered resin covering his fingers. The outside of her cloak appears to be covered with it. The sensation of insects transforms to complete numbness. Cheshire tries to move his fingers, but they do not listen, losing all feeling and control over them.

"What is this witchcraft?"

He dares not move his hands closer to his face, but he can smell the essence of hemlock, henbane, poppy, and something else much more powerful. *Damn it.* The crown of his head tingles. Another gathering of insects spreads down his face and neck. The numbness climbs up his arms toward his chest. His lips and tongue grow numb, spit flying from his mouth. The sensation travels down his spine and into his legs. Unable to support himself, Cheshire falls to the dirt face first, unable to use his arms to brace himself. His vision blurs and focuses at a rapid pace until all is a mix of colors and shapes. Cheshire feels his breath slowing.

The woman reaches for her hood. Cheshire fights against the call of the darkness; he must see her face. She pulls the hood back as if pulling water from her hair. The purple strands are gone, an illusion, and long golden hair falls to her shoulders. Her golden eyes pierce deep into his. Runic tattoos cover the soft features of her face and neck. Cheshire recognizes them, and the woman. She was the apothecary from the Crooked Market he bartered with many moons ago.

If this is how he meets his end, it will be quite furious and disappointing, and he promises to haunt and torment this woman from the next world. However, he is not sure her concoction of ingredients is meant to kill him. If the apothecary wanted him dead, she could have doused him with this powder at any point in time, whether it be at their first encounter or in the city. She wishes to render him unconscious, or so he hopes. Unfortunately, one way remains to find the end of this path and the puppeteer behind it all—through the darkness. Before his old friend fully embraces him in stiff arms and the numbness consumes his body, he forces his lips to heed to obey him, with one last thing to say to the apothecary.

"Fuck you."

CHAPTER 33
JONATHAN

Jonathan counts the stairs as he walks back to the castle to distract himself from the pain of each step, with his adrenaline fading. He can still feel their knuckles against his skin and bones. Beneath a broken gutter, Jonathan scrubs his hands and arms in a small bucket full of rainwater. He sniffs his hands to make sure he did not just plunge his hands into someone's chamber pot. The cold splashes tense his skin, his faded bruises, and those yet to be.

Once clean, he takes a small sip from his elixir and pockets it again. His consumption has increased since arriving in Mirus, which is to be expected, but still bothersome. The elixir numbs the sting of his wounds, or at least numbs his mind to them. The clop of the boots helps to keep time as he climbs through Stonehaven, and the years of cracks and chips on each step keep his mind distracted until he reaches the top.

Something thumps against his head while his gaze is lowered, focused on his feet. Jonathan lifts his arm, prepared to move a low-hanging tree branch out of the way, though none grow here. It takes his eyes a moment to focus on the object so close to his face. Bark does not meet his hand, but the thick soles of another pair of muddy boots. A poor man hangs from a noose, lifeless, swaying in Jonathan's hand, suspended from a beam connecting the neighboring buildings across the stairway. Jonathan lifts his eyes to meet the lifeless gaze of the man above; he knows him and has seen him often in the Row.

The man's neck stretches from the thick length of rope, with bloody scratches marking his skin. The same blood packs underneath his fingernails. Jonathan's elixir temporarily numbs his emotions or he would feel a vortex of outrage, sadness, guilt, anything. All he can wonder is how unfortunate it must be to survive the consuming wave of the cult just to die senselessly at the hands of Lysander and Uriah's petty ambitions.

A distant scream rises in Stonehaven somewhere to the east—a scream filled with the anguish of discovering the body of a loved one. Jonathan's feet move before he can think, running down the stairs, following the street in search of the source of the scream. Before he can reach it, an out-of-place silhouette in a narrow alley catches Jonathan's attention. The body of an elderly man, a well-regarded sculptor, hangs from the iron sign outside of his shop door. His fingers and clothing are splattered with clay and speckled with crimson.

Another scream grows, this time of one woman, soon joined by another from a lower tier of Stonehaven. A third rises from the west. A fourth cry of agony joins the swells, then a fifth and sixth. One by one, they fill the streets and transform the dull muffled air of Stonehaven to a sorrow-filled wailing wind drifting through home, shop, street, and alley for all to hear. Jonathan's ear is not as keen as March's or Cheshire's, but he counts the voices as they join, and loses the count after fifteen.

Locating the first scream seems pointless now. In the alleyway, he uses a nearby crate to loosen the noose around the old sculptor's neck. From what Jonathan can recall, he has no family left. The frozen expression on his face, the sad grimace, suggests a surrender to his fate. It may have taken the soldiers hours or even days to stumble upon him in this quiet alley. The man deserves more respect and care; they all do.

A few painful phrases slip through the cries and weeping, which overrun the harrowed streets.

"He was only a boy."

"Find the rest of your sisters."

"Mother."

"My Son."

"Don't look, child."

"Why?"

"I hate them all."

"Father. Father. Father."

The deep lines of the face of Jonathan's father, Theophilus, suddenly take the place of the old sculptor. A cold sweat washes over Jonathan's body and hands, and his legs become cold and numb. His heart beats in his chest with the rhythm of an army riding into war.

The crate rocks beneath him. He stumbles back, loses his balance on the crate, and falls to the ground. The unforgiving stones reawaken every bruise on his back. Jonathan reaches into his pocket for his elixir, drinks half of the vial, and holds the smooth glass to his forehead as he curls his knees to his chest and hides his face.

"Not him. It cannot be him. It is not him."

Jonathan never saw his father pass, therefore there is no way of knowing what expression was frozen on his face at the end. Over the centuries, he has suppressed thoughts of his father's death, even when people mention him by name. This memory Jonathan keeps locked deep within the recesses of his mind, in an iron trunk with no key. Keeping the memory at bay are a fog of images circling and guarding the trunk: his father's hearty laugh surrounded by friends at the Dry Dock tavern in Rookridge, his warm, generous smile when greeting anyone he passed, sipping his lavender tea Jonathan would make him every morning as a child, and working side-by-side in their family's workshop and the finest hats in all of Wonderland.

The trunk rattles and Jonathan's most painful thoughts threaten to resurface. They have spent far too long in Mirus, where time has no meaning and it feels as if a century has passed since he has looked upon his table sitting under the lone oak in the Hollow, missing him.

“Heavens.” A voice pulls Jonathan back to the here and now. A woman of Stonehaven stands at the end of the alley, staring at the sculptor. One hand clutches her apron, the other covers her mouth, and she runs out of sight, this probably being the first body she has seen despite the many screams across the city.

Jonathan dares to look up once more, and the sculptor’s pale face returns. Jonathan replaces the crate and, with a few quick tugs at the rope, the sculptor’s lifeless body flops over Jonathan’s shoulder. He kicks in the front door to his shop and workspace, ransacked and looted. Still drying busts and vases bear the marks of blades, while others are smashed into piles of clay shards and dust. He lays the sculptor on the thin, threadbare mattress at the rear of his shop and positions him with care to give him the appearance he sleeps. He could never leave the old man uncared for. Jonathan will inform the next soldier he comes across and send him here. The scrapes around his neck and the noose outside will be evidence enough of what happened to the old man. Jonathan must wonder how many other bodies, how many other innocents, swing throughout the city, and how many are yet to be discovered?

Lysander and Uriah struck quickly; a retaliation without reason. They killed and mutilated ten innocent townspeople of Stonehaven and blamed Mirusian soldiers. Now, to those loyal to their cause, these deaths are in some way justified, and more innocent men and women will die, neighbors and friends they have known for over a millennium, though they do not realize it. They do not see what happens right in front of their eyes. To those blindly devoted, would they care if they knew the truth?

The Twins remain in the castle to keep their hands spotless, but this man’s blood, the blood of all the innocent, will stain their skin for all time. Jonathan must question who enacted this violence. There is no evidence of any wound on the sculptor or the man he left over the stairway. A horrible shiver overcomes Jonathan. Many know the knots and the length needed to make nooses, not just soldiers. Any townspeople of Mirus loyal to them could have easily committed these murders. The crowd assembled in the Row easily numbered over a thousand.

On his way back to the castle, Jonathan fears his heart stops, replaced with a cold, all-consuming hollowness. High between two buildings in Stonehaven, another body dangles by its rope, swaying in the wind as if rocked by a lullaby the boy will never hear again. He cannot be further than his tenth year, one boot and one bare foot. Unlike the others Jonathan has stumbled upon, streams of tears cut their way through the dirt on his cheeks. A crestfallen expression forever locked on his face. His final thoughts probably questioned why this happened to him, calling out to his parents. It happened because people who do not even know his name play a game with everyone's lives in the city, himself included. This is the way of Mirus; the city destroys innocence.

The city and its people will not last five days with such tensions brewing and stirred by the Twins. Especially not now. They may have started with treachery, but this will soon turn into a civil brawl, overtaking all of Mirus, with its people demanding answers and seeking retribution themselves. The city was already broken, and so are its people, and what comes next will change the city, unable to recover from it. As long as Lysander and Uriah draw breath, the longer Jonathan and everyone else play at this despicable game, the more lives will be claimed, the more destruction will be wrought upon the city, and all the more innocents will be lost.

CHAPTER 34
CHESHIRE

Cheshire wakes in a void, unable to open his eyes; the embrace of darkness will not release him yet. Sensation returns to his chest first, feeling his lungs take in full breaths, like someone gently dragging their fingertips across his skin. He misses time, disoriented, and does not know if he is standing, lying, hanging right-side up or up-side down. The insects return, and prickles spread to his back and creep down his arms and legs. Curious. As the heat and feeling return to this body, the prickles do not leave the backside of his body. He shifts as much as he can manage, and the slight crunch of grass meets his ears, as do the call of birds, the rustle of leaves, and distant water. Perhaps he has crossed over to the next world, or at least been taken out of Mirus. Cheshire focuses and forces his eyelids open, one by one, to reveal the blurred world around him, somehow light and dark simultaneously.

"Welcome back," a man's voice says from somewhere around him.

Cheshire means to threaten the man's life, curse him, but can only manage a muffled murmur.

"It will take a moment, but all your senses will return, I assure you," the man says.

A moment is too long. Cheshire takes command of his body, gripping the grass and soil beneath him, and forces himself to roll over and get to his feet like a marionette willing life into itself. He collapses back to the earth twice like a newborn fawn trying to walk after birth. Both times, his chest and face skid across the grass. The third time he rises, growls, and roars, tongue still tingling with numbness, forcing himself upright, still wobbling.

An old, thin man with short white hair comes into focus and greets Cheshire with an open palm, his fingers and long beige and gray robes splattered with paint the colors of a sunset.

"Kill you," Cheshire says, before falling back to the ground. "Fuck."

"Calm yourself," the man says as if he knows Cheshire. "All I wish is to have a conversation with you."

"Where is she?" Cheshire pushes himself back to his feet, this time easier, still not yet regaining full control of his body.

"We will get to her momentarily," the man says.

"You speak as if you know me, yet your face is unfamiliar. Do I know you?" Cheshire asks, looking past the man, curious about this mysterious place within Wonderland he has never seen or known.

"I know you. Correction, know of you." The thin man gestures to the cavern. "Welcome to the Groves."

His vision fully comes to focus on the small verdant meadow they stand in, the large crystal-clear lake in front of them, and the lush expanse of oak, sycamore, and ash surrounding them. The soft grass underfoot welcomes Cheshire's stretching toes. High above, at the top of the cavern, an orb illuminates in a pale-blue wash, as if the moon beamed down on to this serene, hidden place, and gives light to the full forest concealed within its walls. Its reflection ripples gently, waving to him in the lake's reflection. Glowing bugs drift in and out of reality, creating warm, twinkling stars.

Across the lake, two rushing waterfalls, at least forty feet high, cascade from the rock face. A small grotto, perpetually sprayed by the falls, sits at the level of the lake between them, to form a giant face within the cavern.

Large golden discs attached to metal arms jut from the walls, catch stray sunlight from unseen holes in the rock face, and reflect its rays to more disks in a maze of orange shafts gently cutting through the blue. The dancing particles in the rays of sun, the false moon up above, and the pulsing glow of the bugs create an astonishing, ethereal place where night and day exist at the same time.

As his senses fully return, he recalls his reason for being here, even if he does not recall how. The woman he followed had a purpose, and if not to kill or imprison him, it must be to meet this man. Cheshire will allow him to live long enough to answer his questions.

"What do you want with me?" Cheshire asks. Not knowing grates at Cheshire's nerves.

The man twists his fingers in the ends of his robe to remove more dried paint.

Cheshire huffs and takes in his surroundings to get some sort of bearing and discovers he does know of this place. It sits on a shelf in the far reaches of his mind—another of his mother's bedtime stories she would tell him as a child.

"T'was once upon a midsummer eve, the gods did grant the world's reprieve. After hearing their plights and burdens great, took mercy on them for pity's sake." Cheshire can hear his mother's voice join with his as he speaks. "They freed the people of the doubt and woe they had fallen under, and instead granted them the ability to dream and wonder. The veil lifted and the weir of woe, one last gift the gods did bestow. New fortune would spring eternal from their transmuted fears, letting new life grow from their Pool of Tears."

"I've not heard the rhyme said correctly in an age," says the old man.

"I remember everything," says Cheshire. "Even made-up stories."

"All stories are made up." The old man chuckles. "I would not discount them. Mothers often create stories for their children to explain the unexplainable and teach them of the world in ways they can comprehend. T'was your mother who gifted us the Geal Stone." He points to the glowing orb above. "She is responsible for the creation of this sanctuary—a gift to those who live in the city's shadow. And it was she who created the rhyme."

His body may as well lose all feeling again. "My mother?"

"You are Queen Dinah's son, are you not?"

The fact this man can say such a thing with confidence and no malice in his eyes causes Cheshire's hair to stand on end, tears and anger crashing behind his eyes and in his stomach. Strangers know more of his mother than he does. "How do you know, old man?"

"Dodge," he corrects Cheshire. "Alderman Dodges, or just Dodge. Your choice. And I knew your mother. She was the only queen or king to ever venture down to the Boroughs. Kindest woman I ever had the privilege of meeting. Though it would seem her fruit fell quite far from her tree."

"You know her. How do you know of me?"

"Honestly, I had no idea you existed; not until recently." Dodge wags his finger at Cheshire's head and chest. "I first saw you atop the gatehouse days ago when the queen-to-be pardoned you for your crimes. There were whispers and rumors long, long ago of a child, if you found yourself in the right circles. I have seen much, and the color of your mother's hair and eyes are unique, unmistakable in fact. The same shade you possess, though a darkness veils their brightness. Not to mention you have her features, and you wear her shawl draped around your neck. She bought it from a shop here in the Boroughs when I walked with her one golden afternoon, and she wore it every day thereafter. Until it came into your possession."

He should take this as a compliment to her kindness, but Cheshire had so little time with her, it is eternally unfair to take it as anything more than another wound. Cheshire fights every curse clawing at his tongue and calms his breath. He forgets his rage and asks through bellowing tears, "Can you tell me more of my mother?"

Dodge walks toward the tree line and waves his hand for Cheshire to follow. "I can do better."

They pass under canopies where blue and yellow streaks pierce through the leaves. The song of insects chirping from the brush mixes with the constant gentle roar of the waterfalls. Dodge leads Cheshire out of the wood to view the rock face of the cavern.

Cheshire weeps instantly—eyes and lips trembling, body shaking, gasping for breath, trying desperately to hold back his tears.

A freshly painted portrait of his mother covers the wall twenty feet high. Her head takes prominence at the center of the masterpiece. A circle of yellow surrounds her head to make her lavender hair shine. A silhouette of her floats below, both arms outstretched, and a painted wind swirls in blues and whites from her fingertips. Her long-draped sleeves and gown whip around her; a moment of history frozen in time. Below her figure, hundreds of arms and hands are outstretched, not painted but left void to take the gray and blue colors of the stones.

The features of her face are exactly as Cheshire remembers: her smile, the color of her eyes, the warmth in her cheeks, the sparkle in her eyes. She shames the beauty of the cavern. So long, the image of her face faded from his memory, but now her visage stands in front of him, and a host of memories return to Cheshire with the crushing weight of the waterfall. The tears come and he does not try to stop them.

Dodge returns to the wall, dips his fingers in small basins of paint set out along a wooden bench, and adds further details to the wind with his thumb, never looking back at Cheshire, allowing him to mourn, to grieve, to feel joy, all mixed together. In this otherworldly place, the only reason Cheshire knows time passes is the movement of the sun streaks in the air. After a great length of time, and after Cheshire's energy is all but exhausted, he sits on the grass and wipes his cheeks and nose.

The tattooed apothecary appears from out of the tree line. Or so he thinks. The tattooed runes and lines upon her face and body give her away, though curled hair the color of strawberry jam replaces the golden locks she presented earlier, and eyes to match. She keeps her distance, cloak open and hanging behind her, draped in thin scraps of gray and red linens and feathers, revealing more of her body and tattoos than they cover.

"This is the Lory," says Dodge. "I assume no other introduction is in order."

Cheshire glares at her, studies her—soft, elegant, and enigmatic. He does not know what else she has prepared for him, so he turns his attention back to Dodge.

"You did all this?"

"Aye." Dodge wipes the paint from his fingers onto the side of his robes.

"Why?"

"Do you really wish to know the answer to the question?"

Of course he does, but the question itself, the confidence of Dodge, gives Cheshire pause. "You are an artist," he says instead.

"At times. I like to create."

"I destroy," says Cheshire.

"Well, we each have our strengths." Dodge chuckles. "You know, creation can come from destruction, from chaos. One cannot happen without the other. Everything has its place. Everyone has their purpose."

"Alright, then. Why? Why all this?" He points to the Lory. "Why the illusions? Why..."—he struggles to form any more words, to describe the breathtaking painting of his mother again—"... this."

"I am no fool," says Dodge. "You would never give thought to parlay with me had I not tricked you down here. I do apologize for the deception. It must have been difficult to endure, however, the Lory is quite proficient at delivering on what I ask."

"How?" Cheshire's curiosity gets the best of him again. He has seen his fair share of magic and tricks, but never someone wearing another's face.

"I touched you." The Lory finally speaks. "You came to my stall, and I traded forks and essence of hemlock for a chance to touch your body. You were sweating. More than the mind holds memories. Different bodily fluids have their uses and can create several simple incantations, depending on their potency. The sweat of a prince is difficult to come by and a prize in any hand."

"I am no prince." The disdain spits from Cheshire's mouth.

"And now we arrive at the *why*." Dodge picks at some of the dried paint on the top of his hands. "I have met with this woman who would be queen, Mary Anne, and the twin brothers. Both parties play games with the lives of the townspeople, vying for a throne none have claim to."

"You think the throne interests me?" Cheshire laughs. "I come to destroy this city." These words Cheshire has repeated hundreds of thousands of times, yet for the first time sitting in this place, the phrase holds less meaning. Especially if this was a gift from his mother. "Destroy the city, and everyone in it for what was done to my mother," Cheshire continues.

"What wrong was done?" Dodge asks pointedly.

"They forgot her," Cheshire snaps.

"Have you ever considered the best revenge is none? Hurting them won't heal you, and becoming like them won't bring your mother back. Let them live with what they've done. You can walk away. Break the cycle."

The alderman does not believe Cheshire's mother to be alive, which angers Cheshire further. "Those responsible sit in her place. They live with what they have done, and all the while enjoy luxury and comfort. I will walk away when the city burns."

"May I ask, why do you hold on to this pain?" asks Dodge. "This hurt must consume you."

"It has. It does."

"It is all you know," Dodge cuts him short. "You find comfort in your rage and in this pain. So much so, I wager it terrifies you to let it go."

Cheshire's blood boils at Dodge's words. He speaks the truth, and Cheshire will not accept it. It is all he knows. It drives him and gives him purpose. He has spent more time in life knowing hate than love. The pain is the last constant reminder of his mother, and he will not release it until his work is finished.

"They forgot her," he repeats.

Dodge puts his hand on the painting. "Not everyone."

Cheshire twists the frayed edges of his mother's sash. "What does it matter?"

"What does it matter?" Dodge repeats Cheshire's question as if to someone slow of the mind. "She and you are not the only forgotten people in Wonderland. The people of the Boroughs outnumber the combined population of Stonehaven and the Crest, even before the attack of the cult. Wager a guess how many of our number we lost?"

"One hundred," says Cheshire.

"Two," says Dodge. "Two unfortunate souls who happened to be in the Row. The rest of us, while still concerned, remained ignored, because every vile and evil force in this world climbs toward the castle."

"On this we can agree."

"The Duchess speaks of women from another world who have the gift to be chosen by Wonderland to be queen."

"This is true," says the Lory. "It is the old magic of the Grand Arcana, created by the Old Ones."

"The brothers peddle the story of being the last blood of the line of kings," says Dodge. "They are false, and you know this to be true. Dinah herself was—"

"Is."

"Is of the blood of the kings. It was her grandfather, King Muiread, she dethroned. Lysander and Uriah, the sons of his brother, are her cousins. Your cousins. Your blood."

"Also true," says the Lory.

"Wonderland, the Arcana, the Old Ones, whoever the fuck is in charge and pulls at our strings, chose your mother, imbued her with the power to topple a tyrannical ruler, and then blessed her with a son, an heir. Wonderland's rightful heir."

Cheshire squirms in his skin. He knows this. Deep within him, he knew this and buried it down with any thought of his wayward father, content to not accept any of it. Cheshire thinks of the hidden stone door in the grotto. It opened at his touch. The catacombs of Wonderland welcome him and feel like home. Was this not just a gift of his mother, but of Wonderland as well? Blood does not matter. He found his rightful family—Jonathan, March, Dormy, and at times Ogden.

"No," Cheshire says from under his brows. Someone else knowing his secrets greatly vexes him and claws at his bones. This man may need to die for his stolen knowledge.

"Think of it. What if Dinah's, Queen Dinah's, son reclaimed the throne?" Dodge asks with a newfound intensity.

"No." Cheshire rises and dusts off small pieces of grass from his backside.

"The skein of your life was woven a long time ago. Why fight it? Her legacy echoes through you. Do you realize the number of people who would follow you if they knew who you were?" Dodge picks up a large bucket of water by the wooden bench holding his paints.

Cheshire cracks his neck and back. "Mention it one more time and the Boroughs will be in need of a new alderman."

Dodge shrugs. "Then, you are correct. It does not matter." He rears back, ready to fling the bucketful of water at his masterpiece and wash it from the walls forever.

In half the breath of a second, Cheshire imagines the paint smeared, running down the cavern wall, and marring his mother's face. In the other half of the breath, he grabs the old man's wrist to stop him. The water sloshes and spills onto the grass.

"What are you doing?" Cheshire asks, heart pounding and chest heaving. "Please." Cheshire stares at his mother's face.

Dodge drops the bucket and the rest of the water spills onto the ground. He waits for Cheshire to release his wrist. "I won't say another word about it. Just sharing a thought. And not to worry. The painting will stay. It's calming to look upon Dinah again, both in the painting, and in you."

Cheshire releases his wrist.

"You and yours are welcome here any time," says Dodge. "The Lory will show you the way out."

"You have nothing more profound to say?"

"I wanted to say my piece, and you have heard it. You disagree, therefore there is no need to continue the conversation. But return any time if you would like to hear more about your mother. I am more than willing to share the small memories I have of her."

Damn Dodge and his fucking theories. Cheshire follows the Lory along the cavern wall, glancing back at the painting of his mother as it grows smaller. Eventually, the grass beneath Cheshire's feet turns to the viscous sludge of dirt and mud common in the Boroughs. His pace quickens, trying to unhear Dodge's words. Fate bound him to be a player in this game, but he has his own motivations, and he will see them through to the end, and no amount of paint on a cavern wall will change his mind. No matter how much the likeness of his mother looked down, smiling at him.

Fuck legacy. Hunt the Gryphon. Find my mother. A sliver of doubt pierces his heart. *Kill the Duchess. Destroy the city. Leave this gods forsaken land behind.* Looking upon his mother, even a painting of her, shifted something inside of him. Are these reminders, or does he try to convince himself? *Fuck... hunt... find... kill... run, leave, mother. Mother. Mother.* He plucks the doubt like a splinter with his teeth. He knows nothing else. His life is dedicated to this cause. *Fuck. Fuck. Fuck!*

The Lory leads him to a small opening in the cavern, zigzagging back and forth several times before he steps ankle-deep into mud at the back of a wide drainage pipe hiding underneath the base of the Long Bridge.

"I trust you know the rest of the way." The Lory ushers him forward.

"I trust you know what will happen if you ever dare wear my mother's face again."

"Yes," the Lory answers simply.

"Before I leave, I have a request. Two, actually. Consider them repayment for the pain you caused."

The Lory lifts her eyebrows, waiting.

"I know the ingredients of the powder you used on me—most of them. Hemlock. Henbane. I assume dehydrated milk of the poppy. All of them are used to render someone unconscious. First request: what was the paralytic infused with it and why did it act so quickly and thoroughly?"

The Lory laughs. "Monkshood, Nightshade, Mandragora Root, and small amounts of newt secretions."

"Damned woman. You might as well have opened the door to the afterlife and kicked me through yourself. I have never heard of a deadlier concoction."

"It is not concocted to take lives," she says, walking away. "In fact, it can't. I am good at what I do. I am sure it wouldn't have worked on you anyway."

"My second request—"

Before Cheshire can finish, the Lory pulls a small leather pouch from the cloak and drops it into Cheshire's hand.

"In return, perhaps you will return and gift me something more. Sweat works wonders, but you would be surprised at what I can create with other fluids from your body."

"No."

"Worth an ask. Perhaps you will reconsider." The Lory wipes her hands over her hair and the golden waves return. She blinks three times and the red of her eyes fleck to gold. She leaves Cheshire and heads toward the Crooked Market.

He tosses the pouch in his hand. There is little heft to it, but then again, it does not take much to be effective. Cheshire used to be the biggest threat to the Queendom. This cult and the Twins have distracted the people from this most important fact, and Mary Anne robbed him of his power.

Cheshire summons the Mask of Shadows to his face, walks into the shadow of a large culvert in the city wall, and appears in the chamber full of looking-glasses and statues. He slips through the secret passage and collects his clothing, donning his barely held together trousers, his vest, and cloak.

He walks through another shadow, emerges from a large cupola above one of the tallest buildings in Stonehaven, and climbs to the pointed top of a nearby chimney. The cooler air high above the city fills his lungs, and his cloak flaps in the wind. This feels right. The city once again beneath him.

Dodge's misguided intentions were to remind Cheshire of a past and a life he never knew. He has never been a prince, or considered himself one. Difficult to think of yourself as royalty when hidden away and scurrying through tunnels. Their conversation has the adverse effect the alderman wished for, fueling the vengeful spark within Cheshire to a roaring fire. It is time he reminds everyone of who he really is—not a prince, but a murderer. The demon who struck fear into the lives of all across Wonderland. Mary Anne and the Twins had their time to make their proclamation. The time for Cheshire's silence is over. He will make his voice heard and his intentions known.

And thanks to the Lory, he has everything he needs.

CHAPTER 35

MARY ANNE

The lawn and the outside of the topiary maze are freshly trimmed and mowed; the faint, foul odor hangs in the air, the last fading evidence of the Cult of the Mother no more than cinders and ash in the harbor below. The smell grew rank days priors, but in a day or two more it will fade.

Mary Anne waits at the far side of the croquet court. A dozen members of the Castle Guard raise thin poles around the lawn and farther into the garden, connected by lengths of rope with small pennant flags. Lanterns hang at the center of each rope swag. Mary Anne must remember she promised the townspeople a festival. She must remind herself in spite of the continued restlessness of the city.

She paces back and forth on the southern end of the field, closest to the overlook to the harbor. By her measure of the sun setting, nearly an hour passes before Lysander and Uriah round the corner of the hedge maze to join her. They most certainly have changed for the occasion. Besides their boots, they hardly wear anything at all: long half-tunics covering half their bodies, kept in place by two leather belts around their torsos connected by a golden ring. A set of three glass orbs hang from their belts. As they walk, weapons over their shoulders, the fabric of their tunics, placed precariously close to their cocks, shifts to reveal themselves to the world, without a care.

Behind them, a dozen armored soldiers of Adamas walk in procession and stand in a line on the opposite side of the court. Lysander and Uriah lay their weapons, almost ceremoniously, in the waiting arms of two of their soldiers and take their time crossing the lawn to meet Mary Anne.

If not for their vile personas, Mary Anne would find their bodies and faces attractive, more than attractive, falling into the same trap as every other woman and servant throwing themselves before them. In some strange way, they are a warped looking-glass reflection of Jonathan and Cheshire. Lysander, with his broad shoulders and heaving chest, and Uriah with his slender but muscular build. Mary Anne looks away, searching for the large woven basket containing the spiked croquet balls, and discovers it out of place at the eastern end of the court.

"I invited you two for croquet." She selects a mallet from their stand. "Not a battle or any other activity. I am not March."

"You most certainly are not." Lysander looks her up and down.

They antagonize from the start. Mary Anne should have been prepared. Must she always be compared to March? In truth, it is Mary Anne who compares herself. The Twins merely make her thoughts vocal.

Mary Anne stands tall, and the deep V of her gown widens. "I am woman enough."

"This remains to be seen," says Uriah.

"Woman enough to be queen."

"Indeed. And we are more than willing to find out." Uriah grins, and his cock pushes against the edge of his tunic.

"Disgusting."

"What disgusts you about the idea?" Uriah moves closer and taps the tops of the mallets with his fingers. "After all, we are willing to fuck you while the man you fawn over has yet to claim you as his own?"

Mary Anne's stomach sinks and her face flushes with heat. "You know nothing."

"We know more than you think." Lysander prowls around her.

She will not give into fear or intimidation. In the distance, the Castle Guard climb down their ladders, drop their baskets, and buckle their belts and swords around their waists.

Uriah's tone turns to jest. "We have been around enough women to know when they are in drought, shall we say. And you, my dear, most certainly are dry."

"I did not call you here to talk about fucking," Mary Anne snaps.

"Pity," says Lysander. "Very well. What confidence do you wish from us?"

Mary Anne wastes no time. "You are knowledgeable of Wonderland's history."

"Of course," they say together, mulling over the mallets.

"Educate me."

"What an intriguing request." Uriah selects a mallet from the stand and spins it effortlessly in hand, each turn a thought. "What do you wish to know?"

"Allow me to answer a question with a question of my own. What should I know?"

"Fascinating." Lysander selects his mallet and holds it over his shoulder as he would his sword.

The twelve members of the Castle Guard slowly inch closer and assemble on Mary Anne's side of the court. She nods to them to hold their position and remain steadfast.

"There are things you should know," says Uriah. "Others you need to know. And others you must know. Which would you like?"

Mary Anne hardly sees the difference, but chooses anyway. The answer will more than likely be the same, no matter her choice. "Should."

"You should know the reason we will be victorious," says Uriah, strolling onto the court.

She will suffer their goads and jabs in order to discover and learn. "The reason?"

"Wonderland has a deep connection to its traditions and history," says Uriah, his tone too casual for Mary Anne. "Its lore journeys back thousands of years, passed down by stories and legends. The people of this country are raised by them. We know the stories all by heart. We can tell you when this castle was built, why the Wilds broke off from the mainland, where the Knights of the Draughts came from, the secret of the Garden in the Everwood, and so much more."

"You possess information," says Mary Anne, "nothing more. Information differs from knowledge. All this proves is you are well read."

"We can also tell you in which region of Wonderland which Old Ones are worshipped, and the traditional meals eaten on their high holy days, the difference in the air between Rutrum and Clypeus, and we can tell you what it is like to be forged in the heat of battle, armor and swords clashing, blood spilling, and we can tell you why so many fear a queen retaking the throne. And being a woman has nothing to do with it."

"Then, why make it such a contentious point?"

"Simple people understand simple things," says Lysander. "Complicated arguments and reasoning boggle the mind of simple farmers and merchants who care only where their next meal or coin comes from, the condition of their crops, or the shoes for their horses."

"You talk of the people as if they are simpletons."

"Are they not?" asks Lysander. "It is true we cannot wield the power of the Arcana, nor would we want to if given the chance. If we can convince the masses to choose us, the old ways, over someone who, for all intents and purposes, is all powerful, then tell us, who are the simpletons?"

At every turn they confound Mary Anne. How many years have they deceived and manipulated the people with their lies? How can Mary Anne believe what they say is true now?

"We have experienced this world," says Lysander. "Though you think you have some misbegotten right to it. There are answers you will never find in books. You will never learn within these walls. And when put to the test, the people of Wonderland will see through your frail claim."

A familiar feeling fills Mary Anne's stomach—hopelessness. A pit forms and falls beyond her feet. Even if these are half-truths, what chance does Mary Anne have if they know the people, know the world, and Mary Anne cannot risk leaving the city?

No. No. No, she tells herself, banishing the void. "Wonderland chose me. If Wonderland wanted you to claim the throne, the doors would have opened for you long ago. Yet, they remained shut, and the throne beyond your reach. In your vast knowledge, can you explain why?"

Uriah sighs heavily. "What does your book say?"

Mary Anne keeps silent. She does not want to let on; she does not know or even if the answer is in the book.

"The Grand Arcana proves more troublesome than beneficial," says Lysander. "There are still mysteries yet to be uncovered. Imbuing a person is one matter. Controlling the fates, binding wills, and forging the design of the world is quite another. Surely you can see why people would not accept a ruler who can control them?"

Mary Anne has no choice but to believe them, thinking of Jonathan, whom she named her counsel while on her path to become queen. Wonderland bound him to her. Mary Anne knew this but did not consider the breadth and hold of the Grand Arcana. Her focus was too narrow.

"Binding," says Mary Anne.

"Yes," says Lysander. "In the old ways there are many rituals and contracts that, once spoken, Wonderland, or the Arcana, sees them through to the end."

"An unearthly covenant," says Uriah. "Words have power and consequences."

Mary Anne feigns ignorance to gain more information besides her connection with Jonathan. "What is an example?"

"Now, we journey into the category of things you need to know," says Uriah. "There are many. Most spoken in the old tongue. Invoking Ciorcal Nocta would have eight of your choosing stand in a circle and watch or take part as you consummate your marriage, as many times as you require."

"Why would anyone wish for such a thing?" asks Mary Anne, shuddering at the idea of her round bed, the sheer curtains, and the stage it may have been previously.

"We did not say these all had positive intentions." Uriah smirks. "There are multiple possibilities."

"Anything not having to do with sex?"

"If Cuir-Mar is invoked after a battle by those who were defeated," says Lysander, "the victors must give proper burial to the slain."

"And if they do not?"

"Wonderland will claim the number of lives slain from the victors." Lysander bows his head as if in reverence.

"Keep in mind," says Uriah, "these are of the old world. There is also Aon Praelium, a duel between two combatants, champions, to determine the outcome of any battle or war to spare senseless bloodshed."

"And we cannot forget Sors Corgnat, granting a person the right to fuck any and all in their spouse's family."

"Enough of the barbarism," says Mary Anne, repulsed at the Twins' fixation with fucking.

True, she asked, but these are not the answers she wants to know. It is the past queens she must learn about. Whether or not it is a half-truth, Lysander and Uriah mentioned the people of Wonderland fearing the queens; a possibility Mary Anne never gave thought to. Before she can question any further, Jonathan calls her name and lifts her heart and thoughts.

"Mary Anne." Jonathan rounds the corner of the hedge maze and runs to her just as he left this morning: with only trousers hanging low on his hips and a soldier's boots. He does, however, carry his sword holstered on his back; its leather harness wraps around and under his arms, making his chest appear larger than it normally does. Behind him, a procession follows—March, the Gryphon, the Duchess, Bronwen, and the Chamberlain. Bronwen and the Duchess bicker behind Jonathan, as do the Gryphon and Chamberlain. March stands farther behind them, squinted eyes in the direction of the Twins, plotting another private rendezvous, no doubt. It appears there will be no further questions or answers about the queens until a later time. The most pressing question now is why have they all assembled?

Mary Anne lifts her mallet up and points to those following Jonathan like a scepter. "What is the meaning of this?"

"Ask them," says Jonathan, brow pinched and mouth twitching, pointing at Lysander and Uriah. "Ask them about the nearly sixty innocent townspeople—men, women, and children—hung throughout Stonehaven."

What has transpired while Mary Anne stayed in the castle? She promised the townspeople they would be safe; a fool's promise. Lysander and Uriah play their followers like a fiddle and set them into motion without ever leaving these walls. The thought of children dying at the hands of their followers crushes Mary Anne's chest, unable to breathe, and makes her want to snap her croquet mallet in half and stab both brothers through the chest. She scratches at the bare skin of her chest and neck.

"You will answer for your misdeeds. You will answer for their lives," Mary Anne commands.

"Dare to raise your voice at us again and you will lose it along with your head," says Lysander.

"We are not accountable for what those loyal to us do. Our soldiers had no part in this. Ask Carter yourself. Were any of our soldiers on the streets of Mirus? If the people grow tired of this nonsense and take matters into their own hands, you cannot blame us."

"You empowered them, emboldened them," says Mary Anne.

"I suggest we begin our game while the daylight stays with us," says Uriah, ignoring Mary Anne completely. "It is why you invited us here, after all. Everyone here is welcome to join us." Lysander and Uriah cross the lawn to the large wicker basket containing the croquet balls.

Mary Anne's hand rises, ready to command the Castle Guard to detain the brothers.

The Twins pause before reaching for the lid and exchange intense glances with each other, then turn back to Mary Anne, their expressions stone.

"Wait." Jonathan grabs Mary Anne's free wrist. "Something is wrong."

Lysander kicks the lid from the large basket. His eyes narrow and turn to steel. They would slice through Mary Anne if they could. "What do you mean by this treachery?"

March tilts her head and then looks to Jonathan with their damned invisible speech.

"You finally have the nerve to play the game the way it should be played," says Lysander. "You dare speak to us of blood spilled, and dare think to hold us accountable for others' actions, while you plot in front of our faces. I must say I am impressed." Their demeanor shifts, their posture changes, eyes darken, no longer players, but hunters.

"What does he speak of?" Mary Anne whispers to Jonathan. "What does March say?"

"Be ready," he whispers, and backs toward the bench with Mary Anne, unsheathing his sword.

Lysander kicks the large basket over, and what must be a dozen severed heads thud out and roll onto the grass in different directions, mouths agape, eyes glossy, skin pale, and jaws askew. He picks one up by the hair and holds the lifeless gray screaming face toward Mary Anne. Hard, shriveled tears of skin dangle from the neck. "These are our men. Loyal men. If we are to answer for others' crimes, so must you."

"By the heavens. We had no hand in this," the Duchess protests.

"This is Cheshire's work," whispers Jonathan, a hint of guilt hiding in his words.

Bile rises in Mary Anne's throat. The acrid smell from earlier came from the dead hidden on the field, not the harbor. She expects Lysander and Uriah to show more outrage. Instead, they smirk at her from below their brows, which adds to her nausea and quickening heart.

"No!" shouts Mary Anne. "We will not have bloodshed here."

Uriah gestures to the heads littering the grass and drops his mallet. "Too late. If you wish for no more blood to be spilled in the city, it can be spilled here just as easily."

The soldiers of Adamas widen their stances and unsheathe their swords, ready for an order. One tosses Uriah his glaive and whip. The Gryphon holds up a hand, and the Castle Guard on their side of the court bring their steel forth as well. Bronwen runs from the field and disappears around the corner of the hedge maze.

"We will have none of this!" the Duchess shouts. "Return your steel."

The Castle Guard heed her command, cautiously. Lysander and Uriah's men do not.

Lysander snaps the croquet mallet with his hands, tosses it aside, and pulls his longsword from the hands of a soldier. "Blood for blood."

"Nothing of the sort," says Mary Anne, trying to defuse this powder keg they tread upon.

Uriah holds his glaive out and slowly points to everyone. "Clever girl. Why would you assemble your forces, your best fighters here—as if numbers would give you an advantage—if not to attack us?"

"Do not give this pathetic woman credit for my deeds," Cheshire's voice calls from behind them.

No.

They all turn as Cheshire appears out of nothing with a wave of his hand and stands on the wooden bench at the edge of the court. His hood drapes over his face, concealing his eyes, but leaves his dark smile for all to see. His cloak billows behind him as if he creates his own wind. For once, Mary Anne would prefer him without clothing. Returning in his old garb, he brings with him something different, filling the court with ominous tension, as if sucking the air from the field. The last time they all were present was the council room when their brawl erupted. No side could claim victory during their previous exchange; they all stopped fighting. It is difficult to believe it will happen a second time.

"Why do you do this?" asks Mary Anne.

Cheshire turns his attention to Mary Anne. "Question me again and I will take you to the tower and the marvelous announcement system where I shall peel the flesh from your face to your toes for every other disrespecting wretch in this damned town to hear your screams."

"You are pardoned," says Mary Anne. She looks to Jonathan for aid, a word or action to stop Cheshire. Instead, he lowers his head, resigned, knowing as well as Mary Anne, Cheshire cannot be stopped.

"Pardon me. Savior of Mirus." Cheshire laughs. "I did not care for it. My other monikers suit me better."

"Do you include 'bastard' among them?" Uriah scoffs. He and Lysander turn to join their soldiers.

"Do not turn your head from me," says Cheshire. "Lest I add it to the pile on the grass."

"You are nothing without your tricks, child," says Lysander. "The masks make you no less dangerous than you were before. After all, you are only a scared child playing at war. We live it."

"You think so?" Cheshire steps down from the bench. "I had many names before Mary Anne so foolishly gave me the masks. Queen Slayer, they called me. They may call me this yet again. You can add bastard among my names, should you like. But you can also add the title of god-killer at the top of the list."

A chill in the air grips them all. Mary Anne looks to Jonathan for an explanation—surely this cannot be possible—but he and March engage in their silent conversation, worry upon their brows.

"If I can kill a god, what chance do you two stand? I have slaughtered thousands in my time." Cheshire walks to the center of the lawn where the long shadows of the eastern wall and thin juniper trees slide across the ground as the sun sets. "Be they soldier, guard, townsperson, or anyone unfortunate enough to stand in my way."

"Cheshire," says March.

"Please," says Jonathan.

Their words fall on deaf ears. For the time Mary Anne has known him, when Cheshire smiles, it is already too late.

"Stop this, Cheshire!" Mary Anne shouts. "You sound no better than them."

Cheshire laughs loudly, and it shakes Mary Anne to her core. Both sets of soldiers turn their blades to Cheshire. He ignores them and looks to Mary Anne, Lysander, and Uriah, and finally at the Duchess.

"I am better. I am pain. I am fear. I am chaos. I am your death. Welcome me."

"Prove it, then." Lysander swings his sword overhead with both hands and takes aim at Cheshire.

"No!" shouts Mary Anne.

Cheshire waves his hand over his face, summons his mask, and drops into the shadow of a tree as if a trapdoor opened beneath him in the earth.

Jonathan turns his attention to the soldiers of Adamas, standing in the long shadow of a thin juniper tree. "The shadows. Watch the shadows!"

Too late. One by one, the soldiers fall into the darkened ground and disappear. Quick screams from the line fade to nothing. The last two of the twelve try to run, but one of each other's legs falls into another shadow. They scream and claw at the grass as if pulling themselves from a cliff. The soldiers of Mirus and Jonathan run to their aid. Too late, again. They pull the soldiers from Adamas from the shadows, who are missing their entire legs up to the hip bone—blood gushes and spurts from the wound. Their lives bleed out in a matter of seconds.

Lysander and Uriah abandon their men and move to an area of the lawn away from shadows of the trees, shrinking by the moment. They thrust their blades into the ground, into each other's shadows. Should Cheshire try to appear from them, he would impale himself.

It does not end. Mary Anne can scarcely make out the slaughter. Cheshire's arms reach up from the earth and pull at the soldiers of Mirus, yanking them part way into the ground, severing arms, legs, and heads without ever wielding a blade. Half-men slump to the ground, without time to scream, let alone realize what fate has befallen them. A fortunate, or unfortunate, soldier walks away from the pile of the dead. Both his arms are gone, severed just below the shoulder. He screams, mouth agape.

In shock and horror, Mary Anne catches a glimpse of Cheshire's eye in the soldier's open mouth a second before his fingers reach out, grab the soldier's top jaw, and jerks it to the side with a loud crack. He falls to the ground—the last of the soldiers, dead.

He is no demon; he is a devil, perhaps the devil himself. But, if he can accomplish all this, perhaps he can rid them of the Twins once and for all. Lysander and Uriah, bodies tense, stand back-to-back and remain calm in the turmoil and deaths unfolding around them.

"Now?" Lysander asks.

"Now," says Uriah.

They untie the small glass orbs hanging from their belt and smash them to the ground one after another in a circle around them—six in all. The glass breaks, and pressurized gas or smoke explodes into white clouds spreading across the lawn and choking the air.

"What have you done? Have you poisoned us all to kill him?" The Duchess covers her mouth with her dress and urges Mary Anne to do the same.

"No," says March. "Smoke—odorless, tasteless, harmless." She unsheathes her swords and stands her ground. "Similar to those used to extinguish the fires in Mirus."

The Gryphon descends upon Mary Anne. "Pardon the intrusion, but your safety is most paramount," he whispers.

"Go with him," says Jonathan. "He will protect you. The farther away you are from this, the better."

"Forgive me." The Gryphon's mighty arm wraps around Mary Anne's waist, lifts her from the ground, and holds her to his side. He cautiously steps back toward the Duchess and Chamberlain at the edge of the field.

The smoke sucks the breath and sound from the lawn. Everyone waits, heads shifting side-to-side, preparing for the worst. Cheshire aims to take out the Twins. However, she and the Duchess are also on his list, no doubt. He may take advantage of this opportunity to wipe them all from the board at once.

Jonathan and March soon become nothing more than hazy, dark silhouettes in the smoke. Mary Anne's eyes dart back and forth once she loses sight of them. Her faith in Jonathan's skill does not lessen her worry for him. She holds onto the Gryphon's forearm, waiting, searching, listening. Mary Anne's heart thunders in her ears, and she releases her breath when the first resounding clash of steel against steel rings somewhere in the all-consuming white shapeless void where all are predator and all are prey.

CHAPTER 36
MARCH

The swirls of smoke hang around them, frozen in time like ghostly waves of the sea, so dense the walls of the hedge maze cannot be seen. Small particles swim away with each of March's breaths. The murky silhouettes of Lysander and Uriah, back-to-back, wait for Cheshire, and perhaps Jonathan and March to come to them.

Cheshire chuckles playfully, somewhere unseen to their left. She welcomes the chaos he brings, encourages it, especially now with so many players in the game, but for one who conducts his work in the shadows to lash out publicly, something has happened. This is different; this is troubling. His laugh continues somewhere off to their right, and she and Jonathan creep forward with quiet footfalls, swords at the ready.

Jonathan takes his place by her side. "We have fought in worse conditions," he jests. "The fire he created in Ilex was a sight to behold. Made for a quick retreat, though. At least we can breathe here. Why can we breathe here?"

"This smoke was manufactured," March whispers. "They are too damned cunning. This is not diversion or subterfuge; this is a countermeasure against Cheshire. They discovered a way to combat the power of the masks. Look down. Our shadows are all but gone."

Jonathan waves his hand in front of him. "Any movement Cheshire makes, visible or invisible, will displace the smoke and give away his position."

Cheshire's calm voice permeates through the smoke, addressing the Twins. "You two can fight all you wish. It is futile. This is merely a prelude. Mirus will burn, and I will watch as the townspeople try to quench the flames with their tears before the pyre claims them as well, scorching their bones."

"Rather grim"—Jonathan chuckles, to hide his worry—"even for him."

They fear not for their own safety or Cheshire's—they will survive this—rather, it is the condition of their lover which fuels their shared concern.

The smoke ripples in the wake of Cheshire's unseen figure to their right. Uriah thrusts his glaive, aiming at the height of his chest, while Lysander swings his longsword at a twisting wisp of smoke charging toward him. It slices through nothing. Uriah twirls his glaive in hand before he strikes at the same mark. The smoke bends to their will, commanded by every gesture—a hurricane unto themselves.

Cheshire is skilled and elusive, but Jonathan and March will take no chances with the Twins. Lysander strikes at the smallest disturbance in the smoke, and Jonathan deflects each blow with his longsword. Uriah takes aim, ready to thrust his glaive into what he hopes is Cheshire, but March deflects his attack with both swords, sending the blade skyward. She takes command of the smoke, swinging wildly, strategically, in different directions, creating a maelstrom from within. The muted storm rages around them, making it difficult to spot what moves if everything is in motion. Jonathan joins March and together they swing their blades wildly, not at the Twins, but at the smoke, creating ripples and waves in the white cloud to frustrate Lysander and Uriah. The Twins stab at the air, at nothing.

The Twins continue to strike and lash out in every direction, keeping their weapons in constant motion. March's and Jonathan's blades meet theirs every time, ringing out in wonderful chords March's soul has longed for. *Clang* after *clang*, their song continues, punctuated with grunts and snarls.

"Damn you both." Lysander growls and turns his attention to Jonathan and tries to bring his longsword down on him. He sidesteps as the blade embeds into the ground with a loud thud.

Uriah dances around March, stabbing at the air, testing her, but her steel catches his every time.

"Darling," says March.

"Yes," Jonathan and Uriah respond.

March glares at Uriah, who shrugs.

"Darling," she calls to Jonathan again.

"Agree," he says, being of one mind.

Jonathan widens his stance and swings for Lysander's neck, who narrowly escapes the blade's tip, pulling his sword free. Uriah, ready for the attack, spins his glaive in hand, blocking the barrage from March's blades one after another. The Twins' speed and skill are at the same level as March. She knocks away attacks from Uriah and simultaneously blocks strikes from Lysander intended for Jonathan. Her lover is powerful, but not as quick as her or their opponents.

Strikes, slashes, and lunges come quick and furious in the smoke. March darts in close and rolls against Uriah's back. His exposed neck calls to her blade, begging for it. Instead, she slaps his shoulders with the flat part of her blade, to let him know the opening was there and she could have easily sliced the back of his neck, severing his spine, ridding them of half of their problem. The temptation was great, but he unfortunately still has information she needs.

His muscles pinch, and he rolls his neck at the pain, turning to face her. She spins both swords in hand, beckoning him forward.

The Gryphon's shout from somewhere behind them stops them both the moment before they charge at one another.

"Carter. To Mary Anne. To the Duchess."

March has never heard such a timbre in his voice. Jonathan is gone by the time she turns to see him, his silhouette fading into the smoke. A pang of pain hits her chest, as if struck with steel. Watching him run to her hurts more than any pain a blade can inflict.

A look of concern pinches Uriah's brow. Lysander and Uriah rest their weapons over their shoulders, knowing the fight to be done. They will bring no harm to March. Not now, at least. There is nothing to say. March fears if she dares utter a word, she will crack. Her swords sing as she puts them to rest in their sheathes.

Realization settles in. March and Jonathan played their part well and served as a distraction for Cheshire, but March stands alone on the field with Lysander and Uriah. It has been some time since they heard Cheshire's laugh. If he meant to attack Twins, he would have done so already. He is no longer on the field with them, which means he took advantage and used the Twins' smoke against them all, for he must have another target in mind.

CHAPTER 37

MARY ANNE

Swords clang against each other like church bells, and the cloud vibrates with every clash. As long as the bells continue to toll, Mary Anne knows Jonathan perseveres. For the briefest of moments, she felt safe in the Gryphon's arms. It does not last.

"Mary Anne, please heed my words." The Gryphon's steps become heavy, as if drudging knee deep in thick mud. He stumbles back and stops, not yet reaching the end of the court marked by the form of the Duchess.

"Run," he struggles to say. He releases his hold on Mary Anne, and she falls from his arms. "Run to the Duchess."

She catches herself and quickly gets to her feet, frantically searching for any sign of Cheshire—a curled wisp of smoke, his piercing eyes, clawed fingers reaching for them. Nothing. "What is the matter?"

"I cannot move." He falls to one knee and then the other. A strange white powder covers his face.

Mary Anne checks her arms and hands, believing it might be residue from the smoke. This is something different. She reaches out to wipe it away.

"Do not touch it," the Gryphon snaps at her.

Greater lengths of silence fill the space between the bells.

"I will not leave you here." She hooks her hands under the Gryphon's arm and tries with all of her might to pull him to the edge of the smoke, but they collapse together on the grass. Mary Anne kicks and pushes at the earth, barely able to move him at all.

"Go." He struggles for breath. He gasps, and with a loud roar, cries out, "Carter. To Mary Anne. To the Duchess."

His body falls slack and his arm slips from her grasp. Did the Gryphon meet his end in front of her? And here she stands, powerless to do anything. The general of Wonderland fell with a whisper, unable to take a single swing of his longsword. What chance do the rest of them have against Cheshire?

"Mary Anne!" Jonathan shouts from somewhere unseen.

Lips trembling, legs shaking, Mary Anne obeys the Gryphon's command. She does not look back as she runs toward the Duchess, who waits with outstretched arms. Out of the corner of Mary Anne's vision, Jonathan sprints toward her, gait wider than she has ever seen. He left the battle and ran to her, to protect her. She is not sure if it is the smoke or fear burning her lungs, but she knows it is Jonathan's lasting bravery which causes the tears to swell.

She runs with her hands out in front of her, though it would offer little protection coming face to face with Cheshire. The chill of memory's cold nails climb up Mary Anne's spine. She screams, remembering she can scream, believing the devil himself grazes her back. The memory, the terror, the smoke, no fog, and the running—it all seems so familiar yet so distant. Her breaths come quick and short with every footfall.

The thoughts and images of being queen filled Mary Anne with a premature hubris, believing herself untouchable within the walls, the army, the Duchess, the Gryphon, and Jonathan. Whatever the memory, this new situation sets into stone an immutable fact Mary Anne forgot:

she is not safe.

The Duchess catches Mary Anne and pulls her into a mother's protective embrace. Jonathan slides on the grass and stops in front of them, sword at the ready. She can feel the heat and sweat of his back upon hers. Together, they have faced mercenaries, soldiers, and the cult. At this moment, when they all should fight united, they cannot be more divided. A new, unsettling thought creeps into Mary Anne's mind. They are not enough. She is not enough. In order to stop the Twins, stop this take over—stop Cheshire—she must become more. Her want to become queen became a need, and now it becomes essential.

Cheshire's disembodied voice drifts through the air with sharp, biting clarity. "I speak to you, Duchess. I will save you until last. You will watch as I destroy everything you hold dear. Then you will have my permission to die. And nothing grieves me more heartily than after your death by my hands; I cannot continue to torment you a thousand times more."

"Never!" the Duchess shouts into the void. "You will never succeed. Mirus has survived your every attempt and we will continue to do so."

"You believed my previous attacks were meant to topple the city? No. They are merely an opening salvo. There is one thing you have all forgotten. Know it well and never forget it again. The only reason any of you still draw breath is because I allow it."

Mary Anne swallows and huffs out loud to make sure she still has the ability to hear. Besides Cheshire, no other sound except the heavy breaths of the Duchess and Jonathan exists. The smoke muffles the world. Or does Cheshire will it to be so?

The smoke slowly lifts from the court like a sheer curtain caught in a strong breeze. March stands suspiciously, yet expectedly, close to Lysander and Uriah. The Chamberlain hides behind the bench, sprawled on the ground. The somber, lingering silence pulls at Mary Anne's heart beating in her throat. There is no way of knowing if Cheshire remains invisible among them or not, ready to strike at any moment.

Mary Anne pushes away from the Duchess's arms, who tries to keep her close.

"Wait," she urges her.

"No," says Mary Anne. "I have acted rash and foolish for too long. No more. I do not fear Lysander and Uriah. And I most certainly will not fear a petulant child and his empty threats."

However, his threats are not empty; far from it. Cheshire decimated twenty-four armored soldiers on both sides without mercy in a matter of seconds. He struck fear anew in all of them. Even Jonathan's and March's expressions weigh heavily with frustration. Mary Anne must come to terms with the fact she already knew: the only side Cheshire is on is his own. He made it clear countless times. The word impossible may not have hold in Wonderland, but Cheshire's presence gives meaning to the word.

Worst of all, another grave realization comes too late as the last tendrils of smoke lift. In the heated, sobering seconds, everyone notices the empty lawn and the irreplaceable loss they have all suffered. The Gryphon is gone, taken by Cheshire.

CHAPTER 38
JONATHAN

The next morning, unable to get a full night's rest after the events on the croquet course, Jonathan tries to force his eyes open, still caught in the hazy realm between waking and dreams. He stretches the bruises of his sore muscles and welcomes March's warmth, curled against the front of his body. However, Mary Anne's is curiously missing on his back. As he wakes to discover what fresh hell this day has in store, soft blades of grass tickle and brush against his skin.

"Hello? You are not supposed to be here," he says to the grass, with a deep morning gravel in his voice.

Waking somewhere unknown has never ended well for them; until now, perhaps. His vision finally comes to focus on the small verdant meadow they lie on, the crystal-clear, still lake in front of them, and the lush expanse of oak, sycamore, and ash surrounding them.

"We are not supposed to be here," says Jonathan, despite its beauty.

"She is not supposed to be here," March mutters, more asleep than awake, speaking of Mary Anne.

Jonathan glances over his shoulder to find only grass—whatever power brought them here did not intend for Mary Anne to join them. This is not the time for them to separate. Jonathan kisses the top of March's head, slips from her warm embrace, and stands in awe of this ethereal landscape. The cavern is considerably larger than Jonathan first thought, containing a full forest hugging the shore of an expansive lake fed by twin waterfalls at its far side. Questions should flood his mind, but not a thought forms, his mind incapable of questioning the wonder and magnificence.

March wakes, stands by his side, and takes his hand in hers. "Is this real?"

"It is a waking dream," says Jonathan.

"It most certainly is real," Cheshire's voice calls to them from the middle of the lake.

"What in all of Wonder?" Jonathan whispers. Jonathan neither wants nor needs explanation; dreams can be real. His loves have proven this.

Cheshire walks from the lake, dripping water tracing every hard curve of his body, hands pushing his wet hair back, widening his muscular shoulders even more compared to his slim waist. His gloves and sash rest coiled together at the base of a nearby tree. He brought them here some time in the night; this is the only explanation, and why Jonathan and March are bereft of clothing as well.

Jonathan's and March's bodies cover with gooseflesh from the caress of the cold chill of the sprawling nature. He is reminded of the days, weeks, and months in the Hollow, when their trio would spend every minute of the day without a stitch of clothing in their lost, secluded world.

"I know of this place," says March.

Cheshire approaches, and if Jonathan's cock had not already been hard from waking, the sight of Cheshire would have kindled the fire within him, watching the thin streams of water trickle and glisten in the deep recesses of his muscles. Cheshire tenderly runs a hand behind March's neck and kisses her, long, soft, yet forceful.

Beautiful. A beauty to rival this place.

Cheshire parts with March, sharing breath from close lips, and then looks at Jonathan with hunger in his eyes. His hand tickles Jonathan's neck as it slides around, pulling him in and pressing their lips hard together, kissing with the same intensity, before parting and allowing their tongues to intertwine.

Out of instinct, Jonathan reaches down and takes hold of Cheshire's shaft, joining March's hand, already there. Cheshire reaches around March's waist and pulls her in to join their kiss. They stand in this magical paradise, turning to each other, tending to each other with their tongues and lips, until their trio join in a singular, soft kiss. Jonathan grabs Cheshire's and March's asses in his hands and pulls them closer, pressing their bodies together; three flames—purple, blue, and pink—combining to make a brilliant white.

Time means nothing in moments like this, sharing each other, relishing in the enjoyment of one pair kissing as their third watches, back and forth. Laughter and soft moans intermingle with their kisses. Hands caress and massage backs and backsides and trace hard muscles. At moments, they refrain from kissing and stare down the glorious tunnel made by their bodies.

Cheshire is the first to pull away and crouch by the water's edge, leaving Jonathan's mouth wet and wanting more. A melancholia weighs heavy on their love. Jonathan and March shared the same thought in the midst of battle—something is different, something is wrong. There are so many unknowns; questions needing answers. What did Cheshire do with the Gryphon? Does the Gryphon still live? The way he spoke yesterday, it sounded as if he had a plan in mind, and whatever it is will most certainly spell disaster for any in the castle. Jonathan would start at the basic questions he should ask: why and how are they here? But at the sight of Cheshire before him, looking so small, distant, staring out at the water, Jonathan knows the answer—he needs them. The day prior does not matter, the Twins' retribution does not matter, Mary Anne's worries do not matter; they must tend to Cheshire.

March lifts an eyebrow and shifts her eyes from Cheshire to Jonathan. *We are together. Cheshire is not in the city. We stay as long as we must.* She kneels behind Cheshire and leans on his back, wrapping her arms around his shoulders and rubbing her face in the back of his wet hair.

While the worry of the world outside this breathtaking cavern should weigh heavy on Jonathan, he cannot help but enjoy the relief of a great pressure on his shoulders. This unknown place outside of time gives him and his loves the moment they desperately need. They will deal with the consequences soon enough.

Cheshire reaches behind him, hooks his arms under March's backside, rises, and carries her, her legs hooked around his waist, back to Jonathan. Together, they lie on the small incline of soft grass on the forest floor facing the lake. Cheshire sits with his legs spread, Jonathan lies between them, head resting just below his stomach, and March straddles Jonathan's torso, legs tucked. Jonathan turns to kiss Cheshire's hard shaft, leaning against his neck. His own cock flexes behind March.

Though the world may burn around them, this is what they need: the opportunity to lose themselves, sitting together, hands tracing over each other's bodies in the breathtaking sounds of nature. The curious soft-blue light from high above frames March's figure in an angelic glow. He tilts his head back and watches the orb shimmer in Cheshire's eyes.

"Can this last forever?" Jonathan asks.

"It can," says March.

"It does," says Cheshire. "This moment already lasts forever. Time has no hold over us, dear heart."

Jonathan closes his eyes, at peace with his loves, and cannot tell how much time passes when they open next. He feels his bare hips for his pockets which are not there and thinks of his timepiece and, more importantly, of his elixir in the castle, gods know how far from this place.

"All has been arranged." Cheshire caresses Jonathan's cheek.

As if on cue, a rustle of footsteps upon the grass catches Jonathan's ear, and March tilts her head, looking past Cheshire, waiting for the unseen visitors to clear the tree line. She looks back at Cheshire with a raised eyebrow, then down at Jonathan; her playful, beautiful smile and her tongue placed at the edge of her teeth tell Jonathan *this day will not be as restful as they first believed.*

Pat and Bill, wearing naught but their boots, emerge from the trees and join them at the water's edge before the grass turns to smooth gray rock. Their green eyes sparkle in the light of the blue orb, though their expressions remain as enigmatic as ever. Cheshire's intentions become more clear and more enticing. Jonathan knew, after his comment days ago, Cheshire's curiosity would win him over, but he did not think it would be this soon.

"You invited them," says Jonathan

"It is only fair," says Cheshire. "You both have had the pleasure. Why not increase our fold?"

"Do they not have business to—"

Cheshire places a finger over Jonathan's lips, slides it into his mouth, and runs his other hand down Jonathan's chest. "Your thoughts race and attempt to escape this place. You have nowhere to go, nowhere to be than here."

Jonathan nods, helpless to suck on Cheshire's finger.

Pat and Bill carry large woven baskets, one in each hand. This is the first Jonathan recalls seeing them without their hammers, though, unlike him and March, they are close by with the rest of their clothing. They make a sensual pair unto themselves: Bill's slim yet muscular build and Pat's petite frame with arms to match Cheshire. They place the baskets down near the trio and unpack small wooden bowls of fruits, a silver tea service, breads, tarts, and biscuits. Bill pulls Jonathan's timepiece from one of his baskets to show Jonathan and places it back with care. Pat pulls a small bottle of Jonathan's elixir from her basket and hands it to March. Cheshire has thought of everything. He should not be surprised.

March holds the bottle out for Cheshire to uncork with his teeth and then taps on Jonathan's bottom lip. Cheshire slides his finger from Jonathan's mouth, and she touches the cold glass to his lips and pours in a small amount. He swallows the cold liquid, and a flash of warmth radiates through him, relaxing his nerves further.

Bill pulls a stopper from a wineskin and pours its contents into a waiting tea pot. Jonathan knows the contents of the cup with no need to see the liquid: his most aromatic and rarest of his teas—golden raspberry, honeyberry, medlars, pomegranate, and lemongrass from the Everwood. His jaw tingles at the thought of it. Bill pours a cup and hands it to Pat. March motions with her head, and Pat stands behind March, straddling Jonathan's legs.

"Tea time, darling," says March.

Jonathan tries to sit up, but Cheshire holds his shoulder down against his legs.

"By the heavens," Jonathan pants, smiling. "Yes."

March slides up Jonathan's body and positions herself over his face, the heat radiating from her body palpable. Even Cheshire's cock throbs against Jonathan's neck, trapped by March's thigh, matching the thumping heartbeat in his own.

"Oh, yes."

Jonathan's heart thunders with anticipation. March, her love, her strength, has always filled his cup, but now she is his gilded chalice. Pat holds the rim of the cup at March's neck, between her collarbones, and tips it toward her body. The beautiful light-amber tea trickles down her body, in the soft valley between her breasts, down the middle of her flexing stomach muscles to her lips, and into his waiting mouth. Jonathan, parched, laps and drinks from her, taking in the combined, exquisite, exotic taste of her and the tea. His tongue presses tight against her in long, heavy strokes from bottom to top and back again, kissing every time he swallows, collecting every sweet drop. Her taut, tender skin fills his mouth, and he hooks his arms around her thighs, pulling her down onto his face, craving her moans, yearning for everything she has to give. Her legs and ass tighten around his face and shoulders the wilder he laps and drinks.

Unable to resist, Cheshire leans forward and licks between March's breasts before focusing on her right nipple, tongue circling, while Pat's hand massages her left. Bill kneels behind Cheshire, runs his hands under his arms, and massages his nipples between his fingers.

Pat lifts the cup from March with what must be a third of a cup left by Jonathan's measure. The last few drops trickle down, leaving glistening trails upon March's skin. Her thighs quiver from his thirst, but once he catches the last bead of tea, he stops for both of them to catch their breath.

With her hands, March pushes herself down Jonathan's body until the tip of his cock presses against her. She circles her hips, teasing him.

Cheshire slips from under Jonathan and kneels next to his head. He takes the cup from Pat and drinks the remainder of it. He holds the cup away from his mouth, tongue outstretched, for Jonathan to watch the last few drops fall. With a mouth full, he leans forward with a sly grin and grips the sides of Jonathan's face.

"Yes."

Every muscle in Jonathan's body twitches. He nods, waiting, and opens his mouth eagerly. Cheshire remains inches away from Jonathan, puckers his lips, leaving the smallest opening, allowing the tea to flow and drop into Jonathan's mouth. Jonathan dare not close his mouth, lest he lose a single drop. He gulps down the trickle Cheshire gives him. Once there are no more drops to catch, his love bends down and shoves his tongue into Jonathan's mouth, which he sucks on greedily, forcing his lips into Cheshire's.

Pat reaches down behind March and takes hold of Jonathan's shaft and, gripping tight, rubs its head against March, up and down her skin, nuzzling warmth. His love looks down upon him with shimmering doe eyes, biting her lip. Pat holds Jonathan in position, and March pushes back, inhales, and welcomes him home. She sighs loud and arches her back as Jonathan reaches her depths. Pat stays behind her and massages their union.

Cheshire, mesmerized by the moans filling his mouth and those March sings into the air, sits up, tilts Jonathan's head backward, and shoves his cock into his waiting mouth. Jonathan willingly accepts his lover's force and every pump and slide thereafter. Cheshire's own taste mingles with March and the tea and becomes a combination Jonathan has never experienced and never knew he needed, but will crave from this day forward.

Bill kneels on the side of Jonathan's head, cock hard, tapping on Jonathan's neck. Jonathan takes Cheshire's right hand and places it on Bill's shaft—short and slimmer than Cheshire's—giving unspoken permission, though they need none.

March's muscle control rivals only Cheshire's. Her hands grope at Jonathan's chest while her hips circle, push, and pull as if they had a mind of their own. Her breath quickens, as does Jonathan's heart. Any time Jonathan's legs shake, bringing him to the brink, she slows, exerting her mastery of control over him.

Cheshire sits to the opposite side of Jonathan's head from Bill and fills Jonathan's mouth, pumping deep within again and again, his flesh blocking and replacing the air. As far as Jonathan is concerned, he can live off either. Jonathan gasps for air when Cheshire offers him a reprieve, pulling from his throat, and brings the tips of his and Bill's cock heads together over Jonathan's lips. He kisses both—tongue pushing between the two of them, their tastes so different—and tries to fit them both in his mouth, a near impossible feat because of Cheshire's girth, and settles to take and savor one at a time.

Jonathan locks eyes with Cheshire with Bill's cock in his mouth, curious to his reaction. Heavy breaths escape a wide, gleeful, lust-fueled grin, with a dark intensity behind his eyes. Jonathan reaches up and grabs Bill by the neck and pulls his mouth down straight onto Cheshire's cock, accepting its length and moaning to the heavens. Jonathan looks past Bill and enjoys his lover's grin growing wider, kissing his shaft every time Bill pulls to the end. Jonathan holds Bill's head in place as Cheshire fucks his mouth harder, quicker, as he leans over to take March's nipple in his mouth, while Pat attends to the other, wrapping around her body under her arm..

Fingers massage the base of Jonathan's cock, rising and falling with March. Pat reaches around, mouth full, and massages her sensitivity. March looks down at Jonathan with fluttering eyes, gripping the hair of Cheshire and Pat in her fingers, utterly lost in bliss.

Long ago, when March and Jonathan first asked Pat and Bill to create a mold of Jonathan's cock, they did not know they would fuck then, or sporadically throughout the centuries. Now, having Cheshire with them, Jonathan does not know why this has not happened sooner. Then he remembers they could never be in the capital at the same time.

Jonathan reaches and grabs Cheshire's flexed arms, and looks into his eyes, pleading. "Take me."

Breaking from Bill, Cheshire moves down their line. Bill circles round and, together with Pat, lifts Jonathan's legs into the air and hands them to March. She holds his ankles, smiling down at him while Jonathan bucks beneath her like a stallion, body anticipating what comes next. The wide, wet tip of Cheshire's cock presses against Jonathan's ass, at his mercy. He teases Jonathan only once before thrusting in. Jonathan's stomach cramps from the brief burst of pain and the long pull of ecstasy.

March grits her teeth, smiling, feeling Jonathan swell within her from Cheshire's thrust. Unrelenting, he slams against Jonathan, who has no choice but to moan and scream to the heavens with every deep thrust, rocking their entire trio. If there is anyone in earshot, Jonathan cannot be sure, but he can restrain himself no longer. Cheshire snakes his way under March's arm, wrapping his around her, and takes her breast back into his mouth, biting and sucking one and then switching sides to not neglect the other. Her moans and spasms collide with Jonathan's in the air, accompanied by Cheshire's low growls.

Pat and Bill kneel at Jonathan's sides and take control of his hands. Pat takes two fingers of his left hand and slides them inside her. Jonathan's thumb finds its mark, and she flexes her stomach over and over, grinding against him. Bill slips Jonathan's other hand behind his legs for his fingers to massage his ass; two fingers tense his body, just like Pat.

Even with Jonathan's feet aloft, at their bidding and mercy, March's and Cheshire's passion, along with Pat and Bill, drive him to the brink. He thrusts his own hips, no longer willing or able to be passive in this quintet, thrusting up into March, who grips his ankles tighter, screaming with a parched tongue, and down onto Cheshire, taking every inch. Cheshire's body shakes, mouth cupping March's breast. Her eyes drift back, as do Jonathan's.

His legs burn. He can feel Cheshire swell. March becomes wetter with every thrust. His lungs burn from quick, long breaths. The tingles start in the back of Jonathan's head, almost making him black out, and rush down his body to his cock, throbbing uncontrollably. From the shake of everyone else's body, he knows it is time for them to climax, to fall like dominoes.

Pat and Bill fall first—a warm shower from both drizzles across his outstretched arms as they continue to grind harder. Cheshire follows, thrusts becoming excruciatingly pleasurable. The slam of their bodies together, and his against March's, is too much to bear. Cheshire pushes in until his body presses against Jonathan and gifts him with his amazing climax, filling his body and his spirit. Even if Cheshire will not, Jonathan keeps moving. Cheshire grits his teeth, biting at March's breast as Jonathan takes control of the sensitivity of his cock.

Without letting go of her breast, Cheshire reaches down, circling his fingers at March's sensitivity. His touch pushes her over the edge. She stops breathing as she climaxes and gifts Jonathan with her warmth over his body. She laughs and moans when she catches her breath. Enough, but never enough. The sight of his loves and their friends is too much for one man to bear. Every muscle in Jonathan's body tightens as he erupts, unable to stop moving. March gasps, wetting her parched mouth, accepting every bit of Jonathan's gift.

Labored breaths fill the forest. Their sweat-drenched bodies glisten in the orb's light. A living portrait of the divine. Whatever plans Jonathan thought would transpire today escape him. This all-consuming moment in time begins a never-ending day Jonathan will not part with. Everything else does not matter.

CHAPTER 39
MARY ANNE

Mary Anne races through the corridors with Grace close behind, heart beating louder than the clacks of her heels upon the stone floor. *Alone,* repeats in her mind, over and over, like a skipping record on a victrola, but a new thought overtakes the previous. *Abandoned.*

The servants pass by, attending to their early morning duties, and she asks each for the whereabouts of everyone, anyone. Jonathan and March disappeared without a trace from their bedchamber before she woke, and whether they are in the city or in some peril, she cannot be sure. They keep their plans and damned secrets and never inform Mary Anne unless she presses them. This is possibly the worst time for them to disappear. The Gryphon, mightiest of them all, has been abducted, if not murdered, by Cheshire. And the Duchess and the Chamberlain are nowhere to be found.

At long last, Mary Anne pounds on the doors of the Duchess's bedchamber like she once did to the throne room, nearly drawing blood and leaving bruises.

She beats against the wooden door again and again without response.

Her heart climbs to her throat, attempting to choke her. The echo of her knocks and bangs fades, leaving Mary Anne and Grace alone in the corridor.

After the events on the croquet court yesterday evening, Mary Anne assumed the council would reconvene again, but everyone else has gone on without her, leaving her to fend for herself. Cheshire slaughtered soldiers of Mirus and Adamas without remorse and openly declared war upon the city. Queens may not make mistakes, but she is not yet queen. Mary Anne realizes she made a deal with the wrong devil, not fully understanding his motives and what he is truly capable of.

However, there are still other devils within these walls who may have more than one use. She never finished her conversation with Lysander and Uriah, and with no other council present, she must speak to someone, and Grace is ill-equipped to aid in this endeavor. The Duchess is who Mary Anne needs. Mary Anne does not know what happened to Lysander and Uriah as night fell, but from the number of missing servant girls, Mary Anne knows where to find them. It is a dangerous gamble, but if the Duchess knows she is with Lysander and Uriah again, she, hopefully, will show herself.

"Locate the Duchess," Mary Anne tells her handmaiden. "Inform her—as best you can—I have been invited to parlay in Lysander and Uriah's bedchamber, and I have accepted."

Mary Anne cannot see Grace's eyes behind her mask, but concern shows in her shrinking lips. Grace gives the slightest of curtseys she can manage and leaves Mary Anne to scour the castle. The clack of Mary Anne's heels on the long trek to the opposite side of the castle seems louder, more isolated than normal. Jonathan's heavy boots do not accompany her, nor March's sharp footsteps. She adjusts the low scoop of her gown repeatedly until she reaches Lysander and Uriah's bedchamber.

The thick doors muffle the moans of several women on the other side. Mary Anne, hesitant at first, knocks as loud as she did at the Duchess's chamber. She knows the risk in this course of action, but she tires of remaining in the dark with few pieces to a puzzle so integral to her survival, and hopes her presence here will give her some leverage with the Duchess. She will take their half-truths and their knowledge, along with the Duchess's, and cobble together some sort of answer.

The door clunks open, and a servant girl with long pale-orange hair Mary Anne has often seen around the castle stands before her without a stitch of clothing or modesty. She opens the door wider and returns to the bed with over a dozen other women writhing and pleasuring each other, and where Lysander and Uriah kneel side by side at the bed's center fucking two poor women on their hands and knees, screaming with every exhale. The thick aroma of heavy perfumes and sex waft through the chamber like an opium den.

"Come to finish us?" Lysander asks.

"I had nothing to do with any of it," says Mary Anne.

"Yet you were the one who traded the Mask of Light and Mask of Shadow, ancient relics, to the Queen Slayer, were you not?" asks Lysander.

"I will not explain my decisions to you."

"Join us, then," says Lysander.

"Please, disrobe and climb in," says Uriah.

Their bodies glisten with sweat, and their muscles shimmer from the braziers around the chamber. They converse with Mary Anne without pausing, as if this situation is a regular occurrence. The women on the bed do not stop either; even those who serve in the castle glance at Mary Anne with a hint of shame but continue groping at the Twins and their other bed mates.

"Can you stop fucking for one moment for us to finish our conversation?"

Their continued thrusting is their only response.

"Fine. We touched on two of the three categories you brought up; what I should know and what I need to know. What must I know?"

For a moment, the Twins slow, and Mary Anne believes they will have their conversation, but instead, they slap their women on the ass. They moan as they leave Lysander and Uriah and make room for two more to take their place on their backs. Other women hold their legs up and rub their hands across the women and the Twins' bodies, bite at their muscles, and lick at their nipples and underarms, causing Mary Anne's stomach to twirl—not with nausea, but with something more, a sensation it should not.

"I am done with you." She almost makes it to the door when Uriah stops her.

"What you must know," he says, "or rather what you must question, is who are you?"

"I beg your pardon?"

"You must know the type of woman you are," Uriah continues. "Not all queens of Wonderland have been benevolent. Just because you place a crown upon your head and are gifted immeasurable power, does not mean you will act in the best accordance of Wonderland's people."

Lysander slows his pace to speak. "Our cousin Dinah was revered by most of the land, and despite killing our grandfather, we will not speak ill of our own blood. But the second queen of Wonderland was another matter entirely. She wiped out entire villages, razed them to the ground, and erased them from the map. She destroyed crops, sunk ships, and tortured any who questioned her." The screams of their women punctuate each one of his points.

"Can you stop for one fucking minute?" Mary Anne shouts. "Must you force yourselves upon these women every moment of the day?"

Uriah addresses the women. "Are we forcing you to do anything you do not want to do?"

A smattering of giggles and 'no's' slide from the silk sheets. The silly expressions of the women sicken Mary Anne. "Can we continue this conversation in confidence?"

Uriah sighs and waves the women away. "Make your way to the baths. We shall join you shortly."

"The baths adjoining my chamber?"

"Of course. They are the best in the castle. You speak as if we have not already entertained there in your absence."

"I will make sure every stone surface has a thorough scrubbing."

The women grab near-sheer robes from a stack on a chaise and file from the room. The remaining flowers who work in the Garden playfully size Mary Anne from foot to hair, while servants from the castle keep their heads lowered as they run from the chamber, closing the door behind them.

The Twins rise and stalk toward her, stopping too close for her comfort, Uriah in front and Lysander behind, wet cocks dangerously close to her thighs. Their musk and heat pulse from their bodies. She swallows. Their bodies should not be a temptation, but her body yearns to be touched, instead of constantly teased.

"Must you?"

"You came to our chambers," they say together.

"If it bothers you, slip from your dress and join us," says Lysander. "We will not touch you until you ask. Or beg us."

Mary Anne's body should not stir, but it has a mind of its own, reacting like a drunkard who has been off the bottle for a week. It has been days since her last tryst with Jonathan and March, an experience which will forever change her, and left her craving more.

"Who do you take me for? March? Answers to my question will suffice."

"Interesting," says Uriah. "Continue."

"There have been four queens of Wonderland. Tell me about them."

Lysander's hot breath spreads across the back of her neck. "Such an open-ended question, one does not know where to begin," says Uriah. "I offer a question instead. If the queens were so revered, why is there no evidence of them through the castle, throughout the city? You would think renowned rulers would have some memorial or remembrance."

"There is no evidence of your forbearers, either."

"Have you seen paintings, statues, portraits, or anything else of them, their legacy, their existence? You walk blindly down a path without understanding its importance or history."

A cold emptiness overtakes Mary Anne, filling her chest, then her entire body. Their words cannot be half-truths if they speak irrefutable facts. Besides a bedchamber and clothing she was told belonged to the previous queens, the only evidence Mary Anne has seen were the items presented at her test from the Duchess and Chamberlain. Four queens of Wonderland ruled, yet there is nary a memory of them in the castle, and she receives only obtuse answers from those she questions.

"What is the meaning of this?" The Duchess bursts through the door, sneering at Lysander and Uriah, waving them away. Grace and several of the Castle Guard wait outside the door. "Come along, Mary Anne. This is no place for you."

The Twins take a step back, and Uriah gives a knowing glance to Mary Anne, as if he knew the Duchess would arrive and her intentions all along.

"I believe I am precisely where I need to be."

"Do not tell me you have fallen for their lascivious wiles." The Duchess holds Mary Anne by the shoulders and inspects her front and back.

"On the contrary, she has been quite immune for now. We were discussing the previous queens of Wonderland."

"They are not the sort to trust with this information," says the Duchess.

"I know." Mary Anne pushes the Duchess's arms away from her. "You are; you who I should trust most. Yet after yesterday, when I need you, I am abandoned."

"Mary Anne, this can be disc—"

"And the only two who were willing to speak with me are the two I should trust the least. At every turn, my questions are ignored, avoided, or put off for another time, but they give their answers freely. A half-truth is better than no truth at all. You will answer my questions this day, or I will leave you here and join Lysander and Uriah in the baths to finish our conversation."

"Please do join us in the baths, if you like," says Uriah. "We have other business to attend to."

"Not to mention trading this group of flowers for a fresh bouquet," says Lysander. "No sweeter smell than a freshly plucked flower from the Garden."

The Twins take their leave, and Mary Anne cannot fight the temptation to steal a glance at their backsides as they walk from the chamber.

The Duchess, taken aback and exhaustion heavy in her eyes at this early hour, appears speechless, lips and eyes searching for words. "Mary Anne, you must understand my choices—"

"No. Lysander and Uriah have told me more of the queens in the past two days than you have since my arrival in Mirus. They have also led me down a path of questions I did not even think to ask."

"You think they can be trusted? Look at what happens in our city because of their influence. I saw the glance you took. The woman I have seen grow before me would never have taken a second look at them, knowing how vile they are. They sow seeds of doubt, which is why half the city questions your legitimacy."

Mary Anne questions if, in her haste for answers, she took what the Twins said to heart too quickly. Regardless, the thoughts and questions they have raised cannot be ignored. She locks eyes with the Duchess from beneath her brow, waiting for an answer.

"Very well." The Duchess inhales through her nose as if inflating herself to her correct posture. "Allow me some time to gather more of the Castle Guard, and you shall have your answers."

CHAPTER 40
MARCH

After washing in the pool and enjoying a relaxing lunch, they rest together at the edge of the forest. Jonathan leans back against the trunk of a large sycamore, March leans against his left side, head on his shoulder, his on hers, and Cheshire sprawls across their laps, fast asleep. Jonathan plays with Cheshire's soft, thick cock to keep his mind occupied. She runs her fingers between the grooves of Cheshire's stomach muscles and twists his damp hair.

Cheshire's slow, deep breaths are a peaceful melody, perhaps the only time he ever knows peace—sleeping with Jonathan and March, knowing they will let nothing befall him as long as they are together. She knows this sleep. The sleep of someone who has stayed vigilant for days and nights on end.

March soaks in the relief this excursion grants, away from Bronwen, Lysander, Uriah, and all of their schemes. She hates the thought that she entertains their offer, but hates Bronwen prancing through the castle all the more. From the content on Jonathan's face, the thoughts of Mirus and Mary Anne have faded. The hells may break loose outside, but it is wiser to keep Cheshire here than unleashed on to the city for the time being, and many will die at the hands of Lysander and Uriah, but this is unavoidable and expected long before Cheshire brought them here.

Against the opposite side of the tree, Pat rests back against the trunks and Bill sits between her legs, leaning back on her chest, rubbing her thighs, as she runs her fingers over his chest. Their kinship runs as deep as March, Cheshire, and Jonathan. Inseparable, and living in seclusion for so long, to whom else would they have to turn?

Cheshire snaps out of sleep, flaying, and gasps for breath as if long submerged under water and finally breaking through the surface. Jonathan grabs hold of his legs, and March holds his head to her bosom, but despite their efforts, he bolts from their laps and runs deep into the wood. March and Jonathan give chase without a second thought, weaving through the dense mix of trees. Jonathan falls behind, regaining feeling in his right leg. March continues, trunk after trunk whizzing by in a blur. Far ahead, the warm silhouette of Cheshire's bare body stands in stark contrast against the browns, greens, and blues of the forest. Ever elusive and ever more nimble, he keeps a sizable lead in front of them, jumping from branch to branch with silent grace.

Her body and mind contrary, March chases after Cheshire as if the Ace chased them, but she senses no threat. She loses sight of him—brief flashes of his body between branch and bough disappear—but she continues onward over root and grass. Jonathan catches up, limping and chuckling as the last of the pricks of his legs dissipate. They stop beneath another large sycamore tree, breathing heavily, legs worn from the morning's festivities, and listen to the slight rustle of the leaves and clack and creak of the trees for any sign of Cheshire.

His laugh echoes through the canopy, and distant, unseen birds chirp and join in the joyous choir. Jonathan and March share a glance, as well as the weight in their chests and the tears welling in their eyes. It has been so long since they have heard Cheshire's genuine hearty laugh when he does not use it as a mask. The tone in his voice floats in the air like the fireflies illuminating the speckled shade of the grove of trees, lighter than she has heard in an age. It brings back memories of their times, not just in the Hollow, but adventures to the Warrens, Ilex, Clava, Grey Harbor, Clypeus, and the open roads and dales in between. Adventures she wishes to return to once this horrible game is complete.

Cheshire drops from the canopy and crouches on a low-hanging bough just above their heads. He grins ear to ear, hooks his knees onto the branch and swings below to hang upside down. No words are needed. March twists his hair in her fingers and kisses him passionately. He rubs his face against hers before turning to Jonathan, who must lower himself to kiss Cheshire. They laugh as Cheshire passes back and forth between the two of them. It brings a warm glow to March, watching her men kiss with such intensity. But she wants more, her body reinvigorated.

"We have wandered far from our encampment." She grabs Cheshire by the waist and pulls him down. He flips and lands on his feet.

"Let us return," says Cheshire, "to the rest of our party."

He wraps his arms around March's waist, lifts her from the grass, and walks back toward the lake. She wraps her legs around his waist and feels his cock, hard anew, rubbing against her, its strength enough to support her on its own.

"Wait," says Jonathan, kneeling behind her.

March watches the fireflies drift in the reflection of Cheshire's eyes, matching his grin. They kiss with gentle pecks.

Jonathan lifts March higher, and Cheshire hooks his elbows under her knees to raise her higher. She presses her forehead against Cheshire's, and they inhale each other's breaths as Jonathan's nose and hair tickles between her thighs as it passes back and forth, wetting Cheshire's cock—for her. His head, guided by Jonathan's hand, finds its mark, and she slides lower and welcomes him.

Always, even after Jonathan, she must become accustomed to

Cheshire, who supports her twitching thighs, lowering her ever so slowly. Jonathan's breath heats a trail between her legs from her union to her backside, and his kisses turn to strong wet swaths of his tongue.

Cheshire's eyes tell her, *we have you.*

Yes, they do. They always do. She relaxes, staring deep into his eyes and allows her loves to lower her farther. Jonathan kisses up her back to her neck and steps aside for Cheshire to walk back to the lake with her. With every step, her body bounces off him—the constant rhythm and the pure sensation of Cheshire driving deeper. Jonathan walks behind, holding his own cock, enjoying March's expressions, her quivering eyes, and airless gasps.

The walk is long, and the vibrations take over March, from her flexed toes to the small hairs standing on end at the back of her neck. Cheshire is too much to bear too quickly. Her body spasms, and they are not halfway back to the lake. Jonathan trails behind them and watches, pulling his cock to the side to fight the temptation to finish.

"Look at me," Cheshire whispers in a growl. "Escape with me." For the rhapsody of their lovers' union is the only point in time they can truly escape the world, mind, body, and soul, no matter where they are.

March holds onto the sides of his face. His devilish grin tells her he is not close at all, but every step and thrust from Cheshire reaches deeper than before and pushes her closer to the peak until her breath stops, and lightning crackles through her every nerve. She tries to scream at the rush of her climax, but he steals her breath. It is his heartbeat within her, keeping her tethered to this world.

At last, able to breathe again, March releases a long, screaming, quivering exhale, and falls limp over Cheshire's shoulder. Jonathan does not give her a moment to rest and slips his arms under her knees to take Cheshire's place, carrying her the rest of the way. When Cheshire leaves her, she exhales, stomach constricting, as if a piece of her soul follows. Jonathan kisses her parched lips, while his cock, this time guided by Cheshire, finds its way home.

Jonathan's rhythm in every step does not grant a reprieve, or allow March a full descent from her climax. Unlike Jonathan, Cheshire walks beside them, hand kneading March's breasts and backside. The waterfalls grow louder in the distance, and they reach their small camp. Jonathan stops, keeping her in the air, and pulses within her. Cheshire reaches beneath them, takes Jonathan's shaft, and shakes it vigorously, while his tongue and his hot breath tease her ass, pressing hard against it, in it. Her body shakes involuntarily at the speed of Cheshire's hand, with waves of warm pleasure like hands sliding against her skin, against her soul. Her nails grip into Jonathan's shoulders, shaking, moaning with every exhale. She rests her head on Jonathan's shoulders, vision blurred, ears ringing, and bites into his shoulder.

Again, she exhales at the sensation of her lover sliding from her moments before she reaches her climax again. Cheshire stands beside Jonathan, takes her left arm over his shoulder, and hooks under her left knee, lifting her aloft, legs apart, as Pat and Bill approach.

The cool air rushes to meet the heat between her thighs. Jonathan's and Cheshire's eyes grow wide. They kiss her neck softly, the way the snow kisses the branches in winter. Weightless, March surrenders to the whims of her lovers.

Pat and Bill step in between her legs, and their cold lips and warm tongues cause her body to quake again as both of their mouths forcefully fight for her sensitivity. They press their cheeks together, knowing where to lick, where to suck, where to kiss for March's body to writhe.

Helpless, she looks into the eyes of Jonathan, her fierce gentleman, and Cheshire, her feral animal, so full of love, so full of desire. Their muscles tighten and hold her safely in the air.

Bill disappears between her legs and, from the quick breaths of Jonathan and Cheshire, tends to their needs below her. Her own breaths come quick as Pat takes over, with each well-placed flick and lick of her tongue. Pat's strong arms curl around March's thighs, and she smashes her face against her tenderness. Jonathan, and especially Cheshire, are skilled and gifted in the ways to please March, but Pat possesses secrets only another woman would know. She cups her mouth around March's sensitivity and sucks as hard as she can while her fingers explore and caress inside and out, plucking a long-needed string in March. March struggles against the pull of ecstasy, at their mercy, but not out of control; not yet.

She turns Cheshire's and Jonathan's heads to her breasts, and they cup her nipples in their mouths. The vibrations of three mouths on her body, as if they each handle and play her like a skilled musician, quicken her rise, and she bucks in the air. In this place, there is no reason to bridle or temper her screams, moans, and whimpers. Between each gasp, she sings to the heavens. She pulls on the back of Jonathan's and Cheshire's hair, raising herself higher into the air as she climaxes. Pat presses harder between her thighs, tongue speeding up as she rises into the air. Her back arches but no mouth leaves her body, keeping her at the precipice.

Where chills coursed through her body, a torrent of flames now consumes her, from her stomach to her toes, to her fingertips, to the ends of her hair. The hums of her lovers, their friends, and March's own screams resound in perfect harmony. Her body spasms, and Jonathan and Cheshire lower her back from the heavens to the earth, still keeping her arms over their shoulders, her legs shaking like a newborn fawn.

"Shall we rest?" asks Jonathan, kissing her temple.

Cheshire has yet to leave her breast.

"Never," says March, wetting her dried lips. "You started something you must finish, and you two must catch up."

She pushes Jonathan to his back, turns, and lowers herself down, legs weak. His cock pushes against her ass, warm and flexing. Cheshire squats in front of her, a twinkle in his eye, and reaches behind her, grasping her backside to steady her. She feels the slight playful pull as Jonathan raises his hips off the grass. Her lovers know her mind.

Again, she gasps at the slow, wonderful, temporary pain of Jonathan taking her from behind. Cheshire's strength sits her down. Jonathan grabs her waist to keep her in place and pushes up again and again, slowly, as March whimpers with every exhale, and welcomes more with every inhale. March wraps her arms around Cheshire's neck to hold herself up, legs trembling gloriously. Her breaths increase as Jonathan's pace quickens, and Cheshire breathes every one in.

Her lavender-demon, her lover, waits with a trembling jaw, and cock pulsing against her—teasing each other. March nods to him. He growls in her ear as he lays her back on Jonathan. The tension in her legs eases, but the rest of her body tenses; a prelude to the symphony they will create.

Cheshire thumps his long, thick shaft upon her sensitivity, again and again. Her body jerks with every thud, until in a single heavenly swoop, he lifts her legs into the air, and takes her. March welcomes both of her lovers until there is no room left within her. The momentary pain of Cheshire, combined with Jonathan, opens new doors and streaks through her body like lightning, filling her soul, her body, her core with fire.

March finds herself suspended once more, trapped between their hard, sweat-soaked muscles. Jonathan pulses, kissing at her neck, and Cheshire, on all fours, slams against her, in her, feral and powerful, reaching depths within her she knew not possible, all while he licks the sweat from between her breasts.

Clinging to Cheshire while Jonathan's wide hands tighten on her waist, the crescendo of her moans and screams to the heavens with every thrust, every rock, are accompanied by those of her lovers in glorious, sensual, melodic harmony. Long, drawn-out notes in exhalation and short bursts like prayers as they worship. She screams loudest and her lovers follow her melody. The sound of their bodies and voices in exulted, pure rapture creates a hymn any of the old gods would find envious. Their idolatry of each other knows no bounds.

She finds herself caught in the song, the tempest, her men conjure deep within her. Crashing waves and spiraling sky submerge her, taking her breath and only allowing her air when they calm.

March reaches out, placing a hand on Jonathan's and Cheshire's sides to hold, to let them know she will sing their song throughout the night and into the dawn. Cheshire lays upon her, all three of their heartbeats resonant in her body, growing together like the roaring fire of a smith's forge and intertwine, indistinguishable from one another; three lives shared as one.

Drops of sweat dangle from Cheshire's nose and shake free onto her chest. Jonathan's breathing becomes heavy. He nears his end, but Cheshire needs to catch up. March grips his hair and pulls his ear to her lips, biting his lobe and licking the concentric curves. His body jerks, thrusting even faster, half-screaming, half-moaning filling the cavern.

There. Jonathan matches his pace, and their rhythm reaches a fever pitch equilibrium, one thrusting and one pulling contrary. Her body hums, stomach twists, lost in the choir of her loves, and her hands and feet feel like ice while the rest of her ignites with fire. Jonathan and Cheshire are deliciously relentless, getting as much pleasure as she does, feeling their shafts rub and pass each other through her.

"Yes," she pants. March barely has the faculties to form thought, let alone words. "Yes." She nears her end, but not before they will.

Her tongue traces the inside of Cheshire's ear, and he is done. He pushes deep with all his weight and roars. Jonathan follows a second after, his hands pulling at her backside. His climax joins with Cheshire's exquisite song, and their warmth fills her body and her soul. Cheshire's beautiful whimper amid his guttural growls mixes well with the higher timber of Jonathan's moans. Their pulses nearly push March to the brink of what she can bear physically.

Finally releasing his ear, Cheshire collapses atop March, out of breath and rubbing his open mouth across her chest. Jonathan nuzzles her neck and rakes his fingertips up her sides. They did not give her time to rest, therefore neither will she.

"Once more makes us even," she whispers into Cheshire's ear, tracing its curve with her tongue, and then glances at Pat and Bill, who have knelt nearby, hands tending to each other.

Pat and Bill kneel behind Cheshire, and from the familiar, punctuated gasps her love makes, it would appear Bill's fingers find Jonathan's and Cheshire's asses. Helpless, they push back against them, this time in unison and increase in intensity. It takes much to surprise March, but the quick licks by Pat at the exceedingly tender area of March between Jonathan and Cheshire's cocks curls her toes and fingers.

Pat and Bill match rhythms, and Cheshire rears back, raising up as he thrusts wildly, taking hold of her waist. Every muscle of his body is taut, covered in sweat, and veins bulge from his forearms, up his arms to his neck and down below his navel. He looks over his shoulder, then back to March with a devilish grin, reveling in the company. Jonathan wraps his massive arms across her chest and takes hold of her breasts. The muscles and veins of his forearms ripple. His heartbeat pounds against her back, and Cheshire's within her.

Unable to fight against the will of her body any longer, March grabs onto Jonathan's arms, succumbs to the song of her lovers, and cries out. Cheshire blurs, and her vision almost falls to darkness. Sparks like steel against steel radiate from between her legs to the back of her head. Her love combines with theirs, and the unbridled song March sings pulls Jonathan and Cheshire to the climax and coda of this phase of their symphony.

Pat pulls Jonathan from March just as he climaxes. His warmth fills the heated space between their bodies and runs down her thighs. Bill pulls Cheshire from her and strokes him vigorously, bathing her and Jonathan in his almost never-ending love.

March sucks at her dry lips and slides off Jonathan's body and lies beside him in the grass, turning to kiss him and enjoying the sweet, blissful look on his face. Cheshire, chest heaving, lies on both of them. Pat finds a spot next to March, Bill beside Jonathan.

They need to rest, but their day is far from over. Like Cheshire, if March had her way, they would remain here as long as possible and return to survey the destruction. She shakes the thoughts of the outside world and exchanges a long, simple look between their trio, sharing the same thought, linked for all eternity, as if lying on the grass of the Hollow at twilight.

More.

CHAPTER 41
MARY ANNE

After a hearty meal of turkey legs, roasted potatoes, and several cheeses, Grace escorts Mary Anne to the Chamberlain's study. Twenty guards stand shoulder to shoulder outside the door, part for Mary Anne and Grace to walk through, then close again once they pass.

"Make sure the door latches firmly behind you," says the Duchess, sitting in one of the four chairs at the center of the chamber, sipping a cup of hot tea.

Once the latch clicks shut, a quick crunch of armor clatters together on the opposite side of the door, blocking any entry. Dozens upon dozens of candelabras and single candles spread their glowing light throughout the study, reflecting off the amber stacks of parchment, lessening the shadows almost to the point of nonexistence.

"Come, sit down, join us," the Duchess beckons with a soft voice.

Mary Anne joins her and the Chamberlain, already seated, with a circle of candles placed at their feet, illuminating the underside of their chairs. She has seen the Duchess affected, but never to this extent.

"Why all this?" she asks.

"Do not act naïve," says the Duchess, sipping tea from a tiny porcelain cup. "You know the reason as well as I. You have unleashed the Queen Slayer within our ranks and allowed him to run free, unchecked."

"If I had not made a deal with Cheshire, most of the citizens would have succumbed to the cult and the castle would most certainly have been overrun. Queens do not make mistakes. Remember? Hard choices are made without thought of the consequences, and now we must act accordingly. And if you believe these candles will keep Cheshire at bay, I regret to inform you once his mind is made up, little can be done to stop him. Curious. You still refer to him as Queen Slayer."

"It is what he is. He earned the title himself."

"Why do you fear the Queen Slayer, since you do not hold the title?"

The Duchess briefly chokes on her tea, coughing, and sets it back on its saucer on her lap. "It would be silly for anyone not to fear a murderer whose body count rivals, if not surpasses, most armies."

"Yet, as the smoke lifted yesterday, he addressed you, not me. He holds you responsible for something."

"Yes," the Duchess says, head lowered. "He blames me for the death of his mother. You wanted the truth; here it is. His mother was a servant in the castle some years ago. She served the court and queen well, until one day, years into her service, she fell ill. None of the castle physicians could decipher the ailment. Some thought the plague, others the pox, and others the sweating sickness. Her health faded over the course of months, and we could do little to save her."

"Does the queen's power not allow for such an act?"

"No, my dear. While queens hold dominion over all, all does not mean everything. Death in Wonderland is quite final. Because of this, Cheshire, as you refer to him, never recovered from his mother's death. He held the queen and all those close to her responsible, and exacted his revenge. Hence his title as the Queen Slayer. It took a miracle and cost the lives of hundreds of soldiers to banish him from the city, and for many years, the soldiers and castle guards fought to keep him from returning. So, you can see why his presence and proclamation has put me somewhat on edge."

"I did not know."

"He is more dangerous than any other threat you have faced or will ever face in Wonderland. Lysander, Uriah, their grandfather, and a host of others have tried to take the life of every queen; only one has succeeded: the young man you let wander our castle and streets."

"I did what must be done for the greater good," says Mary Anne. "Now we move forward. I shall ask a question and you will answer without lengthy explanations or tangents unless I ask for them. Do we understand one another?"

"Yes."

"How many queens of Wonderland have there been?"

"Four: Dinah, Catherine, Isabella, Beatrice. They were all deemed worthy by Wonderland land—"

Mary Anne holds out a hand to stop the Duchess. "Previously, you said the Arcana manifested itself differently in each one. Explain, and now you may go into detail."

The Duchess sighs heavily, humoring Mary Anne's stipulations, unaccustomed to limiting her words. "First, allow me to say, the royal decrees of the queens stand apart from the Arcana. After all, words have power. For Dinah, the first queen of Wonderland, the Arcana granted her the ability to control the wind, and with it, the breath of all those around her. The second queen, Catherine—"

"Hot tempered to be sure," says the Chamberlain.

"Catherine could hear the thoughts of others, as if they were speaking clearly to her. I believe she could not control the power, and it took its toll on her mentally, making her vulnerable. Isabella, the third queen, had power over nature, and could communicate and manipulate flora and fauna. The fourth queen, Beatrice, could control the earth we stood upon, able to topple buildings and create great chasms. The Arcana gave each a unique set of abilities, which is why it has been so difficult to explain what it may look like for you, because we cannot tell; we cannot know."

The information Mary Anne asked for all seems too much to take in at once. Perhaps the Duchess was right about giving it to Mary Anne in breadcrumbs to consume rather than shoving the whole loaf down her throat. It makes sense why, as Lysander and Uriah said, people feared them, and it's why they do not want a woman to reclaim the throne. How could they possibly fight against a force of nature?

"Something Lysander and Uriah brought up. A question continued to fester over dinner: Why is there no evidence of the queens, besides what you pushed in on a trolley days ago? Surely there must be a memorial of some sort. The Triumvirate has statues in their honor, yet not a trace of any queen remains."

"Not a simple answer," says the Duchess, "but I shall tell you. First, you must understand, Dinah, our first queen, did not quest for wealth or lavish living. Unlike the kings of old, she never had busts sculpted of her, or any other monument to her greatness or likeness built or constructed. She did not need them. The Chamberlain and I eventually convinced her to pose for one portrait. It hung in the main corridor of the keep. After her death, Lysander and Uriah's father and his forces invaded the city and sacked the castle. You have seen evidence of this outside the Reliquary. Their forces tried their hardest, but the Arcana would not allow them entrance. During the invasion, they shredded Dinah's bedchamber and destroyed all her belongings. The soldiers passing by her portrait each left their mark, slicing at it with their blades. Out of respect, we took it down."

A clearer image forms for Mary Anne.

"The second and third queens required a much more lavish presence and had portraits, statues, busts, vases with their visage on them, and banners throughout the city, which remained flowing in the wind for years. Yet it was the fourth queen who grew jealous of those who came before her and had every trace of them destroyed, while she planned grand designs for her image. If you know the way through the hedge maze, you will come across large slabs of stone where statues of the first three queens once stood. Beatrice did not live long enough to see her visage displayed in Mirus, so I, along with the Gryphon and Weiss, made the decision to stop all commissions before their completion."

Their conversation continues into the night, and the candles shrink to nubs of wax with flames struggling to stay alive. The Duchess warned her about the Twins' half-truths, and Mary Anne did not comprehend the full dangers of listening to them. They gave Mary Anne enough information to question the Duchess and doubt her own journey, even though the throne room doors opened for her.

"I think it time you retired to your chambers," says the Duchess. "If you do not mind, I will retire somewhere else in the castle."

"I understand. Tomorrow, I plan to have the Gryphon's archers and the same number of guards accompany me into the city to check on the progress of the festival."

"Oh, Mary Anne, do you still intend to go through with this? It is no longer safe."

"No, it is not; not for anyone. But I made the people of Stonehaven a promise, and if I back down, they will believe I fear Lysander and Uriah, which I most certainly do not. In such a time as this, when morale and hope are at its lowest, there must be a beacon, like a lighthouse, to shine on the path ahead, regardless of treacherous waters. And I will require your help."

"But I must—"

"You need not fear Cheshire for the time being. For the time I have known him, he may be many things, but he is not a liar. As dark as it may seem, he said he will leave you until last, until Mirus burns. As long as the city stands, and the people celebrate, I dare say you have nothing to fear."

The Duchess inhales deep and huffs, resigning herself to Mary Anne's macabre comfort. "When did we trade places and you offer me solace?

Well spoken. I shall not hide, not when you are so close to becoming queen, though I hope you will humor an old woman and allow me to keep a small regiment with me at all times, just in case."

"Of course. Thank you for speaking with me."

"My apologies for the vagueness of my answers. I thought they would only confound you more, but you are brighter than I could have ever imagined. I hope you understand why. All was to be revealed to you, but over time, to not overwhelm you. Now, get some rest." The Duchess rises and pats Mary Anne on the top of her hand. "Tomorrow is a new day, and we shall begin anew."

Mary Anne returns to her bed chambers with Grace by her side, instead of behind. She slows her pace. She has not walked side by side with Grace for some time. "I have not treated you fair these past few days. I became so focused I chose, willing or not, to neglect too many, including you. You have been by my side since I arrived, and somewhere I stopped treating you as a friend and started treating you as a servant. Queens are not supposed to apologize, I am told, but I hope you will allow me to break the rule this one time. I am sorry. Thank you for everything."

Mary Anne reaches out and takes Grace by the hand. She recoils at first, but her soft palm soon settles. Grace's lips quiver, and though Mary Anne does not turn to look upon her, a tear reflecting the braziers of the corridor rolls down her cheek.

When they reach the bedchamber, Grace slips her hand slowly from Mary Anne's, as if guilty, and closes the door behind her. Mary Anne half-expected, hoped, Jonathan and March would be here, but the candles are unattended and the bed remains undisturbed. She craves his touch, especially after her encounter with Lysander and Uriah and their harem. Mary Anne slides the gown off her shoulders, pooling at her feet, and slides under the covers, with thoughts of Jonathan, Lysander, and Uriah, and somehow March. She tosses and turns well into the night, unable to fall asleep. In order to relax and release these pent-up thoughts, Mary

Anne must take matters into her own hands, parting her legs and caressing the curves of her body, fingertips gliding down her skin between her legs, with thoughts of Jonathan above her, muscled arms pressed into the bed, but the chamber door flies open with a crash. Mary Anne instinctively covers herself, even under the sheets, wrapping herself in them.

The Duchess, dressed in her robe, gray hair hanging in loose curls, and a candle in hand, rushes into the room. She looks around the chamber, confused. "Where are Carter and Lady Adrianna?"

"Where indeed," says Mary Anne.

"Damn it, never mind. Forgive the intrusion. As I feared, our guests exploited our quarreling and moved against us. Dress yourself. This will be a sleepless night, my dear."

CHAPTER 42
CHESHIRE

The shafts of sun overhead disappear, passing afternoon into evening. Jonathan and March splash and wrestle each other in the Pool of Tears while Cheshire watches from its banks. Jonathan picks March up and falls back with her, both laughing, and splash into the crystal waters. They scoop handfuls of water and fling them at each other, but any time they are close enough to embrace, they do and share a kiss before the game begins again.

There are a multitude of questions brimming at March's and Jonathan's lips. He would answer every one if they ask, but their love for him runs so deep it keeps their questions at bay, and they spend the day in silence. It is the profound silence of knowing. Knowing so deeply, words become unnecessary. Knowing so deeply words would only diminish the truth.

Cheshire looks into the surface of the water, and his reflection returns his smile—a smile he has not seen on his face for an age. Jonathan and March bring this out of him; through the darkness they find him. There are several types of unseen strings binding them all to Wonderland, the past, the present, and the future, but none compare to the strength and pull of their heartstrings, forever woven inseparably into each other.

Pat and Bill lie end to end farther off, tending to each other.

The night will soon be upon them, and their time together will soon come to an end. But not before Cheshire has his way. He rummages through the one basket he packed, instead of Pat and Bill, tucks the crumpled scroll the Gryphon gave to March underneath one of Jonathan's shirts, and pulls out March's harness and the mold of Jonathan's cock. They were in such a frenzy the last time March used it, Cheshire did not have time to appreciate the accuracy of the details. Pat and Bill captured every ridge and vein. He squeezes the hard yet pliable material and briefly holds it next to his own hardening cock. While he is still larger and wider, Jonathan's remains beautiful to observe, especially in action.

Once March catches sight of it, she leads Jonathan out of the lake by his hand. Jonathan lies on his back and props himself up on his elbows, ready to fulfill Cheshire's desires. Cheshire wraps the harness around March's waist, grazing her skin as often as possible. He helps her buckle the brass and leather and must stand back to admire the gorgeous and fearsome image of her, standing tall, dripping wet hair, breasts tight from the cold water, and Jonathan's cock hanging from her waist.

Pat and Bill join them and lift Jonathan's legs and roll his hips into the air as they did in the grotto. Cheshire's cock throbs and his body aches at the sight of so much bare skin around him. He stands behind March, kissing her neck before she kneels between Jonathan's legs. She rubs the tip of the mold against Jonathan's ass, and he laughs and pants. It would be a simple matter to have Bill fuck Jonathan, which he still might suggest, but there is something extremely erotic in watching Jonathan's own cock bring him pleasure, and watching March be its deliverer.

She spits on the mold and rubs it thoroughly before sliding it into Jonathan's waiting body. Cheshire walks around the sculpture of lust, never having experienced Jonathan's pleasure from these angles, watching different parts of his body flex and relax as March fucks him. He returns to stand behind March and peers down between her breasts to watch the mold slide in and out over and over again, slamming hard against his body, because he can take it. Cheshire stands next to her and guides her mouth to his cock, which she welcomes without question and without interrupting her rhythm. Over the centuries, they have tried many positions and scenarios, but this is new and exhilarating to Cheshire. March takes hold of Jonathan's ankles and pounds against him harder, rocked by every thrust. His cock smacks against his stomach, leaving beads and strings of his love behind.

Spoiled for choice, for once, Cheshire does not know what to choose, as if standing before a lavish banquet for the first time. Luckily, Pat and Bill decide for him. They return to another basket and pull out a second mold and harness—of course they would have multiple—and Cheshire's toes dance with the possibilities.

At first, wanting to kneel behind March, Cheshire elects to lie on his back on Jonathan's chest, who lifts Cheshire's legs into the air. March wastes no time and, with a lustful grin, pulls from Jonathan and plunges into Cheshire, over and over again. With each thrust and pull, March steals his breath with her prowess and beauty. Her breasts and stomach flex, trickling sweat, and her hair, wet from the lake, sticks to her skin. Bill kneels next to them and takes Cheshire's cock into his mouth to the base. Cheshire grabs ahold of his head and thrusts deeper, pressing Bill's face against his body as March ravages him.

Pat kneels behind March and slides her mold into March's waiting ass, and reaches around to roll her nipples in her fingers. March's hips become wilder, pushing back into Pat and into Jonathan and Cheshire

Cheshire wants more. Once March thrusts into Jonathan again, he lowers himself onto Jonathan and welcomes his cock into his own ass—its warmth, the heartbeat, the ultimate difference between the mold and the genuine article. Rising up and down, enjoying Jonathan's pull, Cheshire stares deep into March's eyes, lost in their shared euphoric, heavenly state. Bill kneels facing away from Jonathan and lowers his ass onto his face, and his tongue makes quick work of his ass.

So much—almost too much—Cheshire does not want this to end, but he can see March nears her climax in the fluttering of her eyes. He grabs the side of her face and kisses her as she reaches her pinnacle and screams in his mouth, and he inhales every breath she gives. Jonathan follows soon after, March never stopping her rhythm. His hips rise into the air, raising Cheshire higher, and fills him with his warmth.

Cheshire wants to sample everything, even if some experiences must wait until later. More animal than man, he stands, pulling March and Pat to their feet, standing them side by side. He has never had another breast in his mouth besides March's before, but why let this experience pass him by since it has presented itself? His mouth jumps back and forth from March to Pat, kissing, licking, sucking at both. Cheshire rubs his face against both of their chests, consuming all he can. Eventually, they face each other, breasts touching, allowing his tongue to play with both simultaneously, sliding his tongue between them, intensifying every one of his senses and blocking out every thought.

Not satiated, but yearning for more, Cheshire turns his attention to Jonathan and Bill, who stand side by side waiting for him. He kneels before them and takes Jonathan's cock and then Bills's, back and forth, squeezing their asses with his hands. Like March and Pat, Cheshire places their heads together, to taste them both, tongue passing between and circling each. March and Pat kneel next to them and touch his shoulder to get his attention. He no longer thinks, he feels, experiences, and craves, jumping back and forth to their breasts and cocks, insatiable. Four pairs of hands massage his shoulders and run through his hair. He grows light-headed at the exertion of his debauchery but pushes himself, growling, grunting, licking, and biting.

Jonathan and March bring Cheshire to his feet while the rest of their party kneels, and all four of their mouths descend upon his cock, shaft, head, and balls. The sight of all four attending him is too much to bear.

He barely lasts a minute's time before the tingles and butterflies take over his body. They brace his legs and squeeze his ass as he climaxes and, smiling, each take a turn swallowing his shaft as far as they can, gulping from him, sharing him, until he has nothing left to give.

He falls to his knees and kisses Jonathan and March, licking at their faces, reluctant to kiss Pat and Bill, though the temptation presents itself after everything they have experienced together. Cheshire's shoulders slump, exhausted and spent.

"Once more," says Jonathan.

Who is Cheshire to argue? Unable to rise from the forest floor, all five join in a beautiful ouroboros of carnal desire, lying on the grass, mouths and exploring hands connecting them all. Their mouths tend to each other while enjoying the attention of one another. Everyone around him divides and pulls Cheshire's focus. Jonathan's cock fills his mouth while Pat swallows most of him. Then there is Jonathan who takes all of Bill, Bill whose tongue teases March, and March who circles her face between Pat's legs.

One by one, they climax with muffled exhalations, unwilling to release the others—first Bill, then Jonathan, Pat, March, and finally Cheshire. He did not know what would transpire when bringing Pat and Bill here, but now Cheshire imagines even more possibilities and positions when the five are together.

Spent and exhausted from the exhilarating bliss of their union, Cheshire rolls back on the grass. Jonathan and March lie next to him, legs draped over him, covered in glistening sweat. Pat and Bill lie together not far off.

"Fuck me. This was much needed," says Jonathan, feeling the end of their day, like the rest of them.

"Always needed," says March. "But rarely ever available."

"Is that in reference to me?" Cheshire jests.

"If you were to stay in the Hollow with us, think of what our every day and night would be," says March.

"Tempting," says Cheshire. "Always tempting. Perhaps one day, but until such time, I am capable of handling my own urges while away."

"What ever do you do without us?" asks Jonathan.

"Well, I do not have the luxury of a spare cock around. Or these two." Cheshire grins. "Why have the five of us never played together before?"

"Because we have all never been in Mirus at the same time," says March.

"Cannot argue with the truth," says Cheshire. "But after this is all over, they will need to visit the Hollow on occasion. For now, while I am away at my work, I shall continue to resort to my own means."

Jonathan rolls to his side and rests on his elbow. "Please, tell us."

March drapes her arm over Jonathan, curiosity piqued. "Or better yet, show us."

Cheshire raises an eyebrow, rolls back on his shoulder, ass in the air, and lets his knees fall to the grass, bringing his cock to his mouth. He opens, swirls his tongue around its head, and then welcomes and wraps his lips around a third of its length. He wishes he could take more, but it took decades to make it this far.

"Oh, fuck," says Jonathan.

"And fucking beautiful," says March. "Why have you never done this around us before?"

"Because..." Cheshire releases himself. "I have you two."

Jonathan and March scramble to their knees and take hold of Cheshire's thighs, keeping him locked in this position. "Keep going." Their eyes fill with an intensity Cheshire cannot resist.

Cheshire grins again and takes his cock back into his mouth, slowly moving his head back and forth, sucking and massaging while he stares up at Jonathan and March. Their wonder, disbelief, and lust causes Cheshire to swell harder. He puts on a show for them, playfully using his tongue and kissing and licking his swollen head.

Jonathan, unable to help himself any longer, leans down and licks at Cheshire's shaft and then takes his balls into his mouth, teasing and sucking them. March kisses and bites at his ass; her tongue circles, laps, and presses against his hole.

Cheshire loses control, growling and moaning the best he can with his mouth full. His body, beyond sensitive, instinctively tries to fight against them, but his lovers have him pinned with their bodies, their hands, and their mouths. He bucks against them, but they hold him tighter, pushing him to the brink again. He sucks harder on his own cock, enjoying the sweet taste seeping into his mouth. Not yet; or at least not alone.

He reaches up and grabs Jonathan's shaft with one hand, hard as stone, and with the other, reaches behind him to find the warmth between March's legs, and slides three fingers inside her while using his thumb to massage her sensitivity. They both gasp, and all three laugh at their current situation. Nothing exists outside of their connection, their lovers' knot. Their spirits melt together, indistinguishable from each other, not knowing where one begins and one ends; as it should be.

Jonathan and March take small breaks for air to kiss each other above Cheshire and watch him, enjoying the show as much as Cheshire enjoys the audience. He sucks harder, faster, and growls louder. His legs tremble, and his stomach tightens and flutters.

Watching the twinkle in their eyes, Cheshire pulls Jonathan closer to him by his cock, slides his hand between his legs, squeezing the base of Jonathan's shaft with three fingers while the other two slip into his ass. With a grip on both of his lovers, Cheshire shakes his hands, unrelenting.

March gasps, barely able to breathe, and punishes Cheshire for his wickedness with her tongue returning to his ass, fingertips digging into Cheshire's backside. Jonathan rocks back and forth, throbbing against Cheshire's hand, as a drop of spit falls from Jonathan's open mouth onto Cheshire's cock, before reclaiming it in his mouth. It slides down his bulging shaft until Cheshire welcomes it onto his tongue.

Tingles race from Cheshire's cock to the back of his head. His eyes roll backward.

"Yes," Jonathan whimpers.

"Yes," says March, through rapid inhales.

Cheshire shakes his entire arms, untamed, and Jonathan's and March's moans border on screams. In playful retaliation, before their shared moment, they both slip a finger into Cheshire's ass.

There is no turning back, no time to pause. The explosion of their love happens simultaneously. Prickles of energy wash through all of their bodies, connecting them all. Warm ribbons from Jonathan's cock drop along the length of Cheshire's arm and thigh. The sound of Cheshire's hand between March's legs becomes wetter, and she bathes him in her glory.

Cheshire screams against his own cock, welcoming every pump into his mouth. After climaxing so many times, he thought there would be less to give, but March and Jonathan force every drop from him as if it were his first time. He grows light-headed, his mouth fills, and his eyes flutter shut.

Through his labored pants, Jonathan says, "Give it to us."

They sit Cheshire up so quickly the blood rushes from his head and he loses all sense of his bearings. He does not need them, because Jonathan and March are in control. Once upright, Jonathan grabs Cheshire by the jaw, turns him back toward him, and kisses him deeply, sucking on his tongue, pulling the taste from his mouth, and leaving his moans behind. March continues to stroke Cheshire, causing his entire body to spasm until she grabs Cheshire by the jaw, turns him, and brings his mouth to hers. She kisses him passionately, sucking on his tongue, drinking the rest of him, filling him with her moans as well.

Cheshire pulls away for the briefest of moments to catch his breath and for his eyes to focus on his loves. The shimmer in their eyes is as brilliant as their first time together; every time together. Cheshire wishes he could say he wants nothing more than to retire with them to the Hollow and live out eternity with moments like these, but in his heart, he cannot. Through everything they endured in recent days, this moment, the celestial moment, stokes the fire within Cheshire to complete his mission.

He kisses March and then Jonathan gently on the lips and brushes the tip of his nose against theirs. Their trio rest their foreheads together, feel their heartbeats sync and slow, and breathe in unison.

Unfortunately, what he wants will impede Jonathan's work with Mary Anne. The quicker the world burns, the sooner he and his loves can be lost for all time together.

Cheshire's lip quivers, and worry fills the eyes and pinched brows of his loves. They both reach out and caress his cheeks with their thumbs, and he cannot hold the tears back.

"There is nothing here for us but tragedy and pain. You need to leave."

"And we will," says Jonathan. "Soon."

"No. It cannot wait. You must both leave. I have learned these past days and nights my attention is all but fractured, and I need you out of the city."

"What is it you fear?" March asks, ever intuitive. She does not ask what he has planned, or the whereabouts of the Gryphon. Instead, she cuts straight to the core of the matter.

Cheshire catches his breath. "My biggest fear is you will come to know me as I know myself. You see kindness where I see emptiness. You see strength when, in actuality, I am at the end of my rope." Cheshire glances to himself in the pool. "I am a broken reflection of the man I should have been."

Tears swell in Jonathan's and March's eyes, and they lean their foreheads against his. Cheshire has shared more with Jonathan and March during their stay in Mirus than the entire expanse of their relationship. The truth pulls at him and wants him to divulge more. Does he show them the painting of his mother on the other side of the grove? If he did, they would know all, and he cannot have this. Secrets hold power, even if they are from his loved ones. He does not cry because he has ruined this day, but because it must end; he knows what he must do.

"Thank you both, truly. But it is time I returned you all. You have your business to attend to, as do I."

"You are mistaken if you believe we will leave you now," says March.

"Return us in the morning," says Jonathan.

March and Jonathan lay Cheshire back on the grass and wrap their arms and legs around him, tighter than ever before. They hold him, and their breaths and heartbeats become a lullaby, like a siren's call to slumber and dream. His body relaxes, and he free falls into the realm halfway between dreams and waking. When the morning comes, the city will be his, but until the dawn, he shall be theirs.

CHAPTER 43

JONATHAN

Early the next morning, Cheshire returns Jonathan and March to Mary Anne's bedchambers through the shadows. Jonathan expects Mary Anne to wait for them, confront them on their whereabouts after the hangings and the aftermath of Cheshire, but the bed shows little sign of a peaceful night's rest. A quick glance from March lets him know he is right in his assumption: Mary Anne did not slumber here. He must attend Mary Anne today, who will undoubtedly be cross from their absences. The scales in Jonathan's mind swing off balance, not wishing to trade the day he shared with his loves, but also knowing the world, Mary Anne, and the Twins moved forward without them.

March stretches, callous to the predicament they face, grabs a near-empty bottle of rum from the floor, clicks it against other empty bottles, and finishes the contents in a single swig. "I can add a restock among my tasks today." March circles the last remaining drops around the bottom of the bottle. "Decisions, decisions. Go to the Boroughs for stronger spirits and risk hallucinations or steal lesser quality from the vats in the distillery of Far Side."

"Vats, you say?" asks Cheshire, wiping the Mask of Shadows from his face.

"Two nearly twenty-ton casks, twenty feet tall, at least. Passable quality, but it gets the job done. Sometimes quantity outweighs quality."

"Do not fret over such minutia," says Cheshire. "I shall replace your stock from Far Side. You have more important tasks to attend." Cheshire pulls a long length of twine from one of Jonathan's chests, used to secure his boxes of teas, and ties it around the neck of several bottles, creating a beautiful and bright clicking wind chime when he picks them up from the floor.

March shows her thanks with a lasting kiss. Cheshire rushes to kiss Jonathan goodbye, summons his mask, and leaps into the shadow of one of the large pillars around the bedchamber, off to wreak more havoc upon the city.

Jonathan pulls a fresh pair of leather trousers from a trunk and slips into his favorite, tattered blue longcoat while March laces her trousers, wraps the linen top around her, and pulls up her bracers.

March grabs Jonathan by the collar and kisses him. "Every step away," she says, lips pressed against his.

"Is a step back to you." Jonathan returns her kiss harder.

"And you." They both look to the shadow where Cheshire disappeared.

Jonathan slips his longsword over his shoulder and leaves the bedchamber in search of anyone, yet again, to give him any news of the past day's events. With Mary Anne's handmaiden nowhere to be found, he journeys deeper into the castle. The servants passing by possess an anxious gait about them. He stops a young girl headed toward the Chamberlain's study.

"Excuse me. Would you know where I may find Mary Anne this morning?"

The servant blushes and stutters. "Have you not heard?"

"Heard what?"

"I... I should not say. You will find her by the castle gates."

What the fuck has happened?

Jonathan emerges into the bailey to find Mary Anne standing beneath the gatehouse, surrounded by a dozen soldiers and double the number of archers. She catches Jonathan's gaze with pressed lips, not her normal greeting, while she commands the attention of the soldiers and archers with every word and gesture.

Almost every minute of the day, Jonathan wishes he were lost—lost to the world—however, this sensation as he walks to join them churns in his stomach and brings an anxious sweat to his brow. The solution to cure this malady is to know. He must know, because knowing is how he keeps the intrusive thoughts and assumptions at bay. He catches every third or fifth word of what she speaks—overrun, necessary, streets, force, preparation, losses.

What the fuck have I missed?

The soldiers and archers part to make an aisle for him straight to Mary Anne. Her appearance signals strength, wearing a long, thin crimson coat fastened with a wide brown belt, its lapel pulled wide to reveal the pale skin of her chest—as March would.

"Thank you for joining us," says Mary Anne, without an ounce of warmth, though her eyes reveal her hurt.

"I must apologize—"

"While I appreciate the gesture, we do not have time at the moment."

Jonathan shrinks inside. Mary Anne has never spoken to him in such a cold manner, and even though she is feet from him, he has never felt so distant from her. *Distant.* Words beginning with D flood his mind: dejected, dereliction, downcast, despondent, doleful, disappointed. Whatever orders Mary Anne gave the soldiers and archers are lost to the torrent of spiraling words. They file out of the gate, leaving the last few to flow around Mary Anne, like water around a river stone.

"Mary Anne, I must—"

She holds a finger to his lips. "I want to be cross with you, really I do, but I forgave you the moment you walked from the keep. Through a sleepless night when I should have been focused on Lysander and Uriah, all I could think about was your safety and missing your warmth next to me. But you are here now, when it matters."

Jonathan cannot help but feel a pang of guilt with his relief, like another fist to the gut, which will leave a new bruise, a fresh scar. He wraps Mary Anne in his embrace, and her tense body melts with his heat. After breathing him in, she nestles her face in his chest, nose running up and down between his muscles.

"I did not mean to make you worry." He lays his chin gently on top of her head. "Cheshire absconded with us during the night. After the debacle the prior evening, not to mention his unwillingness to release us, we figured it was better to keep him occupied than unleash him onto the city."

"Occupied?" Mary Anne questions for only a moment, but the half-grin gives her the answer she needs. "Ah."

"This morning, however, is another matter."

Mary Anne steps back and fusses with the top of her jacket. "How the dickens does March keep hers open?"

"Open?" Jonathan reaches his hands up to her collar. "May I?"

"You never need to ask permission." Mary Anne grabs his hands and places them on her collar.

He tugs her coat open slowly. His thumbs graze against the inside curve of her breast, and her body tenses at his touch.

"Apologies."

She grabs his wrists to keep his hands in place, pressing them against her. Jonathan's heartbeat quickens with hers.

"The secret is to alter the front, removing a few inches of darting from the top between shoulder and collar, so it will stay open on its own. The trick is tapering the alteration to the waist, so it can fasten if need be."

Her eyes dart from his lips and return to his gaze.

"Back to the matter at hand." He gives one last tug to her coat and drops his hands.

Mary Anne shakes her head as if snapped from a trance. "Yes, well, perhaps we can use a little of Cheshire's chaos this morning, or at least aim it in the right direction."

"Tell me what has happened."

"It would be better to show you."

At the lowest tier of the Crest, soldiers of Adamas, armed and in full polished armor and tabards, form lines and block the entrance to the high ways and the staircase leading into Stonehaven. The back of Jonathan's neck and arms tingle when he tenses them, ready for a confrontation, but the soldiers face away, toward Stonehaven. Their quarrel is not with the castle, not yet at least. They intend to cut off and keep those from the lower city from the Crest. The soldiers make way for Jonathan and Mary Anne when they approach and close behind them like a scraping door, leading to another set of soldiers at the base end of the stairs.

Halfway down, Mary Anne squeezes Jonathan's arm to stop him. "Lysander and Uriah's men position themselves at every entrance along the border of the Crest, and from the reports of the scouts this morning, they have created a full barrier between the Crest and Stonehaven."

"You sent soldiers and archers out this morning; will they not clash with the soldiers of Adamas?"

"Our soldiers will, at every stairway as planned, as they are meant to, in order to serve as a distraction for the archers to take to the roofs, where the soldiers of Adamas cannot reach. They will monitor us and search for any other innocent lives lost."

Jonathan rarely finds himself speechless, but again he sees a different woman before him—wiser, more knowledgeable, a strategist, and, more importantly, a player, not just a pawn, proving herself capable without the Gryphon, the Duchess, or him. Part of him misses the gentle woman he walked through gullies and hills within the Rookwood, but her change was inevitable; nothing in Wonderland stays innocent.

"You are a wonder," says Jonathan.

Jonathan and Mary Anne pass through the next gate of soldiers and find the information of the scouts horrifyingly true. Every ten paces, three rows deep, soldiers of Adamas stand at attention, gleaming sentries, alternating with spear and sword down their line until out of view. If they continue at this count around the curve of the city, there would be roughly three thousand men on foot alone. Soldiers on horseback stand in the middle of the street every thirty paces and hold the white banner of Adamas.

"The Adamas occupation of Mirus has begun," says Jonathan.

"From the information given this morning, they stay on this tier for now. I wonder how much of the city is aware of this?"

"Oh, we are well aware." Lacha climbs to the street, leather apron unhooked and dangling at his waist, carrying two hammers larger than Jonathan's thighs in each hand, standing with splatters of blood.

Several more blacksmiths, each as large or larger than Lacha, follow up the stairs. Sweat, grease, and dirt cover their broad, bear-like muscles, and they carry hammers, chisels, and chains.

"They tried to move to the lower tiers of Stonehaven. We let them know it would be unwise. After thirty-seven of their number had their arms and legs broken, and chests and heads crushed, they listened."

The soldiers of Adamas widen their stance and reach for their swords. The blacksmiths spin their hammers in their hands or by the leather straps at their ends. Jonathan and Mary Anne find themselves caught between an imminent clash if not diffused immediately.

"We cannot shed more blood," says Mary Anne. "Blood will only beget blood."

"They should have considered this before standing idly by while friends, family, and neighbors I have come to know my entire time in this world were strung up."

"The soldiers did not hang them?" asks Jonathan.

"No. They watched and laughed. A sin greater than killing them with their own hands."

"What of the townspeople who committed these atrocities?" asks Jonathan.

"They are not people, not anymore. Not if they are capable of such evil. The ones we tracked down, we took care of, and we will find the rest and put their heads to our anvils for all the city to hear the ring of justice; justice you fail to bring us."

"I am so sorry," says Mary Anne, but her words fall on deaf ears.

"Don't give excuses, words, or condolences. Your words mean less now than our last conversation. I foolishly let myself believe you stood a chance, but you have just started this game of politics, while your opponents have won countless times over. You play games with people's lives like we are pieces to be sacrificed, welcoming and hosting our enemy when their necks should be sliced, faces crushed, and drowned in their own blood."

"There is more you do not know," Mary Anne pleads, whispering to keep her words from the soldiers. "It is more complicated than just taking their lives."

"Have you tried? Or just thought of what will get you the throne before them?"

Mary Anne looks to Jonathan for help, but the blacksmiths crack their necks, breathing heavily and gripping their hammers tight. The leather bands of their handles crackle. They grow restless, and any answers to their questions will not appease them when they thirst for actions and results. Not even Jonathan's silver tongue will win them over when they are done listening, yet he must try.

"We face a greater threat on the horizon," adds Jonathan. "It is about negotiations and playing the long game to ensure victory and survival."

"Whose survival? Yours?" A larger smith flexes his arms and chest, veins bulging. "I lost my daughter. Our neighbor tied a rope around her neck, tied it to the post of her bed, and threw her out her window. She was in her seventh year, eighth this winter. I kicked down his door and buried my hammer in his forehead."

"Know this," says Lacha. "I have no love in my heart for the Twins or you. As far as I am concerned, as many in the city are concerned, you can all die, kill each other with your own hands, but at least we would be done with the lot of you."

"Give us time," says Jonathan. "We save it, bide it, mark it, often waste it, and it always still passes inexorably. Despite everything, we still have time, even if you cannot see it, because your passion, rightfully placed, blinds you. We cannot make things right, but we can make them pay."

In the distance, a horse trots against the street, keeping time like a ticking clock.

"We can make them pay now," says Lacha, pointing one of his hammers at the line of soldiers.

"And what would this achieve?" Jonathan stands between them.

"You protect them?"

"I protect you, sir." Jonathan risks placing his hand on Lacha's hammer to lower it. "Over a thousand soldiers line this street alone. While your intentions are noble, we cannot suffer your sacrifice. Your band of brothers may lessen their number, even by half, but they, like the swarming insects they are, will overcome your number. As an alderman, your people need your leadership and guidance, which they cannot get from a corpse."

Their conversation has drawn the eyes of Stonehaven, peering down at them from between cracked shutters and behind curtains, watching and waiting to see how this exchange ends. Lacha catches Jonathan's eyes darting to them and turns to see them as well. He waits long enough to worry Jonathan before lowering his hammer and looks over his shoulder at his men, his brothers, and with a glance they loosen their grips, though their nostrils flare and eyes wish death upon the soldiers.

"This is their line. They can keep the fucking Crest and the castle. Should they dare descend any farther into my territory, for any reason, their bones will become the powder for the mason's mortar. My words go for soldiers and servants alike from the Crest."

"You dare threaten us?" The Red Knight approaches on horseback, pulls on the reins, and stops between them and the soldiers. "Such words would be considered treason if my Lords heard of such things."

His voice scratches deep into Jonathan's mind, thankful, and wondering when he would have the opportunity to face the turncoat. "I am glad to see you again. I am told you were behind the kidnapping of Mary Anne and held her and March, my love, in the dungeons." He unsheathes his sword, forgetting his words to Lacha. "Dismount your horse."

"Jonathan, did we not just talk about staying our hands?" Mary Anne reaches for his arm, but he steps away.

"Your whore?" The Red Knight chuckles.

"The woman who claimed your eye. For what you have done, I will take much more."

Snickers and scoffs ring from beneath Adamas helmets.

"I do not need to lower myself to your level. At my command, the soldiers will run you through. You, this worthless lot of laborers, and the false queen. In fact, I shall be rewarded for it."

Jonathan searches the faces of the soldiers, and many of them appear bored, uninterested, and, if Jonathan reads the rolling of their eyes and their snarled lips correctly, fed up with the Red Knight and his opportunistic ways. Mary Anne's words repeat in his head, but looking upon the Red Knight's smug face, knowing the state he found March in the dungeons, all Jonathan can think of is taking his life. It would be easy.

"Excuse me, gentleman." Jonathan addresses the soldiers. "Does this turncoat command you?" They remain silent. "So, since he is not of Adamas, and actually from Mirus, if I killed him here and now, would you take up arms?"

The Red Knight circles his horse, searching the soldiers for an answer. None meet his eyes. The clacking of the horse's hooves increases with his irritation. The frantic side-to-side movements of his head, the huffs, the way he jerks at the reins cannot hide what he truly feels—embarrassment.

"How dare you?" His scold runs off the helmets of the soldiers like drops of rain.

"You see," says Jonathan, leaning his sword over his shoulder. "Even though these soldiers find themselves on opposing sides from us, one thing can be certain of almost any soldier: loyalty is key. Loyalty is life. And once someone like you brands themselves a traitor to their own, you will forever be a traitor, untrustworthy, especially to those who do not claim you."

"Aye." Lacha slams his hammer in his palm. "If Carter doesn't do the job, I'm more than willing to knock your head clean from your shoulders."

"You will pay for your threat." The Red Knight cannot mask his growing panic, turning to the soldiers. "And you sons of whores will pay for this insubordination."

Mary Anne tries to get Jonathan's attention; his name muffles in his ears, as he does not drop his gaze from the Red Knight. Jonathan brings his sword down and grasps it with both hands, twisting its grip as if it were the Red Knight's neck.

"I shall request again." Jonathan points his sword at the Red Knight's throat. "Get down from your horse."

"I am done with the likes of all of you." The Red Knight pulls back and rears his horse up, summoning a pained whinny from the animal. "The next time you look at me, it will be with the point of my blade at your throat." He snaps the reins and rides off to the east.

"At least I will have two eyes to look upon you," Jonathan shouts after him.

The shutters and curtains no longer conceal the townspeople of

Stonehaven. They watch, chests held high and chins up, at the act of defiance between Jonathan and the Red Knight. Even the soldiers of Adamas glance up at their audience. The faces of the smiths soften, brows raised—a vast distinction from the scowls prior to the knight's arrival. Jonathan did not mean it as an act of rebellion or to incite or elicit any reaction. He simply wants to repay the Red Knight for what he did to March.

"Thank you." Jonathan extends his hand to Lacha. "Thank you for standing up for your people."

"It is the right thing to do." Lacha hooks the leather strap of his hammer on his belt and shakes Jonathan's hand.

"How fares the rest of Stonehaven?" asks Jonathan.

"They are aware of this turn of events. Most stay in their homes, for fear of being strung up, or assaulted by Adamas soldiers. Some move their families to the lower tiers or leave the city with packed wagons and carts. Those who try to go on about their day do so with trepidation and fear in their eyes. And for them, and all the rest, we will make sure they can."

Mary Anne extends her hand, and though hesitant, Lacha stands on good form and takes hers as well, consumed by the width of his grip. "This will all be handled by the time of the festival," says Mary Anne.

"You plan to go through with the damned festival? Will you push it further to add more days of mourning for the dead?"

"We must show strength." Mary Anne glances back at the uniformed soldiers. "They have unity, so shall we. Try as they might, they will not break our spirits."

"Be that as it may"—Lacha signals to the other blacksmiths to return to Stonehaven—"whatever festivities you have planned, we will not be in attendance. And before you try to object, you have your duties and obligation, and I have mine. We will leave on those terms. Agreed?"

"Agreed." Mary Anne has no choice in the matter, and no leverage to sway Lacha's stance.

The larger smith turns back before descending the stairs. "You want him? The Red Knight?"

"You know where he hides?" asks Jonathan.

"Not difficult to miss," the smith says. "The fuck has been giving away gold and silver coins throughout the city, like tossing pebbles in a pond. He's been holed up in the Garden for days and always comes out with full pouches."

"The flowers," says Mary Anne. "Women from the Garden come and go from the castle every day and pass the Twins' orders."

"And the chests of coin March mentioned," says Jonathan. "They were never brought into the castle. No better place to conceal them than a business where money flows in and out like a spring without question."

It makes sense why the Twins remain on the castle grounds and how they continue to plot while keeping their hands clean. This entire time, their women have passed information to the Red Knight, their informant outside the castle, and he attempts to buy the loyalty of those suffering and in need. The soldiers' reactions prove they have taken orders from him out of necessity, not loyalty. And even though a traitor, no one believes he could pose anywhere near a threat as the Twins or Cheshire, therefore he is forgotten. Jonathan himself almost forgot he skulked somewhere in the city. Little does he know how expendable he is, and he will soon find out.

CHAPTER 44
MARCH

From the moment she sets foot in the bailey, the jarring difference hits her ears, and even more so once outside the castle walls. Every cacophonous, ambient sound of the city is hushed, as if muffled by a heavy damask curtain. Few distant sounds permeate through—voices and footsteps, the caw and cackle of birds, just as there are visitors in a graveyard.

In the highest level of the Crest, townspeople move about with their same pompous air, purses jingling with coins, the ripple of thick woven fabrics, and hushed chatter. In the distance, outside the manor, Bronwen converses with the Twins with an exaggerated expression and feigning concern. March has never known a sincere moment or bone in her mother's body. She flaunts her connection with them to those who walk the cobbles of the Crest and prying eyes from the balconies and shuttered windows of their garish manors. Although Bronwen's fingers traipse across her exposed cleavage from her fur-collared gown to gain the Twins' attention, they glance at March to get her attention. She plays the scene in her mind from before when the Twins spoke to the soldier in the bailey, wondering if this is a distraction from something else or if this is part of their plan. Unfortunately, either way, she must discover what this triad of conspirators plans.

March walking unaccompanied in the Crest draws attention of its own—lustful gazes from married men, and some women, the upturned noses of those who know well her reputation, and something new, with which she is not familiar.

"Congratulations." A woman in a feathered, plumed coat and hat rolls her eyes.

Congratulations?

A married couple from around the curve walk arm in arm and look at March from head to toe. "Too good for a strumpet like her," the wife tells the husband, who concentrates more on March's body than his wife's words.

A portly man passes close to March, and she can smell his foul breath despite the copious amounts of perfume. "If I did not already wish to be like them," he says, "now all the more, knowing they will share you."

"Congratulations are in order," says a young man, no older than Cheshire, with the sickly lecherous tone no doubt taught by his father. He would be considered handsome if not for the man March sees him becoming. "I cannot wait for the wedding night. I am told they will make it a public event, and I would pay handsomely to be nearest the bed."

If Bronwen wishes to get a rise out of March, she succeeds. The hatred festering in her sets her skin ablaze, the heat palpable from her face. Bronwen's mouth spews falsehoods for every person in the Crest to cling to and spread, just as she did years ago. Nothing changes.

March approaches the trio, ignoring the other side glances and congratulatory lies. The Twins turn to greet her, eyes devouring her, reverting to their old ways or back to the game they play.

"Morning, Audrianna," says Bronwen. "Gentlemen, would you give us a moment together? Mother and daughter."

They nod together, pass on both sides of March, leaving her with one last glance, a warning to prepare herself—their concern troubles her and oozes across her skin.

"What the fuck are you telling people?" March slaps Bronwen's hand when she reaches out to adjust her braces. "Telling everyone I am to wed both Lysander and Uriah?"

"Just trying to repair the reputation of my wayward daughter," says Bronwen, her eyes surveying the prying eyes of the other manors and homes on the street.

"Do not pretend you ever have anyone's interest, especially mine, in mind but your own, you self-serving bitch."

"Will you never have a kind word to say to your mother?"

"Never."

"If not a kind word, then perhaps just a word."

"You have spoken too many already and waste my time."

"Can we not have a conversation—"

"No."

"—without snide comments. I would like to have a genuine conversation with my daughter."

"Seek elsewhere. You shall not find her here."

"You can run and disown your lineage, but do not think for a modicum of time it changes the fact you are my daughter; you are of my blood."

"I believe I have threatened your life if you dared speak to me as if I am any relation to you." March tilts her head, eyebrow cocked. "You need a slit throat more than a daughter."

"Do it," Bronwen challenges her, arms spread wide. "Kill your mother in the streets for all to see."

"I am sure you would like me to strike you, cut you, kill you to add to every growing lie you spread about me. Do not think I am not tempted. Your death would bring me such peace."

"But when I am gone, you will have no one else to hate." Bronwen steps dangerously closer to March. "If I died tomorrow, if you killed me, your hate would persist and poison you for all time."

March laughs out loud in order to restrain herself from grabbing her swords, fingers twitching. "And you were the alchemist who administered the poison; years of it. I am tainted by both your blood and your poison. Inside the city walls, I am known as a whore because of your words, while outside of this city, I am known for something quite different. I have killed thousands of men and sleep well after each one. Despite all they have attempted, none of them have wronged me the way you have. Do not be foolish enough to believe my thoughts will linger on you for a second after you are gone from this world, and neither will anyone else's. You will be forgotten, as father was. No one speaks his name, and no one will remember yours. I will see to it."

The corners of Bronwen's eyes tighten revealing more of her age. Any mention of hatred or relation has no effect on her, but the thought of her absence from this world gives March the reaction and the satisfaction she wants. A word her mother used previously jumps to the forefront of March's mind—legacy. Bronwen does not fear her own death, but the loss of her estate, her reputation, her legacy.

"I have one of two theories why you press this matter so hard," says March. "The first being the most obvious, why you throw yourself at the Twins: you try to sire a child yourself, but you are well past your prime and cannot carry a child. The second, probably the more likely: no matter how many times you let the Twins fuck you, they refuse to finish in you. If you have not noticed the sheer number of women they bed, if they were not smart enough, they would have heirs running around in every city, village, and hamlet of Wonderland. You are no different."

Bronwen's smug smirk fades and lines around her mouth become more pronounced, as if March's words age her.

"Let me wager a guess; they finish on your face? Your chest? Or probably your back. Why would they want to look at you when they fuck you?"

"How dare you speak to me in such a disgusting manner?" Bronwen flicks at her underdress and robe to adjust it to take out her anger. "I have simply accepted the conclusion we all know to be true. The brothers want you. After all, you are the prize of Wonderland, not just because you came from my womb, but also because of the fearsome name you have made for yourself. You can try to deny it, run from it, but you are cunning and ruthless like your mother. Think of what an heir your union with them would create. Power, skill, and, most importantly, royalty—the ability to sit upon the throne. All you need is to accept their seed."

March unsheathes Brynjar from her back and slaps the flat part of the blade against the side of her mother's neck and turns to catch the gazes of several more prying eyes from windows, balconies, and passersby. Curtains draw closed, shutters click shut, and those on the street turn their gaze and quicken their pace.

"You must ask yourself one thing, Bronwen." March presses the blade harder against her skin. "Who will save you? The soldiers of Mirus I have trained? Lysander and Uriah—the men who want me rather than you? Their soldiers? Any citizen of the Crest? I could slay you now and no one would give two shits about what happened to you. What, then, would be your legacy? Bleeding out on the cobbles in front of your immoral home from where you whored your daughter."

Bronwen slaps the blade away. "How dare you?" she growls in a whisper.

"You say that so often, and as if you have any means to back up your challenge."

"Be reasonable," says Bronwen, unwilling to yield. "Will you not even consider the future of our family?"

"No." March sheathes her sword and turns to leave.

"Fine," Bronwen calls after March. "Continue to share your bed with your two degenerates. You disparage the quality of Lysander and Uriah, yet you lower your standards, acting like some hedge-born whore to fuck a murderer and a nutter. I am surprised you have not spawned a bastard with either of them."

In a single motion, March draws Flynn, grabs the back of Bronwen's hair, bringing her close, and sets the edge of her blade across her throat.

"Say another disparaging word about them. I beg you. Say it."

This time, Bronwen cannot bring herself to reach for the blade. She stands frozen, chin up, and neck trembling.

"If you speak of them ever again, in my presence or not, I will slide my blade across your throat, giving you a wider, deeper grin than Cheshire, and sip tea with Jonathan as you drown in your own blood. Do I make myself clear?"

Bronwen's pride wants to win out and not give March satisfaction or a response, but she finally succumbs in defeat with a nod. March sheaths Flynn and steps away from Bronwen, who grabs at her throat and the slight cut across it.

"Burns, does it not?" No, it does not burn enough. Her mother must suffer more. "Oh, and on the other account, you need not fear. There will be no surprise or offspring; I have made quite certain of it."

Bronwen furrows her brow. Her eyes grow wide. "What do you mean?"

"Before returning home after being given to one of your business associates the first time, after I killed him, I knew he would not be the last man you sold me to and he would not be the last life I would take. Every time you sent me out to be a whore, I became a better killer. But in case, for whatever reason, I failed, I took precautions, and fate, into my own hands. I traded all the jewelry you adorned me into an apothecary, a woman, in the Crooked Market, for one simple physic. Because of your and father's depravity, I made sure I would never bring a child into this world."

If Bronwen could shed a tear, she tries desperately to summon them. Not out of sadness, but rage. Her hands turn to claws, ready to lash out at March's face or her own, realizing the sand in her family's hourglass does not run low; March has shattered it.

"This should draw our conversations to a close and bring an end to your plans. I hope this knowledge brings you some comfort. Your daughter, forged of steel, as cunning as you are, made sure long ago your line ends with me."

March leaves Bronwen in the street, and every curse and foul name her mother can conjure chases after her on the breeze. Those she passes look at her in shock and disgust at what Bronwen shouts, probably still believing half of them to be true. March can only laugh. The priceless expression of despair in Bronwen's downcast face will forever bring March joy.

There is power in the lies and vulnerability and the drowning feeling of being powerless in the truth. However, this encounter, no doubt planned by the Twins, has renewed March's interest in the gift they offer, and her need to see Bronwen punished. For too long, March has found comfort hiding within the lies, just like her mother escaping the truth. If March must relinquish part or all of the power to bring her mother's truth to light and watch the old woman powerless, vulnerable, weak for the first time, it is an easy price to pay.

CHAPTER 45
MARY ANNE

The verdant lawn and vibrant flora of the Corolla Garden blossom among the grays and browns of the surrounding storehouses. Beautiful beds of flowers line the iron fence's perimeter and create walking paths through the expansive lawn. The white and pink manor reflects a storybook facade despite the carnal and immoral activities within. Men and women of Stonehaven and the Crest walk freely into and from the entrance without a care in the world, as if visiting a brothel is not out of the ordinary, even though almost all conceal their identity with hoods or scarves.

Mary Anne walks arm in arm with Jonathan, circling around the city block where Mary Anne points out the Red Knight's horse tied to the post by the rear door among seven others. "There. He entered through the back door. Should we follow?"

"No. He likely tied his horse, thinking it would blend in with the others. And yes, we follow, but through the front entrance. This is not a place one sneaks into," says Jonathan.

They continue around the block and up to the large front doors. The natural, beautiful fragrance of the flowers disappears behind a heavy, invisible cloud of opium and other spiced fragrances.

"I must prepare you," says Jonathan. "This establishment has certain requirements. The madam will not let any one enter unless they intend to make use of their rooms with her flowers. If we are to gain entry, we may have to act out of character, which will require us to be a bit more physical than usual, put on a performance, so to speak. But please understand, I do not want to put your reputation at risk being here."

Reputation be damned. Mary Anne's heart lodges in her throat. "As I told you before, you have my permission to do whatever you deem necessary, whatever you wish, or want."

"You mistake my meaning. It is I who gives permission to you. When you open the doors, lead me in by the wrist," says Jonathan. "Treat me like your object. Make it convincing."

Mary Anne's face does not move, but she screams in her chest and enjoys its cascade of vibrations down her body. She wonders why, when they finally have a moment between them without March, it must be a charade and not genuine. No matter; it may be an act for Jonathan, but Mary Anne need not try hard for a convincing performance. She has always thought of Jonathan as a gentleman, her hero—never an object, unless the object of her idolatry counts, but for this day, she will gladly oblige.

Mary Anne takes Jonathan by the wrist, and his pulse throbs into her fingertips. She pushes open the thick oak door to reveal a decadent, yet unnerving, hazy world of crimsons and purples, with sculptures in the shape of human arms holding large lanterns from the walls, and heavy damask curtains muffle moans and screams from down the long hallway. The humid air weighs down Mary Anne's breaths and immediately pulls sweat from hers and Jonathan's exposed chests.

A full-figured woman with a tattoo of a rose on her breast bursts through a set of curtains—the madam of the brothel by her demeanor. Her fingers dance upon her decolletage, and she bites at her heavily painted lip. "As I live and breathe. Carter, come back to fulfill your fantasy of an older woman who knows how to handle a strapping man. I can even use straps if your taste so desires."

"Mind your tongue." Mary Anne's tone surprises herself. "He belongs to me."

"Dangerous words, knowing the company Carter keeps."

"Do you see March here? Stop wasting our time and show us to a room."

The madam guffaws and waves them off. "You have no clue, do you, woman? I run my establishment the way I see fit. Patrons, like you, do not pay for the use of a room, you pay for the time with one, or more, of my flowers. The room is merely a stage. Ask Carter, he and Lady Audrianna shared three of my best Pansies, who are now solely engaged with Lysander and Uriah. I hardly see them, and do you think I see my cut? Not a single coin."

The thought takes a moment to form—Jonathan with four women both intrigues and infuriates Mary Anne, jealousy bubbling in her veins. She wonders how long, how often, and why March would willingly share Jonathan with courtesans, though she is not surprised. Yet another reason to fuel Mary Anne's hate and drive to free Jonathan from her enchantments.

"And if you expect me to believe you two want to fuck? I've seen more sexual tension between a sandwich and a slob. You want in, prove it. Put on a show for us and I may let you both prune some of my flowers."

While they wait, at least twenty men and women slip by them, escorted to the entrance by flowers without clothing, where they cover their faces before they cross the threshold, while others enter, greet flowers with a sack of coins and disappear into the depths of the house. The madam clicks her nails on a side table in the hallway. One flower after another crowd behind her to watch, massaging their bodies and biting at their lips, making an utter spectacle of themselves, waiting for the show to begin.

This is Mary Anne's moment. She pulls Jonathan's coat open to reveal the body chiseled from marble she has thought of, dreamed of, and lusted after for so long. His chest is warm to her touch and his heartbeat thumps against his chest in her hands. Her fingers press and squeeze his tightening chest, flesh into marble. Being ever the gentleman, he opens the coat wider, putting his body on display. Mary Anne's eyes and fingers drip down his torso as a drop of rain would trace every groove and valley of his godly figure until they reach and tuck into the waistline of his trousers. Inches from her face, the heat of his sweet breath gently blows the loose strands of hair in front of her face. If Mary Anne raised her head, their lips would meet, and the taste and brush of his lips would spark such ecstasy in her body she would never recover. March is absent, and Jonathan has given himself over to whatever she wishes, whatever she lusts after. Yet, she hesitates.

She knows this is not real, at least on Jonathan's part, performing like a carnival act for the likes of the madam and her workers in order to gain entrance. While her previous encounter with Jonathan wrapped her in bliss, she could not help but feel tawdry at the act, controlled by March, all but ignored by Jonathan. Mary Anne is sure he would heed any command given, but she wants to feel his touch, his passion, when it is his decision and impulse, and no one else's. Still, there must be something stirring within him, reciprocated yet held back, and unable to express it, otherwise he would recoil at her touch, her mouth, and the experiences they share.

Mary Anne raises her eyes to meet Jonathan's innocent, sparkling gaze, catching the lantern light, eyebrows lifted, chest heaving. Damn him. She closes his coat and holds it shut, like curtains keeping out the dawn. They came here with a purpose, not to fulfill someone else's voyeuristic pleasure.

"You bore me," the madam says.

"Enough of your lip," Mary Anne commands. "Show us to a room."

"You think I do not know who you are, Mary Anne, would-be-queen? I do; I just don't care. We run our own small township here, and I am mother, proprietor, and mayor of the quaint hamlet I have created within these four walls. It has outlasted every king and queen of Wonderland, and it will outlast you. You want access, you pay the toll like everyone else, one way or another."

"Everyone else except Lysander and Uriah."

"You misunderstand again. I said I do not get a cut of the Pansies and a few other select girls to which they stake claim. But they have paid me handsomely. You think those snobs up the hill in the Crest are wealthy. You've no idea what real wealth is, my dear."

"Madam Rose," says Jonathan, adjusting his coat. "Please, we seek a man."

"He speaks," she says. "Always knew about you. Adventurous. I like it. I have some in my employ who would tickle your fancy, along with your ass and balls. But it would be such a waste since my services come free of charge." She pushes her breasts together, and they bulge over her corset.

"We seek the Red Knight," says Mary Anne. "What we request is simple: show us where he is or hand him over to us."

The madam laughs heartily, and the flowers behind her follow suit, giggling and covering their mouths. "You make no demands here. Your authority, which you don't have, means nothing." She snaps her fingers, and the sounds of moans and screams subside. The thick curtains concealing the activities in the large salons slide open, and at least twenty flowers, men and women, crowd into the hallway with barely enough clothing to make a single garment among them. "If you think you can walk into my house and make demands of me, you are sadly mistaken." Their customers shout and curse from within the rooms, questioning if this interruption will cost them extra.

"Coins," says Mary Anne. "Coins are all you care about."

"We are not so base. Gold, jewels, and precious stones are also welcome."

"Allow me to speak your language to make my intentions plain. We are aware Lysander and Uriah keep the wealth brought from Adamas here for safekeeping."

"Safer than any money lender in town, and especially more secure than the castle since your arrival. What's your angle? Do you think you can pay more than the brothers?"

"No," says Mary Anne. "You may have operated with impunity, and I can see this arrangement continues. However, since you claim I have no authority within your house of ill repute, I will show you the authority I have in the city and send my soldiers to your establishment."

"They frequent here already." The madam laughs. "Some are my favorite customers."

"They will not enter. I shall station them around your entire property, not touching a blade of grass. Their orders will be simple: require anyone who tries to enter to show their face and give their name."

"Anonymity is a professional courtesy we provide here."

"And you can continue." Mary Anne smirks. "But the moment they step foot onto my streets, they are subject to my soldiers. I am sure you service many lonely men and women in need of company, but I wager there are married men and women here who wish to keep their activities secret. I dare say, after a day at most, the flood of customers will dwindle down to a trickle. I would hate to think how light your purses will be then."

The madam's painted lips twist into a puckered scowl, and she runs her finger along the edge of her corset, pulling out a crescent-shaped silver coin. She taps it against her lips, turns it over her fingers, and then thumps at the side of her nose with her index finger. "Shrewd, a bit of a bitch, but I can respect a woman who can stand up to me and have the means to back up her words." She glances at the other flowers, who close the curtains and return to their clients, where fake moans and screams resume throughout the hall. "Fellow's a prick anyway, and a limp cock, from what some girls say. In my office. Door past the weapons closet."

"Is he alone?" asks Jonathan.

The madam nods.

"Does he have his sword?"

"Don't care how much you pay, I give no one the chance to harm my girls. Now, seeing as how I am being so generous and all, gracious, some might say, how about a small preview, Carter?"

He humors the madam, lifting the strap to his sheath over his shoulder and slides his blue coat off in a single movement. Mary Anne sees Jonathan more often without clothing than with anything on, but the grace, strength, and sensual stretch of his body as he undresses brings a racing flutter to Mary Anne and a tingle to her body, briefly rethinking her decision to be noble. She takes his jacket from him and folds it over her arms. He hands his sword to two of the flowers, not ready for its weight.

"Fuck me," the madam says. "I know I've said it before, but I will say it every time I bloody see you. Fuck me."

Jonathan chuckles and takes Mary Anne by the hand.

"You can leave her with us," says the madam. "Or we can take her farther in, get her acquainted with the staff."

Mary Anne wishes desperately to say, 'where he goes, I shall follow,' but knows she presents only a liability for him. "I think the weapons closet you spoke of will suffice."

With the madam's permission, Mary Anne steps into the closet, which is large enough to be a small bedchamber. It is lit by candlelight with swords, daggers, knives, and clubs of all types laying on tables, hanging from hooks, and leaning against posts. A flower with tan skin, curly purple hair, and large spectacles polishes the long blades with oil-soaked rags.

"Mary Anne, I must ask for your help in this matter." Jonathan kisses the top of her hand. "You choose this place because you think the weapons grant you safety. Know, if the Red Knight gets past me, he will come here first to claim his weapon, any weapon."

"Should I have chosen someplace else?"

"No. You are brilliant. If you will take part, position yourself behind the door, feet propped against it. Should I shout to you, kick it with all your strength to shut it. Do you understand?"

Mary Anne nods, and Jonathan lifts her by the waist onto the table behind the door before whipping out of sight. It does not take long for the flower, wearing only a sheer wrap around her waist and a thin gold chain, to approach Mary Anne.

"He will be fine," she says. "Not to worry. Until he reemerges, care to pass the time?" The flower leans forward quickly and kisses Mary Anne full on the mouth.

Out of instinct, Mary Anne pulls her away and slaps the flower across the cheek. "I did not mean to," Mary Anne stammers, wafting the heavy scent of daisies and oils from her nose.

"Don't apologize." The flower returns to polishing the blades and runs the top of her fingers on her face. "I enjoyed it."

A loud crash from the neighboring room causes Mary Anne to jump, hopeful, yet still worried for Jonathan. "Be careful."

CHAPTER 46
JONATHAN

The door to Madam Rose's office slides inward quietly. If there is any noise to be heard, the performances of the flowers in the salons cover it. The incense and haze diffuse the sunlight from the tall windows on the left side of the office. At the far end, the Red Knight, in armor from the waist down, stands in front of twenty-two giant chests stacked along the back wall. His breast and back plate, gauntlets, pauldrons, and helmet sit on Madam Roses's long-legged, clawfoot desk. With his back turned, he grabs handfuls of coins and drops them into a deep leather satchel, muffling their clicking. This man, who kidnapped his love and held her and Mary Anne hostage, deserves far more than death.

Jonathan reaches for the back of a polished oak chair by the right side of the door and, with a single swing, catapults it across the room. The Red Knight turns, ready to block the attack, but the weight of the chair and the power behind Jonathan's throw are more than he expected. It slams him back against the chests like a thunder crack and breaks apart against his crossed arms. Coins fly and flip in all directions like sparks from a bonfire.

Before the splinters of the chair or coins fall to the floor, Jonathan darts across the room, but the Red Knight dodges and screeches with frustration, swiping stacks of papers, ledgers, and sacks of coins from the desk.

"You dare follow me here. Who do you think you are? I owe both you and your whore a swift retribution, but I suppose I will settle for you now. And once you are gone, she will be easy to find, and I will not be as gentle—" His face jerks, not expecting how swift Jonathan moves.

Jonathan's fist collides with the Red Knight's cheek with such force his head snaps to the side, sending ribbons of blood across the wall and the Knight sprawling into the wall, sliding to the floor.

"Speak of her again, and I shall break every bone in your body one at a time. And if you pass out from the pain, I will wake you to feel the next break."

"You think you are superior to me in some way, you fuck? The last of the Carter legacy, favored son of Wonderland, revered by all. Not all of us are born under a great star with a family name to exploit."

Jonathan's muscles burn and his knuckles pop with the clenching of his fists. "Never speak of my family."

The Red Knight spits blood at Jonathan's face, and in the moment Jonathan closes his eyes, he rushes forward, wraps his arms around Jonathan's waist, and shoulders him in the stomach, pushing him back against the opposite wall, rattling the coins in the stacked trunks. Jonathan wraps his arms around the Red Knight's body and tries to lift him, but their slick bodies from the moist air make it difficult to keep hold of him. Instead, Jonathan brings both fists down on the Red Knight's back, knocking the wind from him, and thrusts a knee into his chest. The Red Knight releases his hold, blocks the attack, and grabs Jonathan's inner thigh, twisting and digging his fingertips into his skin.

Jonathan grunts with pain through gritted teeth. He must stop thinking of the Red Knight as just a traitor and remember he is still capable of being an adept fighter. Jonathan brings his fist down on the back of the Red Knight's skull with enough force to crack it in half, but the knight throws himself back to avoid the fatal blow and collides with the desk.

"What the fuck do you want?" the Red Knight shouts. "Money? Take it, for fuck's sake. You have already deprived me of everything else: my position, my reputation, my status. Why do you torment me?"

"You stand in my way." Jonathan thrust kicks at the knight's legs but catches the desk leg and shatters it. "You are a sad man, if this is all you care about."

"I have to, you damned twat. You have left me with nothing else."

"Not yet," says Jonathan. "There is much more I can take from you. There is much more you have to answer for—to pay for."

The Red Knight grabs the broken desk legs and swings it at Jonathan's head like a club again and again. Jonathan ducks, grabs a large handful of crescent-shaped coins from the open trunk, and flings them at the knight's face. Taking the opening when he raises his arms to shield his face, Jonathan delivers punch after devastating punch to the knight's midsection. The Red Knight does not lower his arms to allow his head to become a target and suffers the barrage as Jonathan backs him across the office with each blow.

The knight lands two sturdy strikes against the side of Jonathan's head with the desk leg, dazing him and blurring his vision. Jonathan loses sight of him. The next blow comes from the back. The Red Knight brings his iron breastplate down on Jonathan's back. He fights to regain his senses and staggers toward the door, ready to cut off the knight's escape and call out for Mary Anne. However, the Red Knight runs to the trunks instead, grabs the large satchel of coins, plus others laying nearby, throws them over his shoulder, and picks up his helmet. He throws it through the window, raining shards of broken glass onto the wooden floor.

"Coward." Jonathan grabs the side of his head, throbbing at his touch. "Run to save your own hide until you find the next lord or lady with a bigger purse. If I see you in Mirus again, if I hear word or whisper of your presence, I will hunt you down and kill you myself."

"Fuck you. You make a mockery, a fool, of me again and again, when all I try to be is loyal."

"Loyal to yourself, you self-serving son of a bitch."

The Red Knight steps onto the window ledge. "You are mistaken. It is you who will suffer at my hands for the disgrace and ridicule you and yours cause me. Mark my words." He jumps from the window, and the sound of clinking coins grows distant in the shouts and screams inside the Garden.

The Red Knight will not remain in Mirus, which means one less player on the board. Jonathan never heeds Cheshire's advice: to always finish the job, take the kill today, so they will have one less adversary to face tomorrow. He should listen to his lover, but whether it be Jonathan's own hubris or a misplaced sense of mercy, he often cannot follow through. Perhaps it is because he seeks a form of grace or forgiveness to equal out his scales, though he knows in his heart he deserves neither. Everything catches up, the bill comes due, and he knows it is only a matter of time.

Moments later, Mary Anne runs in and throws her arms around Jonathan. Madame Rose and other flowers crowd the room, complaining about the mess and whose purse will pay for everything.

"How much do Lysander and Uriah pay you for your service? Your banking services," says Jonathan.

Madam Rose pats a sealed chest. "Twenty gold, thirty silver, and forty copper, each day these remain in my care."

"Keep it all," says Mary Anne. "Distribute it as you see fit, and quickly. I would rather it be in your hands than used by Lysander and Uriah. Trust us. If they have their way, your home will not survive."

Madame Rose looks to Jonathan, concern furrowing her brow, knowing he will not lie.

"She speaks the truth," he tells her.

"Damn it all. Well fuck them, then." Madame Rose's sour face brightens, and she gives orders to the flowers. Some grab pouches from a nearby chest of drawers, while others meticulously count each piece, and more run off to bring more flowers for the task.

Mary Anne drapes Jonathan's coat over his shoulders and takes his face in her hands. He winces at her touch.

"You are hurt," she says.

"I have suffered and survived worse."

"Will you two get the fuck out of my house?" Madam Rose shouts. "Take your business elsewhere."

"Seeing as how I have given, and you have accepted, every coin in this room, I think we are permitted to do whatever the fuck we want."

Madame Rose presses her lips, thinking and nodding. "Fair point."

Mary Anne gently brushes Jonathan's face with her fingers, on the opposite side of where a welt will form. "You were magnificent. You are magnificent. Let us return home."

If only. Jonathan tells himself. *If only.*

CHAPTER 47

MARCH

At the border of the Crest and Stonehaven, Adamasite soldiers in full armor create a blockade to the Crest, cutting off entrance from the high ways and stairways. While Cheshire absconded with them to their small paradise—odd, she would call a place such as the Pool of Tears paradise—the Twins seized control of a portion of the city without much resistance. Those of the Crest probably cheered at the sight, being able to keep anyone from the lower city from their tiers.

The clacking of her swords in their scabbards keep time and rhythm as March pushes through the soldiers and meanders through Stonehaven's back alleys. The familiar sensation on the back of her neck returns—eyes following her since the Crest. She makes sure they remain on her until she reaches the tier above the Row, away from any prying soldiers. March stops outside of a mercer's shop and turns around to confront her stalkers. To her right, water drips from a broken gutter into a full barrel, behind her, townspeople shop in the Row, to her left, in the distance, a white cat purrs as it lies with its calico mate, and in front of her, Lysander's and Uriah's heavy breaths cannot be missed.

"Do not walk in secret. You never walked farther than the edge of the Crest, then waited for me to pass, and followed me the entire way. You might have been less conspicuous had you taken the high ways."

Lysander and Uriah emerge from an arched alleyway. "And lose the opportunity to watch you walk from behind?" Lysander runs his fingers through his beard.

"Neither of you are as sly or cunning as you both believe yourselves to be."

"The streets of Mirus would sing a different song," says Uriah.

Before March turns to leave, Uriah steps in her way, and her fingers find their way to the hilts of the daggers on her thigh.

"Wait," says Uriah.

"Move. Or I will step over your corpse."

"It is difficult not to lust after you." Uriah laughs. "You know this. Your wit, your skill, your body. However, your purposeful allure may work as a distraction to others, but it will not work on us."

"Will it not? I could have called you out from where you lurked in the jeweler's before I stepped foot from the Crest. You thought you tracked me, but I wanted you to follow me far enough from the Crest, from your men, and my mother, to finish our conversation."

Uriah breaks eye contact with March for the slightest of moments, knowing her to be right, knowing he fell for the bait she laid out.

"But it was our glances which brought you to us in the first place," he says. "You needed to hear your mother's—"

"Bronwen."

"Forgive me," says Uriah. "You needed to hear Bronwen's thoughts about your future. All her ideas, mind you. A conversation to spark your need to speak with us again."

March continues to play their game. "Yet, I already knew you wished for me to speak with her because you already played this hand in the bailey to see if I would bite. Your glances were not subtle. Since we never continued our conversation, you would have sought me out again eventually, so I chose the time and place. Now, here we are. You are welcome."

"Here we are," says Lysander, moving to Uriah's side. "So, you have thought about our gift?"

March wishes she was not tempted, but she must know if they hold the key to Bronwen's ruin. However, if the Twins are distracted by her, they are unaware and away from Jonathan and Mary Anne. If she must play this game, once started, she will see it through to the end.

"Show me," says March.

Lysander reaches into a pouch around his belt and produces a worn, rolled parchment, and the sight of it steals her breath. The idea they would go this far must give her pause. It could be a fake or a forgery for them to use and manipulate her. March takes it from Lysander and unfurls the crackling scroll. The parchment bears the signature of her father and mother at the bottom—hard, unkind strokes of their quills. Next to them, her family's seal, faded and smashed, but unmistakable. It is real.

"Last paragraph," says Uriah.

A knot made of burning coal grows in her throat as she reads the last lines of her father's script.

"Therefore, in addition to the exchange for three-hundred and twenty-five custom, hand-crafted weapons of the finest quality for the agreed upon price of five thousand gold pieces, ten stone of pink diamonds, emeralds, sapphires, and golden pearls, the dealers allow the company and use of their daughter in whatever manner they see fit for the term of one week's time, excluding travel, under the conditions the purchaser return her unblemished and without imperfection."

A quick slash of ink from her mother and father determined her future—words void of emotion, cold, and final. This was the last contract they scribed, but there were many, many more before it, each with the same ending clause but a different price. The parchment pulls her mind to her youth to replay a memory she has locked in the back of her mind, but never wishes to remember. A nightmare come to daylight.

Young Audrianna stood before the towering, silver-framed looking-glass leaning in the corner of her mother's bedchamber. Bronwen stood behind her and straightened the arms of her small gown, flaring out the long, draping ends of her sleeves, and fastened a small diamond necklace around her neck to match her bracelets. Audrianna shifted in the uncomfortable gown, scathing and picking at her skin.

"You look absolutely priceless," said Bronwen. "And you are. Never forget this."

"Where are we going?" Audrianna asked.

"Not us." Her mother stood behind her, hands resting on her daughter's shoulders. "You are going on a special journey today."

"To where?"

"Almost done." Her mother pulled Audrianna's hair into a bun and kept it in place with a silver hairpin in the shape of a basket-hilted sword almost as long as the span of her mother's hand. A calling card of her parents' trade.

Her father told others they were pure silver, but she watched the smith deliver them from the Forge. Nothing more than an iron core with the thinnest coating of dipped silver.

"You will journey to Clava," her mother continued. "One of your father's associates, the Castellan, has a daughter your age and wishes for you to spend some time with her and train her in the ways of proper upbringing. I am sure you two will make quite the pair. I have heard so much about her."

"Clava is so far away. What of my studies? What about my training?" Audrianna pulled at her fingertips.

"I know, but you will resume your studies, music lessons, everything, once you return. This is a grand opportunity for you."

Audrianna followed her mother through the manor, passing servants who greeted her with a nod and hurried to their duties. Something felt different. The sounds of clatter and life, which filled her home daily, faded into a muffled hum as if water filled her ears.

Her mother opened the front door and led her into the bright afternoon sun, where her father and the Castellan, an older man with white hair starting halfway back on his head and a stomach so bloated, it tested the strength of the buttons on his brocade vest, conversed in hushed tones and shook hands by his large gray carriage, door open and waiting. In front of the carriage, several of their house servants loaded dozens of long wooden crates, painted a glimmering black, with her family's coat of arms on them, into a row of six wagons, then covered them with wide burlap tarpaulins used by farmers to keep birds from their crop as they came to market.

"We shall send the shipment out of the city before you," her father told the Castellan. "They will ride to Clava spaced from one another and yourself, to quell the temptation of any along the roads." Her father handed him a scroll, which the man tucked into the inside breast pocket of his coat.

"Agreed," said the Castellan. "And the other agreed upon package?"

Her father looked back toward the manor. "Here she is," her father said, arms wide. "My pride and joy."

Audrianna swallowed. She had never been on any a sort of journey without her parents and expected the trip to be awkward until they arrived in Clava, but she will do her best to remember the decorum both her mother and father taught her.

"Hello, young one." The Castellan stooped and offered his hand. Audrianna placed her hand in his. "Soft," he said.

"Quite," her mother said, placing her hands on Audrianna's shoulders again. "And her tutors say she is the brightest of anyone they have instructed, already versed in the old tongue and skilled at writing and arithmetic."

"Smart and beautiful," the Castellan said.

Audrianna's skin crawled with unseen fingers along her arms and back.

"Up we go." The Castellan ushered Audrianna up one step and into the carriage. Its blue cushioned seats and thick curtains stood in contrast with the oak of the rest of the interior. He climbed in after her, holding onto the silver handles outside of the door, rocking the entire carriage, and grunted when he sat, lips blustering. Then he smiled at her.

"Are you ready, my dear?" he asked

"Yes, sir," said Audrianna. "I look forward to making your daughter's acquaintance."

The old, bloated man chuckled. "Daughter? I do not have a daughter, silly girl."

A chilling realization rushed up Audrianna's body, unable to hide the panic on her face, but the old man continued to laugh. She bolted for the door, but her mother waited for her, hands out to catch her.

"Mother, no," Audrianna pleaded, on the verge of tears.

"You shall not embarrass our family." Her mother forced Audrianna back into the carriage. "Sit down this instant," Bronwen commanded.

The old man grabbed her by the upper arms and seated her back on the bench opposite him. "There you are."

"Please," begged Audrianna, her small voice barely escaping the lump in her throat. "No, please."

Her mother reached into the carriage and tucked the loose strands of her daughter's hair behind her ears. "Not to worry. You will eventually become numb to it." Bronwen's smile never left her face.

The carriage door slammed shut and locked with finality from the outside. The bloated old man knocked on the wall of the carriage behind him—a signal to the driver. Reins snapped, and the carriage lurched forward. Audrianna sank into her seat, while the old man leaned forward, too far for the movement of the carriage to justify. A puff of his breath—pork and whiskey—assaulted Audrianna's face.

The man lingered for a moment and smelled her thrice, before he took his seat again. A pleasant kind expression on his face. "Your scent is sweet." Not kind. False.

In that moment, and the instance with her mother, March learned a smile was merely a mask to wear to hide someone's true intentions and to trust no one who gave them freely. Besides the intentional lean forward, the old man remained in his seat the entire winding descent through the streets of Mirus. At times, he peeked out the windows of the carriage, fiddled with their curtains, and waved to passersby. In between, his gaze returned to Audrianna with a sickening dull glaze over his eyes. After they crossed the Long Bridge out of Mirus and the rhythm of the cobbles was traded for the crunch of dirt, the old man pulled the curtains closed, darkening the cabin and his smile with it.

"Since we are now clear of the city, we have a long road ahead of us to Clava." He adjusted his collar.

Audrianna remained silent, eyes on her hands, but she focused on every subtle movement he made.

"Tell me about yourself."

The clops of the horses and the creak of the carriage filled the silence between each question.

"What is it a girl of your age and stature does for entertainment? Do you have many suitors? I bet you have. Look at you. You are quite beautiful. Quite beautiful, indeed. Your parents speak highly of you. I cannot wait to get to know all about you during our time together. I live on a large estate with a large courtyard and lawn, and high fences. Quite private."

The numbness Bronwen spoke of comes sooner than Audrianna thought, though not in the way her mother intended. Audrianna felt this man's ill intentions the moment his eyes turned to her after speaking with her father. Her parents did nothing, nothing to save her, their own daughter.

No. No. They did everything, orchestrated it all. She was the agreed upon package the man spoke of and her father agreed to. Smiles hide, but eyes reveal all. The numb filled her like a silver goblet, starting at her toes, past her hips, drowning the worry in her heart, and crawled up her neck and past her ears, blocking out the man's questions. It finally reaches the top of her head with tingling fingers until it consumes everything about her. Once submerged, the man's grating voice returns to her ears.

"Will you answer nothing I ask? You prefer to remain silent? This simply will not do." The somewhat pleasant tone of the old man faded away to reveal his real voice—darker and sloppier. "I can bring forth sound from you, mark my words. You are in my care now, and you will do as I command."

Audrianna's hands rested calmly on her lap. Where once fear gripped her heart, hatred took a foothold, as easily as lighting a brazier, twin flames fighting for the same kindling. It felt strange, but also gave her solace. Hatred was clear. It gave her focus.

"You look uncomfortable," the old man said. "We have a long way to travel, and since you will not speak, you will provide me with entertainment. This is the reason your parents gifted you to me. You will serve in any way I see fit. Do you understand?"

Audrianna's fingertips tingle.

"Undress," the man said. "Slowly. I want to savor the tenderness of your body."

Audrianna swallowed again. Hate and Fear clawed and ripped at her chest as her heart raced.

"You have a choice to make," the man says. "You mock my generosity. Undress, as I have so politely asked. Or I will tear the clothing from you and give you nothing in return when we reach my home. I had meant to spoil you, pamper you, dress you in the finest gowns Clava has to offer.

But if you wish to be so disrespectful, you will spend the duration of your stay confined to my bedchamber and wear nothing at all."

Audrianna let every word the man said sink into her soul. She reached behind her head to let her hair down.

"Yes," the man hissed. He unbuttoned his trousers and his bloated belly flopped forward from under his vest. He grunted and pushed his stomach aside to reach a hand in his trousers to rub himself. "Yes. Slower."

Her hair fell to her shoulders, but she kept hold of the hairpin; a silver-wrapped iron sword in her small hands. The carriage rocked on the uneven dirt road. Audrianna stood up, keeping her balance, lowered her arms, and concealed the small sword against her right wrist.

"Fuck, you are beautiful." The man groaned, shifted, and squirmed on the bench. "I will use you unlike any other before you. Fuck. Yes. More."

How many others had there been? Had they all been her age? What fate befell them? One burning flame smothered the other, ended the struggle, and gave way to the pure stillness of hatred.

March reached for the man's face to scratch him with her left hand. He caught and squeezed her arm with his free arm. The other was still buried below his stomach. Audrianna winced and thought he may snap her wrist. He wet his lips with his fat tongue, and the sickening slurps and clicks of his saliva crawled across her skin as if they were his hands.

Before he could retract his vile tongue, Audrianna stabbed him through the fat hanging below his chin. The hairpin was long enough to pierce through the fullness of his neck and *tink* against his spine. He batted her away, back to the other bench with a swipe of his arm, panicked and gurgling, but Audrianna pulled the sword with her, knowing she could not let go of her only weapon.

Blood spewed from the man's throat between his fingers as he tried to stop the bleeding. He tried to shout for help to his driver, but blurts of blood sprayed across the cabin and Audrianna. Face twisted with shock and anger, he lunged and fell with his full weight on top of her. One strike would not finish the job, so she stabbed him in every vital place she could reach—his left eye, inside his ear, the side of his neck. The blood spurted and leaked from his wounds and rained down upon Audrianna, soaking her gown.

Audrianna stabbed him over and over again and pierced the fat bag hanging from his neck sideways, the point sticking out the other end, and pulled with both hands. The blade was not sharp enough to cut, but with enough force, it ripped through his flesh, slitting his throat. After a mile on the road, his obese body slumped down on her, silent, without the sound of a heartbeat. It took her several more miles to pry and pull herself from beneath his dead carcass. Covered in his blood and short of breath, she sat on the opposite bench, his bench, and gripped her hairpin with both hands.

Dealing in weapons, her father made sure his daughter had the finest tutors, not just in education, but in training with blades as well. His mistake; her providence. She never thought she would take anyone's life this early in her years, but this man deserved to die. She had *no choice. Her parents made the choice for her.*

Audrianna wanted to scream and ponder how they could do this to their daughter, but came to the conclusion, henceforth, she was no longer their daughter and they were no longer her parents. Audrianna wanted nothing more than to disappear from the world and stared at the blade for miles on the road, considering how it pierced the man's flesh and how it could easily pierce hers as well.

She opened the curtains to allow the sun in on the gruesome scene before her. All she wanted was to be lost to the world. Outside, birds sang and flitted in the distance. She could run, but her parents made deals with hundreds of people across the country, and too many people knew of her, so she could not simply disappear. There would be a time, but it could not be now. She relinquished herself to the numb void and listened to the rhythmic crunch of the road, the trotting of the horses, and the song of distant birds.

Once started, she must see it through to the end. She could not return home now. *Home.* The word twisted her stomach like spoiled meat. The Castellan said he lived alone on a private estate. He did not speak to his driver, only knocked on the board behind him. The driver did not see Audrianna enter the carriage, and the rest of the wagons traveled to Clava ahead of them. To every other man working for the Castellan, she did not exist.

A tavern stood not far outside the outskirts of Mirus. Audrianna would risk jumping from the carriage unseen, find a way to clean herself and make her way back to the city. She could return to Mirus and hide in their manor—it was large enough. If her parents—if Bronwen and Seamus—did not need her, they did not look for her. She worried about her lessons, but they taught her the harshest of them all.

"Will you accept our gift?" Uriah draws March back to the present. "You seemed to have drifted off for a moment."

"Can we offer you a place to lie down?" asks Lysander.

"Shut up." March closes the scroll and fights the overwhelming urge to crush it in her hand. She taps the roll in her palm and then pockets it in her trousers.

"We have an accord," says Uriah.

"We have no accord, remember? This was a gift."

"A gift with one condition," says Lysander.

"No," says March.

"The condition of this gift is that you use it," says Uriah. "If you have no intention of taking advantage of our kindness, hand it back and we shall never broach this topic again."

Damn them.

Uriah watches March's fist in her pocket, waiting for her decision. She waits as well, unsure of what she will decide, but eventually, she pulls her hand free, keeping the scroll in her possession.

"A condition and a consideration."

The thought of being indebted to these two makes her want to drink herself into oblivion and walk into the sea for a last briny call. "What if an opportunity of my choosing never presents itself?"

"It was still a gift," says Uriah. "Still, we stand to gain from your use. Do not let it go to waste."

March leaves the Twins behind and makes her way to the Row, sparsely crowded and devoid of the kind banter between neighbors. No one knows who to trust any longer, hands on the hilts of their swords, ready for a fight to break out at any moment.

"Normalcy," March scoffs to herself.

Chatter calls to her from the one stall where every townsperson knows how they will be treated, no matter what side they find themselves on—Dormy's wagon. March waits across the street while the people of Stonehaven crowd around to buy necessities and oddities from Dormy.

"Normalcy," she says again. March has missed her friend and joins Dormy behind the tables and immediately heeds her commands.

"Two cast-iron pots," Dormy tells March. "Sack of potatoes. One left-handed gauntlet. The dented one hanging by the pipes. Large pair of used black boots."

March cannot keep her laughter contained as she makes her way through the maze inside and tosses item after item to Dormy from the open side of the wagon. They continue until dusk, when the shadows spread across the market, and the few open shops close and patrons return to their homes. Usually, some vendors' hours extend into twilight. Not anymore. For now, at least.

Once Dormy's last customer leaves, March helps her disassemble her tables and return everything into her wagon. With a pull of the large switch, the side of the wagon closes, concealing the warm candlelight within.

"Thank you," says Dormy, hair wild and panting.

"You are most welcome. Quite a busy day, little mouse." March fusses with Dormy's jacket and straightens the neck of her linen shirt.

"Oh, indeed." Dormy yawns, one eye squinting. "Most of the day, the other vendors and shopkeepers barely had any customers. I felt bad, only I didn't. They kept coming to me. I couldn't help it."

"I will return to the castle. Will you stay here?"

"Yes. I can handle myself."

"Of course you can." March kisses Dormy on her sweaty forehead and walks from the stall, hands in her pockets. "Do not waste it," she whispers to herself and turns back, knowing why she came to the Row, why she came to Dormy in the first place. It was not merely for her companionship, but for her skills as well. "May I call upon you for a favor?"

"Anything. Whatever you are in need of, I got, or if I don't, I can have it for you by morning, only don't ask where I got it from?"

March pulls the scroll from her trousers and hands it to Dormy. "I need you to scribe the words and signatures exactly as they are, as only you can."

Dormy laughs and starts to open the scroll. "I haven't done this in an age. I thought you were going to ask for something difficult."

March places a gentle hand on her wrist. "Please, read it after I leave."

"Of course. How many do you need?"

"As many as you can manage."

"Done." Dormy climbs onto the back porch of her wagon and reaches for the back door.

"Thank you," says March. "No one tells you," says March, "though we ought to more often. You are the constant amongst us all."

Unsure how to take any compliment, Dormy laughs nervously and disappears into her wagon with the slamming of her door.

"For fuck's sake."

Lysander and Uriah wait for her several stalls away, stealing her peace.

She does not say a word to them, nor they to her as they climb the stairs back to the castle. There is nothing she can say; March accepted their damned scroll and puts plans in motion for it—they are witness to it. Another line will soon be crossed, from which there is no return.

The fire, the inferno, spawns anew within her chest, the hatred rekindled. She wishes to seek out Bronwen to not waste this purest moment, but realizes if she kills her mother, she will learn nothing, and will not suffer the way March needs her to. If not her mother, then may the gods have mercy on the poor soul to cross her, for while the fire rages, she will scorch any who cross her.

CHAPTER 48
CHESHIRE

After dusk, sitting atop Dormy's wagon, the pensive, bottled chaos of the empty market is more delicious than Cheshire imagined. While there are still signs of life from behind closed doors, or distant weeping, which could be mistaken for the whistle of the wind through the treetops, the near solitude and hush of the city gives Cheshire a glimpse of the future—devoid of life.

His only regret—this is not of his making. Despite destroying the Hanging Cells, decimating the harbor, and even after the attack of the cult, the daily lives of the Mirusian people went on—limping—yet still inching forward. Only when neighbor turns against neighbor, and they hang bodies across Stonehaven, do they let fear consume their hearts and make them hide within their homes. Perhaps it is the thought of the women and children dangling above the city streets that undid the last frayed knot of bravery; something Cheshire could never bring himself to do. If whispers find him of the persons capable of such evil as to hang children, he will make their deaths long lasting, keeping them alive, removing piece by piece until they no longer have the will to live and beg for death, which will not come. When they die, if they have a family, he will wait a week or month, just long enough for their sorrow to ease, then he will leave their bloody stump propped against their door, to rekindle their suffering anew. Cheshire will take advantage of the division and harness their fear.

He turns his gloved hand upside down and produces the eight tall, clinking bottles he took from March, freshly filled with rum from the Far Side tavern, corked, and tied together with twine. He sets them down quietly on the small balcony of Dormy's wagon near the planter with herbs mixed with flowers and then banishes the Mask of Shadows back into his glove. As powerful as the masks are, he wishes his gloves could hold more than one item at a time.

Cheshire slips into the wagon's top window, steps down onto full sacks of flour, and knocks on the wooden shelves to give Dormy notice of his arrival. Jonathan and March he can surprise any time he wants, but to do so to Dormy would be cruel in his mind. With the Row empty, her wall remains shut, shop closed, and her wares and sundries returned to their nests, hooks, barrels, and crates.

Hanging pots and pans clink, wooden crates and boxes rub against each other, and feet scamper across the floorboards in the wagon below. Once the clatter subsides and the soft swing of rope suspending sacks of vegetables and pans returns, Cheshire slides down the ladder. Dormy waves and tries not to disturb the candles around her and the stacks of hundreds of pages of parchment. Those to her left blank while those to her right scribbled upon. She covers the pages with her arms to keep the writing from Cheshire, piquing his curiosity and making him want to see it all the more.

"I remember a time, years ago, before the fire in Breighton, you forged a letter from their magistrate and posted it on every door in the town square and surrounding homes telling the villagers to assemble in the grand hall to await an announcement on the reduction of taxes, I believe. The fools could not leave their shops and storefronts quick enough, thinking their corrupt and greedy magistrate had turned a new leaf. Little did they know, while they were waiting for a magistrate March already killed, you and I snuck in and looted every store."

Dormy laughs nervously.

"Up to told tricks?" asks Cheshire. "With the market empty, I would keep myself busy."

"March asked us a favor, so I am being helpful where I can. Always helpful."

"Yes, you are."

"I have a similar favor to ask." Cheshire's fingers dance toward the top page of the written stack, but Dormy instinctively slams her hand down on it.

"If you promise not to read what I am writing," she says, with a forlorn look in her marmalade eyes.

"A hard bargain, but as you wish." Cheshire retracts his hand and reaches to the stack of blank parchment, asking Dormy's permission. Once she agrees, he slides the top piece free and grabs a spiraled glass quill, one of three, in a large inkwell in the middle of the table.

Cheshire scribbles quickly, only needing to dip the quill twice more. "That is not your penmanship," he says, glimpsing a corner of the original scroll hiding under Dormy's arm.

"No. I copy something for March, and it would be best if I matched the lettering on the parchment." She shrugs. "But she asked me to keep it secret."

"You are a wonder. And of course you will. I shall not pry." Cheshire plucks several red and green grapes from a nearby hanging basket and pops them into his mouth. The sweet and tart juices flood his mouth with every bite.

Cheshire pushes his parchment closer to Dormy, careful not to disturb any others. She twists it on the crowded table to read, eyes darting back and forth. Her nose scrunches, and her head tilts back and forth as if sifting through the idea in her head.

From his inside cloak pocket, Cheshire produces the crumpled scroll he took from March and drops it on the table, the Gryphon's seal facing Dormy. Her fingers tick in the air, curious but cautious at the sight of it. Curiosity wins out, and she unrolls the parchment to read its contents.

"This is a summons from the Gryphon to March."

"Yes, and also a sample of his handwriting. You can copy it, can you not?"

"Of course I can," says Dormy, examining the parchment close to her face, lit by a candle behind it. "But what you plan will not work. It can't."

"Do tell."

"Because you don't have—"

Cheshire pulls the Gryphon's ring with his seal from his cloak pocket and presents it to Dormy.

"Oh, shit." She snatches it from his hand, grabs a pair of spectacles with several circles of glasses for magnification to scrutinize its details. Her eyes grow four times their normal size behind the glass. She inspects it an inch from her face, twisting it in hand, and rubbing her fingers over the grooves and ridges.

"Is this real?"

"The genuine article and difficult to come by, I might add. You can keep it when you complete my favor."

Her already enormous eyes light up through her spectacles. "Truly?"

"Of course. I have no further use for it, and if I do, who better to keep it safe than you?"

"How many do you need?"

"As many as you can manage. I will handle the distribution. However, I predict I will need it at the same time March will need hers."

"I can handle it." Dormy removes her spectacles, setting them on the table, and takes the glass quill from Cheshire and returns it to the inkwell with its two matching sisters.

He reaches out and cautiously takes hold of her iron wrist and squeezes and presses the unforgiving metal, studying each finger, knuckle, their range of motion, and checking how far back and forward her wrist bends. His fingers slide down the iron bands of her forearm until they reach the ring and bolts securing it to her flesh just below the elbow. Cheshire worries for her, knowing of what she is capable of. "Of course you can. You can handle anything. And I will see this city suffer for what it has done to you, my dear friend."

Dormy rolls down the sleeve of her oversized coat to cover her arm up to her knuckles. "Need to get back to work," she says, grabbing a quill.

"Yes," says Cheshire. "We all must. I shall return soon."

Leaving Dormy to finish, Cheshire climbs back to the balcony, summons the Mask of Shadows to his face, picks up the bottles by the twine, and flips his hand upward, banishing them into his glove. The detour to Far Side and the information from March were quite educational in more ways than Cheshire initially thought. His lovers provide him with so much, and unbeknownst to them, help spread the chaos he so craves.

CHAPTER 49

MARY ANNE

Mary Anne stops Jonathan before the hallway leading to their bedchamber. They spent the climb back to the castle in silence, Jonathan perhaps not knowing what to say, but for Mary Anne, she held in her thoughts until now but makes conversation anyway to pass the time.

"Were you worried?" she finally asks. "During your battle with the Red Knight."

"No," says Jonathan. "I was focused. What he said narrowed my thoughts and vision to where it needed to be."

"What did he say?" Mary Anne cannot help but ask. "If I may ask."

"He had choice words to say about March, of course, revenge and all, and in a roundabout way, brought up my family—my father."

"You never speak of your father."

"I suppose I do not."

"Is it one of the secrets you prefer to keep?"

"No, not a secret," says Jonathan. "More unpleasant memories. Not of his life. He was a great and kind man. It was his passing that often brought the nightmares, and still does. To be fair, I speak about my father about as often as you speak about your parents."

"My parents." An odd tingle washes over her, as if rocked on a ship sailing through a dense fog, unaware of her bearings, unsure where her compass points. She tries to push away the fog to find an image of her mother or father. Faded silhouettes shrouded in the haze are all Mary Anne can make out. "Odd..."

"Something the matter?" asks Jonathan.

"For the life of me, I cannot seem to recall what my mother and father did here in Wonderland. Perhaps it is the stress of the past several days. Regardless, they must have been quite important, nobles, landed gentry at the least."

Jonathan tilts his head with a quizzical and confused look; almost worried. A question sits just behind his lips, but will not pass.

Why can she not remember? A flurry of emotions swells within her, a sense of love fills her chest, yet with the weight of fear, melancholy, and longing. What happened? She shakes the thought from her head. What is past is prologue, and what is before her, the castle and Jonathan, are the next chapter of her future.

Mary Anne's mind returns and races with her thoughts from earlier, the pressure in her body building in the Garden, holding it in until they enter the keep. She wants to return to their bedchamber but worries March may arrive at any moment to interrupt Mary Anne's time together with Jonathan. She takes his arm and leads him to the center of the eastern interior courtyard, where the last rays of sunlight bounce off the arches, pillars, and the deep silo of stone and brick above them, casting everything in a warm glow. The soft crunch of grass beneath their steps is a welcome break from the harsh stone of the city.

This is her moment, alone with him, in the fading light of a golden afternoon. "May I confess something to you?" Mary Anne stands toe to toe with him, heart thundering in her throat.

"You never need to ask, Mary Anne," says Jonathan.

"Precisely what I wished to speak to you about. Earlier, in the Garden, you gave me permission to do as I wanted with you. I know it was all part of the ruse to fool the Madam, but for a moment I felt free, unrestrained for the first time. I wanted, I yearned, down to my heart to reach out and touch you, and, damn it, I wanted you to touch me. Not because I commanded you, but because you wanted it as well."

"Yet, you did neither."

"It did not feel right in the moment." She opens his jacket to look upon his body without protest from him. "My heart beats so loudly you can feel it through the air."

"Take your time."

"It was not the right moment. I am not sure there ever will be a right moment, but it is time the truth must see the light of day, even in the fading light. I know you said secrets are necessary at times and the truth can be more dangerous, but if I do not speak from my heart, I fear I will explode."

"Mary Anne—"

"Please, allow me to finish." She unbuckles her wide belt and lets it drop to the grass. Her hands pull open her coat, revealing herself to Jonathan, and let it drape down and hang from the bend of her elbows. "Somewhere, in all the madness, my heart became yours, though you were not aware. You have so much love to share." Mary Anne leans in, takes his hands, and brings them to her chest and thundering heart. Puffs of his sweet, warm breath caress her face again. "Can you not spare a portion for me? I will admit, I do not particularly care for sharing, but if this is the way I can be in at least a corner of your heart and know you return my love, I shall suffer it, perhaps learn to enjoy it." She moves his hands to cup her breasts. "But to know I have at least a piece of your heart reserved for me, for us, it would make me—"

March appears like a phantom and digs her nails into the front of

Mary Anne's neck, the sharp pain stopping her breath, let alone any word. The burn in her throat soon travels to her lungs, rasping for breath.

"What has come over you?" Jonathan grabs her wrist, but March will not relent. When he pulls at her arm, Mary Anne's neck follows; March's nails embed deeper.

Uriah and Lysander applaud from under the arcade, barely audible over Mary Anne's gasps for breath.

"Well done," says Uriah.

"Finish this," says Lysander.

"I am done with her, with this city, with this entire fucking scenario."

March has made her intentions and lust for Mary Anne's death clear, never mincing words or threats. This is the first time death seeps in the growl of her words. Jonathan grabs March around the waist and lifts her off the grass. Mary Anne, coming to her senses, uses both hands to pry herself loose from March. Jonathan walks with March to the far side of the courtyard.

"Stop it," he pleads. "Please. I will not let you do this."

"Will not? Will not? Not cannot?" March rages in his arms, unable to break free. "This is your choice."

"Stop, please, dear heart."

Mary Anne slumps forward and grabs her neck. When she pulls her hand away, blood covers her palms and fingers. The world spins as she reclaims her breath.

"How boring," says Uriah. "What a disappointing end to an eventful day. Let us find more fulfilling entertainment elsewhere." He taps his brother on the shoulder, and together they retire into the castle.

Mary Anne, March, and Jonathan are left to pick up the pieces of their confrontation. Mary Anne should fear March, and at one point she did—but no longer. The sight of her own blood enrages her, and the pounding in her chest and head fills her with newfound courage. She started this conversation resigned to share Jonathan, but this back and forth is over; Mary Anne will see to it.

"How sad. Your audience of admirers has left." Mary Anne straightens her posture, picks her coat back up to her shoulders, and wipes the blood on it as if wiping away dirt. Previously, Mary Anne hinted at March's indiscretion and used it to her advantage, gaining access to their bed, but now she will use it to banish March from it.

"You think you hold power over me?" March shouts. "Over us? No one controls me. No one. Do you hear me?"

"Darling, what is the matter? What has happened? Please."

"I do," Mary Anne says coldly. "And I am tired of pretending I do not. We have tried your attempt at control; now you experience mine. Jonathan deserves to know the truth."

"What truth is this?" he asks, still struggling to keep March from Mary Anne.

The words bubble up in her mouth like fire in a dragon's stomach. "The deal she made with Lysander and Uriah, for their help in dealing with cultists. She fucked them. She fucked them both."

"Stop her talking." March claws at Mary Anne from yards away.

Jonathan turns to Mary Anne. "Why do you say these things?"

"Because they are truth. I saw her with my own eyes." Mary Anne embellishes, only having glimpsed March's pink hair through the spyglass. More than enough to lay blame on her. Mary Anne has seen no one else in Mirus with a similar color. "She fucked them both," she repeats. "And this was not her only indiscretion."

The struggle diminishes in March, and she falls slack in Jonathan's arms for a moment but shakes violently. It pains Mary Anne to see the pinch of his forehead, the worry in his eyes, and the twitch of his lip, nevertheless, she will tend to his wounds once they are rid of this malignance.

"She, who is supposed to love and cherish you, cannot remain loyal, despite the quality of man you are, Jonathan. Ask yourself, how often has she been alone with them? How often has she soiled herself with their lust and then returned to you?"

Jonathan sets March down, arms supporting her—the fight gone from her. She hangs her head, hair obscuring her face.

"Please, stop this, Mary Anne," Jonathan pleads.

"Do you not think it suspicious she suggested handling them herself? She suggested the brokered deal and sealed it with her body and her dignity. You should wear your shame with pride," she tells March. "You see how she has no rebuttal?" Mary Anne recalls Bronwen leaving Lysander and Uriah's chambers, hair askew, and clutching at her robe, and the words come without warning. Or perhaps Mary Anne does not care anymore. "Just like her mother."

March slides from Jonathan's hold in the time it takes Mary Anne to gasp and knocks both legs out from under him with one swift kick, sending Jonathan to the ground. Her hair swoops from her face to reveal a veil of hatred. March draws three daggers from the holsters on her thigh and tosses one into her free hand.

Time slows, as if the world itself submerges in deep water. Seconds turn to hours. March cocks her arms back, ready to release her steel claws. Mary Anne glances at Jonathan to be her savior. He reaches for her, but she evades his grasp.

March lunges forward and throws her first dagger at Mary Anne with the marksmanship of an archer. To Mary Anne, it appears little more than a sliver of sunlight headed straight for her face. She flings herself to the left as the dagger embeds itself in one of the stone pillars beside her.

Thlink.

The blade missed her head by inches. Mary Anne turns to look at the dagger meant to end her life, but the glint from the second dagger already spinning through the air catches her eye. She narrowly escapes again, losing her footing and stumbling back.

Thlink.

Icy terror burns through Mary Anne's veins as her pink-haired assassin shoves Mary Anne beneath the arches of the arcade, against the unforgiving stone wall and pins her there with a hand to her chest, the impact knocking the wind from her. She gasps for breath and rebounds off the wall, but March catches her, palm on chest again, and slams Mary Anne back against the stone. March flips the third dagger in hand and holds the tip to Mary Anne's throat.

"No!" Mary Anne shouts, and time begins again.

March's eyes vibrate with anger, near insanity. Her nostrils flare with every fiery breath. The tip of the dagger picks at Mary Anne's bloody skin. She stretches her neck in retreat, but Mary Anne has not yet regained her breath. Each deep, painful inhale ends with a pinprick to her throat.

Jonathan does not pick March up this time. He shoves his towering body between them, a barrier knocking the blade and March's hand away.

"Stop this," he whispers. "Please."

Mary Anne cannot see his face but hears the tremble in his voice. The tense silence carries on longer than Mary Anne can bear. Jonathan's arms reach back and encircle her, shield her. She dares to peek around his shoulder.

Tears run down March's cheeks, face frozen in utter anguish. "You choose her over me?" March asks with a tremble to match his. "After what she said to me?"

"You leave me no choice," says Jonathan.

"You have a choice. You have always had a choice." Tears stream down her face. "I kill her and we all return home. Is this not what you want? I could have killed her so many times, yet you stop me. It has always been your fucking choice."

"You know the choice is not mine," Jonathan pleads. "I am bound to her. I will not allow you to lay another hand on her."

Mary Anne has never seen either of them in such a state, let alone at each other's throats. There was the one previous argument she walked in on in their bedchambers, but nothing ever like this. Pain fills their every word.

"You have chosen her," says March, all will to fight gone.

"No," Jonathan says. Tears obstructing his words. "Do not—"

"Yes!" March shouts. Her words cut through the air like her dagger and silence the birds and the wind. "You and your damned honor have chosen her since she appeared in the Hollow. You throw away years of our life together for her?"

"I throw away nothing. I am caught, bound, chained, tethered, unable to move, unable to breathe, unable to think. This is not what I want. But we must all do things we do not want to do in order to survive." Jonathan speaks March's words back to her. The words she spoke before leaving for her mother's home to meet with Lysander and Uriah.

March looks past Jonathan to make sure Mary Anne sees her eyes—bloodshot and full of tears. Mary Anne once looked upon her own reflection in a looking-glass in the town of Briarwell, looking thus, while March paraded around arrogantly. How their positions have switched. Not as quickly as Mary Anne would have liked, but time reveals all.

"You doubt me, now?" March asks Jonathan in less than a whisper.

"I never doubt you." Jonathan's voice wavers harder than before. "This is how I know you will always do what is necessary to protect us. Even if it rips my heart from my chest."

Mary Anne can still not see Jonathan's face, but she can see his heartbreak in March's eyes.

March drops the dagger to the ground and walks from the courtyard without looking back. The bond they shared, perhaps not severed for good, not yet anyway, but severely damaged.

Once she is out of sight, Jonathan finally turns to Mary Anne. Her moment of victory shatters when Jonathan turns to look at her; his eyes, once brilliant blue, darkened by the red of his tears.

Mary Anne wraps both arms around Jonathan's neck and hugs him tightly, and after what feels like an eternity, he returns her embrace, his massive arms pulling her against him by the waist. His stomach spasms as he tries to swallow his grief. Mary Anne did not want to make him feel this way, but he deserved the truth, and the truth always brings pain—pain she will help him heal from. After all, regardless of if Jonathan denies it now, one thing is perfectly clear: he did choose her.

CHAPTER 50
MARCH

March storms from the courtyard, mind reeling from the thought she was so close to taking Mary Anne's life. She can feel the heat of her pulse on her face and in her eyes. Table, vase, chair, and every other gaudy piece of furniture and decor flies by in a blur. When she passes them, March pushes every tall candelabra to the ground, and if she still had a blade on her, would rip every tapestry. Servants and the Sarafan, who unfortunately enter the same hallway, take one look at March and run in the opposite direction to escape. She must destroy something, break something, but fears what must break is herself.

She waits until she is far enough away from the courtyard, in one of the lesser traveled areas of the castle, the chamber of the Triumvirate, to collapse and scream out and release the fire, the hatred for Mary Anne, before it consumes her. Her stomach cramps and she doubles over, holding herself, and resting her forehead on the cold marble floor.

"Who has done this to you?" Cheshire asks with a dark tone. He gently grabs her shoulders and lifts her up. "Tell me, and I will kill them here and now and lay their body at your feet."

The temptation pulls at March with the force of Cheshire's gravity. She has already unleashed him onto the city; why not have him kill Mary Anne as well? Her lover would not hesitate, but to set *Cheshire* on Mary Anne would place Jonathan dangerously close to his wrath. Before Cheshire can ask again, March pushes him against the stone wall and holds him there. She hangs her head, hair hiding her face, not ready to share his gaze for fear of his reaction and the resulting aftermath.

His chest flexes beneath her hands, hard as the marble behind him, striations rippling. Though she cannot see his face, she can hear his sly grin in the hiss of his lustful inhale. Tears swell in her eyes, and the void in her chest, with no fire left, aches. A tear slips from her eye and tickles the tip of her nose. Cheshire traces his hands along her arms from wrist to shoulder, barely touching her skin, but enough to send shivers over her body. The tear falls from her nose. Her ache grows as it becomes smaller, falling, falling, until her pain becomes a dark stain on the stone floor.

Cheshire parts her fallen hair and lifts her face to his with a gentle, bent finger. She struggles to keep her lips from quivering or more tears from falling—as futile as trying to stop the rain. Their eyes meet, and the mischievous grin he had moments ago melts to the stone-faced, wide-eyed expression of rage.

His eyes shake. They ask, "Who?" He tries to lurch from the wall, but March holds him firm. She cannot let him go as much as she wants to. He tries again and again, not wanting to push her, but wanting answers. It is not his gentle touch she needs. March grabs his wrists and slams them against the wall above his head. She kisses him roughly and passionately, dragging her nails down his arms and torso, pulling his cloak and vest from him and dropping them on the floor.

He returns her fury, harder and wetter. Her mouth parts for his, and she forces her lips still and breathes deep. Her voice will not waver. "Make me forget," she commands. "Please." She needs to break, and it is Cheshire who can both break her and heal her at the same time.

The swell of tears in his eyes matches her own, full of rage and sorrow. He understands. He spins March to place her back against the wall, kneels, and rips the laces off her trousers, lowering them just below her backside.

She can feel his heavy breath against her sensitivity, and grabs his hair, shoving his face between her thighs. His lips slide, tease, and kiss her tender skin, and his rough, skilled tongue sends wave after wave of warmth from her legs to the top of her head.

Cheshire wraps his arms around her thighs, smothering his face, and March twists her fingers in his lavender hair and pushes her hips away from the wall. The harder she holds him in place, the harder he envelopes her, ravenous as an animal, finally sinking into her. This is the side of her lover she needs.

His grunts and her moans fill the chamber with deep, resonating harmony, shaking their bodies. March grinds her hips against his glistening face until his grunts turn to guttural growls and purrs, tongue flitting as fast as a hummingbird's wings. March gave him a command, and he fulfills it with every fiber of his being. She can think of nothing else, look nowhere else, but the sight of her lover kneeling before her. The lavender shimmer of his eyes catches her, grounds her, while his tongue sends her to the heavens.

The world spins, her eyes flutter, and legs quake. Cheshire's hold on her thighs keeps her upright despite her knees begging to buckle. Her moans intensify to screams of pleasure, echoing through the chamber and connecting corridors. Their melody attracts the attention of servant girls and a castle guard, who peek around distant corners. Some disappear quickly and others remain to fulfill their curiosity.

Cheshire brings March to the brink of her tolerance.

Not yet.

She pulls his face from her and enjoys the fight he puts up to stay in place. March brings him to his feet, pushes him back against the wall with a thud, rips his tattered trousers from him, and guides his hard, dripping cock between her thighs, trapped together by her trousers. Her body jumps as it glides against her.

March grabs his wrists again, pinning them over his head, and slides back and forth against his shaft, pressing her body against his, feeling his head rub against her ass, then pulling away until his tip teases her sensitivity. By the fourth time she slides to his head, she can take it longer. She holds both hands over his head in one, and with the other, guides him, welcomes him into her. Normally, Cheshire takes his time for her to adjust to his girth, but she slams against his body, taking every inch at once. She loses her breath, and her stomach contracts from the shock and searing mixture of pleasure with delicious pain traveling through her muscles like lightning strikes to a tall oak.

Cheshire pushes his hips forward, as March did before. She can only feel him, all of him, every pulse, every flex, every heartbeat through his body. The deep grooves of his stomach muscles run with his sweat. She looks down between them and pulls away to watch his beautiful shaft slide from her until she thrusts forward again, taking all of Cheshire. Again and again, she slams harder and harder against her lover's hips, watching his cock grow wetter, feeling it swell within her. The pain subsides and gives way to a crescendo of unexplainable ecstasy.

She grits her teeth and roars as she thrusts faster, legs trapped together by her trousers, unable to stop herself, unable to satiate her need. The sweaty sight of her lover, the fragrant scents of their love, the rhythmic slapping of their skin, and the pulsating ache through her body take March from this world and send her over the edge. Her climax steals her breath, and, unable to control her body, continues to slam against Cheshire harder until she finally releases her breath with a long quivering scream.

The muscles of her stomach shake with every contracted breath. She raises her eyes to Cheshire's beautiful gaze, more animal than man. They are not done. March stands and waits with Cheshire twitching within. He understands.

He pulls her top up, uncovering her breasts, nearly ripping it in the act, and takes her left nipple in his mouth. He reaches down and grabs hold of her ass and starts thrusting harder than she had before, not allowing her climax to decrescendo. Cheshire gives her no time to recover and keeps her suspended in a state of bliss, unable to think, only able to feel him. She leans back, held up by Cheshire's strength, and grips her hair as she screams. Every thrust, every inch, rocks her, fills her, breaks her.

His growling on her breast, tongue swirling, lips pinching, grows stronger, as does this grip on her ass. Cheshire's pace quickens as he grows within her. The heavenly pain returns, and Cheshire grunts louder and thrusts faster until he climaxes. March finds herself beautifully helpless, but securely caught in the wake of his lust. The warmth grows within her, and in turn she climaxes again, unsure if she moans, screams, or cries; perhaps all three.

Cheshire stands her upright, face to face, breathing in each other with heavy pants. His eyes ask if she is alright.

March wraps her arms around his neck and gives him a gentle kiss on the lips. "Get me out of here," she whispers. "Get me out of the city."

Without hesitation, Cheshire raises her trousers and pulls her top down, grabbing his own clothing, and leads her to one of the large woven tapestries hanging from a gold bar in the hallway and pooling on the floor. She cannot help but watch the shift of his bare ass as he walks in front of her, round and firm, and the dimples above it. With a wave of his hand, he brings the Mask of Shadow to his face and flaps the tapestry away from the wall, revealing the shadow behind. Together, they travel through the darkness, and the wall and tapestry narrowing on her shoulders instantaneously transform to smooth, solid rock.

The scent of earth, stone, and fresh water greets March. Cheshire leads her out of a narrow crevice into a damp, lush grotto covered with mosses, fen violets, and creeping marshwort. A beautiful, clear waterfall rains down from an unseen cliff above, and a brook rushes by beyond its curtain. *Has he always had this place to escape to?* This place is unknown to her, though it does not surprise her in the least that Cheshire has his own secluded spaces. After all, they all hold secrets from each other.

Cheshire waves the mask from his face, helps March undress, sliding off her braces, slipping off her boots and trousers. She pulls her top up over her head, but while her hands and linen block her eyes, Cheshire grabs her arms and kisses her exposed lips. Her animal has become a man again.

He lays their clothes and his purple sash on a large nearby slab and leads her beneath the waterfall. The rush from the water is a welcome reprieve from the heat coursing through her body. She closes her eyes and feels the water trace down her body—down her neck, down the middle of her back, around her breasts, and between her legs. The water is soon joined by Cheshire's warm hands, delicately washing her skin and worries away with the brook. She tries to wash him as well, but with a caring glance, he lets March know this is his time to take care of her, to heal her. He rubs and caresses every part of her body, hands cascading down her like falling leaves.

Even in the waterfall, she feels the tears form without thinking. Cheshire sees them, and though it makes little difference with the pouring water, he still wipes them and their trails from her cheeks.

Fatigue takes over, and peace, but also emptiness, fills her. March has fought thousands of battles and would fight thousands more to be physically rather than emotionally exhausted. The former heals, the latter lingers. The tension held in every part of her body dissipates like the fading echo of a hymnal sung in the temples. March leads Cheshire from the waterfall to the slab with their clothing. He lies down with open arms, and she lies beside him, using his upper arm to rest her head, and hides her face in his neck. Cheshire wraps his arms around her and pulls her close.

She loses herself in the song around her—Cheshire's breath, the thump of his heart, the distant trickling of water, and the wind rustling through the ravine above. This is where she belongs—where they belong.

Cheshire, unable to control his cock, or never willing to, grows hard again. An endearing quality March would never do without. She still needs him, so she wraps a leg over him, slides a hand down between the warm cocoon of their bodies, and though March's eyes weigh heavily, she guides him, whispering a slight whimper until she welcomes him completely. Cheshire grabs her backside and holds her against him, as if the water, the wind, or some unforeseen force might steal her away.

Unable to fight the temptation, March rocks her hips back and forth. Her body relaxes, safe in Cheshire's arms.

"Stay with me," she whispers as she succumbs to her exhaustion, little more than a mumble, but he understands.

"Always."

"Do not leave me."

"Never."

Part III

CHAPTER 51

JONATHAN

The following morning, after a sleepless night, Jonathan walks the streets of Stonehaven, unmoored, adrift, rudderless. He loses time, looking up from the ground to see the three-story tenements on the middle tiers of Stonehaven, then blinking, walks by the Verdant Inn on the lowest tier, and seconds later, or what seems like seconds to him, he passes the charred remains of the Temple of the Old Maid.

After the argument with March, the castle did not seem the right place to be, despite Mary Anne's attempt to keep him there. He does not search for March; she does not want to be found, which spreads the cracks in his own heart. Instead, he chooses isolation, to be lost in the numb void for however long he can be. He hurt her, and for such an act, Jonathan cannot and will never forgive himself. The thought repeating in his mind to the point of mumbling the words every five paces, which they both know to be true, brings no solace to the hollow chasm in his chest. *They have no choice.*

The void brings into striking clarity the severity of their present predicament. Two days from now, the armada arrives, and they all have done little to prepare, just as Lysander and Uriah planned. The council should convene, but the Duchess refuses to leave her guarded escort, Weiss cowers in his study, the Gryphon is still unaccounted for, March is heartbroken, and Cheshire lurks somewhere as the calm before the storm. Even Pat and Bill have hardly made an appearance since their time together in the Pool of Tears.

Jonathan pulls his elixir from his pocket and swirls the half bottle between two fingers, and for a moment sees himself screaming in its reflection and torrent within. He finishes the contents, waiting for the last drop to fall onto his tongue. The elixir works quickly, spreading through his mind like fingers searching and sifting through a sack of grain.

The city hums with life again—busy bodies with anxious eyes and steps, still weary of the dangers. They emerge because the soldiers of Mirus finally make their presence known by the dozens and more, patrolling, standing, and conversing with each other or townspeople. None wear their uniforms and armors, but the Mirusian steel at their hips gives them away. The soldiers give the townspeople peace from the threat within the walls, while Jonathan thinks of the impending threat sailing toward them.

"Jonathan," Mary Anne's voice calls from atop the high ways. "Jonathan." She runs down a nearby stairway, still wearing the longcoat and trousers from the day prior, and hesitates, the temptation to kiss him plain on her face, yet decides to throw her arms around him instead. "I have been worried all night."

"My intention was not to make you worry," says Jonathan, caught in a senseless haze between his exhaustion and his elixir. "How did you find me?"

"The archers." She points to the roofs of Stonehaven, where the blurry silhouettes of four of the Gryphon's archers perch. "We must return to the castle to finish preparation. The festival starts today."

Yet another important aspect overlooked in his own guilt and wandering. Above, ropes of colorful red and white pennant flags zig zag over the street. Hooked from building to building, pine and leaf garland swags with flowers— thistles, daffodils, roses, daisies, and cornflowers—drop between buildings as well. Wreaths of the same variety hang from lampposts and above shop doors. Jonathan never noticed—prone to missing details, so Cheshire says—and he is not sure the citizens have taken notice either.

Mary Anne follows Jonathan's gaze from the festive decorations overhead to the downtrodden faces of the townspeople. "They do not seem to be in a celebratory mood."

"Fear carries a great burden, a weight to it. Its most dangerous attribute, veiled in its simple complexity, is its power to steal people's lives without having to take them. There are more out today than days prior. When did the soldiers appear?"

"They finally reemerged from their homes last night, and several hundred others returned on horseback before dawn. Just in time."

Jonathan has failed so often these past few days, he must find a way to see Mary Anne's vision through. He must occupy his mind with something, anything, to keep himself from sinking, spiraling. After what transpired yesterday, he understands there is not a way to unite the townspeople—not yet anyway, not in time for the festival. In order to find success, they must risk a further divide.

"Excuse me, gentlemen." Jonathan calls over several nearby Mirusian soldiers, who each speak with a small crowd of townspeople. Five join them. "I ask you to spread the word to every person you pass, and send soldiers into the Boroughs as well. The celebration will commence as scheduled. Let there be music, tell every shop and tavern to supply food and drinks for all in the Row and the Crooked Market at the castle's expense, and above all else, tell them there will be nothing to fear."

"Easier said than done," a soldier says.

"Agreed, but we will take the opportunity away from our adversaries to do any further damage. We shall have two celebrations: one on the castle grounds for those loyal to Lysander and Uriah, as first intended, and the other, a proper celebration, in the streets of Stonehaven and the Boroughs for the people. Make sure it reaches every ear."

"I do not believe dividing the people in such a way, at this point, would benefit us," says Mary Anne. "You draw a deep line between the two. And what guarantee would we have each would attend their intended celebration?"

"Excuse me," Jonathan calls to a man of Stonehaven still conversing in the small groups. "Given the choice, would you choose to celebrate on the castle grounds or in the streets of Stonehaven?"

"There ain't no choice at all." The man starts hesitantly but builds in confidence. "I wouldn't step foot in the castle. Me and mine would dance and drink in the streets until we woke up the next dawn."

"Would you like the chance to do so again?"

The hint of a contentment brightens his cheeks and his eyes sparkle as if catching unseen lamp lights, remembering a time long, long before any of this.

"Spread the word," says Jonathan. "When the sun starts its descent, we remember those we have lost and celebrate their lives." He has the attention of every ear on the street and new additions on balconies and in windows. "So much has happened, and we have become a shadow of ourselves, allowing fear to rob us. Reclaim your lives. This is not a time to fight. This is a time to dance and to live."

The buzz and hum of the street grows, whispers pass through windows and doors, and a few townspeople run off to tell others the news. Words fly farther and quicker than any bird or leaf on the wind.

Before Jonathan dismisses the soldiers, he asks, "Who amongst you is without a wife or companion?"

One of the soldiers, a younger man, raises his gauntlet. Jonathan asks him to remain while the other soldiers leave for their tasks.

"I must ask you for a different favor. Journey to the Garden and tell Madam Rose, Carter and Mary Anne require their best—fuck it—all of their flowers dressed in their finest, at the celebration in the castle by dusk. When she asks for payment, tell her the price has already been paid."

"And me being single, sir?" the young soldier asks.

"Since it is such a long walk to the Garden, should you want to find rest and relaxation there before this evening's festivities, let Madam Rose know we have already paid for those services as well. For your troubles."

"Yes, sir." The soldier tries to contain the excitement in his steps, running off to the east.

"Plans are in motion," says Jonathan to the air.

Mary Anne stares at him with admiration. "You are a wonder. You created the plan so quickly, even after a sleepless night."

"It was your plan. I embellished on it. It also helps to have something to focus on. Considering..." Jonathan trails off. He offers his arm to Mary Anne. "This is important to you. I was with you when you bore the idea, and I will see it through."

Mary Anne slips her hands down Jonathan's arm, interlocks her fingers with his, and leans against his shoulder as they climb back to the castle. Jonathan intentionally walks slower than they should to allow the whispers time to reach the castle and the Twins before they arrive.

The parapets of the castle are sparse of guards, undoubtedly helping with the last details on the croquet court. In their place, soldiers stand at attention—curious, but understood. The Gryphon's archers slip through the door of the gate behind Jonathan and Mary Anne and retake posts. Across the bailey, Lysander and Uriah wait at the top of the grand stairs, arms crossed, with a servant girl and flower fawning over each of them, heads leaning on their shoulders, and rubbing their chests. The Twins' robes hang down by their belts, and they carry no weapon with them. With victory within reach, they do not see the point, believing all they must do is wait.

"March allowed you to live? How droll," says Uriah.

"Must we continue with this charade?" Lysander gestures to their left at the pathway around the castle, lined with posts and more draped garland and lanterns creating a tunnel to the gardens at the rear.

"We hear you plan to keep us caged within the castle walls," says Uriah.

Jonathan was correct to take their time walking back to the castle. The Twins, having heard the news, prepared rebuttals and snide remarks. Regardless, no matter what they say, the Twins must agree to the plan or it is all for naught.

"This scheme of yours will not work," says Lysander.

"There is no scheme." Mary Anne climbs the stairs with purpose and unyielding confidence. "Unlike your selfish ambitions, I came to this decision for the people of Mirus."

"You fool yourself if you believe your ambitions are not as self-serving as ours," says Uriah. "We just have the confidence to admit it."

"I had to remind myself I do not need to quest for the throne. It already belongs to me." She looks to Jonathan. "Wonderland has made its choice, and it was not you. To the matter at hand, this is not about me or the throne. After everything the people suffered these past weeks, they deserve a chance to enjoy themselves without fear, regardless of whom they follow or what tomorrow or the next day brings," she says pointedly.

"Well said," says Jonathan.

"You would allow all those loyal to us into the castle grounds?" Lysander's tongue plays with the inside of his cheek.

"If it ceases the fighting and deaths for an evening, yes."

"As we said in the council chamber, our arrangement could be amended," says Jonathan. "Your followers will be granted access for one night but must leave by festival's end or twilight, whichever comes first. Can we agree?"

"Agreed," says Uriah. "But every one of our soldiers will be armed, considering the ambush we faced upon our last visit to your croquet court. Agreed?"

"Agreed," says Mary Anne. "Ours as well. Agreed?"

"Agreed," says Lysander.

"Now that is settled, we must take our leave to prepare," says Jonathan, wishing to end this potential loop before it continues. "We will see you this evening on the lawn."

"We look forward to it," says Uriah.

Jonathan takes Mary Anne by the hand, her grip on his arm growing tighter, and together they walk into the keep to her bedchamber. Inside, her handmaiden waits by the bed with a gown, or rather selection of gowns, Jonathan has seen hanging in the wardrobe, spread out across the sheets. Mary Anne waves the gossamer curtains away, lifts the crimson fabric, and lets it fall back to the bed.

"It is exquisite," she tells her handmaiden. "Thank you."

"You shall look wonderful in it," says Jonathan.

Mary Anne leaves a silence hanging in the air, fiddling with the ties to her coat. "Jonathan."

The air weighs heavy between them, thick, as if the door to the baths stands open, and the humid air fills the bedchamber. He hears her swallow and knows what she means to ask before her eyes raise to meet his. He rushes to the trunks, picks up a full vial of elixir, the red longcoat, and his patchwork hat, then returns to her and kisses her on the temple.

"I shall meet you on the lawn."

As much as Jonathan has been by her side from the beginning, and wants to be here for her before the festival begins, he cannot indulge her fancies. His heart cannot bear it. For so long, Jonathan focused on the here-and-now in order to escape the past and not summon the worries of what is yet to come, but the present stabs at him with blades of the past. The only place he can turn to is the future, however uncertain, because now, he will take uncertainty over what has been done.

CHAPTER 52

CHESHIRE

Cheshire perches on the railing in the backrooms of the Far Side Tavern, swaying side to side, waiting. Its owner, dead from a twisted neck, vacant wide eyes, and mouth twisted and frozen in a scream he never had the chance to start, lies broken on the stones of the first floor below. The thick wooden walls of the distillery will keep any noise from escaping, and Dormy ordering rounds of drinks on the owner's tab keeps the masses entertained and sloshed in the tavern. A muffled shanty, an unintelligible knot of laughter, and out-of-tune singing hardly makes it into the back room.

There are only two important noises Cheshire focuses on: the twisting and groaning of the thick rope in front of him and the heavy, slow breathing of the Gryphon, hanging from his feet, hands bound, above the largest vat of whiskey. The dishonored general appears less imposing, thinner, without his sweeping longcoat and pauldrons, which were a feat to remove from his unconscious body. The rope travels through several pulls and ends at a large wood and iron crank and lever to Cheshire's right.

A multitude of questions persist, but only one matters—one question will answer all others, no matter the Gryphon's attempts to avoid the truth.

An hour elapses before the Gryphon finally stirs. His deep groans increasingly grow louder until his eyes open one at a time. The ends of his long, gray braided hair dance upon the surface of the dark, shimmering whiskey. He sniffs the air, eyes coming to a sharp focus to assess his surroundings, and panic overtakes him at the sight of the vat below, though unable to move yet. Over time, he struggles but regains the strength to swing back and forth and, after many failed attempts, builds up enough momentum to swing up and grab the ropes around his ankles, flopping around like a long-haired salmon.

"Impressive." Cheshire rocks back and forth on the rail of the walkway. "The powder I doused you with has a potent paralytic quality. Yet, it lasted a far shorter time on you than me, more than likely because of your size. I had to keep administering it every few hours. But alas, its effects begin to wane, and I dare not waste the rest of my store on you. Do not struggle too hard. I shall release you once you have answered my question."

The Gryphon thrashes frantically, his senses restored and more sensation returning to his limbs. "Do not do this," he mumbles, trying to regain control of his face.

"Do what?" Cheshire points to the vat below. "Drop you in the vat of whiskey? I thought you were partial to spirits. First of all, give me more credit. I will not drop you in. I am going to lower you in slowly, forcing you to drink, drown, or answer my question truthfully. You see, I thought to myself, as much as I wish I could, I may never overcome you at your best. Therefore, the only recourse is for me to face you at your worst—the way I found you."

"No, please."

"Also, I must thank you for your help in conducting an experiment with the Mask of Light. You see, the power of the mask extends to those I keep contact with. It has its limits, but you, being the largest person in

Mirus, except for the gatemen, presented the perfect subject. While the panic ensued on the croquet court, I took the risk and rather than escaping with you immediately, I sat on your chest and watched everyone else run around the field and flee, not knowing you still lay there. It was quite amusing."

"You cannot do this."

"I can. And I am. For someone so intelligent, you are quite slow—"

"No, you little shit. I mean you cannot afford to do this, with the battle looming, the armada approaching, the Twins poised to strike, all of what is coming in Mirus."

"Little shit?" Cheshire's fingers dance upon the crank. "You dare dishonor my mother by dishonoring her son."

The Gryphon mutters quickly under his breath. "Forgiveness. Forgiveness."

Cheshire cocks his head and squints at his prey. This fearful, not fearsome, side of the Gryphon is one Cheshire has not seen before. His grin masks both the hatred and enjoyment burning in his soul. He killed a god, only needing to figure out how. The Gryphon will stand no chance.

"All I require are answers, one answer actually, and yet you fight me, lie to me, send me across the country, deception in the guise of compassion, having me dig up what I believed in my heart at the time was my own mother's grave. No child should ever endure such a task. Each claw full of earth and dirt caked under my fingernails, wet from my tears until I hit bone. Yet, you allowed it without conscience or shame."

"You are one to talk of shame." The Gryphon releases his ankles and swings back and forth violently, still not in full control of his faculties—an erratic pendulum. He reaches for Cheshire with each pass, gaining more height.

"True, I know nothing of shame. Shame is a learned trait often taught by one's parents." Cheshire shrugs. "Of which I seem to be in short supply, with a derelict father and abducted mother. But not for long. Once reunited with her, I shall tell her of your lies and the way you throttled and beat me. What do you think she will have to say when she finds out how you treated her one and only son?"

There. There it is. Amid the flailing for his freedom, his entire body jolts ever-so-slightly, his eyes widen as if some unearthly figure yanked at his eyelids, and his skin grows pale even with the blood rushing to his head. He would not fear it if his mother were dead. Confirmation of the Gryphon's lie and his mother's truth. Yet, the question remains.

"You give the game away. My mother lives. Where is she?" Cheshire, with grim and gleeful confidence, places his hand on the crank. "The sooner we begin this game, the sooner it ends. For one of us at least."

"Your mother is dead, wretched boy. Her body slumbers in the crypt below the city, below the castle with the rest of her ancestors. I am sorry I—"

"Lies."

Cheshire releases the handle, and it spins one revolution until a metal latch catches the next thick wooden tooth of the gear. The Gryphon plunges headfirst into the dark liquor, up to his collarbones. The Gryphon thrashes, a fish caught unexpectedly on the end of a hook, splashing and drizzling whiskey in giant waves onto the stone floor. He summons his strength, bends at the waist, and pulls his face above the surface of the whiskey, releasing a mist of spit and whiskey into the air.

"No. Do not do this. Bring me up," the Gryphon pleads. "My skin itches, my mouth waters. My mind reels."

Cheshire remains silent.

"I cannot return to the state I was in. The prison of the bottle was far worse than the oubliette."

"A prison of your own making. Was it so bad? Did it not dull your senses and your shame?"

"It was all provided to me. It was drink or die."

"Then, you should have died in the service of my mother. Fortunately for you, you now have a chance to rectify your decision."

"Stop." The Gryphon's body convulses. "It calls to me."

"Like a warm embrace. Your dependency was quite apparent when I discovered you in the dungeon," says Cheshire. "Even after you sobered, you could not stomach walking by me in the harbor when I doused myself in liquor before I set it ablaze. The perfect camouflage against a recovering drunkard."

"Stop. Please. It pains me. The temptation. I could not administer help to Carter in his time of need, tempted by the hemlock and henbane."

The hair on the back of Cheshire's neck bristles. "You hesitated to help him?" He releases the crank three notches and drops the Gryphon deeper into the vat, nearly up to his waist.

It takes longer for the Gryphon to resurface the second time. There is fight in him, but the whiskey does its intended task, enticing him, luring him like a siren's song. The Gryphon reaches up, grabs his trouser legs, and pulls himself up for air. He does not spit the liquor out this time, eyes wild, and an expression of disgust on his face for surrendering to his weakness.

"Enjoy your drink?" asks Cheshire.

"Stop."

"All it will take is the truth to end this. Now tell me. Where is my mother?"

"I cannot tell you." The Gryphon swipes wildly at Cheshire with one arm, gaining more control over his fingers.

Cheshire ponders the curious choice of words purposefully chosen. "Interesting to say you 'cannot tell me' instead of 'will not tell me.' So, it is not just stubbornness and pride that stays your tongue, rather, something else. Or someone else." Cheshire knows precisely who holds the Gryphon's strings. The same person who orchestrates all in Wonderland. He wants to hear it from the Gryphon. "Who keeps you from speaking the truth?"

"No one!" the Gryphon shouts. He looks around the room as if specters listen in on their conversation from every shadow in the rafters. "No one."

The grin from Cheshire fades, as does the sparkle, any light, in his eyes. "I almost took my life because of your lie. The sea at the Wrecks called to me from the crashing waves below the Sorrows. My mother would have lived on without me had I believed you. I would be gone from this world, leaving her behind, alone." He looks to the door to the tavern to make sure no one hears the Gryphon's pleas. There can be no interruptions. Cheshire's arm tenses on the handle. "I would ask what a poor wretch you are and what poor soul you used to fill my mother's false grave, but alas, I care not. I just want to hear the truth from your lips. Does my mother live?"

Body shaking, fighting fatigue, and licking the liquor from his lips, the Gryphon relents. "Yes."

A deafening silence follows, blocking out the music and cavorting from the tavern. Cheshire dares not disturb it. A cold emptiness fills his chest, then his entire body. A dull calm fills the room like a still lake on a moonless and starless night. He thought the admission would bring the slightest amount of solace. Nothing. Only a parched mouth, sore muscles, a throbbing head, and a numb heart. Cheshire stares into the Gryphon's eyes, waiting, commanding more.

The Gryphon continues. "The Duchess, before my imprisonment, would speak of the queens as if they still lived."

"Where is she?" Cheshire asks coldly.

"I do not know." Before Cheshire can turn the crank again, the Gryphon blurts out, "This is why I cannot tell you. Because I do not know where she is. She is the reason I have not left Mirus. Even after her disappearance, I searched to the point of suspicion. The price for my loyalty was the damned oubliette and drowning at the bottom of a bottle."

"And now?"

"I search still to the best of my abilities, when not pursued by you."

Desperation fills the Gryphon's voice. "Trust me, when I tell you we work together toward the same end."

"You are mistaken. Your search for my mother comes from nothing more than the shame or regret for your greatest failure."

"No. No, there is more."

"I assume you want to seat her back on the fucking throne."

"How else will all this end? She was the one beacon of light in this entire damned world. Queen Dinah brought balance. She can do so again."

"Herein lies the crux of the problem. You still see her as a queen. I see her as my mother. When I find her, we will walk away from this city as it burns and crumbles into the sea. You and I, our paths do not align. You, like everyone else, have your own purpose, your own agenda for her. I want her only as a mother, and you or anyone else will not have her."

"What will she think when she hears of everything you have done in her name? The atrocities, the murders, the lives you have ruined?"

The emptiness in Cheshire fills with hot, searing coals, bringing his blood to boil. "In her name? Her name? The world has forgotten her name."

"No, they have not. Those of us still loyal—"

"Shut up! All I have ever done, every life I have taken, is in my name. At least the name I assumed after I was forced from the castle. My mother will know her son loved her to the end of the world, to the end of Time, and back." Cheshire watches the Gryphon's eyes tick back and forth between his own eyes and the crank. "Put it together, have you? Longer than I expected."

"Damn you. You do not have the strength to pull me up." The Gryphon snarls. "You had no intention of letting me go."

"I believe my words were, 'I would release you'. Never doubt the conviction of my words. There are many liars in this world, but I cannot and will not be added to their number. Every fiber of my spirit wanted to bind your hands behind your back and drown you after this conversation.

However, you can still be of use to me. I cannot believe I go against my advice to Jonathan, to put an end to our enemies so they do not return later to attack again. If what you say is truth, which will already be difficult to believe because of your propensity for falsehood, then with every additional breath I allow you to take, you better keep your word and search for my mother. Pray you do not lie to me again."

"Please, do not do this." The Gryphon's tone shifts to bleak sincerity.

"It is already done."

Cheshire flips the crank, and it spins, whirring uncontrollably, round and round. The deep splash of whiskey silences the Gryphon's blood-curdling plea as the rest of his body submerges in the deep vat. He resurfaces, gasps for breath, and digs into the water with his bound arms to keep him afloat until he reaches the chain. His long hair floats on the dark surface, and his breaths push and pull the whiskey from and to his face.

Cheshire pulls the lever next to the crank and a thick iron grate lowers into place across the top of the vat, used for the tavern owner to walk upon to inspect the gears and pulleys above, and keep any other workers from falling in. It will serve to keep the Gryphon in until Cheshire returns.

"Fear not. I will come back for you. In the meantime, should you not want to drown, I suggest you drink heartily. But for now, I must leave you. You see, I am late for a party, and it would be such a shame if I missed the hard work you and I put into it. Thank you, again."

CHAPTER 53
MARY ANNE

The door to their bedchamber shuts, and the pressure of Jonathan's kiss remains on Mary Anne's skin. Her stomach sinks, and the heat of embarrassment flushes her face. He must have known Mary Anne was about to ask for his help to undress and change into her new gown. It would be an innocent gesture, though Mary Anne admits she hoped it would lead to a more tender moment between them. Jonathan is not ready, and Mary Anne realizes she chose poorly. There will be time enough for them. Jonathan needs his time to process yesterday's events, and Mary Anne must focus hers on the celebration at hand.

Instead, Grace unties her coat, pries off her boots, unlaces her trousers, and holds up the beautiful, crimson jacquard gown. Mary Anne slips her head and arms through and walks to the looking-glass, where Grace tightens the laces on the back. As she pulls, the top forms to Mary Anne's figure and the two high slits become flare from the empire-style band crossing under her chest to reveal her body. Mary Anne runs her fingers down her skin, starting at her ribs and down to her thighs. She sweeps her right leg out and turns her hips to discover the limits and modesty of the dress. When standing still, the slits give a peek at her body, however, with the heft of the fabric, and with the right movement, the gown swings open around her hip to show her entire side with only the front panel to conceal her, but only just. Grace helps Mary Anne step into a new pair of knee-high leather boots and clasps wide silver bracelets around her wrists to finish the ensemble.

A thought crosses her mind. Somehow she previously would have objected to this cut and style of dress, though she cannot seem to remember why on earth she would not wear such a beautiful gown. Mary Anne meets the gaze of the woman in the looking-glass and marvels at the elegance of Grace's craftsmanship. This ensemble would never grace the pages of a storybook princess or queen with so much exposed skin. Nevertheless, Mary Anne cannot help but feel powerful and, dare she think it, dare she believe it, regal. Tonight she must be, being surrounded by those who want to see her fail, and every eye scrutinizing.

Grace holds the chamber door open, and Mary Anne takes a deep breath before stepping into the hallway. She stops, expecting Grace to follow, but her handmaiden stands dutifully outside the door.

"Are you not coming?" she asks.

Grace shakes and lowers her head, fidgeting with her clasped hands.

"I need you there," says Mary Anne.

The amount of growing unease in Grace's bites at the corner of her mouth is almost too much for Mary Anne to bear.

"Is it the crowd?"

Grace shakes her head so fast it is almost unnoticeable.

"I wish you could tell me what you think, what worries you, so I can help. Please, come with me." Mary Anne offers her hand. "We shall give each other strength. I cannot do this without you. Please."

Slowly at first, Grace steps forward, calculating if there may be some consequence for her action, but finally reaches out and takes Mary Anne's hand. What a pair they make. The metal slivers clink inside Grace's dress as they journey to the rear of the castle. Mary Anne grew concerned about these weeks ago and, like so many other things, let it slip from her mind. The remarkable work Grace did on Mary Anne's wardrobe deserves a reward. *What a horrible thing to think.* Basic comfort is not a reward, it is a necessity. When this mess with the Twins concludes, Mary Anne will change Grace's wardrobe to reflect her own and free her from the gilded cage she wears.

The bustle of clanging dishes, pots, trays, lids, and goblets meet their ears long before they reach the kitchen and the door to the garden. Inside the kitchen, twenty cooks at least, commanded by the head cook with bushy yellow and gray hair, toil and sweat, stacking all manner of pastries, biscuits, fruits, and cheeses on wide silver trays, some already covered. A great number of Mirusian soldiers assist in the preparation and ferry out the trays into the garden.

Outside, the Duchess and Castle Guard have outdone themselves, creating a beautiful, tunneled archway of flowers and lanterns along the path between the hedge maze and the castle's outer wall leading to the croquet court. Rows of potted lilies and small iron candelabras with glowing candles run along the edges of the path. Combined, they create a miraculously lighted gateway to another world. In the distance, the voices of a great number of people clash together with beautiful music.

Citizens from the Crest pass Mary Anne and Grace with little acknowledgment, whispering about the Twins. Mary Anne, on the other hand, walks casually to enjoy this peaceful moment before the night's misadventures begin. She would much rather be in Stonehaven, dancing in the streets and celebrating with the townspeople, rather than here with the upstarts and pompous peacocks from the Crest.

Once Mary Anne and Grace round the corner, the music stops, and the reality of her plan sets into her bones with cold finality. Hundreds upon hundreds crowd the croquet court and the lawn beyond, stretching from the wall of the hedge maze to her left to the edge of the cliff above the harbor to her right, and yet there is still plenty of green between them.

Those from the Crest dress in their finest feathers, furs, and jewelry, the flowers from the Garden wear long sheer dresses of various colors, and the townspeople of Stonehaven attempt to match the splendor of the upper tiers, wearing dresses and coats of fine fabrics without the jeweled embellishments. Hundreds of soldiers from Mirus and Adamas glitter the most in the lantern light. Random glares of judgment from wandering eyes find Mary Anne.

In the middle of the crowd, the Duchess's hat pokes above everyone's bouffant hair styles, accompanied by the Chamberlain's tall personage. Lysander and Uriah gather the largest crowd, in a half circle, not to be blocked for any others to gaze upon them.

Always the preening cocks of any situation. Besides their boots and bracers, they hardly wear anything at all; long half-tunics leave half their bodies uncovered, kept in place by two leather belts around their torsos connected by a golden ring. The slightest breeze or quick movement would expose them to the crowd—a prospect they care little, or nothing about, knowing it will keep the attention on them.

Not quite all the attention. On the opposite side of the lawn, March walks between the separate crowds with a drink in hand. Her sparkling white gown, if it can even be called such, hangs from a silver ring below her neck down between her breasts, swooping down and draping to her knees and back up to another ring at her back. Two other swaths of gray fabric connect to the silver ring, encompass half of her breasts, and must connect in the back. Apparently, they all have the same taste and style of wardrobe, or they are all more similar than Mary Anne would like to believe.

Dormy, with freshly braided hair and wearing her oversized coat, stands behind a small table covered with white linens handing out small scrolls tied closed with twine to every guest who passes. Hundreds of scrolls cram four buckets on the tabletop like a floral arrangement at a wedding, and dozens of empty buckets are stacked on the grass behind her.

Dormy hands one to Mary Anne and to Grace. “Gifts for all those who attend the party. Do not open them until later.”

Mary Anne twists the scroll in hand, curious how Dormy was brought into this and by whom. With no pockets or easily accessible place to hide her scroll, Mary Anne gives hers to Grace to hold then leaves her handmaiden to join the treacherous sea of guests, whose judgment fuels her spite to glide elegantly along the grass.

The deeper she travels into the crowd, the more the thumping of her heart in her ears drowns out the chatter, snide comments, and scoffs. Her heartbeat rather than her words makes her confidence falter. The mask she presents stays intact, but her breaths betray her, quickening, and sending pin pricks up the back of her neck.

A hand slips into hers—Jonathan’s hand—and his smile outshines every lantern in the garden and the moon itself and focuses her thoughts. He leads her to an open section at the center of the lawn and steps in front of her. If her rapid breathing were not enough to buckle her knees, the sight of Jonathan in his crimson longcoat, top hat, and no shirt certainly would.

His icy blue gaze peers out from underneath the brim’s shadow. “May I have this dance?” He brings her hand up and reaches the other around to her back. His presence draws the eyes of everyone else who did not already stare, and a hush falls over the crowd.

“There is no music.”

He motions with his head toward the small orchestra at the far end of the lawn. “This gathering may be for those loyal to Lysander and Uriah, but those who work and support it are loyal to you. Nod to the conductor. He waits for you.”

The conductor, arms poised gracefully in the air, indeed waits for a signal from Mary Anne. She does as Jonathan suggests, and the conductor brings a joyous melody to life. The crowd forms a circle around their makeshift dance floor and watches, intrigued yet still judging. Lysander and Uriah push their way to the front with their pansies. The Duchess and the Chamberlain make their way to the circle's edge.

"You look wonderful." Jonathan sweeps Mary Anne off her feet—the footwork similar enough to a waltz for her to follow. "Let your nerves calm," he says without moving his lips. "I can feel your heart race. Keep your smile to defy all those around us and let me take care of you."

Mary Anne melts into his arms and allows Jonathan to move her as he sees fit, guiding her across the lawn. After several circles, Lysander and Uriah step out with their pansies on their arm and join the dance, not wanting Mary Anne to be the sole focus of the evening. Bronwen appears out of the crowd and joins with a young man from the Crest. More townspeople follow and fill the lawn while others continue to drink, converse, and watch.

"Look what you have accomplished," he whispers.

"What? Gathering all those who despise me in one place?"

"Take a closer look."

Jonathan takes deliberate steps and turns to direct Mary Anne's attention near the hedge maze, where Lacha converses with members of the Crest, along with several other smiths spread out among the crowd, and a great number of her supporters from Stonehaven. Near the cliff, yet more laborers from Stonehaven, clear from their garb, stand with drinks in hand.

"Steady yourself," says Jonathan.

"For what?"

"Dances are often used to hide conversations underneath the music. And I dare say you will have a fair few this evening because you are about to be asked to dance."

"I will decline. We have just begun."

"You feel safe in my arms, and as much as I would like to continue dancing with you throughout the night, you must show strength. You need not worry, I will be close by at all times. Do you trust me?"

"With my life."

Lysander approaches with the blue-haired pansy. “May I continue this dance?”

“Certainly,” says Mary Anne.

Mary Anne does not hesitate, parts with Jonathan, and slips into Lysander’s gargantuan hands. Jonathan trades places gracefully and dances at a distance with the pansy, glancing in Mary Anne’s direction between the other dancing couples as they circle the lawn.

Lysander, tall bear of a man, towers over Mary Anne and does not attempt any pleasantries. His dancing is heavy-footed, and he does not possess half the grace of Jonathan, as Mary Anne believes everything about Lysander would be.

He does not say a word but says volumes with his silver eyes, piercing down at Mary Anne. His hulking figure keeps Mary Anne in his shadow, the sinews of his exposed thigh crawl beneath his skin with every step, and his chest heaves with every low, growling breath. If he believes his presence intimidates Mary Anne, Lysander’s assumption is correct. Fortunately, the direction they turn keeps his tunic in place. His eyes never break from Mary Anne, while she looks to the crowd and meets the gazes of citizens of the Crest and continues to nod at them respectfully. Most women have a quizzical look, and the men keep their gaze lowered on the movement of Mary Anne’s gown, waiting for it to open, and Jonathan, who she seeks often, always finds her with a smile no matter where he is in the dance.

“May I cut in?” Lacha asks, creating a wall with his body.

Even though Lysander was not one for words, Mary Anne may need to endure hours of conversation to this never-ending song. Lysander steps away and wanders off to reclaim his pansy. Lacha takes Mary Anne in hand and does little more than sway and turn their pair in place. Until now, she never noticed how similar he and Lysander are in build, though Lacha’s arms and hands are the larger between the two.

“You came.”

Lacha's eyes drift around the crowd while they dance. "Not to enjoy ourselves. I would much rather be with my people."

"Are they celebrating?"

"Yes. The streets are packed with the people of Stonehaven and the Boroughs. Before coming here, for many, it was the first time I have seen many of them enjoy themselves in a fortnight. This division of yours has served its purpose as a distraction. Only a skeleton crew remains between Stonehaven and the Crest."

"I am glad to hear their spirits lift and hate I must miss it."

"On that, we can agree with all which has transpired, it is time I played my hand. I believe there are several supporters from the Crest who can be swayed, encouraged, or coerced to your side."

"Would anyone?"

"The smiths hold more influence than we like to let on. I am not an alderman because of my size. You can speak to those in the Crest about rights and magic until you're dying breath, but if you do not speak a language they understand and care about, your words fall on deaf ears."

"Money."

He nods. "I do not appreciate being drawn into this fight, but defending Stonehaven is no longer enough. There are several families in the Crest whose businesses heavily rely on the Forge. Threaten to play with their purse strings, and some here will have no choice but to listen and show where their true allegiance lies: with themselves."

"Thank you."

"I do not do this for you."

"Of course. For your people. Hopefully, you will see, despite this current conflict, this is where my intentions lie as well."

"We shall see." Lacha releases his hold on Mary Anne, steps back, bows his head, and rejoins the crowd.

"Perfect timing," says Uriah from behind her, leaving his pansy.

"Care to dance?" Mary Anne asks before he can.

Uriah slides one arm around her body and the other up her wrist to her hand like a coiling snake wrapping around a branch and whips her back into step with the churning dance.

"I must say, this celebration is quaint, yet entertaining. However, I must wonder what purpose you believe this will serve? How does it feel?" he asks, cutting to the point. "To know you have squandered your time."

"You still ignore the fact Wonderland chose me."

"It will matter little in two days' time when our fleet arrives. You have been so consumed with worthless minutia, you forgot the threat looming at your door."

"The people of Mirus are not worthless, and the threat to Mirus and all of Wonderland is not at the door. It is in my hand."

"Of course." Uriah drags her closer. "The townspeople of Mirus can enjoy a night of frivolities to escape their woes. They will only return with the dawn. Do us all a favor: concede this evening, here in front of everyone, and no harm will come to anyone else in Mirus. I give you my word."

"Gracious of you."

"And those who do not wish to remain will be given the chance and adequate time to leave the city peacefully without interference from us."

Mary Anne cannot help but feel the icy fingers of hopelessness crawl down her spine. His damned half-truths are still truth nonetheless. The armada will arrive in two days and they have done little to prepare. Was it folly to believe winning over the people would have any effect on the outcome?

"There will be no concession. You shall not win," she says from beneath her brow.

"My dear, we already have. It is you who have not caught on yet. But you will soon. And the blood in Mirus and Wonderland will be on your hands."

Jonathan appears out of nowhere. "May I finish this dance?" he asks Mary Anne.

"Please." She pulls away from Uriah and welcomes Jonathan's embrace. "I believe there is an unattended flower who needs tending."

Uriah nods with his arrogant half-grin and disappears into the crowd.

Mary Anne lays her head on Jonathan's chest. "What have we done? What have I done? Words, as powerful as you say they are, cannot overcome cannon fire."

"Do not question yourself now." He rests his chin on the top of her head. "Words are still the sharpest of weapons, even more so when whispered. From what I heard dancing around the circle, Lacha and the Forge move against the Crest, not the Twins directly, disrupting the precarious balance they believe they possess, tearing down the pillar propping them up. Despite their threat of warfare and their ships laying siege to the city, they remain, enjoy themselves, and make no preparations to leave. Does this seem as though they are ready to destroy the city?"

"Would they have time? Their treasury, as far as they know, still resides in the Garden."

"Yes, which they would not carelessly leave behind. And amongst all the chatter around the lawn, no one mentions the fleet headed our direction, even in whispers."

Mary Anne finds the smiths and Lacha in the crowd, walking away from those they talk to from the Crest, leaving them in silent bewilderment or frustration, fidgeting with their small scrolls. Their strategy has merit, it works, and Mary Anne can see the pillars crumbling before her eyes. Lysander and Uriah, with pinched brows, look into the crowd at the confused guests, no doubt sensing something amiss. Words indeed have power, as long as there is power to enforce them.

"The truth is dangerous," says Mary Anne. "Words are dangerous. Perhaps it is time we used them as a weapon against Lysander and Uriah instead of remaining silent. Why let such a gathering as this go to waste, when we can announce the Twins' secret to everyone and let them pick off the pieces?"

Mary Anne pulls Jonathan to a table at the far end of the lawn where castle servants distribute drinks among dozens of bottles and casks carted from the cellars. She places Jonathan's hands on her waist, and as if reading her thoughts, he lifts her to stand on the tabletop—her own dais. The conductor stops the music abruptly, leaving the guests in a lurch. Their attention turns to Mary Anne like a slow wave coming up the shore. From across the lawn, Lysander and Uriah narrow their eyes, somehow expecting this but annoyed at Mary Anne's play nonetheless.

She reaches down and cups Jonathan's cheek. "Thank you for everything."

Now is the time. She rises, inhales deeply, ready to lay bare Lysander and Uriah's secrets to all in attendance, but before she can utter a word, Dormy's voice rings through the night air and steals everyone's focus.

CHAPTER 54
MARCH

March drinks a dark rum from a silver goblet, swirling the last drops at the bottom, wishing she swiped the bottle from the tables with various libations, ports, wine, rum, ales, and beers. The soft breeze tickles the small of her back and the curve of her hips. The lecherous eyes and lewd comments of men and women of the Crest, soldiers, and several flowers follow her. Half the guests are hard and the other half are uncomfortable; predictable all around. March deflects their lustful comments and glances as if they were slings and arrows, all unable to pierce her skin. At least in this city of lies, it comforts March to know where everyone stands.

Her heart wanders through the crowd. Jonathan, wearing Mary Anne's damned red coat, scans the crowd in his precious, oblivious nature. March keeps her distance for now. The farther away from him, the less her heart aches.

Adamasite soldiers, fully armored and armed, mill about the guests, each with six glass orbs clicking at their waist, prepared for another attack from Cheshire. If they knew him well, they would understand he will not attempt the same strategy twice because the game has already been given away, and the next will be far worse. If he wanted, he could swallow the entire lawn in a shadow as he did the cult. However, March's and Jonathan's presence limits his action, unwilling to harm them.

The glint of lantern light on the soldiers' swords calls to March. Although comfortable in her wardrobe, she feels naked without her steel on her hips and at her back. Fortunately, March had the foresight to hide two of her own among the casks at the edge of the lawn.

The young Mirusian soldier with the blue hair sporadically catches her eyes through the crowd. He hides something and overcompensates for it, making his erratic head movement all the more suspect. Serving girls walk amongst the guests with silver trays piled with biscuits, tarts, and small cakes. Curiously, soldiers of Mirus join them, carrying platters covered with silver cloches.

A thin young man from the Crest wearing a white cropped jacket reaches out to run the curve of his fingers across March's hip. She grabs the tips of two of his fingers before they can touch her and brings the goblet down onto his knuckles—*crack*—and March snaps his fingers to the side. The guests around him snicker and guffaw at this reckless and stupid attempt. Before he can curse, March grabs the back of his neck, flips her goblet upside down, and shoves the wide base into his mouth, clicking against his teeth and stretching his cheeks.

"Is this what you wanted?" she asks him. "To be close to me? Is it everything you dreamed of?"

The crowd around her falls silent as the man whimpers in pain.

"All I need to do is press down and flick my wrist to pop your jaw from its socket. Would you like that?"

He attempts to say 'no' the best he can, with tears running down his face and snot seeping out of his nose. March pulls the goblet from his mouth, clacking against each of his teeth and chipping his bottom front pair.

"Get the fuck out of my sight."

He holds his wrist, fingers bent at odd angles, and cries, running from the garden. When the spectacle is over, the crowd does not return to their vulgar gestures or fantasies; instead, the refreshing, frozen expressions of fear fill March's cup. But snaking through the crowd, the fear fades, replaced by the salacious thoughts plain on every guest's face.

Bronwen makes her rounds through the crowd, making her presence known to all. The sight of her bears down on March's shoulders. Bronwen questions her neighbors about the scrolls and attempts to pry one from their hands. They find it amusing to hold something over Bronwen, to have something when she does not. Their selfish and competitive nature keep March's plan in motion and Bronwen in the dark.

Dormy appears by March's side, a small lantern in hand, and taps her arm with a small scroll, saving her from the drowning pressure on her chest. "I did as you asked. There are still quite a few left over, but everyone from the Crest and the soldiers has scrolls. Everyone except Bronwen."

"You are a wonder, little mouse. Are you prepared for the second part?"

"Yes, but speaking in front of everyone frightens me, if I am not selling something to them."

"You will not be in front of anyone. You shall be alone in the tower. And you spoke bravely when you defied Lysander and Uriah."

"Oh. right. I can do it. When should I be off?"

"The sooner the better. Best to take your leave now. I do not want you here for whatever is to follow."

Dormy nods and scurries into the crowd, but returns. "I never had the chance to tell you. I am sorry."

"Whatever for?"

Dormy holds up the scroll. "I had to read it over a thousand times, and it hurt me every time, knowing you had to endure it. I can't imagine what you must feel, what you must have felt."

Tears rise in March's throat like unexpected bile, and she swallows to keep them at bay. "You do not need to apologize."

"I know. I do because I know the ones who are responsible never will."

"Off with you." March waves Dormy away, lips pressed and quivering, before her marmalade, doe eyes break her further.

Dormy walks through the crowd, holding the lantern high with a straight arm. A signal, but a signal to what? March glances up at the tower, expecting to see another lantern, another signal, but who else would there be?

Finally, Mary Anne arrives late to her own celebration with her ever-present odd mixture of natural superiority and false confidence. March purposely stretches and slinks through the guests to keep their eyes on her instead of Mary Anne. Despite her attempt to mimic March's wardrobe, she will find herself a pale comparison. She does so to anger Mary Anne and to distract herself from seeing Jonathan approach her.

"Fuck."

March's wiles attract the attention of two she hoped to avoid since arriving. Lysander and Uriah saunter up to her with the two remaining pansies on their arm.

"You are a vision," says Uriah, admiring the curves of her body, fingers fidgeting, wanting to reach out. "You make it quite hard."

"I make *you* quite hard, apparently. The both of you."

Their cocks press and bulge against their hanging half-tunics and come precariously close to slipping out the side completely.

"Do not worry, I doubt anyone would notice."

"Lie to yourself all you like," says Lysander. "You have watched when our prowess is at its prime."

"Still, my men are more than you two shall ever be, in every attribute."

"But where are they?" Uriah asks pointedly and looks toward Jonathan and Mary Anne.

The small orchestra seated nearby brings sweet and lively music to the air at the command of the conductor, who summons his own magic with the wave of his hands. She would enjoy the melody on the wind if not for Jonathan taking Mary Anne in his arms to dance. Her skin crawls with the legs of a thousand darkling beetles.

Uriah adjusts his tunic over his cock, but the more he tries to conceal himself, the harder he becomes. "We could not help but notice the small gifts distributed to all who attend. Almost all. You mean to go through with it."

"Do not let it go to waste," says March.

"Indeed," says Lysander. "Save us a dance."

He and his brother wrap themselves around the pansies and join the swirling torrent of the dance, propelling themselves closer to Jonathan and Mary Anne. The blue-haired soldier finds her again through the crowd and nods as if given some silent unknown command, amongst the other continued wandering eyes of men and women.

March turns sharply, gown flaring. The less attention on Mary Anne, the better, especially now, dancing with Jonathan. March cannot see it as anything more than it is: an insult. For which Mary Anne will pay soon enough. She wants to slice the smirk from Mary Anne's face with the daggers she has hidden in her boots, but Jonathan's smile cuts deeper.

March, consumed by her thoughts, loses time, unsure of how much, but aware everyone around her has moved positions. She cannot see Jonathan and Mary Anne in the dancing area. Instead, she locates Lysander and Uriah and follows their grimaces far to the left, where Jonathan hoists Mary Anne onto a table. *Damn it.* Whatever spontaneous whim Mary Anne has will derail March's plan already in motion.

"Hurry, little mouse."

She pushes one of the Mirusian guards carrying a tray out of the way to watch Mary Anne reach down and caress Jonathan's cheek. If not so wrapped in what is about to transpire, March would cut her hand off. She does not need both to be a queen, and Mary Anne can return to her world with a permanent reminder.

Dormy clears her throat in the announcement system. March sighs with relief and a shred of panic, looking at the stone songbirds perched atop the castle walls.

"Ladies and gentlemen, I am sorry to interrupt your revelry this night, but there's an important matter to address. To those in Stonehaven, you can find the same parchment nailed to several of the doors on the outskirts of the Row. Those of you on the castle grounds were handed a scroll this evening." A great huff of breath fills a long break. The seconds may as well last a week. "Please, open them now."

"What is the meaning of this?" asks Mary Anne, upset that her moment has been stolen, though it was never hers to begin with.

"What you have in your hand is a reproduction of a contract scribed by Seamus and Bronwen March."

The scratch and cracking of parchment fills the lawn. Everyone looks down at the parchment—all except March and Bronwen. The white of Bronwen's eyes surrounds her pupils, and her bosom heaves against her corset with each breath. She understands and realizes, helpless, there is nothing she can do.

"May I direct your attention to the last paragraph," Dormy continues. "It reads, 'Therefore, in addition to the exchange for three hundred and twenty-five custom, hand-crafted weapons of the finest quality for the agreed upon price of five thousand gold pieces, ten stone of pink diamonds, emeralds, sapphires, and golden pearls, the dealers allow the company and use of their daughter in whatever manner they see fit for the term of one week's time, excluding travel, under the conditions the purchaser returns her unblemished and without imperfection.'"

The breeze rustles through the hedge maze. Not a piece of armor scrapes against another, nor does parchment roll back against itself. The world has stopped as the truth settles.

March turns to find Jonathan, tears in his eyes. He knew, he sensed, but this is the first time he has heard the words out loud. His heart breaks, and so does hers, standing so far apart from each other.

"This is the last of many contracts signed by Seamus and Bronwen promising me to grown men." March raises her voice to address the crowd, fighting the unfamiliar quiver in her voice and accepts the power in the truth, despite the uneasy vulnerability clawing at her back and neck. "The first was written when I was in my thirteenth year and the last in my eighteenth, with several hundred in between. They stopped because I fled. She would have you believe I am some whore to cover up her own actions. The rumors you hear began with her."

"She lies!" Bronwen screams, pushing her way through the crowd toward March. The calm demeanor she wears like a protective coat slowly unravels. "Look at her, my wanton strumpet of a daughter. The proof is before your eyes. She parades around for all of you to lust after her for one reason. You can trust nothing out of her mouth."

"But you can trust our words," Uriah shouts, taking all by surprise and stopping Bronwen in her tracks. "The contract you hold in your possession is real and perpetrated by Bronwen and Seamus."

"If you know us," says Lysander, "you know we hold family and honor in the highest regard. You, Bronwen, have betrayed and sold your own blood for your financial gain and status, and parade through the city with not a hint of shame or guilt for your actions."

"Reprehensible and unforgivable," says Uriah. "To your own daughter."

"You dare turn against me?" Bronwen screeches at the Twins, her coat threadbare. "After all I have done for you?"

"True, you have done a great deal for us, our family, and this city," says Uriah. "But we cannot and will not have any further dealings with the likes of you. Vile, loathsome, and base serpent."

The silence of the crowd turns to murmurs, murmurs to whispers, and whispers to shouts, all directed at Bronwen. They all call down every manner of horrible curses on her, wishing plagues, loss, death, and suffering.

"Wait," Bronwen pleads on the edge of tears. "Wait, this is not true. This is all a lie orchestrated by the three of them to see my house fall so theirs can rise. You know she plans to marry both of them."

"Untrue. Another lie from Bronwen," Lysander shouts.

"Please listen to me. Hear me." The roar of the crowd overtakes her words. Music to March's ears. "You dare turn on me? My family's wealth built the Crest. I will reclaim everything. I will see you all living on the streets of the Boroughs, groveling for food, stained with shit, sleeping in gutters."

The crowd pushes against her like the tide against sand, inching her toward the exit. No matter how much Bronwen screams, no one will hear her. From across the lawn, she meets March's eyes once more, eyes and face red, unwillingly accepting defeat and walking, refusing to run, from the garden. Once gone, the crowd turns back to March, their faces washed with confusion, shock, guilty understanding, and pity as years of lies and truth bubble up to the surface and take shape. Lysander and Uriah alone nod to her. Damn them.

Sensing his presence, March turns and falls into Jonathan's embrace. His heart thumps against her cheek, and his staggered breaths raise and lower her head with an uneven rhythm. For a moment, all the world and everyone else in the garden vanish, leaving her and Jonathan alone in the back and forth of their hearts.

He could say a multitude but will not, not here, perhaps never; he does not need to. Jonathan understands, and this is most important. "Another drink?" he asks.

"More than one," says March.

Together, they walk to the cluster of tables and hundreds of bottles and casks, coincidentally where Mary Anne waits. Moonlight and lantern light contour the smooth necks and bodies of multicolored glass. March takes an unopened bottle of rum, to no protest from the servants pouring drinks, uncorks the bottle with her teeth, and spits it onto the lawn. Jonathan catches it on its downward arch and pockets it with a wink.

Silver slides against silver as the Mirusian soldiers scattered throughout the crowd uncover their platters to reveal stacks of elegant powder-covered tarts with the aroma of custard and treacle. Jonathan reaches for a tart from a nearby tray, but the soldier moves it beyond his reach. He tries again, and the blue-haired soldier grabs Jonathan's wrist while the other soldier walks into the crowd.

"Apologies. Do not touch the tarts," the soldier says.

March searches the crowd and discovers the Mirusian soldiers distribute the tarts exclusively to the Adamasite soldiers and citizens from the Crest.

"What is the meaning of this?" she asks the soldier.

"What do you mean? We follow the plan."

"Whose plan?"

Confounded, the soldier reaches for his belt, produces a scroll, and holds it out for March. "Why, the Gryphon's plan."

"The Gryphon is missing, you damned fool."

March snatches the scroll from the soldier, recognizing the Gryphon's seal instantly. *Fuck.* Unfurling the scroll, Dormy's expert, counterfeit penmanship is plain. *Damn it.* Before she can read it, Cheshire appears atop one of the tall posts connecting the string of lanterns, balancing on the narrow, rounded top. The moon outlines his dark silhouette, hood up, face in shadow, cloak swaying in the wind like a clock's pendulum counting down, and arms spread out as a conductor, ready to start his own morbid dirge.

The screams begin slow, rising from the crowd like smoke, and crescendo into wails of horror to chill the marrow. Adamasite soldiers thrash as if a netherworld spirit possesses their bodies, grabbing their swords to attack whatever specter torments them, but they lose control of their faculties and some slice through the well-dressed citizens of the Crest. The rich are not immune. They scream and fall to their knees, eyes wide, and mouth agape, never experiencing genuine fear before. One by one, they collapse to the ground like rag dolls until their screams fade. Once one disappears, another set rises to take its place, ebbing and flowing like an unholy choir, and all the while Cheshire waves his hands back and forth, enjoying this new chaos he wrought.

Those not affected, including the Duchess, Weiss, and the flowers, should escape the garden but crush against the castle walls and hedge maze, watching with morbid, horrified curiosity. The smiths hold a line in front of the cowering guests, hammers from their belts at the ready. Lysander and Uriah take up their weapons from nearby soldiers and stand back-to-back. Jonathan pulls Mary Anne behind him.

"What is happening?" Mary Anne asks, as confused as the rest of them.

March has no fucking idea what affects them, but Cheshire does. He orchestrated everything: the kidnapping of the Gryphon, his forged seal, Dormy's script, and now this. It is seldom, but March saw it in his eyes and heard it in his voice the last time they were on the croquet court; he needed to remind the world what he is capable of. Pardon be damned. At least he had the courtesy to wait until after her confrontation with Bronwen. Servants behind them scatter, knocking over bottles, casks, and goblets. The orchestra flees with a discord of notes and thuds, unwilling to leave their instruments.

With no time to read the scroll, March chokes the blue-haired soldier with one hand. "What was the order?"

Mirusian soldiers drop their trays, outnumbering the conscious Adamasite ten to one, unsheathe their swords, and force the remaining soldiers toward the edge of the cliff.

"A counter offensive." The soldier lowers to one knee, taken aback by March's reaction. "The Gryphon gave us the means to fight back. We were given specific instructions, and we followed them, and even went further."

The Adamasite flail their arms when their steps find the edge of their world, the end of their world, the edge of the cliff hundreds of feet above the harbor.

"Seeing as how few soldiers remained in the city, we planned a coordinated strike here and in the streets. To strike a blow to cripple the occupation of Mirus once and for all."

Several soldiers of Mirus follow behind the curving, crunching wall, driving the Adamasite soldiers to the cliff, and plunge their swords into the necks and heads of the unconscious soldiers on the grass. This is not a fight; this is a slaughter.

Familiar plunks followed by unmistakable, faint whistles signal the next attack. The Gryphon's archers conceal themselves somewhere in the hedge maze and rain down death with diabolical precision. Arrows puncture soldiers' necks, spurting with blood, breastplates to pierce lung or heart, and legs to topple their enemies to the ground.

Uriah, with the hells in his eyes, swats arrows away with his whip, a whirlwind as wild as a dragon's tail, snapping them in midair. Lysander picks up one of their soldiers and uses his body as a shield. Adamasite soldiers fall behind them, from the arrows, or from taking one step too far, dooming themselves to a more horrific fate, wishing for an arrow instead of the rocks and timbers below. Their screams fade into the nothingness of their descent. Hundreds upon hundreds of Lysander and Uriah's men greet death this night. All the while, Cheshire stands unmoving, waving his hands back and forth, with the glint of his wide grin beneath his hood.

"We have done it!" the blue-haired soldier shouts.

The Twins turn toward their trio. They are predators, and nothing is more dangerous than a predator who is cornered.

March pushes the soldier to the grass. "You have done nothing but pry open the gates to every hell and unleashed them all into the castle. You believed you quelled a threat, but all you did was spark a raging, all-consuming inferno."

CHAPTER 55
JONATHAN

Jonathan pulls a sword from a dead soldier and leads Mary Anne over the field of corpses strewn across the grass in order to leave. March retrieves her swords from behind the table and follows close behind. Their eyes meet, and together they know while hundreds of Mirusian soldiers stand between them and the Twins, the soldiers stand no chance. Provoked, Lysander and Uriah turn their attention to Mary Anne, Jonathan, and March, and they will cut through anyone in their way.

"Bitch." Lysander holds his sword out with a single arm and points it at Mary Anne. "Falsifier."

"Face us!" shouts Uriah.

The Mirusian soldiers assemble in between the Twins and the trio to block their advance, but they fall as easy as chaff before the reaper. Each swipe from Lysander's longsword, fueled by his rage, cuts no less than two men in half, flinging swaths of blood through the air. Soldiers split in twain fall to the ground, arms flailing, screaming, and crawl on the lawn, pulling at the short grass until the blood and life seep out of them. Lysander's broad sweeps cleave through bone—a master butcher—slicing thighs and shins as easily as if they were on the chopping block. Riotous screams of anguish fill the air from the injured and dying and mix with the shrieks from the guests made to watch.

What Uriah lacks in size and strength compared to his brother, he far makes up for in dexterity and cruelty. With the first crack of his whip, he breaks a man's face and skull in half, split open like a melon. The long leather tendril bends to his will and wraps around another soldier's neck. With a single yank and roar, his head rips from his body. Uriah's glaive slices at the throats and jabs at the inner thighs of Mirusian soldiers, covering his and his brother's tunics in ribbons of blood. They cut a path through the soldiers like a field of wheat, making their way toward Mary Anne.

"It appears we may have no choice but to fight," says Jonathan.

"We are ill-equipped to do so at the moment," says March. She looks to the post where Cheshire stood to find it empty.

The Twins continue their slaughter unabated. Uriah wraps his whip around another soldier's neck and propels himself forward, kneeing the soldier in the jaw while plunging his blade into the face of another. Lysander brings his longsword down and splits a man from shoulder to stomach. The Mirusian soldiers, loyal to the end, swarm and fight to the last breath to keep the Twins at bay, to no avail. Each strike deflected, each swing blocked, and each arrow broken.

"You see, the treachery of your would-be queen." Lysander lifts a soldier by the neck, crushes it in hand, and flings the dead body against the others, leaving them open for a gaping slash across their faces.

Uriah summons thunder with every loud, deadly crack of his whip.

"We must face them," says Mary Anne. "Otherwise, we appear the villains, and they appear justified in their actions."

"Again, you speak as if you will lift a sword against them," says March. "Look at the massacre in front of you."

"We can speak to them."

"Enough with your delusion."

"Stop. No matter what you say," says Jonathan, "they will not listen. They are beyond our words."

Lysander bursts the line of Mirusian soldiers and barrels straight for Mary Anne. Jonathan pushes her away toward the crowd of guests and prepares to take the brunt of the attack.

"Dodge," March shouts.

Jonathan heeds her words on instinct. He steps out of the way in time, but Lysander's strike breaks the Adamas sword Jonathan carries and buries itself deep into the earth. Jonathan meant to block the attack, but he knew the quality of Adamas steel would not hold up to the force behind Lysander. Taking the brief opening, Jonathan strikes Lysander across the face with the pommel of his sword and evades a wild backhand from Lysander's stone of a fist. March slashes at Lysander's hand at his grip, but he pulls it free a second sooner for their steel to clash.

"Stop, this instance!" Mary Anne shouts.

Lysander swings wide, and Jonathan and March dart in close to avoid his swords. She stabs at his torso but holds back. If she followed through, her blade would deflect and hit Jonathan. They are out of step. In such close quarters, their swords lose their potency, so they try to rake the edge of their blades across his skin. March drops one of her swords, pulls a dagger hidden in her boot, and plunges it in the side of Lysander's thigh. Unfazed, he bats her away with his forearm, sending her skidding across the grass. She stops herself right before Uriah's whip digs into the earth, right where her head would have been.

Uriah keeps March pinned, trapped, at a distance, his whip cutting off her path in both directions, digging deeper with every crack. Soldiers who risk attacking him from the rear fall victim to the quick slices of his glaive. He handles both weapons with the ease of an artist's brush.

Jonathan must reach March, but Lysander blocks his way. He drops his broken sword and lands blow after blow to Lysander's face, and finally swings upward with clasped fists, causing the brute to stumble back for the first time. A thrusting kick to Lysander's knee allows Jonathan the time he needs to circle around Lysander, pick up another fallen sword, and launch it at Uriah like a spear. He knocks it out of the air with the end of his glaive. March takes the precious seconds she needs, gets to her feet, and hurls a second dagger at him, clacking against the staff of his glaive, barely missing his neck.

In his haste to regroup with March, Jonathan made a grave mistake: placing them both between the Twins, which will make evading their combined attacks difficult. However, only Uriah faces them, whip cracking at their heads. Lysander, with Jonathan out of the way, stalks toward Mary Anne as she backs closer to the crowded guests. The sharp, biting sting of Uriah's whip wraps around both of Jonathan's ankles, trapping him, and bringing him crashing to the ground. The whip would have broken his bones if Uriah did not have to dodge a strike from March's blade to the chest, lessening his power.

Jonathan unwraps the whip from his feet and twists it around his hand, robbing Uriah of one of his weapons. He may be skilled with this weapon, but Jonathan is far stronger. The metal core within the leather whip digs into Jonathan's fingers. He pulls Uriah off balance, giving March the opportunity to face him properly, blades rebounding off the staff of his glaive.

With March closer to Uriah, out of the whip's destructive reach, Jonathan leaps on Lysander's back, wraps his arms around his trunk-like throat, and steps on the back of his knee. Despite all of Jonathan's strength, Lysander resists and swings an elbow back, connecting with the side of Jonathan's head. Dazed but unwilling to release the beast of a man, Jonathan reaches over his head and scrapes upward at his face, fingers pulling at his nose and eyes. No matter the size or thickness of muscles, there are parts of the body that will always be vulnerable, and Lysander and Uriah are not accustomed to facing opponents in close quarters with their ranged strategy. Lysander screams as Jonathan brings him to a knee.

Unfortunately, Lysander uses his lowered position to his advantage, reaches back, knocks the hat from Jonathan's head, grabs him by the hair, flips him over, and slams him to the ground. In truth, Jonathan had no choice but to succumb and leap, otherwise, Lysander would have pulled his scalp from his skull.

Mary Anne trips backward over one of the unconscious women of the Crest. Jonathan, using the momentum, rolls away and scrambles to her and another nearby sword. Hanging lanterns cast Lysander's growing shadow over them as he stands—an enveloping death shroud. Mary Anne's face loses all color, and her eyes grow beyond saucers.

"Jonathan!" she screams.

Is this it? he wonders. After the countless lifetimes he has lived, everything he has done and endured, is this where he meets his end? With a woman from another world by his side instead of his loves? If it is, he will not surrender—raising the sword—and will not die with his back turned.

He spins, and Lysander's blade plunges into flesh and carves bone with a deep and final wet squelch and snap. Both Jonathan and Mary Anne gasp and hold their breath as the world stops. Blood spurts onto Jonathan's face.

Lacha, grimacing with anger more than pain, stepped between them and blocked the deadly blow. Why the giant smith chose to be a shield instead of a weapon, Jonathan will never know. The crowd gasps, screams, curses, and everyone, including Lacha, cannot take their eyes away from the wide blade jutting out of the center of his chest.

CHAPTER 56
MARY ANNE

Tears swell in her eyes, mind tumbling, speechless, and in utter shock. One word manifests in her mind over and over again. *Why?* Mary Anne will not speak it out loud and sully Lacha's bravery and sacrifice.

He raises his eyes to her. "For my people. For our people," says Lacha, with gargled, labored breaths, then turns and, blade still piercing his chest, manages to strike Lysander across the face again and again, backing him across the lawn, with the same loud cracks of Uriah's whip.

Each blow snaps Lysander's head from side to side, until he throws both forearms up to block any further attacks, claps the blade in between his hands, and twists with a jerk. A loud and final *crack* sends Lacha crumpling to his knees. Lysander walks around him, puts a boot to his back, and pulls the longsword from his body. Lacha, their savior, crashes to the earth like a felled tree in the forest.

Jonathan, sword in hand, unleashes a barrage of thrusts and overhead strikes, screaming with each, using the sword more like a smith's hammer, only giving Lysander the time to block, not recover. Not far behind them, March leaps through the air to avoid Uriah's swirling whip and dances around him, two swords in hand once again, spinning and slicing at him—two cyclones in combat with each other.

On the verge of tears, Mary Anne pulls at the grass and claws her way to Lacha's body. It takes all her strength, grunting, and struggling to roll his massive body over to his back. All color fades from his face, and his vacant stare searches far over the horizon to the next world. Her heart thunders in her head, and her eyes throb in and out of focus from the pressure. She wants to cry out or release some primal scream, but it will mean nothing. This must end one way or another.

The crowd behind Mary Anne, despite being from the Crest, shed tears at the loss of the alderman—a man truly respected throughout the city. The other smiths grip their hammers in hand, ready to snap the wooden handles into kindling. Veins bulge from their arms and neck, sweat cascades down their brows, hate fills their bloodshot eyes, and they stalk forward to avenge their fallen leader, their friend, their brother, and join the remaining soldiers of Mirus. The Twins put on the defensive, dodge attacks from all sides from hammer and blade and fend off the combined forces of Jonathan, March, soldier, and smith.

Mary Anne rummages through her mind to pluck out a single memory she believed to be insignificant at the time. *What was it?* The word dances behind her tingling lips. "Aon," she says, trying to pull the memory from the mire. "Aon." The thought clicks into place like the gears in a clock striking the end of the day. "Aon Praelium." There it is. "Aon Praelium!"

The guests whisper and murmur to each other. The Duchess finally runs up to Mary Anne. Mirusian soldiers, those who remain, stop fighting and back away. The Twins, Jonathan, and March lower their weapons but remain locked in a battle within their eyes, wishing death upon their opponents. This is old magic; the same that binds Jonathan to Mary Anne. All must obey.

"A duel between two combatants, two champions." Mary Anne rises and dusts off her knees. The smiths gather around Lacha. "I have had enough of this and enough of the both of you, your schemes, lies, and deceit."

Uriah recalls his whip and wraps it over his shoulder. "You dare accuse us of lies when we attended your fucking festival, knowing one of yours already slaughtered our men, and yours, on this very ground. We laid our trust at your feet and you stepped on its neck until you suffocated it. You accuse us of being malcontents when you and yours plot against us? Does this not reinforce the reason she should never take the throne?" he asks the crowd.

Mary Anne glances over her shoulder. The guests look upon her in fear, others hatred, others disgust. They will not understand all this was Cheshire's doing, and even though he said not to take credit for his atrocities previously, Mary Anne must take responsibility in her own way.

"It does not matter now. Aon Praelium has been invoked," she says, not even knowing if this is fully true or not. All Mary Anne has to go on are the words of the two biggest deceivers in Wonderland. "Two will determine the end of this feud once and for all." She looks to the Duchess, who nods with confirmation.

"To the death," says Lysander, rising to his feet.

"No." Mary Anne seethes. "I called upon the old magic. I set the terms. There has been enough bloodshed on both sides. This is not what we wanted. You blame me, but your challenge to the throne began this trail of blood and tears. The champion who bests the other in single combat will be the victor and determine who sits upon the throne."

"Agreed," the Twins say together. A suspicious smile creeps across their faces.

"Choose your champion," says Lysander.

There is little choice in the matter. Perhaps she should consider the Gryphon, but with him unaccounted for, her best choice is her first choice. In truth, she would select no other.

"Mary Anne, wait," says the Duchess.

"Jonathan Carter," she says, without hesitation. "My champion is

Jonathan Carter." After all, he has been her hero, and she has seen him overcome insurmountable odds since they first met near Rookridge—brigands, the Ace, mercenaries, the cult, and now, facing off against Lysander without the interference of Uriah, he proves to be his match. If anyone possesses a chance to defeat one of the Twins, he does.

"Mary Anne, no," he whispers. He turns to her, brow pinched, anguish and gloom dulling his brilliant eyes.

The Duchess places her hands on her shoulder. "Moving first in a game of strategy gives the game away."

"Audrianna March," Uriah says with unwavering confidence and a sinister grin. "Our champion shall be none other than the greatest sword in all of Wonderland."

"No!" shouts Mary Anne. "What trickery is this? Why? Why would you? I will never allow—"

"Accepted." March steps forward and brushes her sweat-soaked hair from her forehead.

"What?" Mary Anne clasps her hands over her mouth.

"Dear heart," says Jonathan. "Why?"

"You question me now? To be done with this. Done with her. What will you do, dear heart? Will you strike me down for her?"

"I... I cannot. I will not."

"You must, because she chose you as her champion. Do not blame me more than my choices, when the reason stands there behind you, hands clean as always. I accept," March repeats. "Time and location."

"One hour hence," says Lysander.

"The Long Bridge above the Boroughs, for all the city to assemble and watch," says Uriah.

"Done." March leaves the field without so much as a side glance at Jonathan, signal, secret conversation, hint, or plan. The Twins follow her without a look in Mary Anne's direction.

This is perhaps the gravest mistake Mary Anne has made. She had the most honest and true of intentions; how could she have known? During

Jonathan and March's last confrontation, she could not see his face, only the effects. Here, she bears witness as his sweet face plunges into utter despair, and a cold apathy washes over March.

From Uriah's smile, it is as if he believes he orchestrated and predicted Mary Anne's decision, and she fears he did. Mary Anne would know nothing of the old magic decrees if not for the information provided by the Twins. Their presence kept Jonathan and March apart, emboldening Mary Anne's advances toward him. Earlier they arrived together, suspicious in itself, in time to catch Mary Anne and Jonathan together, fueling March's hatred, giving her a genuine reason for retaliation.

Jonathan can best one of the Twins, Mary Anne is sure of it. However, a chilling spike of doubt stabs into Mary Anne's heart. Can he defeat March? Could he? Would he? An impossible, paradoxical choice. She wanted to separate them, but not this way, inadvertently placing her own fate in the hands and steel of the man she loves and the woman he loves.

CHAPTER 57

CHESHIRE

A single candle sits in its holder on the dirt-covered ground, flame slowly dancing, and creates a small pulsing world in an expanse of darkness. The edge of the warm glow reaches out and laps at the Gryphon's bare feet up to his ankles like the soft tide of a pond. Cheshire squats and picks up pebbles between his toes and tosses them across the circle at the Gryphon's head. They thud on his hair, bounce off, and click and plink across the ground. Finally, the drunkard snaps from this stupor, roars, and clumsily punches and claws at the air and ground without his bearings, thinking he is still in the vat of whiskey, and desperately tries to save himself. He takes nearly a minute to realize he is no longer in danger of drowning and falls limp onto the floor again. Cheshire picks up a larger stone between his toes and hurls it at the Gryphon's forehead. It clacks against his head and skids away.

"Welcome back." Cheshire's voice echoes throughout the darkness.

"Damn you, boy," says the Gryphon, or at least this is what Cheshire makes out through the slurred and garbled mess. He grabs at his head and groans from the slap, the pain from the stone, and the headache from the whiskey. He searches his thighs and back for his sword and finds only bare skin. "Where the fuck are my clothes?"

"Ah, you see. Since you have had your fill, and I have your confession, I need you to sober yourself again. With everything you wore soaked to the thread with whiskey, it would not be prudent to leave you with such temptation. I cannot have you prolong your stay here any longer than necessary, twisting the ends of your sleeves and coat tail to leech the last drop of liquor on your tongue and licking at the seams. Worry not. They will be laundered and returned to you when you prove yourself ready to be released. And please do not try to suck at your beard or hair; I made sure they were thoroughly washed and oiled."

The Gryphon gathers his strength, claws at the ground to turn around, and pulls himself into the light, wincing as even the dim light of the candle hurts his eyes as if he stared into the sun. His head wobbles, like a newborn babe, unable to support its weight. He heaves several times but cannot vomit, but probably wishes he could.

Cheshire steps into the light. "We also made sure you had nothing left in your stomach. You drunkard"—Cheshire laughs—"you must have imbibed at least twenty bottles' worth of whiskey. I do not know the bounds of your sickness and addiction and cannot have you lapping at your own sick like a dog."

"Where have you brought me?" The Gryphon succumbs to the dizzying flop of his head and rolls onto his back.

Cheshire follows the Gryphon's gaze, past the candle's warmth, to a small circle no larger than a cork high above them in the darkness—the grate to the oubliette.

"No. No. No. I cannot be here. Free me at once. Take me from this hell."

"All in due time." Cheshire walks the faded perimeter of the circle, halfway in the light and halfway in the dark until he stands behind the Gryphon. "I am not sure how long it took you to dry out after the first time I found you. Rest assured, there will be no infirmary or physicians to attend you. It will be you, the bottles of water lowered down to you, the darkness, and your thoughts. But, since you must cleanse yourself of only a day's worth of debauchery instead of centuries, it should not take long."

"Damn you."

"Yes, yes, I have heard it all before. You have naught but yourself to blame for your predicament and penance. Think of all the lives you could have spared—all of your soldiers, castle guards, and archers—had you told me the truth from the start?"

"Laughable coming from you." The Gryphon fights against his shaking body to get to his feet and collapses three times before managing to remain upright on a knee. "Do not speak as if you are capable of mercy." The Gryphon shakes with the legs of a newborn fawn. His shadow spreads across the ground and reaches out for Cheshire. "You would have killed them sooner or later."

"I said spared, not saved. Quite the difference. And do not assume what I am capable of. But back to the topic at hand. You will be proud to know the loyalty of your men, soldiers, and guards knows no bounds, and they followed your orders better than expected."

"I gave no orders." The Gryphon sways, able to stand yet still hunched over, swaying like a blade of grass in the wind and having to catch himself with pitiful small steps to keep his balance. He looks at his hand and the discolored space where he wore his ring. "What have you done?"

"Of course you gave no orders. However, they believed so. What a glorious slaughter a forgery, your seal, and a little creativity can be wrought. It was a bloody gambit and masterfully played, if I do say so myself. The forces of Lysander and Uriah are a fourth of what they once were, by my count, and the soldiers of Mirus fought bravely, valiantly even—to the death. Your side suffered great losses as well, not as many, but the Twins, forces to be reckoned with, put the soldiers of Mirus to slaughter before I left to come here to check on you."

The Gryphon's back cracks over and over as he straightens and forces himself still. His long shadow dances at Cheshire's toes. "You play with life so meaninglessly, as if they, we, are pieces in your game."

"Are you not? And how dare you say what I plan out and suffer for, namely at your hands, is meaningless? Every death is carefully thought out, even in the moment, and there are still many more to come."

"And I am to be included among your number?"

"You are, but not yet. The reason I grant you life, and why you must sober yourself, is because I will give you a chance at redemption. A chance to put your greatest shame to rest. My mother lives, and you will continue your search for her. It will be your first and only priority."

The Gryphon slowly turns to face Cheshire. His long damp hair swings back and forth in front of his eyes. "I serve Wonderland."

"And my mother is Wonderland." Cheshire bites every word.

"I serve Wonderland."

Cheshire's tone brightens as quickly as the flit of birds' wings. "Wonderful. And since you are already strong enough to stand, it should not take you long to fully recover."

"Damn you, boy. Damn you." The Gryphon stumbles forward clumsily and reaches out his long arms for Cheshire's neck.

The lesser the distance, the farther his shadow from the candle travels up Cheshire's body—knees, chest, and head. With a wave of his hand, Cheshire summons the Mask of Shadows and takes a step forward, traveling through the Gryphon's chest and into the brazier-lit dungeon above, emerging from one of the tall stone supports of the broken bridge overhead. The Gryphon screams and rages far below. Despite the echo, he may as well shout for help from miles away.

Around the far side of the support, Pat and Bill sit on a nearby wooden bench, their overalls askew. She waits, arms crossed and arms flexed, while he polishes the Gryphon's pauldrons with a linen rag. Since their time together in the Pool of Tears, Pat and Bill have worked tirelessly at Cheshire's request to restore the dungeon for its new prisoner.

"Thank you for making the preparations for our guest." Cheshire walks behind them and sets a hand on each of their bare shoulders.

"It was only a matter of time before we made use of the dungeon again," says Pat. "It was on our list."

"We are to be prison guards, now?" asks Bill.

"Hardly," says Cheshire. "A temporary nursemaid. Check in, feed him, water him, whatever. I guess that makes you more of a gardener. Either way, do not let him die. I am off to see what remains of the bloody field of battle. I may collect Dormy for her to have her pick of the spoils littered along the grass."

"You return to the croquet court?" asks Bill.

"And not the Long Bridge?" asks Pat.

Before he asks, their tone brings an unsettled feeling in Cheshire's chest. They know something he does not, and there is nothing he hates more than not knowing. He left too early. There should be no need for the fight to move locations if everyone had done their jobs correctly. He has been gone from the croquet court for half an hour's time.

"Everything was in motion. The killing spree was underway. What, or who, must I hold responsible for ruining my plan? I do not know why I ask. Mary Anne? My gut tells me I must charge Mary Anne with this mischief and thank her quite gruesomely for it."

They nod once and say nothing.

His skin burns as if he stood with a pyre. Why does this woman meddle with the affairs of a world not hers?

"What the fuck did she do?"

CHAPTER 58
JONATHAN

On the bottom tier of Stonehaven, Jonathan drinks an entire bottle of his elixir and sets it on top of a barrel he passes, and leans on it, fighting the urge to vomit. Despite the quick effect of the elixir to calm his mind, his hands and legs continue to shake. The roar of the crowd ahead, larger than any gathering Jonathan has ever seen or heard, crests over the city like crashing waves. Townspeople crowd the street, peer from balconies and windows, and pack the roofs of tenements and businesses of the lower three tiers of Stonehaven as spectators.

The gathering on the croquet court was almost too much to bear, but this cacophonous noise and the sheer amount of people are enough to drive Jonathan beyond the help of his elixir. Jonathan rests his longsword over his shoulder and pushes his way through the crowd of thousands of eyes, ticking side to side, watching him. It crushes the breath from his lungs. Townspeople pull at his shirt, reach out and touch his arms and chest as if he were their savior. He is anything but, and they would think differently if they knew him.

He meets Mary Anne, the Duchess, and Weiss at the edge of the crowd and the start of the Long Bridge. Mary Anne gives some words of encouragement, or perhaps concern. Her lips move, but the thump of his heart and the high-pitched whistle in his ears drown not just her out, but the crowd.

At the far end of the Long Bridge, no larger than his small finger, Lysander leans his longsword over his shoulder and Uriah holds his glaive like a shepherd's crook. They wear gleaming iron pauldrons and a cropped breastplate with long silver and red tabards hanging down from its center to cover their cocks. Their sides and thighs are exposed except for leather straps around their waists, disappearing behind the tabards, perhaps for some iron codpiece. And dangling from their breastplate, the glass orbs they used on the croquet field.

March waits between them, two swords on her back, one on each hip, a belt of daggers on her right thigh, and a thick leather breastplate down to her trousers and matching vambraces. Her hair is pulled back into a high braid, except for a handful of strands sweeping in front of her eyes.

Jonathan moves onto the bridge first. March matches him step for step. Mary Anne and the Duchess follow close behind, and Lysander and Uriah strut closer behind March.

"Can you best her?" asks Mary Anne.

"She trained me."

"You are a match for her skill."

"No. I have never beaten her."

Mary Anne swallows and asks nothing further.

Watching Lysander and Uriah walk so close to March brings a newfound heat rippling over Jonathan's skin. Before, chills accompanied gooseflesh, but these burn like the core of each large iron brazier lining the Long Bridge. The flames dance and illuminate March's eyes. Jonathan lowers his head, unable to hold and withstand the disappointment in her gaze.

To focus his thoughts, Jonathan counts his steps and notices the faded dancing shadows spiking out in all directions from each footfall. He does not remember this many braziers along the bridge—one every five paces. These are recent additions to keep Cheshire at bay. The number of flames washes out every shadow, not allowing it to grow past a few inches. Besides their orbs of smoke, this time they have taken his use of shadows into account as well.

Both parties stop at the center of the bridge, battle lines drawn with their bodies. Whatever exchanges and words happen around them, the world stops while Jonathan focuses on March's lowered eyes. When he lowers his, she looks up, and contrariwise. They continue to miss each other, out of sync.

"Dear heart, how did it come to this?" Jonathan asks.

"Choices were made," says March. Every word cuts like the sharpest of her daggers, not just at Jonathan's heart, but hers as well.

"Did you hear us, Carter?" asks Lysander.

He could not.

"No one yields or bends the knee," says Uriah. "There must be a victor. Aon Praelium demands it. Since Mary Anne decreed the battle shall not be to the death, the loser shall be determined by the combatant unable to continue in the fight. However, much can be done before one reaches death."

"Fight well," says the Duchess. "Both of you."

"I am sorry," says Mary Anne.

"Speak not a word." March draws the swords from her hips. "Nothing you say can change the fact this is your fault we are all here."

"We shall leave you to it," says Lysander.

Neither move until everyone else clears the bridge. The crowd's jeers and shouts mix with the crackle and growl of the braziers. Jonathan's body already drips with sweat, and his linen shirt sticks to his body. This is not the Hollow, this is not their meadow, and this will not be a training session with his love.

Jonathan flexes his arm to reposition his longsword, and March strikes with both swords from overhead. In order to avoid her blades, Jonathan drops to a knee, leaving his sword in the air. Using the momentum from the rebound, she circles and swings underneath to bat Jonathan's blade away. He rolls to get to his feet to block every new strike March delivers with every step she takes; all without mercy.

"I cannot allow you to win," says Jonathan. "If the Twins reign, all will be lost."

"Will it?" March punctuates every sentence with another strike and clang of steel when their swords meet. "I foresee us leaving Mirus together with Cheshire and Dormy."

"You know I cannot."

"You can if she is dead." March takes a dagger from her thigh, side steps Jonathan, and flings it through the air at Mary Anne.

Jonathan barely has time to swing upward with the tip of his longsword, and knocks the dagger from its trajectory, sending it skidding across the cobbles of the bridge. "I must succeed. All we have worked for depends on it."

"All of your work." March spits her words. "You brought her to our table, you left me standing at the door to our home, and you left with her. Your choice has always been her. Blame your damned honor, it makes no difference."

"Jonathan, fight back!" Mary Anne shouts from the end of the Long Bridge.

Mary Anne does not know what she asks.

"You heard her." March takes a step back to allow Jonathan a moment to right himself, widen and lower his stance, and rest his longsword back on his shoulder. March laughs. She taught him everything he knows about fighting and can prepare and predict each of his movements. "What do you fear? Pretend it is one of our sparring matches in the Hollow."

"You are not fighting like it's a match." Jonathan swings at March's swords, avoiding the risk of hitting her, but she evades and dances around him, fiercer than he has ever seen.

"Because I do not fight to win. I fight to rid our world of her."

March swipes with both blades across Jonathan's torso, slicing his shirt open, close enough for him to feel the cold wind behind her steel. It does not matter how strong Jonathan is. If she wished, March could land six strikes in the time he takes to attack once.

"Do you think this a game?"

"I do. So, raise your fucking sword and fight me." March clangs her swords together twice.

His ears perk, and she charges at Jonathan with no quarter given. Jonathan swings wide with the flat side of his sword. March ducks and follows through. She slaps the back of his hand holding the sword and his forearm with the flat side of her blades. The sharp sting brings a looming dread of finality.

"How long did you think I, we, would put up with her before the strain was too much to bear?"

Five quick strikes he deflects before they puncture his stomach.

"Mary Anne does not belong here, and every day she remains, it puts our world in jeopardy."

Two overhead strikes. followed by a swipe across his face, slice the air in front of Jonathan.

"Together, we can overcome them all and leave this place behind once and for all. Right now, make your choice." March breathes heavy, shoulders hunched, swords down, sweat-soaked hair sticking to her face. Her ferocity burns hotter than the surrounding braziers. "You do not have it in you; or did you decide this long ago?"

March clangs her swords twice again and the reverberation sinks into Jonathan's marrow.

"As you wish." Jonathan does not need to make contact with her, merely end the fight. He circles his sword overhead and swings it with the force of a smith's hammer.

March flips her swords in hand and braces the flat edge on her vambraces to block Jonathan's strike. Its strength slides her back on the cobbles. Jonathan does not, cannot, stop and puts more power behind each swing. March has no choice but to evade rather than block, side stepping and swatting away Jonathan's swings. Despite her fury, March hesitates. Jonathan's power comes at the cost—openings where a quick, non-lethal stab could end the fight.

Their display of skill and vitriol, blades clanging, clinking, and scraping elicits cheers and shouts from the roaring crowd. For a moment, they both forget anyone else exists. March and Jonathan continue a barrage of near fatal stabs, swings, and swipes at each other, as they have thousands of times before in their matches. No matter the outcome, one thing is clear: everyone loses.

Jonathan side steps an overhead strike with March's sword quickly followed by the other, both chipping the cobbles. He brings his sword down on top of them, pinning them to the ground. The pause gives them both a chance to catch their breath and ease their burning lungs.

She could let go and grab at her other swords, or the daggers at her thigh. Instead, March tries to free her blades, but Jonathan's longsword slams to the ground by some unseen weight, pinning her blade and all of their fingers beneath them.

"Get up!" shouts Mary Anne.

"No tricks!" Lysander shouts from the other end of the bridge.

"What devilry is this?" asks Jonathan.

"Fuck," says March.

"Speak of the devil"—Cheshire manifests out of the crackling air and stands on their blades, cloak flapping in the wind—"and he shall appear."

Jonathan raises his eyes to Cheshire's, ablaze with far more than the reflection of the braziers. Disgust and chagrin snarl his lip and pinch his brow. Jonathan did not intend, but should have expected, their love to show himself. With a single pounce, Cheshire places both feet on

Jonathan's shoulders and kicks him backward, then leaps over March, flips her across the stones, and pulls her remaining swords from her back. He drops her blades onto the pile between them and locks eyes with Mary Anne, and then Uriah and Lysander.

"This game is over."

CHAPTER 59
CHESHIRE

Whatever tears dare fall from his eyes, the palpable heat from his face, fiercer than the braziers, dries them. This is neither the time nor the place for sentiment nor uncontrolled emotion. He arrived before the match started and watched to see how far Jonathan and March would take this charade. Even if the match is not to the death, he could bear witness no longer. The tension in the air and the look of disappointment in both his lovers' eyes choked him, and the quiver of their lips prompted him into action.

"What bore these seeds of madness that would bring yourselves to this point? Or is it the spectators who stand far off and let you, who should never be torn asunder, fight in their name while their hands remain clean?"

"Cheshire, we—" Jonathan tries to say.

"I do not want or require any explanation."

"You cannot—" says March.

"Nor you."

Lysander and Uriah rush to the center of the bridge and wisely keep their distance. "How dare you interrupt Aon Praelium?" shouts Uriah. "The old ways dictate a victory will determine the outcome."

"I interrupt nothing," says Cheshire. "I ended it. Know your history, you unlearned swine."

"You dare question us about the history of our land? Smug bastard." Lysander snarls.

"Cheshire, you have ruined everything," says Mary Anne. She and the Duchess stop at the same distance as the Twins on the opposite side of the bridge. "You cannot break the law."

"Do not speak of the law as if you know it."

Mary Anne steps forward and tries to present a brave facade. "Aon Praelium dictates two champions shall fight—"

Cheshire cuts her short. "I know the law. And was it your foolishness that pitted Jonathan and March against each other?" He waits for an answer and receives none. "I believed so."

"The fight continues without your meddling," says Lysander.

"The fight is over," says Cheshire. "Do not dare give me a lesson in this land's history. Aon Praelium says two combatants will face off against one another, and a single victory will determine the outcome. Nowhere in the law, written or spoken, does it say the victor must be one of the two combatants."

Uriah slides his whip from his shoulder. "You think you can find an escape or exception to the law?"

"Everything is black and white to the unintelligent. I live and thrive in between, neither black nor white, but a beautiful gray. Good and evil. And it is already done. Both combatants are disarmed and on the ground. Their fight is over." Cheshire points to the Twins and Mary Anne. "I do not give a fuck of your title, upbringing, name, or history. It is time we put an end to all of it. One of you shall fall first, I care not who, and then I will turn my attention to the other. You wish to have a battle for the fate of Wonderland; you have it."

"Why?" asks Mary Anne. "I pardoned you. None of this is necessary. The deaths, the destruction. Why must you ruin everything?"

He looks to the Duchess, her grimace trembling in the firelight. "It is all necessary. Everything must burn, and every breath is the ticking of a timepiece counting down to the end."

Cheshire dashes toward Mary Anne and the Duchess first in order to test his love. Jonathan blocks his path and holds his sword at the ready.

"Predictable," says Cheshire. "And boring."

He bolts for Lysander and Uriah, leaping over March, and closes the distance. They separate to opposite sides of the bridge to keep the braziers at their back and Cheshire between them. Lysander swings to chop Cheshire's feet from his body while Uriah thrusts his glaive at his chest. They unleash a flurry of attacks, and each means to end his life.

The longsword chips at the cobbles and the whip leaves cracks in the stone and dents the thick bars of the iron braziers, teetering them back and forth. Uriah's glaive slides from his hand, aimed at Cheshire's neck, and he recalls it as quickly as his whip. As much as Cheshire abhors to admit it, it takes every bit of concentration and dexterity to evade their attacks while keeping the grin on his face. This strategy, staying between them, is not sustainable and reminds him of his many encounters with the Gryphon—fighting for a draw and his life rather than to win. Which means Cheshire must find their weakness quickly in order to exploit it.

When Cheshire moves down the bridge toward Jonathan and March, the Twins move with him and match his position to keep the balustrades and braziers to their backs and Cheshire pinned between them for their coordinated attacks. Slash, stab, thrust, whip, over and over again. For the smallest of moments, they glance at each other before they attack. Cheshire looks to March to ask the simple question for the realization he discovered. She nods—enough to let him know the Twins are fearsome fighters indeed, but they cannot read, cannot sense each other's movements the way Cheshire, March, and Jonathan can.

The damned braziers keep him from using the Mask of Shadows, so he must make sure they do not use the glass orbs against him as well. Cheshire jumps and spins through their clatter of steel, the breath the weapons make slicing the air so close to his head. He evades with purpose after observing their stances and patterns, slipping the Mask of Light on and off at random times to disorient them. They soon catch on, and Cheshire must dodge, duck, and roll his neck to avoid the blades, which glance off his shoulders, inches from his neck.

The Twins focus so intently on where Cheshire will reappear between them they do not worry about where he goes for the split second while invisible. Cheshire distracts them with his vanishing act long enough to collect the orbs from both of them. He lingers invisible for a moment longer, and they can immediately tell something is amiss, holding their next attacks. The orbs swing from his fist when he reappears next to March. Lysander and Uriah do not look the least bit pleased. With his never-fading grin, Cheshire tosses them over the sides of the bridge to plummet to the Boroughs below.

The moment Cheshire dons the mask again, March, with her swords back in her possession, grabs hold of his wrist and vanishes with him. Together they pass through the crucible of Lysander's and Uriah's attacks and reappear on the gate side of the bridge. Jonathan and his longsword, on the city side of the bridge, prepares for battle, forcing Lysander and Uriah to adapt their strategy, placing them in the middle. The Twins take careful steps to position themselves back-to-back—Uriah facing off with Jonathan and Lysander against March.

Sword and steel clash, ring, and rip at the air along with screams, grunts, and roars fueling the rage behind their strikes. The change of tactic was necessary, but the Twins at each other's back, without the risk of harming each other, proves to be more dangerous. They fight with unyielding, reckless abandon. Jonathan and March, for every strike they land, Lysander and Uriah make them pay for it. The tip of Jonathan's sword grazes Uriah's leg. Uriah slices at his shoulder. March cuts at the underside of

Lysander's arms and he returns a knee to her chest, nearly knocking the wind from her.

Cheshire disappears and reappears in between them, landing punches to Lysander's and Uriah's heads, knees to their backs, knocking their feet from beneath them, and driving his knuckles into their forearms and wrists to deflect and weaken their attacks. Yet, they fight on, mercilessly. Lysander thrusts an elbow behind him and collides with the back of Cheshire's head. In the spaces between Jonathan's attacks, Uriah spins and swings his glaive between him and his brother, cutting into Cheshire's cloak and limiting his ability to maneuver.

The rooftops of Stonehaven spike and undulate in the darkness beyond the braziers, like a hill of ants, with townspeople cheering, cursing, shouting, and throwing their arms into the air, enjoying the death match. The braziers beat down on them as well, taking their toll, tiring and trapping them in a hell of their own making.

There are moments when Jonathan gets the upper hand, his strength finally catching up to Uriah's speed. Uriah calls to his brother, ducks, and Lysander swings behind him while blocking March to cut down Jonathan. The swing would reap an entire field in one arc. Likewise, there are times in the melee March becomes too much for Lysander, and he calls to his brother, who slides his glaive behind him to stab March, while his whip deals with Jonathan. "Brother," they call out to each other when in need. They listen well to each other. The direction they call over their shoulder, their signal, is the direction the attack comes from, allowing them to evade each other's attacks.

As long as Lysander and Uriah work in tandem, a chance remains their trio will not be able to best them and worse. Cheshire thinks of seventeen outcomes in the time he takes to blink. Uriah's weapon and speed are the greater threat, able to keep Jonathan at bay, attack, and in moments of need caused by Cheshire, attack on all sides. Like the Gryphon, Cheshire must use their own strategy against them, against each other. Also, like his encounters with the Gryphon, still feeling the aches in his own body, victories demand sacrifice.

March spins on a knee to recover from a blow from Lysander. In the breath of a second, Cheshire catches her and Jonathan's eyes. It is a risk and a sacrifice Cheshire was not ready for, but it must be done. His arms throb, head pounds, and the heat presses into his body with the intense waves of a smith's forge. The more tired they become, the less chance they have of an opportunity.

Together, his eyes tell them.

Jonathan slams his sword onto the handle of Uriah's glaive and bears down with all his weight. Lysander raises his powerful arms, ready to bring his sword down and deal March a death blow. Cheshire leaps over March, cocks his fist back, and takes aim at Lysander's face, and at the same time, she thrusts her swords up, ready to plunge into the underside of Lysander's arms.

The twitch in the corner of his eyes gives away his surprise, unable to defend against both in his current stance. Take the blow from Cheshire or bring his swords down and have them run through by March. They give him no choice.

Uriah lets the glaive fall, allowing Jonathan's weight to take him off balance, stumbling forward, sending his chin into Uriah's waiting knee. A thrust kick to his chest knocks Jonathan to the ground.

Lysander shifts to his right, ready to call over his left shoulder at his brother. Cheshire opens his fist and smacks his hand flat on Lysander's face, bringing forth the Mask of Light, and with both hands, twists his head to the right as he screams. The brute vanishes.

"Brother!"

The spectators in Stonehaven release a collective gasp. Cheshire drops to the ground and jumps backward, taking March with him.

Uriah, instinctively, dutifully, spins over his left shoulder, glaive at the ready, expecting Lysander to be clear of his attack. His glaive thrusts with so much power behind it, he could not stop it if he wanted. The look of confusion and betrayal flashes on his face the instant before Uriah vanishes with a deep, wet, squelching sound.

Lysander's invisible blade buries itself into the bridge. Thick drops of blood splatter to the ground. Uriah appears again without his weapon. A moment later, Lysander rips the Mask of Light from his face and sprays a mouthful of blood out to the air with the roar of a demon. He shatters the mask into shards with his bare fist. He lumbers forward. Half the blade of Uriah's glaive sticks out the front of his chest, through his breastplate. The handle wobbles out of his back.

"Brother, stop!" Uriah shouts.

Jonathan tries to wrap his arms around Uriah. He ducks under and punches Jonathan repeatedly on both sides of his ribs, the inside of both his thighs, and finally, an upward swing to Jonathan's jaw, collapsing him to the ground.

"Wait!" Mary Anne shouts from the edge of the bridge.

Lysander tries to raise his sword, but his arms answer to the pain, the blade, and the blood. He drops it with a resounding clang and takes three more steps toward March and Cheshire, reaching for them. A ruse. Before they can back away, Lysander lunges forward and punches Cheshire across the face with his anvil of a fist, splitting his lip and nearly breaking his nose. He finally collapses to the cobbles on his side like a felled yew tree. With gargling breaths, he defiantly clings to life as blood seeps from both sides of his wound, his mouth, and his nose.

Uriah releases a long, unearthly scream from the depths of every hell, silencing the crowd and the gods themselves if they still lived. His fists shake, knuckles white, and the muscles and veins of his forearms push against his skin.

The dizzying, burning hum consumes Cheshire's face, like drowning. He blows copious amounts of blood from his nose and spits just as much on the bridge.

"Lost weapon. Lost brother." He goads Uriah with a bloody smile.

"And one loss deserves another." Uriah unfurls his whip and turns to

Jonathan, still trying to regain his footing, and commands it into the air like a dark lightning bolt ready to rain down its full force.

March and Cheshire race for Uriah. Jonathan picks up his longsword to block. It will do no good. The whip will knock the blade from Jonathan's hand and split his skull. Uriah kicks back and takes out one of March's knees. He dodges Cheshire and allows him to stand in front of Jonathan. The same sinister smile Cheshire shared over Lysander creeps across Uriah's face. This is what he wanted.

With a spin of his wrist, he does not bring the whip down like a lightning bolt, but a serpent, its danger in its coil instead of its bite. Its thin end wraps a half dozen times around Cheshire's neck and cuts off his breath before he has a chance to inhale. Cheshire can immediately feel the pressure build in his chest and his eyes. He tries to dig and claw at the whip, drawing blood with his nails. Its coils wind too tight.

Uriah kicks Jonathan across the face, kicks March in her stomach while doubled over, and snatches the belt of daggers from her thigh. He yanks his arm, and Cheshire has no choice but to hold on to the whip before it claims his head or breaks his neck. The power and wave of the whip pulls him off his feet and flings him into March, sending her rolling farther across the bridge.

Cheshire's heart races, suffocating, useless as a child's rag doll. Another vengeful pull by Uriah sends Cheshire careening into Jonathan, who must toss his sword aside not to impale his love. Jonathan's solid build is like hitting a wall. Each collision somehow knocks more air from his body without the ability to take in any more. At least it steals the distance and momentum needed for Uriah's next strike.

Cheshire regains his footing, digs his toes in between the cobblestones, and pulls on the whip, hoping to give himself some reprieve. A rasped inhale is all he can manage, relieving the pressure. He made his choice and pays the price, and he would do so a thousand times over if it meant protecting those he loved.

In the seconds he has left, he must be smarter. If the braziers keep the shadows on the bridge too faded to use, he shall use his own by ducking under his cloak, disappearing, and severing the whip. Cheshire summons the Mask of Shadows and reaches for his cloak, but Uriah cracks his whip one last time at close distance. The ripple of leather and steel slams Cheshire to the bridge face first.

The Mask of Shadows breaks from the impact and partially crumbles from his face. His vision shatters like a kaleidoscope, his head throbs like twenty soldiers drumming inside his skull, and his body hums like a swarm of a thousand bees. Uriah does not give him a moment to rest or suffer.

Relentless, Cheshire gets to his feet first of their trio, disoriented, but ready to claw Uriah's face from his skull. Another yank of the whip sends Cheshire careening into the balustrades, weightless, holding on for his life. His body crunches against the unforgiving stone and shoves him deeper into his daze, deprived of air and mind swimming. He expects another crack of the whip, a kick, or several more punches while in his current state. Instead, Uriah throws and wraps the thick end of his whip around the base of one of the braziers.

March gets to her feet, limping from the blow to her knee to collect her swords. Jonathan, sword in hand, charges at Uriah, who does not move. He stands and waits until the last second to make sure Jonathan cannot stop the fury behind his swing, just as Uriah could not stop for Lysander.

At the last moment, he ducks, and Jonathan's longsword clangs against the brazier so hard, it dents the cage, knocks it loose, and sends it plummeting over the edge, whip twirling through the air—one end attached to its bottom and the other end still wrapped mercilessly around Cheshire's neck. Then all falls to darkness.

CHAPTER 60

MARCH

Cheshire's body falls limp, suffocating. They have precious seconds to act. Jonathan is closer and throws his body forward, grabs the whip while slack remains, and braces his feet upon the balustrade. He tightens his hold on the hissing leather, gritting his teeth to lessen the grunts and eventually screams as the leather burns and rips into his palms.

March's knee throbs and screams at her as if it were the wrong way round.

Uriah stands between March and her swords. He pulls the five remaining daggers from their holsters, tossing the belt aside, and flips them in hand.

The brazier reaches the end of the whip's length and, with a violent lurch, slams Jonathan's body against the balustrades. His ribs hit the top stone rail, and he screams from the pain. Jonathan tries to reach down with his right hand to loosen the whip around Cheshire's neck, but the brazier is too heavy. It slips and raises Cheshire from the stones. Jonathan cannot support its weight with one arm and bruised ribs. He grabs the whip in his bloody hands and pulls at the brazier to lower Cheshire down.

Hate and fire shine in Uriah's eyes. He glances back and forth between March and Lysander. Her eyes tick between the pile of swords to Jonathan and Cheshire. They meet again, and both know she must make a choice, but in honesty, there is no choice. Uriah catches a dagger by the tip, cocks his arm back, and takes aim at her lovers.

March cannot hobble to her swords. She cannot rush Uriah in possession of her daggers. She cannot reach Lysander in time to pull the glaive from his body. And she has no means to save Cheshire.

The dagger flips through the air toward the back of Jonathan's head, on the other side of Cheshire. Damn him. Uriah tries to take them both from her. Uriah does not give her time, and she cannot properly reach him to catch the blade. Before she can think, March is already in the air, throwing herself into the dagger's path. She stretches out her left hand, inches away from Jonathan's head—it is all she can manage—just as the dagger plunges through the top of her hand.

She falls on her injured knee but will not give Uriah the satisfaction of her screams. The pain does not hit at first, but as she tries to move her fingers, the wider part of her dagger cuts deeper into her hand. The searing burn travels up her arm like a dozen rusted blades scraping at her bones. Half the blade protrudes from her palm, and her blood drips down the point onto Jonathan's back. Fortunately, she positioned her hand for the dagger to slip between her bones. If the blade had been twisted to the slightest degree, she would have lost the use of her fingers for good.

The dagger burns when she pulls it from her hand. She searches the whip and finds where the metal chain at its core ends. A huff is the only warning March receives, but it is enough to prepare. She shifts her body to cover Jonathan and takes a dagger to the back of her left shoulder. Her attention returns to Cheshire and slices through the thinnest part of the leather, braiding at Cheshire's neck. The whip pops, frays, and spins. Jonathan releases the brazier and lets it fall to the Boroughs below. A sturdy punch to Cheshire's stomach by Jonathan forces their love to breathe and spit up more blood across the stones. Yet he is far from conscious.

A second dagger digs into her shoulder near the first, embedding into the bone, shooting searing pain across her back and chest. She turns and flings the dagger at Uriah. She throws blindly, only with the sound of his breath to guide it. Her aim was true, just below his face. It embeds into Uriah's forearm, using it to block his neck.

Uriah gives no quarter. He rushes forward. A boot to the back of Jonathan's head smacks his forehead against the balustrade. He lifts his bloody hands in time to cushion the blow, but it is enough to disorient and daze him. With Uriah in striking distance, March pulls the first dagger from her shoulder, flips it in hand, and stabs it through the top of his foot. Its point clinks against the stones. He reaches down and punches her across the face before he falls to his back, cursing into the wind.

Her lovers still breathe—this is all that matters. March gets to her feet and limps to her swords. Every twitch of her left hand and movement of her shoulder rip at every nerve in her arm. The damage is done.

Uriah could have thrown every dagger and killed them all. He took Cheshire and Jonathan out of the game and injured March to hinder her fighting, not to kill her. His pride will not allow it. He wishes to face her.

"What a shame." Uriah mocks her and pushes from the ground, hobbling on his bleeding foot. He pulls the dagger from his foot and forearm. "It would appear your legend has come to an end. The master swordswoman, unbeatable when she wields two swords, or so the stories say. How will you ever be able to do so again with one less hand?"

"I do not hold stories in high regard." She stoops down and grabs Brynjar and Flynn from the ground with her right hand, holding both handles in the same hand, blades facing out. "However, what you hear are not stories. They are accounts of my deeds. I am unbeatable with two swords. However, you may have misheard your stories. Nowhere in them did it ever mention I needed both hands to wield them, you fuck."

Uriah's smile sours, and he fans the daggers in one hand and beckons her to come with the other. Four daggers against her blades. The fifth in her shoulder and the sixth somewhere down the bridge, deflected by Jonathan. Uriah knows he cannot dislodge his glaive from Lysander. If there is any chance to save his life, pulling the blade free will cause him to bleed out in minutes. Instead of killing her with the daggers, Uriah will use them to weaken her to get to the swords behind her. She cannot let him pass.

He beckons her forward again.

"If you wait for me"—March rolls her right shoulder and widens her stance—"we shall consider this a stalemate at the cost of your brother's life. If you wish to fight me, then bring your ass here so I can kill you properly."

Uriah places his full weight on his bloody foot, testing his limits, and grimaces. "As you wish." The bastard rushes forward as if not injured. He flings the first dagger, and March deflects it.

Both swords in one hand are formidable, unpredictable to the opponent if they have never fought against such a weapon. They cut the air, in a deep, rich tone, one she has not played in quite some time, for good reason. This method comes with the cost of speed. March deflected the first dagger, but without being able to pass the swords to her other hand, she cannot block the second dagger. It pierces her breastplate and sinks into her left side above her hip. If not for the breastplate, it would have sunken deeper and done irreparable damage.

She bites through the pain as Uriah descends upon her, wielding the remaining daggers as swords. March twists and turns, despite the dagger lodged in her side, blocks his strikes, and cuts deep where he cannot maneuver, unaccustomed to close quarter combat. While he blocks and deflects with one sword, March can slash at him with the second. Sparks fly, and the high notes of steel against steel sing through the air. March slices him across the chest, the top of his thighs, and across his left cheek. He repays her cut for cut, but unable to cut through her breastplate and bracers. She manages to knock one dagger from his hand, and while it is in the air, bats it behind her with her swords to keep out of Uriah's hands.

Uriah is no less dangerous with one dagger. He flips it back and forth between hands, trading cuts with both of March's blades. She does not care for this song. This fight lingers on for too long, both of them a bloody mess with their sweat in the heat. She will not win this way. Out of the corner of her eye, both Jonathan and Cheshire stir.

In the flurry of her swords, she offers Uriah an opening to her right shoulder, to incapacitate her other arm. He takes it, and at the final second, she twists, and the blade sinks into her left shoulder blade–she was not using it anyway. She cannot hold back her screams and does not try. He pushes past her to reach the swords.

Uriah may be closer to the swords, but he gave her his back. March drops her sword, pulls one of the daggers from her shoulder, and launches it at Uriah, stabbing him just off the center of his back. He winces at the pain, but limps onward, pinching the muscles of his back.

Exhausted, she cannot reach the remaining dagger in her shoulder, and she cannot risk removing the dagger from her side. She drops to the ground and grabs the first dagger she deflected, turns, and throws it. It hits its mark: the back of Uriah's calf, on his uninjured leg.

Too proud to fall, he hobbles and turns to face March, as she wanted. "You fucking bitch. I will kill them both for the pain you have caused. No ceremony. No mercy. Just quick deaths. Mark my words. And after all is said and done, I will claim you to be mine. And you will suffer in such ecstasy, you will wish for death, but it will not come easily."

"Shut the fuck up." March spits blood at him. "As always, your obsession coupled with your delusion of victory, blinds you."

Jonathan leaps to his feet and traps Uriah's arms behind him. He bears down with the weight of his entire body to bring Uriah down.

Despite their size difference and his wounds, Uriah refuses to fall. He roars in defiance, spit flinging from his mouth, and pulls against Jonathan with all his might.

March stands, takes Brynjar in her right hand, and fights through the pain, commanding her hand to heed her in order to hold Flynn with her left.

"Stop!" Mary Anne shouts again.

"Stop this instance!" the Duchess calls out after.

Jonathan dodges Uriah, throwing his head back again and again, while still trying to pull him to the ground. A hit in the head will not do much harm, but it loosens Jonathan's grip.

It is Cheshire, conscious for the moment and wearing half the broken Mask of Shadows, who kicks Uriah's knees out before falling limp again.

The moment Uriah's knees hit the cobblestones with Jonathan's weight behind him, March falls forward, barely any fight left in her, and plunges her swords through Uriah's thighs into his calves, making it impossible for him to rise again. He fights, thrashes, and screams like a dozen wailing spirits. Jonathan pulls Cheshire away. Uriah tries to claw at anyone near him, but the slightest movement causes excruciating pain.

"Do it, you harlot. Finish me. Finish us."

"With pleasure." March backhands Uriah across the face.

Cheshire pulls himself up and pulls March to her feet, his head bobbing.

"Stop!" the Duchess commands. Her words fall on deaf ears.

"Let the line of kings end with us, and let all know what despicable, honorless villains you lot are."

"You should know better than anyone; there are no heroes in Wonderland." She summons the strength and reaches for the dagger in her shoulder, but a set of high-pitched whistles stays her hand.

Four arrows from the Gryphon's archers imbed in the bridge between March and Uriah. Far behind Jonathan, the Duchess holds her hand in the air, responsible for the command. Mary Anne runs onto the bridge. If

March had a dagger to spare, or the fight left, it would find a home in Mary Anne's eye.

"We cannot kill them," says Mary Anne, huffing as if she fought the battle.

"You may be the cause of this conflict, but you no longer have any say in the matter." March pushes her hair out of her face and leaves a bloody streak across her face. "Worry not, I shall end it."

"You will not." The Duchess approaches. "We cannot allow them to die."

Mirusian soldiers crunch and scrape by to attend to Lysander and surround Uriah, who has passed out from the pain, still kneeling and head hung low.

"If they die, we will have no leverage over their armada," says Mary Anne. "Alive, they are a bargaining chip. Dead, their entire fleet will lay waste to Mirus to seek revenge."

It pains her, more than any wound, to admit Mary Anne is correct. Lysander and Uriah must live, if Lysander survives at all. It does not stop March from wanting to doom Mirus just to spite Mary Anne.

"No," says March.

The Duchess's hand raises again, and far in the distance she can hear the creaking draw of the archers' bows.

"Please, dear heart," says Jonathan.

His words cut into March's stomach deeper than any blade. "Again, you side with her."

"We have no choice."

March presses her lips to hide their quivering. She turns to Cheshire and places her bloody hand on his mask to hold it together. Chips fall off at her touch.

"Will it still work?" she asks.

"Perhaps, one last time," says Cheshire in a hoarse, strained voice.

"Every step away." Jonathan's words hang in the air.

She leaves them there. With a broken heart, a knot in her throat, and daggers in her back and side, she leans her head against Cheshire's. "Get us out of here before I bleed out."

"Wait," says Jonathan, stepping forward and collapsing. Two Mirusian soldiers catch him and keep him upright.

Cheshire grabs the side of his cloak and swings it over both their heads, hiding them from the bridge on fire. Once enveloped, March's stomach sinks as they fall into darkness, out of sight, and away from Jonathan and Mary Anne.

CHAPTER 61
MARY ANNE

This is not what she expected, not how she wanted to claim victory, because it does not feel like a victory. March vanishes into the night with Cheshire, and soldiers brace Jonathan under his arms and walk with him back to the castle. Four dozen soldiers surround the unconscious and bleeding bodies of Lysander and Uriah strewn across the cobbles of the Long Bridge. And though so many surround her, Mary Anne cannot help but feel alone. The murmur, sobs, cheers, and shouts of the crowd fade as the townspeople return to their homes to rejoice, sleep soundly, or, for others, to grieve their loss.

A surge of victory should course through Mary Anne, but witnessing Jonathan's trio break apart, and watching him break even further, stifles the torrent of every other emotion within her. Jonathan will heal. March will survive, as will Cheshire, but Mary Anne must think of herself and their people. Lysander and Uriah may be defeated, but their armada still sails toward Mirus.

Long after the soldiers carry Lysander and Uriah off and the streets empty, all except for the blue-haired soldier, the wind blows across the great emptiness dividing the castle wall and Stonehaven, and three distinct pairs of footsteps approach Mary Anne from behind. The Duchess stands by her side, as well as Pat and Bill from wherever they have hidden themselves during this entire mess. She is glad to have them at the moment, but surveying the aftermath of the battle she created, Mary Anne must think of the days to come and send them away.

"You made the correct choice," says the Duchess. "Difficult, but the most strategic nonetheless."

"Why does it feel wrong? They should be dead for everything they have done."

"Yes, but you were smart enough to see beyond the moment, beyond the emotions to the next move. I am truly impressed and proud."

"No. I think I acted too rash, as I often do. And look at what it has cost."

"Look at the bridge you stand upon." The Duchess taps the cobbles with her heeled boot and points to the main gates of Mirus. "Not long ago, Cheshire reduced half this bridge to rubble, yet it stands again better than before. Anything can be fixed with time and enough determination."

Mary Anne calls the blue-haired soldier to her. "Make arrangements for all those who fell on the croquet court. Send word to their families, prepare their bodies for burial. Take extra care with Lacha. What is an honorable funeral?" she asks the Duchess.

"A funeral pyre. It is the old way, but I think it best. It would show great respect on your part."

"Please, make it happen," says Mary Anne.

"I will attend to it myself. I am proud of you, my girl." The Duchess pats Mary Anne's shoulder and walks into the night.

Mary Anne stops the soldier before he leaves. "A slight correction. Prepare the bodies of our fallen soldiers for burial. Take the rest, loyal to Lysander and Uriah, wrap and pile them on the lawn. Do not question."

The soldier nods and runs off, armor clanking.

"I have a separate request of you both," she says to Pat and Bill.

"Name it," says Pat.

"And it shall be done," says Bill.

"You rebuilt the bridge out of Mirus in days. I need you to build something for me on the croquet field nearest the edge of the cliff, facing the harbor. And it must be completed by dawn. Can it be done?"

Without knowing her mind, or perhaps they do, they nod.

"I shall meet you there presently. But on your way, find physicians in the city and have them dress and bind Lysander's and Uriah's wounds. Give them milk of the poppy and hemlock to keep them unconscious, if no more of the powder remains. When the sun rises, take them to the croquet court, conscious or not. Tomorrow is a new day for us all."

CHAPTER 62
CHESHIRE

Cheshire stumbles out of the shadows into the Crooked Market, March leaning against him, her blood running down his arm and chest. The Mask of Shadows continues to crack, nearly breaking in half. As they trudge into the heart of the market, the hooded patrons part to make way to the glowing candles, where he and March collapse in front of the Lory's shop, bloody and beaten. Cheshire expects her to ask for something in trade, and perhaps she still might, but the conjurer waves a customer away and ushers Cheshire and March to a threadbare cot at the rear.

"Before you lay her down, the blades must be removed," says the Lory, carefully collecting small jars and rags from a squat wooden shelf.

"I know," says Cheshire. "Give me the fucking linens." He holds out his hand, and the Lory lays several cleaned strips in his hand.

"Do it." Exhaustion weighs heavy in March's words. "Be quick about it before I handle it myself."

Cheshire grabs the hilt of the dagger in her left shoulder. It is solid—stuck in the bone. March's eyes flutter, her neck twitches, but she does not change her expression. The Lory unbuckles the straps to March's breastplate. Cheshire crumbles the linens in his hand and braces against March's shoulder. With one hard jerk, he pulls the blade free.

"Wait." Before he can make use of the linens, the Lory stops him and pours a clear liquid from a long bottle over the wound.

It looks like water, but its touch brings March to grit her teeth and grunt. While the Lory moves to the rest of the buckles, Cheshire covers March's wound—the linens soak quickly, crimson spreading across every fiber. The Lory hands Cheshire the bottle and replaces his hand with hers. The breastplate is ready to come off, but not before the dagger in her side.

"This one will hurt and bleed considerably more," says the Lory.

"Let's have it," says March.

Cheshire carefully grabs the hilt, pulls it out, drops the blade, and drops the breastplate to the ground. Blood flows freely. He douses the wound with the near odorless liquid, and March collapses to the cot, toppled by the pain. He grabs more linens from the shelves and presses hard on March's side.

"Once more," he says, and pours the liquid on her bloody hand.

"Fuck," she grunts.

The Lory steps behind Cheshire and rummages through the shelves. She could grab any manner of weapon to kill them both. Cheshire's suspicions try to get the better of him, but if the Lory wanted him dead, she would have dealt him a fatal blow days ago when he was unconscious, and she would not help them now. Cheshire will not look from March's wincing face. The Lory returns with a long curved needle and several lengths of catgut and sets to work stitching the wounds closed, starting with March's side, then her shoulder, and finally her hand. March's breaths grow quick and heavy with each quick pull of the needle.

Cheshire sits against the small shelves, vision shifting in and out of focus, watching the Lory's skilled hands move across March's skin, pulling and pushing, almost as if casting a spell. Patrons walk by, curious of the noises, but Cheshire's glares, even from his hanging, exhausted head, are enough to threaten and send them on their way. When the Lory breaks the last piece of catgut with her teeth, she applies ample amounts of thick, clear creams over March's stitches and places thin leaves over them.

After half the wax has run from the candles, March stops fighting and finally sleeps. As her body finally relaxes, surges of pain surround Cheshire's neck, as if someone with gauntlets fresh from a smith's forge throttled him, and his head throbs as if struck against the smith's anvil. With no need to focus on March, he has no distraction from his own pain.

The Lory dips the tip of her finger in March's blood from the wadded linens and draws faint runes of Old Prodigium around the stitches. Cheshire growls and the hair on the back of his neck bristles, bringing forth new sparks of pain.

She looks to Cheshire, barely able to keep his head up. "It is to quicken the healing. I can do the same for you."

"You have done enough," says Cheshire, head bobbing and snapping up again, eyes growing dark for a moment.

"You will not die from this. You will outlive Wonderland itself." She repeats his mother's words from long ago, and they echo in a double voice, half hers, half his mothers. They send an agonizing chill down his body. "Rest, now. Nothing will happen to her, or you, here. I shall make sure of it."

Cheshire still questions if he should fully trust the Lory, this trickster who bore his mother's face and dares speak her words and use her voice. She deceived him before—with a purpose. It may appear this is the only recourse, but despite what others may believe, there is always a choice.

"No." Cheshire struggles to get to his feet, muscles aching, throat burning, and blows out all but one of the Lory's candles nearest the front of her shop, leaving her cast shadow, a streak of darkness, over March.

"This will be your last walk." The Lory traces the cracks of the remaining parts of the mask, never touching the surface.

"It does not matter. They are worth any price."

The Lory offers a small jar with a lamb skin cover secured with twine to him and points to his neck.

His eyes waver, and his vision shakes as if seeing the world through the surface of a lake. It must be now. He takes the jar, swoops his cloak over March, taking hold of her, and together they fall through the Lory's shadow and rise through another on the sacks of flour and grain in the upper level of Dormy's wagon. The mask cracks further, almost completely across.

A lantern from below keeps the loft bathed in enough shadow to pass. He positions March gently on the sacks as a scramble of thuds, bangs, and shuffles bounces around the lower level until Dormy peeks her head up from the ladder.

"I'll watch after her." Dormy scurries to March's side and inspects the stitches.

Once again a fugitive, a murderer, Cheshire cannot stay here and endanger March and Dormy. He slides down the ladder and bumps from table to table until he leaves through the back door of Dormy's wagon. He will not risk passing through another shadow. Should the mask fail, it could be the end of him in two separate parts of the city. Where he needs to return to are the catacombs, and he cannot access them with the mask.

He hobbles through the empty street and finds the nearest entrance to the catacombs outside of the Row, between a tenement and a glass blower's shop, with barely enough room to walk sideways. The release lever is an octagonal stone in a wall of square bricks at the base of the wall. Cheshire pushes it in with his toes, and the stone door releases a deep yawn. He steps inside and closes the passage behind him.

Complete and total darkness welcomes him back with its cold embrace. He slumps against the wall and slides down, giving in to the burning fatigue in his body and his pounding heartbeat rocking his body. March will be cared for through the night. Tomorrow, he will handle Jonathan. No more thoughts. His eyes shut, the jar rolls from his hand across the ground, and all is darkness; as it should be.

CHAPTER 63
JONATHAN

The next morning, Jonathan snaps awake in the dim light of the infirmary again. The pungent smell of camphor oils, henbane, Feverfew, lavender, camomile, and sage hangs like a cloud in an opium den or the Garden. Wounded soldiers, those who were fortunate enough to survive Lysander's and Uriah's onslaught, with injuries ranging from gashes to missing limbs, fill every cot. The castle physicians tread carefully and step over other poor soldiers for whom there were no cots to treat them.

Where is March?

Jonathan does not know why he is among them. His injuries pale in comparison to the Mirusian soldiers. He rises, with sharp pains stabbing at his bandaged ribs. The back of his head and shoulders feel as though they sit in a blacksmith's vise. Heavily doused linens wrap his hands. A physician makes his way toward Jonathan, but he waves her off as he leaves. There are far worse to attend.

Where is Cheshire?

Mary Anne's handmaiden waits for him outside, nods her head, and walks toward the rear of the castle when he appears in the corridor. She means for him to follow, and he will, but first he needs to return to Mary Anne's bedchamber. The air of every corridor and staircase both feels empty and, at the same time, exudes a crushing, foreboding pressure on Jonathan. A knot the size of an apple rises in Jonathan's throat. When he reaches Mary Anne's chambers, he realizes the crushing weight was not external, but a pull of the void in his chest. All of March's chests are gone, taken in the night, leaving a sizable emptiness on the chamber wall and in Jonathan's chest. It is to be expected, but it does not lessen the pain within.

Gone.

Jonathan takes a fresh bottle of elixir from his trunk and stares at the darker color stones where March's trunks sat, keeping the collection of dust at bay. His mind should race and spin out of control with thoughts. None can form in the hollowness. He sips his elixir, pockets it in his trousers, grabs the red longcoat, and places his hat upon his head.

The handmaiden waits by the bedchamber door, huffing through her nose to catch her breath. The sight of her startles Jonathan.

"Lead on."

Jonathan never once raises his head traveling the corridors, counting his steps and listening to the clinks of the handmaiden's dress. She takes him past the kitchens, where the once sweet aromas twist his stomach, and out the back of the castle to the gardens in the midday sun. The handmaiden travels no farther than the edge of the terrace and points over the hedge maze to the croquet court.

The farther he walks between the looming wall of the hedge maze and the castle wall, the thicker the air becomes with the unmistakable iron sting of blood. Dirt squishes beneath his boots, still moist from crimson trails left by the dead when ferried away. In the full honesty of the sun, the severity of battle on the croquet court reveals itself, a gaping wound for all to see. The short grass bears several deep gouges in the earth and dark splotches and swaths where the pools of blood were deepest.

To Jonathan's astonishment, a massive set of gallows sits at the edge of the cliff as if it were some horrible flower having bloomed over the course of the night, watered from the blood of the soldiers. Its platform stands at least ten feet in height, complete with trap doors with separate release levers and four nooses hanging from the thick crossbeam overhead. From the craftsmanship and the speed, it is no doubt the work of Pat and Bill.

Lysander and Uriah occupy the middle two nooses, tight around their necks, swaying back and forth, arms bound behind them with rope, chain, and shackles on their feet. Castle guards stand behind them and often nudge them to keep them upright. They have never appeared so disheveled, clothing filthy, especially Uriah's long silver hair, now a tangled mess. Lysander's and Uriah's ability to stand with their wounds surprises Jonathan.

Atop the gallows, Dormy perches with a spyglass pressed to her eye, squinting and face snarled, searching the horizon. At the base of one support, Mary Anne waits in her coat from the previous night and holds her arms. A sleepless night weighs heavy in her eyes.

She greets Jonathan with a soft, half-smile. "I am not proud of this. Days ago, I hate to admit it, I came to the conclusion I would need to get my hands dirty in these affairs in order to be victorious. I could think of nothing else. This seemed the best way to make sure the message is received. The armada has the choice to turn around or risk killing their lords with any attack on the city."

"Smart. Not only smart, but strategic," says Jonathan. "Not just strategic, but impressive. Shall they stay up there or have you given thought to where we shall hold them?"

"Pat and Bill mentioned the dungeons they previously kept me in. It seems fitting, if not poetic. Now, all we need is for their fleet to arrive and, gods willing, not fire upon us."

"It already has," says Dormy. "I think. Jonathan, will you let me know if you see what I see?"

Jonathan climbs the stairs to the gallows as fast as he is able with Mary Anne in tow, concerned what Lysander's and Uriah's reactions will be. From the vacant stares of their glassy eyes, the large amount of sedatives given to them will not allow them any reaction. After years of their tyranny, it was not the unity of Jonathan, March, and Cheshire to bring the brothers down, but ironically their division.

Dormy holds the spyglass out for Jonathan and points to a specific spot on the horizon. "Wait for it."

"Wait for what?" asks Mary Anne.

Jonathan watches for almost ten minutes by his count, eyes shifting in and out of focus, until the tiniest glint of light flashes where the sky meets the sea. "There."

"You saw it?"

"Oh, yes. You are quite observant. How many times has it appeared?"

"Every quarter-hour for the past two hours, give or take." Dormy takes the spyglass back and returns to her watch.

"What is it?" Mary Anne asks again.

Jonathan wraps an arm around Mary Anne and points out over the ocean. "The smallest reflection out at sea, out of place among the shimmers on the water's surface. It is the reflection of the sun on another spy glass. The ships hold their position and hide beyond the curve of the horizon where only their highest crow's nest, probably from a man-of-war, and a lookout sit above the sea. You are remarkable, Dormy. I would have missed such an obvious detail had you not pointed it out."

"They arrived early," says Mary Anne. "They must have had favorable winds and fair waters."

"Little good it did them. Fortunate for us, everything went to hell when it did."

Dormy lies on her stomach and rests her elbows on the planks of the platform to support the spyglass. "I'll stay and keep a weather eye out and inform you immediately of any change in their position."

Jonathan kneels next to her. "Be sure to keep watch over the entire horizon. If they were clever enough, they would set one ship to draw our attention while others maneuvered in from the sides. But I doubt they will."

"Diabolical, but clever," says Dormy. "How did you know to think of it?"

"Because I believe it is what March would have suggested."

With Dormy near, March's absence becomes clearer while Jonathan's world becomes blurred. The numbness returns, not from feeling nothing, but from feeling everything at once. He takes another sip from his elixir to make sure the feeling does not fade.

On the stairs of the gallows, Mary Anne waits part way down, her head and shoulders visible above the platform. He follows her back to the lawn, where they both survey the blood-stained grass, the gouges of missing earth, and then up to the dangling Twins above them.

She takes both his hands in hers. "Advise me, please. If all of this plays out the way it is supposed to, what happens next?"

"Well, you have played a risky yet advantageous hand, and now you must see it through to the end. The ships will sail back to Adamas, news will spread of what happened here, your victory, their loss, and the imprisonment of two of Wonderland's prized sons." With March and Cheshire gone, he must turn his attention to Mary Anne, however, the course of action Jonathan suggests is as much for him, selfishly, as for her. "Your task now is to get ahead of the controversy faster than a whisper travels, and we are already behind. Visit the other major cities in Wonderland and the smaller hamlets to make yourself known. We must shape the story, tell the truth, before the narrative grows beyond our control. Besides, the fresh air and distance from the city will do us both a great deal of good."

"I cannot leave the city now, when I have just secured the throne."

"This is precisely when you should. Your throne is secure. There is no one to contest you. You have won a great victory and now you must make appearances to the other lands, the Warrens, the Wastes, the Winds, the

Wetlands, and the Wealds. And it would be best if we leave as soon as possible, at most in a day or two, to make sure the ships leave our bay."

It takes several moments for Mary Anne to work through the idea and its outcomes. "I understand. I wish for a moment's peace, but I doubt I shall have one until I sit rightfully, completely, on the throne. The Duchess can oversee the city while we are away. I say 'we' because I assume you will accompany me," she says hopefully.

"I am bound to you."

"Please, do not say such a thing. I know the Arcana binds you to me, but stated in such a way makes me seem like an obligation you are held to against your will."

"I apologize." Jonathan's thumbs rub the top of her hands. "I did not say what I mean, but hear me now, because I mean what I say. I have been by your side nearly every day since we met. I made you a promise and intend to see it through. You have me. All of me."

Mary Anne takes a step closer and stands toe to toe with Jonathan. Her breath puffs over his lips and her eyes hardly break from them. Jonathan cannot deny the temptation, the stir of his body, and the fear of cold nights.

"Mary Anne, before... well, anything, I need to take the evening for myself."

"I understand." She steps back, crestfallen, and pulls her hands away.

She understands, but not for the reason Jonathan means.

"I would like to give you a gift if you would allow," says Jonathan. "Would you meet me at the entrance to the garden after dusk?"

Mary Anne nods and takes her leave.

He cannot be alone with his thoughts and must find a way to keep the intrusive darkness from clawing at his mind, consuming him, and pulling him further into despair. Jonathan must do something for someone else, or her; it is his nature. The more he focuses on another, the less time he has to focus on himself.

CHAPTER 64
MARCH

After twilight, a ring of keys clinks and jostles together from outside the study. Bronwen unlocks the door, candle in hand, as she probably has done every night since his passing. Wisps of hair wave from her usual perfect styling, and the lack of any make-up reveals the bags under her eyes. The flickering candlelight catches the edge of March's sword laid across her lap as she sits, boots resting on top of her father's study desk. She turns it in hand, letting the reflection of the light stroke the length of the blade. Her heavy boots crumple financial papers and contracts she poured through before Bronwen's arrival. She wears her triangle top so no heavy or light fabric or cloth will rub against the bandages around her hand, shoulder, and waist, carefully dressed by Dormy, and the Lory, the woman she sought out in her youth.

Her mother stifles her gasp and hides it in a deep inhale through her nose. It would have gone unnoticed by any eyes, but not to March. The twitch of Bronwen's neck and the slight tremble of the candle's flame give her surprise away.

"Is this supposed to intimidate me? Have you not taken enough from me?" Bronwen asks with a smug grin. She places the candle and its holder on a marble pedestal beside the door. "Or am I to believe after all these years you come to kill me now?"

"Is it so difficult to believe? I killed my father."

"Yes, you did. I should thank you for your service. I would never have amassed such wealth with his limited vision of what could be." Bronwen pulls a small flintlock pistol, no larger than her palm, from her belt and points it at March. "He was only concerned with selling armor and swords, obsessed with wealth, when power is what he should have thirsted for. I would have eventually killed him myself."

"Always willing to do anything," says March, "no matter the cost."

"Damn right." Bronwen pulls the hammer back with her thumb. "Like mother, like daughter."

March twists the sword to reflect the candlelight into Bronwen's eyes. She squints for the slightest of moments and, anticipating an attack from March, leans forward, ready to squeeze the trigger.

Crack.

Her head snaps to the side and her eyes go cross from a quick blow to the back of the head, and she collapses to the ground, unconscious. Dormy stands behind her with her heaviest flintlock pistol in hand and several lengths of rope hooked on her elbow. She and March make quick work of seating Bronwen's limp body in a sturdy, carved wooden chair positioned at the center of the thick woven rug in the middle of the study.

The night carries on, March leans against Seamus's desk, ignoring the dull throbbing ache of her wounds. Dormy paces back and forth on the far side of the room at the edge of the pool of light from newly lit candles placed on the mantle and desk. March uncorks a full bottle of rum, one of three on the desk, and takes a long drink, savoring the sweet taste. She slams the bottle down, and Bronwen finally rouses from her stupor, struggling against the ropes binding her waist, wrists, and ankles to the chair. Her face maintains proper composure, even if hatred twitches at the corners of her mouth and burns in the reflection of the candles in her eyes.

"I hope you are satisfied," says Bronwen, squinting to focus on March. "The blood on your hands is unforgivable. You and your degenerate misfits have ended any chance Wonderland has at a peaceful reign. How could you be so stupid, so selfish, so vile?"

"Interesting." March sighs. "And quite vexing. The relationship, the bond, between a mother and her child is the most unique and sacred of all. Children look up to, worship, pray, and depend upon their mothers. Mothers are the first thought in a child's mind and the first words uttered from their lips."

"What is vexing about it?"

"Two things. The first: you were never a mother one day of my life. You groomed me like a dog and trained me to serve you and your ambition. Second: no matter how hard I tried, how far I ran, how much I wished you dead, some part of me still ended up like you."

"You are nothing like her," says Dormy.

"I appreciate you, little mouse. But, I am. Part of me. Cut from the same cloth, unfortunately. And I wish I could carve this piece of flesh from my body. I am nowhere near as cruel, but just, if not more, ruthless than you."

Bronwen's gaze remains unchanged, arrogant, and defiant.

"I am what you made me. A killer. No, the killer. Unmatched." March stares into her mother's eyes, into the vacant hollow chasm where a soul should live in a pointless contest until Bronwen blinks first. "Tell me. Do you recall how many men you and father *gifted* me to?"

Bronwen does not answer.

"Do you?" March asks after an hour of silence.

No response. Another hour passes before her mother decides to speak.

"Audrianna, this is unnecessary—"

"Three hundred and forty-one." March unsheathes a dagger from her thigh and walks to her mother, blade and bottle of rum clinking together in her right hand. "Three hundred and forty-one men you would have let have their way with me. A child." March bites her words. "Three hundred and forty-one men I put into the ground before they dared lay a hand on me."

March sets down the bottle on the floor and takes the sharpened point of the dagger and flicks it across Bronwen's cheek. Bronwen's face flinches at the pain.

"You will endure a cut for every. Single. One." March flicks her wrist, slicing her mother's forehead, chin, and nose to punctuate each word. Thin lines of blood fill the wounds and run like counterfeit tears down her face. "You raised me to be a plaything, a whore. I became a killer instead. One of the best." March slashes at her mother four more times, across her forearms.

Bronwen grimaces through the pain and fights against the restraints. "Take your pound of flesh if it will satisfy your childish need for revenge."

Seven more cuts in quick succession slash across the top of Bronwen's hands. She finally bares her teeth and snarls at the burning of her skin.

"After a while, your body will grow accustomed to the pain. You will not feel each individual cut, but rather the all-consuming fire overtaking your body."

"Why continue, then?" asks Bronwen.

March takes another long drink of whiskey. "Because it will bring me pleasure."

Dormy holds Bronwen's fingers together in her iron hand, almost crushing them. March runs her blade across the fatty tip of each finger over and over again, spreading her fingers wider with each pass. Bronwen finally cries out in pain through clenched teeth, body convulsing.

"Not to worry," says March. "You will eventually become numb to it. I believe those were the last words you spoke to me before you shut the carriage door in my face for the first time."

Over the next hour and half a bottle of rum, March waves her hand through the air, like a maestro conductor, summoning her own choir. Every wave of her hand brings forth a new swath of crimson across Bronwen's body and a fresh note of pain. Some are quick, detailed cuts, so fast the pain does not register until seconds after the meat separates. Others are long and lingering when March presses the edge of her blade into Bronwen's skin and slowly, methodically, drags and cuts deeper. Each widening gap of flesh reveals the white meat underneath and fills with blood before flowing freely.

"One hundred and thirty-five." March exchanges her bloody dagger for a fresh, bright, glimmering blade from Dormy.

March keeps most of her cuts to Bronwen's arms, legs, and chest.

"Audrianna—"

But any time Bronwen attempts to speak, March slices upward without looking, her aim true, slicing her mother's face, lips, cheeks, and nose.

"Please."

Slash.

"How can you?"

Slash.

"Don't—"

Slash.

After another hour, the candles on the mantle and desk of the study near their end, and March reaches three hundred and forty. She runs out of skin to cut. Her mother slumps forward in the chair, held up by the ropes around her waist, a bloody ragged mess. Not even a glimpse of the former proud woman remains.

"Look at what you have done to me," Bronwen rasps. "How could you?"

"You still do not understand. You are incapable." March takes the tip of her dagger and places it underneath the nail of her mother's middle finger. "Know, the scars you now bear on the outside, I have borne on my soul since I was a young girl." She shoves the dagger in under the nail, splitting it from the skin the farther the blade pushes.

Bronwen shakes violently from the pain, unable to scream through her bloody mouth, and loses consciousness.

"Three hundred and forty-one." March finishes the bottle of rum. "And I would, I should, continue until you are little more than shreds of flesh."

She nods to Dormy, who takes the bloody dagger and slices through the blood-soaked ropes binding Bronwen. Her body collapses onto the rug. Dormy moves the chair, and March drags Bronwen's body to the edge of the rug, and they both take their places to roll Bronwen's body with it.

"March?" asks Dormy. "Would you like me to go with you?"

"No, little mouse. I have asked enough of you. Please return to your wagon. I will meet you on the morrow."

Dormy, with her beautifully innocent smile, leaves the study.

"Thank you," March says after her.

March heaves her mother's body over her right shoulder. Even at the end, her mother brings her pain. The weight of her mother may rip her stitches, but it is of little consequence now. She grabs the remaining bottles of rum from the desk and pours them as she walks through the hall and down the stairs where her family's servants wait, fear and shame shimmering in their eyes.

"Are you the lady of the house now?" an older woman asks, rubbing her weathered fingers.

"Never," says March. "Take anything and everything you want or need from this house, then go."

"We've nowhere else to go," a stout man who worked in the kitchen says. "We've served your family for most of our lives."

March drinks. "There is no family. Take everything. Leave nothing. Coin, jewel, painting, or dish. Sell it, pawn it, keep it. I do not care. You no longer work for this house or this cursed family." She spills the rest of the bottle on the floor.

The servants squirm and fidget, pensive, looking at each other, unsure and afraid.

The stout man steps forward. "You owe us nothing. We all could have said something, objected, stopped them."

"No, you could not. I do not blame any of you. We are all casualties of their greed. Now leave."

"Please," says the stout man. "I did not help you then. Allow me to help you now. Let me carry her for you. You need not tell me where; I will follow."

March finally concedes, and he takes Bronwen's bundle from her and follows to the door.

"I have never given an order to any of you in my life," says March. "But let my first be my last. Leave. Now. Take everything you are owed and more. All I ask"—she looks at every single person, no longer a servant, in the eyes—"is for the last person who crosses the threshold to burn this fucking hell to the ground."

In the street, the prying eyes of her neighbors, who watched March enter Bronwen's manor, with pity and frustration in their eyes, now look upon her and the stout man with Bronwen over her shoulder the way she always intended—with fear.

The descent through the zig-zagging stairs of Mirus is a long enough journey. The stout man huffs from the unconscious weight of Bronwen over his shoulder, but he does not complain. She could have taken a wheelbarrow from the shed, but the twists and turns of the streets would have added hours to their journey. The few soldiers patrolling through the night streets nod as they pass and wipe away the drops of blood from the rolled carpet.

"Can I help you?" a passing soldier on his way to relieve those at the gate asks.

"Just make sure the way is open."

The soldier rushes ahead over the Long Bridge and orders the other soldiers to open the main gates wide.

Before she crosses over the threshold of the city's gate, she turns back to the stout man. "I will take her from here."

"I can keep going. I have more—"

"No. What remains, I must finish. Return to the manor, collect what you can. Make sure you are the last through the door and watch it burn."

The stout man carefully positions Bronwen's body on March's shoulder, before giving one last nod, and leaves her on the Long Bridge. Her added weight digs into every one of March's wounds again. The soldiers, like all others along her trek, stand at attention and nod when she passes through the gates of Mirus, without questions.

Cold air from the Queenwood rushes to greet her, long kept at bay by the towering city walls of Mirus. The way before her is dark, and even if the speckled starlight did not guide her, she knows the path to her destination. A path she has taken many times in the dead of night.

The cobbles of the Long Bridge give way to the rough dirt of the Queen's Way, the main road out of Mirus, and then the cart path curving off the main road, where the air turns rank and heavy. A tingle crawls across the back of her neck. Her back feels as though some unforeseen hands dig into her muscles and pull at them. March struggles to keep her footing through the uneven, rocky dirt but remains steadfast and determined with the end so near.

March's shaking legs become iron with a will of their own and carry her and Bronwen up the small incline and down into the Crags. Instead of stopping at the end of the bog where the curve of cart wheels mark the dark soil, March trudges up a nearby rock outcropping of cantilevering boulders. Its edge juts out over the middle of the dark maw, devouring Wonderland's dead and forgotten. She slides Bronwen from her shoulder onto the smooth boulder and unfurls the rug toward the ledge. Bronwen's bloody and limp body comes to a stop at the edge. March reaches out with two fingers over Bronwen's mouth to feel her shallow and sporadic breaths. Good; she will not be robbed of this moment. She waits until Bronwen's eyes flutter open; she coughs from the stench, winces from the renewed pain, and rolls her head toward March.

Bronwen summons all her strength and claws at March's legs, knowing her fate. Bloody nubs, which were once fingertips, try to grip trousers, rug, or stone. March swats Bronwen's arms away and kicks her in the chest, sending her mother over the edge. A rather unimpressive *plop* and wet *squish* announce Bronwen's fall into the viscous river below.

By the time March climbs down from the boulders and makes her way to the small shore, Bronwen lies face up and all that remains visible is her chest and the front half of her head. Her pitch-covered arms feebly reach up like an insect on its back, ticking away at the end.

"Audrianna," Bronwen's hoarse voice croaks. "Please. You... you... are strong because of me. Because you are my daughter."

"There is a sadness in the truth of your words."

The vile black sludge of putrefied bodies crawls into the corners of Bronwen's mouth. She fights to spit it out but heaves and spurts vomit out over her face.

"Please," Bronwen gurgles. "Please, save me. Do not do this. You cannot do this."

"I spoke those words to you once." March crouches and rests her forearms on her thighs at the edge of the bog. "As a child, I begged and pleaded the first night you and father sold me to the Castellan from Clava."

"Audrianna, please. Please."

"I pleaded, as you do now. After the carriage rolled from our doorstep, how long did it take you to stand at father's desk, goblet of wine in one hand and untying the pouches of gold with the other?"

Bronwen stretches her neck, and she flails her arms to keep her face above the surface of the Crags. The more she struggles, the quicker she sinks. "I tried. I tried to stop your father. Please. Save me now, as I could not save you before."

"Even here, at the end, you still cannot help but lie."

"Please. Be stronger than I was."

March has never heard her mother plead in her life. There should be some modicum of pity for this wretched creature, but that part of March died long ago. "I am stronger in spite of you."

"Audrianna—"

"Let the weight of your lies and your wickedness carry you to the bottom of the mire as dark and lifeless as your soul."

Bronwen's face hardens. Her sliced lips tighten as the festering thick pitch covers her mouth and crawls into her nostrils. She coughs but sucks in as much liquid as she dispels. Her eyes grow wide, knowing she has taken her last breath. Her head shakes in terror yet unwilling to shed a tear even for her own death.

The shrinking circle of her mother's face grows smaller. The black sludge of the bog covers her eyes. She attempts one last scream, amounting to a large gurgled bubble from her mouth, allowing the liquid to fill her lungs. It pops, and without the strength to struggle any longer, Bronwen sinks into the bog and disappears from sight, from Wonderland, from life.

March watches until the surface of the quagmire returns to its stillness. She releases a long breath and hangs her head. Bloody strands of hair swing in front of her face. The tingle crawls up the back of her neck again.

What next?

A terrifying question encompassing her mother, Jonathan, Cheshire, and every next step, once she crosses back over the threshold of the Crags. But this is a question for the dawn.

CHAPTER 65

CHESHIRE

Deeper into the catacombs, underneath the castle, Cheshire leans back against the wall and dabs his neck with the thick concoction from the Lory. The vapors of aloe, thyme, and honey rush into his lungs and soothe his burning skin. Four dead castle guards, necks twisted, jaws askew, and eyes wide with horror, are piled in the distance to his left. Their torches smolder to cinders next to their bodies.

The shattered remains of the Mask of Shadows flake like the pieces of week-old egg shells next to him. At least his last walk in the shadows had importance—to save one of his loves. His body is weary yet rested, however, his spirit remains restless. Lingering questions float in his mind like the glowing bugs floating in the moonlight, and he fears the paths forward fork in diverging directions.

He pulls his clothing off, stiff with his and March's blood. Cheshire examines his mother's sash and thankfully it remains in its perfect threadbare condition. He bundles his trousers, cloak, and vest with it and slings it over his shoulder as he has thousands of times. But when the sash rubs against his neck, the reignited pain nearly takes Cheshire to his knees. He carries the bundle by his side the rest of the way through the castle's winding, hidden passages and eventually into the corridors, where the midday sun reflects harshly from the upper windows.

As fortune would have it, Jonathan emerges from Mary Anne's bedchamber as Cheshire approaches. The latch of the door clicks shut behind him. His linen shirt hangs open, framing his formidable chest. With a quiver at his lip, he rushes to embrace Cheshire, lifting him from the floor. The warmth of his mighty arms and bare chest melt Cheshire like warm wax.

He cannot help but notice Jonathan holds him with his forearms and not his hands. He pushes away to see not just tears but conflict swell in Jonathan's eyes. Jonathan sets Cheshire down and holds up his bandaged hands, blood staining the linens.

"I did not suffer to the lengths of you and March," says Jonathan, with guilt in the quiver in his voice. "How does she fare?"

"Recovering."

"There is more I could have done, should have done."

"It would seem you have done enough." Cheshire's words strike at Jonathan's heart and twist his face, their meaning plain. Without Jonathan's strength, he would have surely died. However, he has hurt March deeply—for the first time in over a thousand years, as far as Cheshire knows. It is easy to guess Mary Anne is at the center of the vortex, which pulls in everything. From Jonathan's expression, Mary Anne is not within her chambers. The temptation weighs heavy on Cheshire's heart to put an end to her, especially after the prior night.

He will, but for now, Jonathan's beautiful, crystalline eyes shimmer with regret. *Please*, they say. Nights ago, March stood before him with the need to forget, to escape. Jonathan stands before him with the same tumbling gleam in his eyes.

"I did not mean for any of this-" says Jonathan.

He grabs Jonathan by the jaw. "Stop. I do not want your words."

Cheshire lowers his arm and brings Jonathan to his knees in the middle of the corridor. He pulls Jonathan's head back with his other hand, twisting his fingers in his hair. Cheshire leans down and kisses Jonathan deeply, roughly. His lover whimpers in his mouth as his broad shoulders relax, giving himself over to Cheshire.

Jonathan turns his head and wraps his lips around Cheshire's tongue, sucking and pulling it into his mouth. He takes hold of Cheshire's cock with both hands, squeezes, but winces at the pain. Cheshire pushes Jonathan's linen shirt down off his shoulders, tight around his upper arms, to his elbows, keeping them restrained at his sides.

Unable to contain his yearning and the pulse within, he stands, leaving Jonathan's mouth agape, and slides his cock in until his face presses against Cheshire's stomach. Cheshire suspends his love there, in the moments of pleasure and penance without air. After the third time Jonathan jolts, Cheshire releases him, pulling from Jonathan to catch his breath. But he leans forward, trying to take Cheshire in his mouth again, tongue reaching out.

Servants pass by at the far ends of the corridor, but their presence or prying eyes do not deter Cheshire in the slightest. He tightens his fingers in Jonathan's hair, the spark of the animal taking over the man in his eyes. Jonathan looks up at him, chest heaving, mouth watering, waiting, and nods. Cheshire returns the full length of his shaft into Jonathan's willing throat, grabs his hair with both hands, and thrusts over and over, fucking his love's mouth, slamming his body against Jonathan's. His gifted tongue plays and glides against the bottom of Cheshire's shaft and teases the rim of its head as it passes. Every moan, whimper, and sigh increases his lust and ferocity.

Jonathan finally pulls back and gasps his breath, then shoves Cheshire back against the wall of the corridor with his shoulder. He forces his face between his legs, lifting one over his body for his tongue to reach Cheshire's ass. Every rough kiss and long swath and press of his tongue cause Cheshire to squirm and writhe at the vibrations Jonathan's mouth sends coursing through his body.

Cheshire pushes Jonathan to his back and lowers himself onto his face. Jonathan does not need his hands to hook his arms around Cheshire's thighs and force him down to his waiting mouth. He obliges and grinds back and forth across Jonathan. His ravenous tongue ignites every part of Cheshire's body with crackling cinders from a bonfire, heightens every sense, and brings his fingers and toes to curl.

He pulls Jonathan's trousers apart, laces whipping through their holes, and pushes them to his thighs. His cock flops out, heavy, hard, and dripping against the muscles of his stomach. Cheshire's fingers dance down its length, and Jonathan's stomach spasms at his touch. Once Cheshire's body begins to shake and his ass twitches, he shifts his hips and slides down Jonathan's throat again—a welcome surprise to his lover. Jonathan grabs Cheshire's ass with his wrist and pulls him in. He cradles the back of Jonathan's neck and slowly pumps in and out, watching his cock glisten every time it appears, until the feral craving takes hold, and he fucks Jonathan's mouth relentlessly.

Cheshire's cock interrupts the long, guttural moans again and again. Jonathan gasps for breath with every reprieve but pulls Cheshire back in and oft times holds him there, sealing off his own breath, using Cheshire's heartbeat within to sustain him.

The temptation, the call of Jonathan's cock as it bounces up and down with every thrust, leaving an ever-thickening string from his muscles to its tip, is too great for Cheshire. He leans down and takes its throbbing head in his mouth, savoring the sweetness of his love. His tongue swirls around the rim and flicks the underside of Jonathan's head. His legs buck and kick. Farther down the hall, the same servant girls pass back and forth. After a few minutes, they stay and peek around the corner, but to Cheshire and Jonathan, they exist in their own world no matter where they are or who watches.

Jonathan pushes his hips up and both men pump into each other, feeding each other's love and lust in an endless loop. Cheshire wraps his arms around Jonathan, under the small of his back. The shirt around

Jonathan's elbows limits his movements, only allowing him to scratch at Cheshire's sides. Jonathan keeps Cheshire's head in his mouth. The quick sucking, control of his tongue, and thrum of his lips over the edge of his cock builds the pressure within Cheshire's stomach and releases the flutter of sparks and crawling fingers across the back of his head. Too soon.

In one swift, continuous motion, Cheshire moves and kneels at Jonathan's legs, flips him over to his stomach, grabs his hips, and pulls his ass into the air. His wet cock lays between the hard mounds of Jonathan's ass perfectly. He slides up and down, teasing Jonathan, who pushes his ass against Cheshire, trousers still around his thighs, leaving his chest on the floor. Cheshire pulls Jonathan's trousers below his knees, giving Jonathan the freedom to widen his knees and arch his back properly. Braziers from farther down the corridor cast deep shadows in the grooves of his back, from his broad shoulders to the dimples at his waist. He reaches back and takes hold of his ass, spreading it farther.

Cheshire's heart, already racing, thunders in his chest and in his cock. He laughs and growls at the beautiful sight. Jonathan's body jolts with every heavy thump from Cheshire's shaft against his hole.

Jonathan looks back over his shoulder with tears in his eyes. *Please*, they say.

He guides his cock into Jonathan as both inhale deeply. Jonathan cries out in a long burst of mingled ecstasy and pain. Both of their bodies quiver, legs shaking at the palpable heat of their union. Cheshire flexes within Jonathan, and his lover twitches every time.

"Please," Jonathan whispers.

Cheshire will not deny him. He grabs hold of Jonathan's wrists and fucks his lover harder than ever before, slamming their bodies together. Jonathan gasps for air as Cheshire pulls from him and screams out, pushing dust across the ground every time Cheshire plunges deep, offering little mercy. Their bodies crack against each other like thunder. Cheshire does not want to leave the warmth of Jonathan, gripping him tight. Both want it, crave it, need it. Together, the rest of the world fades away.

"More," Jonathan begs, with a parched mouth. "More."

Simple words bring Cheshire close to the brink. Chills run across his skin, but he will not stop despite the pain racing across his neck.

Cheshire rises and places his feet by Jonathan's knees, pushing deeper than before judging by Jonathan's whimper and the shaking of his body. He grabs a hold of Jonathan's shirt running across his back like the reins of a stallion. Jonathan's scream from the first thrust reminds Cheshire of the first divine time he fucked Jonathan and stokes the fire within him. Cheshire fucks him harder and faster than before, tip to base. Jonathan can barely catch his breath. His fingers grip his ass tighter, muscles ripple, and the veins in his arms bulge. He turns back to lock eyes with Cheshire. His body would have been enough, but the glint in his eye pulls Cheshire to the precipice.

"Cheshire," Jonathan pants, legs squirming. "Cheshire." His climax nears.

He will look upon his lover's face when they climax and not allow Jonathan's seed to go to waste. Cheshire rolls Jonathan to his back and kneels, staying in him, and not breaking his rhythm. The bunched trousers at Jonathan's boots offer a handle to keep his legs up. Legs trapped and arms pinned, Jonathan locks eyes with Cheshire through the space between his legs. They want this moment in time to last forever—at least longer—but neither can withhold their love any longer.

Jonathan howls, teetering on the verge of tears, as does Cheshire, at the rapture consuming their bodies. They watch and bask in every shot of Jonathan's climax, filling the deep crevices of his stomach and chest muscles, reaching his neck and cheek. Every ribbon quickens Cheshire's hips, holding Jonathan in his climax, drawing more from him. He cannot contain himself any longer. The longing, beautiful look in Jonathan's eyes, his taut, wet muscles, pulls Cheshire over the edge with him, bursting, filling his lover. His vision blurs, and the tingling of a thousand fingers race through his hair down his body and to his cock. Jonathan's eyes grow wider, feeling and welcoming everything Cheshire has to give. Their bodies vibrate so fiercely it is as if the world quakes around them. Cheshire continues to thrust, unable to stop the hunger of his spirit, the lust of his body, and unwillingness to let this moment end. Jonathan breathes heavily, spent, rocking back and forth on the floor from the wave of Cheshire's body.

After both slowly descend from their climax, and the prying eyes of the servants have fled, Cheshire slides through the space between Jonathan's legs and trousers, lapping up every drop of Jonathan, until he reaches his love's face, smiling and panting. With a simple kiss, Jonathan opens his mouth and their tongues share the sweet taste together until they both swallow, breathing each other in until their hearts and bodies calm.

A sadness still lurks in Jonathan's eyes. It pains Cheshire to see it and know he cannot fix it. He runs his hands through Jonathan's hair, gently scratching at his scalp, as he lies on him.

"Where are you off to?" asks Jonathan

"To March. And you must be away to Mary Anne," he says before Jonathan can respond.

Silence widens the gap between them, though they are close enough to share each other's breath. Cheshire grazes his lips against Jonathan's.

"Choices have been made all around," Cheshire whispers. "But do not forget the promises that bind us."

With a final hard kiss, Cheshire slips through Jonathan's legs, collects his bundle, and leaves his love to clean up the mess—in more ways than one. And every step away tugs at the heart string tied between him and Jonathan.

CHAPTER 66
MARY ANNE

Mary Anne exits the rear of the castle to meet Jonathan, as requested. Braziers light the small terrace, and their warm pulsing orbs obscure the topiary garden beyond. No amount of light or dark can conceal Jonathan's silhouette waiting for her on the other side.

She steps down the stairs, and it is more than Jonathan's presence that takes her breath away. Large, Everlast roses bloom on every topiary throughout the garden, speckling the smooth green with beautiful white accents, turning the lush landscape into the night sky with brilliant starlight.

"Jonathan, it is beyond words." There is no longer any question: this is proof of his requited feelings for her. Even if not spoken, his actions speak volumes and shout to the heavens. "You did this for me?"

"For us. They shall serve as a constant reminder of your devotion to Wonderland. And I... I needed to occupy my mind. I know it does not sound romantic in the least, but I needed to do something, something for you."

Hesitant to touch one at first, she cups one in her hands and smells the sweetest fragrance from any flower she has seen. "It is true? What you said earlier about them?"

Jonathan plucks a rose from a short, conical shaped tree, and within seconds a new bud forms and spirals out to a full bloom in all its glory. He takes Mary Anne's hand, kisses her palm, and places the rose in it.

The gentle kiss steals her breath and weakens her knees. Mary Anne's heart pounds in her throat and temples. "I have a gift for you as well, if you will you accompany me to the throne room."

"Of course."

Every step of the excruciatingly long walk through the winding corridors of the castle until they reach the throne room fills Mary Anne with doubt. Sweat runs down her palms, back, and forehead, worried she cannot handle rejection again.

A blurred face, a woman's face, tries to emerge from some obscured memory. A shadow of a daydream. She wafts it away and banishes it like smoke from a candle. For a fleeting moment, she believes she has forgotten something from her past, something important. Whatever, whoever it was, it could not be more important than what and who lies in her glorious future.

For the first time since Lysander's and Uriah's defeat, she walks into the grand throne room, her throne room. She has not looked upon it since the doors first opened for her, and it is just as magnificent as she remembers. Moonlight and a sky full of stars shine through the false windows of the chamber, and soft specks of dust dance and wander like small glowing fairies.

She turns to face Jonathan once they reach the center of the four pillars. "My gift is actually a confession."

"Some secrets are meant to be kept."

"Not this one," says Mary Anne. "Not anymore. I do not know when it happened. We have been through so much together, and you have always been by my side, honestly, as long as I can remember. I grew used to you being there. Then you went from standing at my side to embracing my heart and having a hold on me like nothing I have ever felt. It is as if you grip me by the throat when you are near. You must know the effect you have upon me?"

"I do."

"I can hold it in no longer. I love you, Jonathan." Mary Anne's voice does not waver. "And I do not expect you to return the same words back."

Not yet.

"It is possible to love more than one person. You have shown me this possibility. Giving to one does not mean giving any less to another. Every ounce of me yearns to speak it aloud to you now more than ever."

Jonathan breaks his gaze and lowers his head. This time it is Mary Anne who raises his chin with a bent finger. "We have been through much, but we are here, now, together. This is not coincidence, this is providence. A new chapter unfolds, and I want you by my side in my story." Mary Anne unbuckles the silver belt keeping her dress against her body. It clinks to the floor like a handful of silver coins. "No longer as advisor, companion, or friend. Lover is my new title."

"Are you sure this is what you want?" asks Jonathan.

"More than the world." Mary Anne swallows, for the first time, hesitant. "And you?"

"This... this is what I need."

She reaches for the front of her dress, hanging loosely over her bare body, but Jonathan catches her wrists.

Jonathan grabs her face, pulls her in, and kisses her fully. "Undressing you is my duty and pleasure."

Her legs nearly give out from the touch. Mary Anne burns from within; every part of her sears with instantaneous heat from his soft lips and the powerful swirl of his tongue. Jonathan slides his fingers from her cheeks, down her shoulders, and hooks them under the fabric of her open-sided gown, moving the fabric inward to reveal her breast.

A soft moan escapes into his mouth as his tongue fills her, his mouth envelopes hers. His hands cup her breasts and gently massage them, never breaking from their kiss. Jonathan only pulls away to pull her dress over her head, leaving her only in her boots.

Mary Anne catches her breath, watches, and enjoys every kiss Jonathan leaves on her skin as he kneels—her neck, her breast, her nipples, her stomach, her thighs. She can feel his breath in between her legs, and her toes curl. He slips one boot off and then the other.

She waits for Jonathan to stand. Instead, he nuzzles the small area of hair between her legs, causing them to tremble. He grabs her thighs to steady her and slides his hands to her ass. Each hot breath on her teases and stokes the fire within. She removes Jonathan's top hat, places it on her head, then runs her fingers through his hair and pushes her hips toward his waiting mouth. His lips and tongue accept her, excite her without question, devouring her as ravenously as he kissed her—more so. Jonathan's head bobs back and forth, his silver tongue lapping, sucking, and reaching inside her.

"Remove your shirt," she commands.

Without breaking away, he slides his linen shirt from his body. The muscles of his shoulders and back pinch as it falls to the floor behind him, and the muscles of his arms flex as he grabs her ass again, pulling himself farther into her.

Mary Anne twists her fingers in his hair to steady herself, mesmerized by his back muscles, until he opens his eyes and looks up at her. The sharp blue of his eyes pierce her deep. His gaze and his tongue have captured her. She forces herself to step away and cannot help but to continue to rub at her sensitivity.

"Stand," says Mary Anne, through panting breaths.

Jonathan obeys, never breaking eye contact.

"Undress for me."

He unbuckles his leather trousers and kicks his boots from his feet. He bends to remove his trousers, blocking Mary Anne's view momentarily. When he rises, the tip of his cock, already hard, brushes against her thigh, leaving a small glistening trail. Again, he may not say the words, but his actions, his body's response, betray his silence and prove his feelings.

Mary Anne takes hold of his shaft with both hands, and it jumps and swells in her grasp. She remembers its taste and yearns for it again. She starts to lower herself, but Jonathan stops her, moves the hair from her face, tucking it behind her ear, and holds the sides of her cheeks.

"You kneel for no one."

Confused at first, Mary Anne follows Jonathan to the throne, leaving their clothing in the center of the pillars.

Anyone could walk in on them at any time—the Duchess, Weiss, soldiers, servants. It does not matter to Mary Anne. They can look upon her with envy. As they should a queen. This is the next chapter in her story, filled with Jonathan, as often as she can take him.

He ushers her forward and extends a hand, asking her to sit. A sudden chill rages against the heat in her body. Should she? This is not how she envisioned sitting upon the throne the first time, believing there would be several more people and much more clothing involved. She trusts Jonathan and steps upon the dais, sits on the cold red cushion of the throne, and lays her hands on the marble arm rests. With every emotion fighting for dominance in her, this feels not like a dream but a fulfillment after her long journey and struggles. Damned if she wears clothing or not. She shall do as she pleases as the queen.

"How do you feel?" Jonathan asks, standing with one foot on the raised dais, cock hard and bobbing, smiling at her.

"Correct."

"Shall we continue?"

"Do not ask anymore. Do as you wish."

Unexpectedly, Jonathan climbs onto the throne, knees on the armrests, and holds onto the tall marble back. His glistening cock bounces inches from Mary Anne's face. Her heart thumps so fiercely between her legs and in her face, she fears she may lose consciousness.

She looks up to Jonathan's smile hanging above her, a glorious chandelier to their love.

Mary Anne takes hold of his cock again, reveling in her victory. Her tongue returns the teasing, circling its head and licking at its underside. She kisses his head tenderly, then again, and again, until she opens her mouth, jaw tingling, and takes him in. She runs her hands between his thighs, hard and flexed, to take hold of his taut ass, pulling him closer and deeper into her mouth. They moan together, synced in pleasure. Her mouth travels his shaft, moaning louder the farther she goes, enjoying his taste. Jonathan inhales through gritted teeth.

Soon, he balances himself on the armrests, gently but firmly grabs the back of her head, keeping it in place, so he can push in and out himself. Her body falls slack with the tingling energy of bliss running through it, surrendering to Jonathan, eyes fluttering at the roll of his hips, pushing farther, fucking her mouth.

She looks to his eyes, sparkling in the moonlight, and his wild smile and snarl tenses every muscle of her body, rocked with every long ebb and flow of his cock. The monument of rippling muscles and veins towers over her. This is the Jonathan Mary Anne watched pleasure March, gentle yet commanding at the same time. She swallows his cock as far as she can take it, which is barely halfway down the shaft, back and forth, harder every time, wanting more. Mary Anne forgets to breathe, lost in the moment, lost in his grasp. She has no choice but to wrap her arms around his thighs and brace herself, like a shift at the mercy of a storm, her storm.

Mary Anne pulls away to catch her breath and slides her spit down the length of Jonathan's shaft. She pushes him from the throne, standing him in front of her, kissing his head one last time. "Enough," she whispers. "Fuck me. Fuck me, this instant."

Without hesitation, Jonathan picks Mary Anne's legs up, her back resting on the cushioned seat, and hooks his elbows under her knees, bringing them to her chest. In one swift movement, he rests his forearms on the armrests of the throne and bends Mary Anne to his will—to her desire. Helpless, but content, she wants to look in his eyes, but the pull, the need, to look down at his body wins. The pale moonlight from the large windows and the warm, lit braziers by the door cast Jonathan in harsh shadows, accentuating the curve and valley of every muscle.

His stomach, his beautiful muscles, contract with every breath. He lays his glistening cock upon the heat of her sensitivity, teasing her, as if a warning. Its length almost reaches her navel. Jonathan breathes heavily and rubs it slowly back and forth against her, flexing involuntarily and slapping down on her. Her body jolts each time. Unable to help herself, she grabs his cock and slaps it down on her clit over and over again.

Pinned as she is, Mary Anne pushes her hips toward him, craving his presence within her. He slides his hips back until the head of his cock pushes against the soft skin between her legs, again teasing, but not entering her. Four times he presses against her, and each time Mary Anne gasps, wanting and waiting.

"Please," she whimpers.

"Take a deep breath." Jonathan's deep whisper shakes Mary Anne to the core. The head of his cock presses against her, then slips in.

Her teeth chatter, her entire body shakes, and her stomach cramps. He waits, but Mary Anne can feel his head pulsing inside her. She looks down at his cock, barely in, yet it feels as though he will rip her in two.

"Are you harmed?" he jests. A question Jonathan has needed to ask frequently during their time together.

"No," Mary Anne says in a breathy whimper.

He bites his bottom lip. A hard, powerful thrust pushes the rest of his cock into Mary Anne. She feels him deep, so deep, a sensation unlike any experienced before. She releases a guttural moan or scream, she cannot tell which, and claws at his arms. He stays still inside her, where she can feel his heartbeat.

From the wincing of her face, Jonathan cannot help but ask, "Does it hurt?"

"No."

It does hurt in the best way possible, but Mary Anne dares not tell him to slow down or stop. It hurts with such pleasure she will never tell him to stop.

"Do not ask anymore," says Mary Anne. "Do what you wish to me. I am yours. Make me yours."

He slides out, and her body aches and her stomach sucks in as if he pulls at her soul. He plunges deep again and again. Each thrust, more powerful than the last, confounds every one of Mary Anne's senses. All she can smell is Jonathan's musk. Her ears, like her whole body, fill with her heartbeat, sending palpable waves of heat pulsating out from between her legs. She becomes aware of every part of her body as it vibrates from his ecstasy. Mary Anne can still taste him in the thick mucus in her mouth. Her eyes lose and regain focus as he forcefully rocks her back and forth upon the throne.

With every intense thrust sliding deeper into her, she swears she sees flashes of beautiful crimson light pulse from the runes of the pillars. Yes. Yes, she does. A crimson glow, dim at first, fills the throne room. The red light traces and frames the edges of Jonathan's body, every muscle, every vein, making each bulge and striation deeper than before. His eyes flash back and forth from brilliant blue to red with every pulse, with every thrust. He is the epitome of what every man should aspire to be—his spirit, in his rugged yet soft face, in his giving heart, his exquisite body, and the way he fucks her, and fulfills her.

She should care. The jewels within the columns glow, the Arcana, the throne, but fuck, she does not. All Mary Anne craves is for Jonathan to fuck her until the dawn, until her entire body is numb, and continue on every day of her reign.

"I feel you. I feel you," Mary Anne pants. "I feel everything."

Her stomach tightens and spasms, taking Jonathan's full length, and sucks in every time he pulls from her, leaving her trembling in his wake.

"Your lips are dry," he whispers.

How can a man be so gentle and yet so forceful simultaneously? He wraps his hand around her chin and kisses her. He pulls out, almost completely, and thrusts in again, harder than before.

"More," she says through panting, crying breaths. "Fuck me. Every ounce of passion, anger, sadness, fear, or love, unleash it on me. In me."

Jonathan heeds her commands and slams against her again and again. The sound and sensation of their bodies, their souls, colliding drives Mary Anne close to the threshold of what her body can handle. She wants this moment to last, forever building to her first climax from Jonathan.

He presses his forehead against hers, both covered with sweat. They lock eyes for a moment and together they look down between their dripping bodies, a cavern of lust. Together they watch Jonathan's wet cock swell, its shimmering veins more prominent, as he thrusts harder. His fingers find her sensitive spot, as if he knew where to touch her all along, and shakes his hand across her vigorously, igniting a new, all-consuming, pulsing wave into the depths of her soul.

She grips his muscular arms and gives herself over to him. Tingles start in her toes, her thighs shake, her core spasms, sending a rush of butterflies, no, more like birds, up her body to her head. They dive back down between her thighs suddenly, body frozen, and the flap of each of their wings sends Mary Anne into untold bliss. Unable to close her mouth, Mary Anne climaxes, wanting to scream, unable to breathe for an eternity, until his ecstasy releases its hold on her, letting her scream unlike any known to her before, long, low at first then rising while her body vibrates uncontrollably. Her eyes strain to stay focused to watch Jonathan slide and thrust faster and harder, each slap becoming more wet, splashing Mary Anne's love between them.

"Breathe," Jonathan pants, rising, reaching his own climax.

Mary Anne gasps for breath, held submerged by his power, finally able to resurface. She brings his hand to her mouth, unable to control herself, and takes his thumb into her mouth, sucking on it furiously.

Jonathan continues to fuck her through her climax, keeping her suspended.

Finally, he hisses through gritted teeth and lets out small moans, quicker, faster.

"I want it," pants Mary Anne. "I want to watch."

Jonathan slides from her one last time and lets her legs down. She fights the cramping of her legs and stomach to sit on her throne again. She takes his shaft in one hand, his balls in the other, and strokes him heartily. Her hand swirls around the head of his wet cock and plunges down his length. Every one of his muscles flexes and relaxes until his body shakes.

"Put your hands behind your head."

Jonathan obeys, muscles flaring, bathed in blue and crimson light. Though she has him in her hands, his presence persists within her. His cock grows thicker in her hand, and Jonathan climaxes like a grand, lustful fountain. Beautiful ribbons of his love erupt and cover her chest, shoulders, stomach, legs, and face. His body quakes as hard as Mary Anne's until there is nothing more to give. They finally look up at each other, faces and bodies drenched.

The woman Mary Anne once was no longer exists. This new woman, a queen, stands, confident yet quivering in the fading red glow of the pillars. She rubs and slides their bodies together, feeling and sharing Jonathan's warm gift. Jonathan grabs her by the chin and licks her face clean with long, lingering strokes. Mary Anne pulls him in for a long kiss, taste sweet and tart, sharing his love in their mouths.

Jonathan kisses her gently and carries her in his arms from the throne room to the baths next to her bedchamber, leaving their clothing behind. He sets her down in the middle of the wide bath, and she presses her hands and breasts to his chest, her forehead to his chin, and her hips to his. Jonathan remains hard and did the entire walk back. His large hands glide and press against her skin to scoop up water and let it flow over her. Her hands cannot keep from his cock and the muscles of his chest and stomach. The quiver returns to Mary Anne's thighs.

Jonathan washes their love from their bodies, massaging her breasts, and plunging between her thighs, never taking his eyes from hers, even with her attention in other places. Her body aches and jumps. His absence leaves a void in her body and her spirit only he can refill.

"Once more," she says, squeezing his cock in time with her heartbeat.

"Just once?" asks Jonathan. He pulls her close and kisses her, lowers himself, lifting her left leg with his hand, and with the other, guiding his cock inside her again.

She wraps her arms around his neck, and he stands, hooking her other knee with his arm. Jonathan's strength keeps her suspended in air while he fucks her. Mary Anne screams in his mouth as they kiss. Even muffled, it echoes through the baths.

This. This blessed, beautiful union is how her story will continue—without March, without Cheshire. Mary Anne will please him, and Jonathan will please her, day and night as they journey around Wonderland together. She closes her eyes and envisions the pulsing lights of the pillar with every wild thrust from Jonathan. Now, nothing stands in her way—the Twins are defeated, the Grand Arcana awakens, Jonathan gives her new life, and all that remains is for her to explore and embrace the Arcana and her reign. In the meantime, she will fill her days with Jonathan, her king, fucking to her lust's and heart's desire. After all, Wonderland has spoken. She has won.

CHAPTER 67

MARCH

The crunch of dried needles and rocks on the road accompanies the symphony of insects throughout the Queenwood as March, exhausted, returns to Mirus. The melody covers the vacant area of her mind where she kept thoughts of Bronwen like creeping ivy over a broken garden wall where flowers bloom, yet the hole remains, unseen except by those who tend them.

The rough road soon gives way to the smooth clacks of her boots against the cobbles of the Long Bridge. In the distance, high in the city, a distant bell rings, followed by a second, then a third and fourth. At the top of the looming dark silhouette of the city, past the walls, past Stonehaven, a small yet bright beacon flashes in the Crest. March cannot see it, but the plumes of smoke rising from the city with an orange underbelly prove the former servants listened. If wise, they will find new lives somewhere else outside of Mirus instead of some other manor in the Crest. If not, they will be among the rest of the townspeople who incur Cheshire's wrath and fall before him. Choices were made, and all must live with them. Jonathan is with Mary Anne, Bronwen is dead, and March is here outside of the castle.

Cheshire, her love, the tingle at the back of her neck, leans against the stone railing halfway down the Long Bridge and waits to greet her. He followed her, watched, and did not interfere. She loses herself in the lavender shimmer of his eyes in the moonlight. Cheshire runs his fingers tenderly over the bandages around her waist, shoulder, and hand. She touches the split in his lip. He takes her by the hand, not saying a word yet understanding, and together they continue across the Long Bridge. Even at this late hour, the shadow of the castle and the city consume the night, growing darker the closer they draw to the castle wall. The soldiers beside the entrance signal March's return, but she holds up her hand to stop them. She will not return to the castle or the city this night.

March leads Cheshire down the small dirt path leading underneath the Long Bridge to a long wooden stairway—recently repaired and reinforced after the bridge's collapse. Hands still intertwined, they descend the stairs toward the cabin perched on the cliffside, where a candle flickers within. March savors the thump and creak of each step, the natural yawn of the supports underneath, and the rush of water from the river at the ravine's base. Too long the muffled sounds of stone have assaulted her ears like an incessant, out-of-tune timepiece.

The front door of the cabin opens as they approach, and Pat and Bill stand before them without a stitch of clothing, both covered with sweat, and Bill's cock hard. March and Cheshire walk past them, and Pat and Bill close the door behind them then set to work undressing their company. Bill makes quick work of Cheshire, sliding his vest and cloak to the floor. One solid pull causes his tattered, short trousers to the floor, leaving him only in his sash. Pat takes care to slip March's boots, top, and trousers from her, minding the bandages. When finished, Cheshire and March stand side by side, an arm around each other, while Pat and Bill kneel before them. Pat takes Cheshire's cock into her mouth, little by little, as far as she can, and Bill's tongue twirls and plays at March's sensitivity.

She gazes into Cheshire's eyes as they rock back and forth, pulled in the teasing current of Pat and Bill. They both grab their heads and hold them firmly in place while they kiss—slowly at first, then wildly. Bill lifts March's leg over his shoulder, lowering himself for his tongue and lips to envelope March wholly. The increasing moans of March and inhales from Cheshire prove Pat matches Bill's intensity.

The shaking of March's legs and the tickle of her stomach cause her to break from Cheshire, breathing heavy, lips wet, to enjoy watching Pat and Bill hungrily grunting and pleasing them. March pulls them both away, faces Cheshire, pulls him close, and continues to kiss him. Before long, four warm hands play between their thighs, widen them slightly, and guide Cheshire into March. Her stomach sucks in when she welcomes him fully, completely.

Her hands slide down Cheshire's back to the slope of his ass and spread it. His rough hands match hers, and the cool air colliding with their heat is vanquished by the warm breath and tongue of Pat upon her ass and Bill upon Cheshire's. Her love rocks back and forth, sliding and thrusting further into her soul, and she cannot keep herself from slamming against Cheshire, wincing and whimpering each time, then pulling away and pushing back to allow Pat and Bill to press and grind their faces into their asses, tickling and heightening every sensation.

This is only the second time Cheshire has been a part of their group, though Jonathan and March have entertained Pat and Bill sporadically over the years. For Cheshire, this is still new, and he thrusts into her like never before, with a newfound fervor. His mouth leaves her lips and sucks and bites at her breasts—the sign he has lost all control and given into his animalistic qualities. The way March prefers him.

March looks down between their legs to see Pat and Bill tending to each other. From their moans, Bill climaxes first, soon followed by Pat. Her moans rumble through March's body, and Cheshire growls on her breast, biting at her nipple from Bill. March can feel his shaft and beautiful head swell with every thrust, from tip to base, fully embedded in her spirit, refilling her chalice. Her legs quake, then her stomach.

March wraps her arms around Cheshire's head and holds him tight to her breast as she hisses and grunts unbridled, unhindered, as if they were in the Hollow.

The pressure builds within her, and Cheshire throbs deeper, unwilling to stop as they both reach their climax. Before either can succumb to each other, Pat and Bill pull them apart and turn them side by side, arms around each other's waists again. Pat lifts one of March's legs and unleashes a flurry of licks and kisses, sucking furiously; her body shakes just as fast. Bill keeps half of Cheshire's cock in his mouth and strokes him forcefully. Soon her love takes control, grabs the back of Bill's head, and fucks his mouth as he roars into the night. Cheshire shakes in March's arms, unable to contain himself. He pulls from Bill's mouth, allowing Bill to stroke him rougher than before. Cheshire pushes his hips forward and erupts, slinging beautiful ribbon after ribbon of white across Bill's and Pat's faces.

The sight is more than March can bear, and she screams to match Cheshire as she climaxes, showering Pat and Bill. Cheshire and March glow with their sweat while Pat and Bill glisten with their love. March catches her breath and swallows to regain any semblance of wetness in her mouth.

Following their encounter, all four stand under the spigot outside the cabin's front door. They wash the day from each other's bodies, hands sliding, caressing, scrubbing. The patter of water raining upon their skin and the wooden planks below takes the worries of this day with them into the darkness of the valley below. Pat pulls on a chain to stop the flow of water, and she and Bill retire inside the cabin and leave the door ajar.

The cold air rising from the ravine creates ripples of gooseflesh over March's body, igniting her wounds again. Cheshire stands behind her and wraps his arms tightly around her waist—a hearth unto himself and his warmth eternal. She holds onto his solid arms and leans her head back on his shoulder. They remain in the cold air, bathed in what little soft moonlight dares reach this depth.

"I recovered your swords and daggers. And added a new longsword and glaive. I think they will make fine additions to your collection."

She turns her head and kisses his cheek.

"Will you return to the castle?" he asks.

"No," March answers simply, not wanting to give another thought to the matter. "Should you have need of me, once I redress my wounds, look for me here or Dormy's wagon or—"

Cheshire kisses the back of her neck. "I will always be able to find you, no matter where you are."

March's heart thumps in her chest, jolted back to life by her lover's soft words. "What of you?" She wants to ask him to stay this night, but from the look in his eyes earlier, his mind is already certain.

"I must be about my business. The end draws near, and there is much yet to be done." He slips his arms from around her.

"Find me tomorrow."

"Of course, love. Every step away..."

Her stomach tightens. "Is a step back to you," she finishes. March does not turn around but knows he is gone with the wind, even without the use of his masks.

She, Jonathan, and Cheshire hold their share of secrets from each other. This has always been the way of things, but perhaps the same one they share is not so secret after all. The simple words they say to each other as proof of their eternal love, a promise they will circle the globe to return home if they must, is as bitter as it is sweet, if not more.

In order to return, one must first leave, and no matter how many times over the years her loves leave, they take a piece of her soul with them, and it hurts no less. In truth, it hurts more every time. After so many years together, they all fear, though they dare not show it, it will be the last time they say or hear those words.

CHAPTER 68
CHESHIRE

Cheshire returns to the chamber of statues—men and women frozen in time, as he is, symbols of his path, his youth. Tears return to his eyes, thinking of the past. He will find his mother soon, and he must give thought to what they will do when she walks free once more. He speaks confidently about leaving Mirus behind, but, in truth, the city can wait. All he wants is to feel his mother's embrace, breathe her in, lie with his head on her lap as she tussles his hair, and know she is safe; he is safe.

Grunting, he plops onto the floor, sits cross-legged in front of the looking-glass to join his reflection, and lays the bundle of his clothing next to him. He and his reflection study each other's wounds—the coiled scrapes around their necks, the split on the right side of their upper lips, the swollen noses, the exhaustion in their eyes, and the glimmer of hope peeking out from behind them.

"We almost lost our head back there."

"It is my own fault, though I will admit it to no one except you—well, me. I grew over-confident and over-reliant on the charms and abilities granted by the masks, spectacular as they were. I have not needed them to escape the Ace, a more formidable opponent than Lysander and Uriah, for a thousand years without more than a scratch. It is not until I started using them, became dependent on them, that, well, this happens." He gestures to his reflection. "Therefore, I do not need them any longer. Good riddance."

"We did not need them because we had full reign of the catacombs before."

"And we still do. The catacombs of Wonderland remain a secret only to us and our mother. The loss of those under Mirus, while a nuisance, was only a small piece. After the losses suffered, I doubt mapping out the rest of the catacombs will be high on the Duchess's priority list. Once we purge them of any lingering soldiers, we can also set traps and seal all except the essentials."

Cheshire stares at his reflection in quiet contemplation, knees bobbing, not wanting to think anymore, avoiding himself, but he knows himself too well.

"Something troubles you," his reflection says.

"Far too much than should." He huffs. "I do not regret coming back to Mirus, but everything seems to fray and crack the longer I stay. The longer we stay. I thought the Gryphon's admission of our mother being alive would give me some great sense of relief, of victory, but I remain just as confounded and frustrated as ever."

"Are you?"

"Yes. I may have information, but one step forward moves us twenty steps back. The Gryphon said he remained in Mirus in order to search for my mother. I have searched every inch of this city, above and below, castle and harbor, with not a single shred of evidence, save for what we already possess." Cheshire rubs his mother's sash between his fingers. "Could the Gryphon continue to lie? Would he?"

"You looked upon his face," says his reflection. "Fear and honor were his undoing. Our mother must be here. The Duchess would not risk imprisoning her somewhere outside the city, especially if she worked so tirelessly to keep us out. It could not be only for self preservation. There is more at play."

"Why is it then, we cannot find her? What have we missed?" Cheshire retraces his paths since he has been in Mirus—every catacomb, shop, tenement, castle corridor, chamber, garden, and harbor—until he reaches the first place he searched in Mirus: the hanging cells. A contraption of Pat's and Bill's genius where prisons and their cages move. Nothing is impossible. He turns to his reflection, who knows his thoughts. "The Gryphon and I cannot find her because if she is not in one place, it stands to reason she must be in many. She moves. Rather, the Duchess must continuously move her. But how and by what means?"

"More fucking riddles," says his reflections.

"We do like riddles. Riddles beget answers."

"There you have it. Our next step is obvious. We face the Duchess. You found the Gryphon's weakness. You will discover hers, exploit it, confront her, and force her to divulge the location of our mother."

"I fear as difficult as the Gryphon was to crack, she will be all the more. She will speak as she dies, but no matter the amount of torture, she would die with a lie on her tongue out of spite to keep me searching in the wrong place until the end of eternity."

Cheshire rubs at his temples and scrapes his fingers through his hair. "This becomes ridiculous. My plans to lay waste to the city are once again postponed until I find her."

"Perhaps it is a sign you are not meant to destroy the city."

"It is all I have thought of for a millennium. I shall not relinquish my quest."

"Yet, I sense there is hesitation."

"Of course you do. You are me. I cannot help but feel bound. Not just unseen chains, but actual walls, the walls of the city, trapping me within a maze I helped to create, yet do not know the exit. Knowing, yet not knowing, where my mother is in the city causes further fucking annoyance. I can do even less for fear I shall harm her as a result."

"Something more troubles you."

A deep pit forms within Cheshire, cold, hollow, endless, and unlike anything before. It begins small and grows larger, as if eating at the earth underneath him. At any moment, any slight movement and he shall plummet down this narrow hole forever.

"March and Jonathan recover from injuries, and while they both have suffered wounds on multiple occasions and healed, it has never been as a result of my actions. Mary Anne was undoubtedly the pawn in Lysander and Uriah's plan, but they would not have been forced into the situation, stupid as it was, if I did not orchestrate the culling on the court. I do not know what this feeling is."

"Guilt would be the appropriate response."

"I do feel guilt. I swim in it like a hog in its own filth, and no matter how much I scrub and scrape at my skin, it will not come off."

"Because it is within you."

"I know, damn it." Cheshire grips and wraps his hair in his fingers. "This is different."

"It is fear."

"Fuck you." Cheshire hangs his head, accepting his own words. "Damn you. For the first time, I am hesitant to move for fear of harming Jonathan, March, Dormy, or my mother, or worse, losing any one of them. We all know the risks we take, and we always triumph, together. I killed Time, the last who remained of the Old Ones, not just to give me time to find my mother but to make sure all of us would be here at the end, until the end of all things, if it ever comes. How is it, despite our skills and my deeds, it seems we grow closer to death with each new encounter?"

"Dormy has lost an arm, Jonathan was beaten within an inch of his life, March bears her first scars, and there is something amiss, something unspoken, between us all."

"If I am the cause of any of their deaths, I would never recover." Cheshire laughs nervously, on the verge of tears. "There would be no returning. I fear the pull of my greatest temptation would win with me at my lowest, unforgivable place, and I would give in and join them soon after. I could not live in a world without them. But again, I would find myself stuck in between, afraid to live, but also afraid to die. Tell me how this makes sense?"

His reflection remains quiet.

"What is fair is foul and what is foul is fair. I feel the icy prying stare of Time still on me, though his body lies shattered on the orrery floor. Or perhaps it is one of the other false gods, Life or Death. By all accounts, I should have died a thousand years ago and a thousand times since." Tears run down his face and onto his lap. "Then again, so should have everyone else. But Death, ironically, if he or she still lived, would be satiated by the number of souls I have gifted over the centuries, correct? I feel it is my life that is the imbalance, the chaos, which they, or whomever, wish to claim to right the world."

"There are many reasons to break, and this is not one of them. The world is not right. It does not deserve to be right after all it has done. This is the way of Wonderland, and we shall be no different. We came here for our mother and cannot turn back now when we are closer than we have ever been. You have killed a god, and you will claim the lives of more if need be. You do not need to protect Jonathan and March, but rather come together, for your trinity can overcome anything. The cult; gone, the Twins; gone. The Ace? We will come back to him. But the Duchess is next."

"You speak the truth. But I shall always be there to protect them. They are my life, and at the end of all things, they will stand beside my mother and I as we leave this place to dust. Yet, in order to accomplish it all, defy the odds, and save everyone, I must undertake the most frightening task I have yet to do in my life, and it scares me to the core."

"Which is?"

"To ask for help."

The latch of the door squeaks and lifts. Cheshire would not mind one more death this night, but his body has not recovered from the fight with Lysander and Uriah. He grabs his bundle of clothing, slips into the secret passageway behind the looking-glass, and runs around the perimeter of the chamber to the opposite side without an entrance.

Cheshire's fingers, toes, and neck tingle with anticipation and providence. Though he cannot hear the footsteps through the glass, Cheshire recognizes the unmistakable silhouette, darker than the shadows, of the Duchess.

CHAPTER 69

JONATHAN

Jonathan wakes and looks to Mary Anne sleeping next to him, leg draped over his. He allows his eyes to focus and adjust to the darkness and searches for the large bottle of elixir Mary Anne brought from the Duchess. It is not on top of his stacked trunks in the corner of the chamber where he left it. A horrid flurry fills his chest, worried the rest of his elixir is not there either. Before he gives himself a chance to panic, he eases Mary Anne's leg off his own and slides from the side of the bed.

Mary Anne hugs his arm before he can rise.

"What time is it?"

"Not yet the witching hour, by my guess."

"Witches? Must we worry about them as well?"

"No. Not here. All our enemies are gone."

"Must you go?" She kisses his forearm.

"I do not mean to be crass, but I must relieve myself." He kisses her temple. "I shall return."

"Be quick, darling. I shall wait for you."

"No need. Rest, and I shall wake you when I return." Jonathan leaves a lasting kiss on her lips, pushes through the gossamer curtains, and searches his open trunks. The only bottles of elixir left are empty, even though March brought back plenty from the Hollow. The nails of panic scrape across Jonathan's mind, up his back, and down his chest. He grabs a blue linen robe from another trunk and wraps it around himself as he hurries from the chamber.

Once the door latches shut, he runs past the baths and toilets and continues deeper into the castle. At this time of night, he did not expect anyone else to be awake and walking the castle. Mary Anne's handmaiden proves him wrong. She waits at the end of the long hall, arms crossed, and head hung low.

"Did you take my elixir?"

She breathes hard through her nose and nods.

"Where are they?"

She turns and walks away, and Jonathan knows she means for him to follow her. His feet and face run cold. All the braziers of the castle have been extinguished or gone out of their own accord. All Jonathan can listen to as he follows the handmaiden are the clacks of her boots, the pats of his feet, the clinking of her gown, and his heartbeat pounding out of control.

Jonathan's neck twitches, and he pulls at his fingers the longer the journey lasts without end or knowing the destination. Finally, after several staircases and corridors, the handmaiden leads him to a large arched door where the Duchess waits, holding a single candle. He opens the door for both of them, leaving the handmaiden behind, knowing she acted not of her own accord, but under duress.

The Duchess leads Jonathan into a cavernous chamber filled with couches, incredibly tall looking-glasses, and several statues of dancing men and women.

"How fares Mary Anne?" the Duchess asks.

"She remains resilient."

He lets the following silence linger. He swallows. The air shifts. A chill like daggers left out in winter scrapes up Jonathan's back, inch-by-inch. His hands tingle and grow numb.

"Not the answer I sought, Carter." The Duchess huffs. "I hear whispers from the servants. Those who can speak, anyway. Anything more to report?"

Jonathan lowers his eyes, and shame fills his stomach like rancid milk. "Your plan proceeds accordingly." His heart thunders in his head. "She has all but forgotten about her world, as you foretold. All she speaks of is becoming queen, Wonderland, and..."

"And you."

"Yes."

"Took you long enough to fuck her. Did she enjoy it?"

Jonathan's stomach turns.

"I asked you a question."

"I would say she does."

"Damn your proper upbringing. Did she scream? Did she moan? Did she scratch at your back while you plunged your cock deep and fucked the memory of her world from her?"

"Yes."

"And what of Lady Audrianna?"

"Heartbroken. Gone."

"Good. Though her swords were of great use, we shall have little use for them now. Mary Anne's ascension to queen is nigh. I can feel it. Keep Mary Anne entertained and her mind on Wonderland and your delicious body."

"Yes."

"Yes, what?"

"Yes, your majesty."

"You have more to report?"

"We were in the throne room." Jonathan's neck ticks worse. "I did not face the pillars, but there was a dim red glow that washed over us in the darkness. Brief, pulsing, but it went out."

The Duchess turns the ruby ring on her finger and smiles wide and silent.

"Your majesty, if I may?" He holds out his shaking hand.

She pulls a small vial of his elixir from her cleavage with a flourish and dangles it in the air in front of Jonathan. His jaw twinges, he blinks quickly, and his fingers move erratically at the sight.

"Kneel," she commands.

He drops to the floor without hesitation. What choice does he have? After letting him suffer for a moment, she drops the vial and makes Jonathan catch it out of the air before it hits the floor.

"This is what you need, is it not? Mary Anne actually thought she saved your life, not knowing I supply your elixir. Well done. Risky theatrics on your part. Not to worry, I will return your stock in full to your chambers as long as you continue to play your part, do your job, remember whose hand holds your leash, and get her to the throne, my good and faithful servant."

"Yes, your majesty."

Jonathan follows the Duchess from the chamber. He uncorks the bottle and takes a small sip to let the tepid liquid wash away his thoughts before they can form, but they still slip through the cracks of his mind. Some unseen tether holds everyone he loves captive, chained to the past. After the garden, he knows what chained March, and Cheshire confessed about his mother's disappearance at the hands of the Duchess. This is dangerous. This time is different. March's and Cheshire's secrets reveal themselves, but Jonathan cannot afford to let even a hint of his secrets come to light. If it is revealed the Duchess, master puppeteer, holds his strings and commands him as easily as a marionette, it will mean the end of everything he loves. The end of his world.

CHAPTER 70

CHESHIRE

The chamber door shuts behind Jonathan and the Duchess with an echoing finality. Cheshire sits cross-legged behind the wall of looking-glasses, silently weeping, tears streaming down his cheeks, soaking the floor. Drool slips from his open mouth, unable to stop. His nails claw at the stone floor.

Never in his wildest imagination did he ever expect to see this clandestine meeting, nor did Jonathan or the Duchess expect him to be there. Unable to hear their conversation, he watched his love kneel in servitude to his greatest enemy, the woman responsible for his mother's disappearance, for the life of exile he led.

A maelstrom of every thought, every possibility, every reason consumes his mind in a vast, unrelenting blur, unable to take form, unable to see clearly for the first time. Cheshire's heart thunders in his chest and sends wave after wave of frigid agony through his veins.

He knows everything. He knew everything. How did he not see this? Cheshire looks for his reflection, for some, for any answer, but on this side of the looking-glass, he is nowhere to be found.

Where does he begin? Does he chase Jonathan? Does he kill the

Duchess? Does he throttle them both? When did the lies and betrayal begin? Where do they end? Cheshire must know. He does not want to know. What is real? What is not?

I am...

He is son and slayer, prince and exile, lover, and chaos-bringer.

I am...

He is light and dark; he is laughter and death.

I am...

For the first time in over a century, a sensation takes root in Cheshire's mind and fills his vacant chest, chilling him to the marrow and the core of his soul, a feeling he has not felt since he lost his mother. He is utterly, completely, and irrevocably...

Lost.

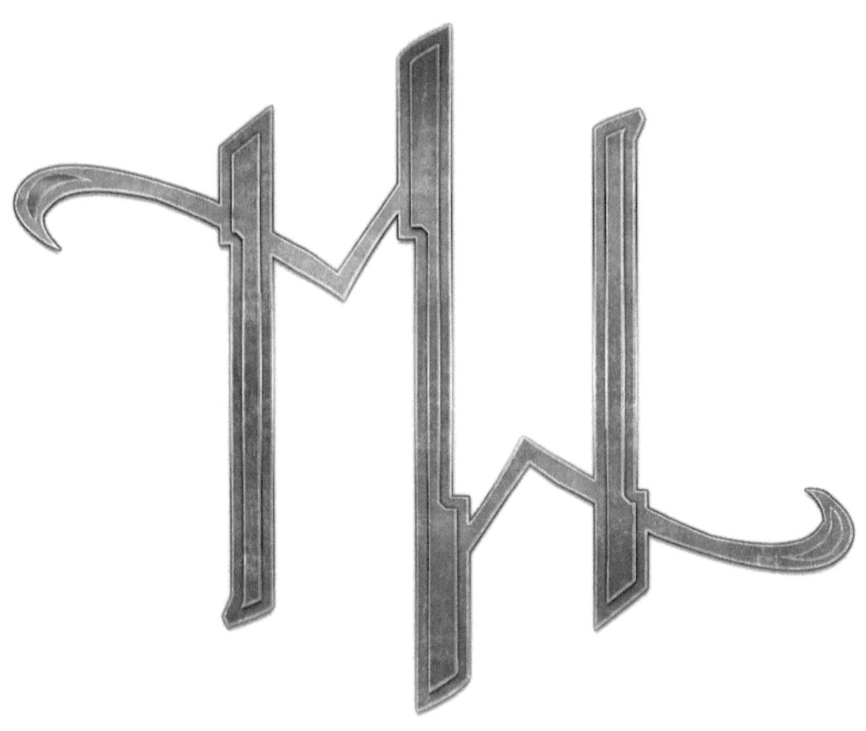

ACKNOWLEDGMENTS

After 4 books, I must still give an everlasting thank you to my friends who helped bring this story to life all those years ago. Dakota, Ryan, Ashton, Abigail, Julie, Lani, Karen, Kristie, and Rachel. This world would never have existed without you.

To Matte, Ismael, Seth, Stacey, Jessie, and Travis for continuing the journey with me and breathing new life into it.

And to Luke, Tommi, Brian, Bailey, Marisa, Katie, Ricardo, Jordan, Tari, and Kathy for making it real.

ABOUT THE AUTHOR

BRANDON T BERNARD is an international award winning playwright and has been featured at the Edinburgh Fringe Festival. The works of Lewis Carroll have been his favorite literature since he was a boy, and cultivated his peculiar imagination. He has been a storyteller and artist from an early age, and worked behind the scenes in the film and theatre industry for almost twenty years. It's now time for him to tell his own stories. Follow him on his journey down the rabbit hole of Mad World.

tiktok.com/@AuthorBTB

instagram.com/AuthorBrandonTBernard

x.com/BrandonTBernard

JOIN THE MADNESS

For exclusive art, music, and shops, visit
www.MadWorldWonderland.com

www.ingramcontent.com/pod-product-compliance
Lightning Source LLC
Chambersburg PA
CBHW020352310726
48979CB00015B/2559/J

* 9 7 8 1 9 6 6 4 8 6 0 0 8 *